HE
REMAINING

BY D. J. MOLLES

The Remaining
The Remaining
The Remaining: Aftermath
The Remaining: Refugees
The Remaining: Fractured
The Remaining: Endgame (coming in spring 2015)

The Remaining short fiction
The Remaining: Trust
The Remaining: Faith

THE REMAINING

BOOK 1

D. J. MOLLES

www.orbitbooks.net

ORBIT

Originally self-published by the author in 2012
First published in Great Britain in 2014 by Orbit

A CIP catalogue record for this book
is available from the British Library.

ISBN 978-0-356-50345-5

Typeset in Galliard by M Rules
Printed and bound by CPI Group (UK) Ltd, Croydon, CR0 4YY

Papers used by Orbit are from well-managed forests
and other responsible sources.

MIX
Paper from
responsible sources
FSC® C104740
www.fsc.org

Orbit
An imprint of
Little, Brown Book Group
100 Victoria Embankment
London EC4Y 0DY

An Hachette UK Company
www.hachette.co.uk

www.orbitbooks.net

To Josh,
Thanks for all your help.
Just remember the plan.

ONE

___

THE HOLE

Lee Harden stood in the center of a knockoff Persian rug. The soft polyester fibers felt like sandpaper on his bare feet. The seventy-two-degree temperature of the room felt hot one moment and too cold the next. His cotton T-shirt clung to his chest. The walls of the room were cloying and stale. Everything was frustrating. Monotonous. The sameness of his prison buzzed in his ears and drove him mad. His body begged him to break free.

His clammy left hand planted in the pocket of his jeans while his right bounced a tennis ball in front of him. To the side, his German shepherd, Tango, sat and regarded the bouncing ball with quiet intensity, his eyes following up and down with the even rhythm of a pendulum counting the endless seconds.

He closed his eyes and tasted brine in the back of his throat. Sand crunched between his teeth and lactic acid coursed through his legs and arms. His lungs clawed for air like someone buried alive. Words punched through the riptide of blood rushing past his ears: *The only easy day was yesterday!*

He opened his eyes and the salty sea and gritting sand fled from his mouth, but the words still hung before him, tangible now. Carved into wood. The 'plaque' was big, about three feet long, and the words were hacked out, like a convict had gone to work with a penknife. Crude and simple. Like the sentiment it bore. Below the chunk of wood was a large steel door that looked like the entrance to a vault.

But it was Lee who was inside the vault.

The only easy day was yesterday.

He wondered how true those words were going to be.

Lee had spent the better part of the day in front of his computer, reading the same news bulletins that had been displayed for the past week. No one had updated the stories. Images of burning cities, overcrowded refugee camps, and violence on the scale of genocide remained untouched. No turnaround. No good news.

No cure.

He had spent most of the past hour lost in thought, gazing at a picture of a very young Honduran child standing in the middle of the street, wearing no shoes, dirty blue shorts, and a yellow shirt stained with blood. He held a half-empty water bottle, likely given to him by one of the humanitarian aid stations. The look on his face was that of someone recovering from a knockout punch: eyes open but not seeing.

Behind the boy and out of focus was a leg. No body to accompany it. It had been sheared off just above the knee and now lay in some dirty Honduran street. The caption under the picture read, *Honduran boy outside Red Cross shelter*. The picture was dated June 28.

It was now July 3.

Most articles on the news websites were dated June 28. One or two were dated June 29. The ones from the twenty-ninth were just blurbs. US military recalling all overseas troops back to the homeland. Martial law was in effect.

Frank had confirmed all of this yesterday, but despite the

look on his face, he had reassured Lee that it would all be over soon. He even apologized for keeping Lee in The Hole for this long. *Maybe another week at most. I'll send you a gift card to Ruth's Chris*, he had said. *Just hang in there*.

Lee realized that he had inadvertently been tempting Tango with the bouncing ball and tossed it in the air. Tango let it bounce once, then snagged it in midair. He smiled and wagged his tail, looking deeply satisfied. Completely ignorant. But that was the beauty of a dog.

Pets were strongly advised as companions while in The Hole, a place where Lee had spent many days. Usually two or three weeks at a time. There had been occasions when national disaster was foretold but averted. Such as when Fukushima melted down after the earthquakes off the coast of Japan. The Washington Worrywarts said fallout could reach mainland USA and cause agricultural collapse, which would in turn collapse the stock market, the economy, and the government.

They kept him in The Hole for eighteen days.

A month after that, Korea created a little nuclear scare that rippled through the various offices in Washington but never reached the press, which always surprised Lee, since the people controlling him made it out to be the next Cuban Missile Crisis.

On that occasion, they kept him in The Hole for a week.

Not that The Hole was a bad place. It contained almost every creature comfort one could think of. It was a little over a thousand square feet, with a great kitchen, fully stocked bar, den with a big TV, a bedroom with a king-size bed, and a bathroom with a large Jacuzzi tub and a sauna next to the shower. It was stocked with a week of fresh food, three months of freeze-dried meals, and three months' worth of water. A battery bank, trickle charged from solar panels on the surface, could run every electronic in the place for nearly a year, and Lee kept it full of entertainment, from books and magazines to video games and movies.

Yes, Lee's bunker had everything. Except human interaction. And the freedom to leave. So far, the Washington Worrywarts had always been wrong. A few weeks after he locked himself in, Frank's face would appear on Lee Harden's computer screen, smiling and telling him to 'come back to the land of the living.' That was his signature it's-all-over phrase.

But Frank would also be on Lee's computer every day at 1200 hours to give Lee an update. Not once in all the days Lee had been restricted to his bunker had Frank been even a minute late to update Lee.

Frank had not appeared today.

Lee checked the digital clock on the wall above his computer. 18:34.

His stomach flip-flopped as he considered the possibilities. His mind took him to a place without controls or any central government. A place where a disease, or a virus, or some kind of plague had brought humanity back to the Stone Age. Complete collapse of civilization. People going crazy, murdering other people, looting and pillaging, warlords seizing control in power vacuums created by fractured governments.

This could be his reality in thirty days. Picturing it all, he felt sick. But anxious. He looked down at Tango, who sat clenching the tennis ball in his mouth and waiting for Lee to do something. The thought of the end of the world was like trying to swallow a mouthful of vinegar. His mind completely rejected it.

'Fuck it,' he told Tango. 'He'll call.'

*

Before all the hell weeks – the pounding, cold surf; and the hot, muggy swamps; and the arid, craggy mountains – there was Primary Selection. Lee was approached, along with 237 other candidates, the proposition coming in the form of a letter, pre-typed and unsigned. It came on the heels of his parents' funerals, and he would later discover that he and many of the others had been chosen due to several factors, not the least of which was the fact that they had no family.

The letter gave no details, but instead spoke of an opportunity to be involved in a top-tier government initiative and some such nonsense about being elite. It provided a number and extension to call, and that was essentially it. When Lee asked his superiors about the weird letter he had received, they just stared blankly and shrugged, apparently not in the loop.

Of the 237 to receive letters, Lee was one of the 191 who called the number. A polite female voice on the other end scheduled a session for what she referred to as the Primary Selection process. Still, she gave no details of what the process would be about or what the government initiative was.

Of the 191 who showed up to their appointments, only 169 signed the waiver that explicitly stated that Primary Selection was a mental test only and would be conducted under the influence of some legally prescribed narcotics, closely supervised by a medical professional.

Lee could never remember the test. He remembered lying down, and the IV in his arm, and something odd flooding his system. Then there was a block of time, filled with snippets and pieces of something terrifying that never made sense to him, and which his conscious mind was unable to make sense of. Then he remembered waking up, heart still pounding.

Of the 169 who took the test, 60 had a conversation with the doctor afterward.

Lee was one of them.

The doctor was a skinny black man. Rather than a white lab coat, he wore cleanly pressed ACUs with no division markings and just a nametag that read COOK and single black bars on his collar. Dr. (or Lt.) Cook was of average height with close-cropped hair and a mouthful of large, incredibly straight teeth. He had a relaxed manner, and he seemed perpetually curious.

'Do you have any questions?' Dr. Cook had asked.

Lee remembered testing his own thundering pulse – touching his fingers to his carotid artery. His skin was clammy and sweaty, his collar wet. 'When do you guys tell me what this is about?'

'Well, today you sat in a chair and received visual stimuli for a period of ninety minutes. Kind of like a virtual reality game. The drugs were to help your mind interpret the visual stimuli as reality.'

Lee stared blankly, not quite sure what to ask from there. He had plenty of questions but really couldn't categorize them or prioritize them.

Dr. Cook smiled and leaned forward, clasping his hands. 'We're testing something I like to call *mental flex*.' Dr. Cook looked thoughtful, as though trying to come up with an apt description, though Lee got the impression that he had already given this speech dozens of times. 'Imagine a dream where you are faced with a life-or-death struggle – a literal fight for your life. Now imagine that this dream fight is against something terrifying, something that you know cannot be real. Even as your logical forebrain is thinking, *This can't possibly be real*, is your dream self still fighting? Or do you stop and wait for the dream to be over?'

Dr. Cook leaned an elbow on his chair's armrest. 'We've found that in certain scenarios or situations, a sense of denial is unavoidable. You actually can't really train it out of some-one. It doesn't matter how elite of a soldier, how much of a badass he is; certain things the brain simply refuses to believe. So when that happens, we've found that most people fall into one of two categories – the flexible or the inflexible. If a person is inflexible, he will mentally stop, almost like he is refusing to entertain the thought because it is so unbelievable.' Dr. Cook laughed a weird little chuckle. 'I'm talking about top-tier operators here. I've seen it happen. Now, granted, the better trained they are, the harder it is to get them to that denial. But you keep pressing the boundaries of someone's reality, and eventually he will reach it. And then most people pop. Like an overloaded circuit.'

Here he stopped and held up a finger. 'But a few – probably about a third – will keep fighting, even when their brain is in that state of denial. And if you're still fighting then you are *flexible*. You have *mental flex*.'

Lee swallowed, felt cold. 'So do I have it?'

Another big, toothy grin. 'Oh, you've got it.'

Lee lay in his bed, still awake at 0200 hours on the morning of July 4.

He had not eaten for the remainder of the evening, not having the appetite. His mind kept replaying his concerns in a dizzying cycle, like a short, annoying song set on repeat. *What if this is it? I can't believe it's the end. It can't possibly be the end. That's bullshit.*

You're overreacting. Frank will call. He's never missed a call before. But what if this is really it?

What if? What if?

Lee tried to turn off his mind but couldn't, and he failed to think of a reason that he needed to sleep. It wasn't like he had big plans, despite it being Independence Day.

That's a first. Locked in The Hole on Independence Day. That's fucking un-American, he thought. *I swear to God, I am going to chew Frank the fuck out ... I hope he's okay. He's gotta be okay. I am a contingency plan. Contingency plans are for contingencies. Contingencies don't happen, at least not on this scale. Not on the scale that requires me to get involved.*

He recalled his commission for this job. He remembered thinking, at first, that it was total horseshit. But in the end you couldn't beat the pay, and you couldn't beat the benefits. The government built his entire house on three acres in the central North Carolina countryside. From the outside, the house didn't look overtly rich, but the inside was large and comfortable. The bunker he now found himself restricted to was a part of this house, buried almost twenty feet beneath the basement. They also paid him an amazing salary to go down into his bunker when they told him.

Seal the doors, they said. *You'll receive more information from Frank during your restricted periods. If you stop receiving communications from command, you will wait in your secure bunker for thirty days from the date of command's last communication before exiting to begin your mission.*

The mission.

The thought of that massive undertaking made sweat break out across Lee's forehead. The parameters of his mission, the whole reason he was sequestered away from what was going on outside, bordered on the impossible.

He shook his head. Frank would call. And so the thoughts cycled and cycled until they had blended into a slur of white noise in his mind, and somewhere around 0330 he fell asleep.

*

When he woke up at about 0930 he felt great.

For a moment he was truly convinced that the previous day had not happened and that it was the morning of the third, only a few hours from Frank's scheduled call, which he would undoubtedly receive. He eventually realized this wasn't the case. But the greasy knot in his stomach didn't return. He felt more agitated, slightly angry. He took a hot shower and thought of all the choice words he would say to Frank when he finally called, which he was sure he would. Lee hoped Frank had a most excellent and entertaining story to explain why he was twenty-four hours overdue for his call.

He hoped Frank was safe.

He air-dried after his shower. There was really no point in rushing to clothe yourself when you were alone, twenty feet underground in a cement-and-lead box.

He made himself a protein shake while Tango dutifully sat next to him in the kitchen. After the shake, Lee put on a pair of athletic shorts, because there was something privately disturbing about doing calisthenics in the nude. He knocked out his sit-ups, push-ups, felt lazy as he looked at his chin-up bar. Then felt guilty and did the pull-ups. He turned on the sunlamp while he did these. It wasn't the same as the sun itself, but it was better than nothing. Being in a sunless environment could mess with your head and your health.

After that he made some egg whites and toast with peanut butter. Then he fed Tango. He made some coffee and took it to the computer. He didn't sit down. Just touched the mouse. The screen saver vanished. The home page of CNN.com was still displayed. It had not changed.

Just to make sure, Lee refreshed the browser window. This time it gave him an error message about the site being down. He checked the status of his Internet connection and found it displaying a good connection. He tried Yahoo! and managed to get the home page, but it was still the same old news.

Nothing posted since June 28. He drank his coffee in silence. It was 1030. He sat down in his computer chair, lifting his feet onto the desk. He rested the warm coffee mug on his bare chest and regarded a flat, rectangular metal box to the right of his computer screen. It contained his mission brief. This was the predetermined contingency plan given to him directly from the Office of the Secretary of Homeland Security. It outlined in detail what they projected the situation would be like on the thirtieth day. Due to the sensitivity of the information contained, Lee was not authorized to open the box until forty-eight hours after his last communication with command.

Frank was Colonel Frank Reid of the United States Army, assigned as liaison between the Secretary of Homeland Security and the forty-eight 'Coordinators' stationed in bunkers in each of the states across the Continental US. Lee was stationed in North Carolina.

Colonel Frank Reid was command.

At 1200 hours today, he would have to open that box and read its contents. That would be it. Project Hometown would do what it was meant to do. He could only assume that the other forty-seven Coordinators had not received communications from Frank either and would also be opening their boxes at their respective forty-eight-hour marks.

The thought of it scared him shitless.

He drank the dregs of his coffee, grabbed a water bottle, and sat down on the couch, facing the gigantic TV. He turned it on and scanned through the cable channels. TV had gone much sooner than the Internet news. Most channels had been

displaying an emergency broadcast screen with a ticker at the
bottom looping the same information: the major metropoli-
tan areas that were under evacuation order and which FEMA
shelter to report to for each area.

Now the channels displayed blank blue screens.

Lee sank back onto the couch and stared, unsure of what
he was waiting for. Perhaps for the channels to start trans-
mitting again. Perhaps for his computer to chime, informing
him that Frank was on the other line. Maybe he was just waiting to wake up from a bad dream.

The blue screen staring back at him felt surreal. He shook
his head. Frank would call. He had to call. A virus couldn't
knock out the United States government. There were scientists, whole departments whose sole purpose for existing was
to identify and eliminate these types of threats before they
even became a problem. He wondered fleetingly if this were
a joke, but dismissed it. Colonel Frank Reid would never play
that tasteless of a joke. Lee didn't even think Frank would play
any joke at all.

He didn't strike Lee as the joking type.

Something was keeping him from calling. The Internet
signal could have been damaged or destroyed where Frank
was, causing him to be unable to contact Lee for the past two
days. Techs would be working overtime to reestablish contact
with the Coordinators so Frank could tell them to hold off on
reading their mission packets.

In the meantime, Lee had no idea what to do with himself.
He would usually busy himself with a book or a movie, but
watching a movie seemed inappropriate and he would not be
able to focus on reading a book with his mind running
through scenarios of what the hell was happening in the world
outside his bunker.

He drank the rest of his water bottle and went to his treadmill. He left the incline flat and brought it up to an eight-minute-mile pace. He needed to waste some time and planned on running for a while.

TWO

THE BRIEF

At 1215 hours he stopped running.

The last few miles were mentally excruciating, and several times he caught himself looking over at the computer. It was past the forty-eight-hour mark. He should be reading the mission packet. Every minute that went by he told himself to wait and give Frank a chance to call. At fifteen after, he realized if he waited any longer, he would be deliberately disobeying his standing orders.

He stepped off the treadmill and took another bottle of water from the fridge, then looped around the couch to his computer and sat down. In the time it had taken him to move to his desk, he had become painfully curious about what information the mission packet held.

He placed his thumb on the small black square on top of the box and, after a brief moment, heard the lock click open. He lifted the lid and looked inside. He had never opened his mission box before. This was a first.

The contents were underwhelming. Just a black thumb drive. He plugged it into his computer and let it load. The program it contained took the liberty of running itself. It was a program he had seen before when completing online training courses. It allowed the user to click though screens like a

PowerPoint, but it was also narrated and contained bits of video.

The first thing he heard was Frank's voice.

For a moment he let himself believe Frank had called. He felt a moment of levity, then a flash of anger for being left in The Hole for so long without contact. But the voice was only a recording. Lee noted that Frank sounded relaxed. Not at all concerned. Just going through the motions.

It was at that moment that the knot returned to Lee's stomach.

'This is Colonel Frank Reid on behalf of the Office of the Secretary of Homeland Security in regard to Project Hometown and to all operatives therewith involved. Your mission has begun.'

The screen displayed the seal of the Department of the Army, which faded to a map of the Continental United States.

'What you will be dealing with topside is what our scientists are calling Febrile Urocanic Reactive Yersinia, or FURY for short. It is a mutated form of *Y. Pestis*, which was the cause of the bubonic plague and nearly every other European plague for the last four hundred years. Because it is a bacteria and not a virus, our experts are unsure of how it transmits from one person to the next; however, the plague has already shown an extreme propensity for contagion. Full Personal Protective Equipment is advised when in contact with infected or possibly infected individuals, and full decontamination afterward.'

Four dots appeared on the map, one each in New York, Florida, Illinois, and California.

'We do not have a patient zero at this time. However, we can infer that the plague is from a source outside the country, due to the first cases in the US being centered on our largest international airports in New York City, Chicago, Miami, and Los Angeles.

'From the research we have available at this time – June fourteenth – the prodromal stage symptoms of infection are fever, shaking or trembling, overt salivation, diarrhea, extreme hunger and thirst, rash on the torso or trunk of the body, projectile vomiting, some loss of fine motor skills, difficulty speaking, and sleeplessness. As the plague progresses into the illness stage, symptoms include complete loss of speech and understanding, pallor, hallucinations, loss of sensation, hyper-aggression, uncontrollable screaming or yelling, and insatiable appetite – which we've seen result in the patient attempting to feed on their own limbs or on anyone within arm's reach.

'During the late illness stage, the patient will often go into a stupor, walk with an unsteady gait, and display slow reaction time. Respiratory rate declines, and in several cases, blindness has occurred. Not every patient will display all of these symptoms. In certain cases we have observed little to no aggression in the patient, except in cases of hallucinations; however, these are the exception and not the rule.

'The plague acts by infecting the cells of the body and quickly multiplying within the lymph nodes. The bacteria then causes the catabolic breakdown of urocanic acid and spreads to the brain and nervous system, causing hemorrhaging in the frontal cortex of the brain, which stimulates aggression, hunger, and thirst and suppresses the patient's instincts for self-preservation. It also affects cells of the thalamus and cerebral cortex that perceive pain, making patients unresponsive to painful stimuli. The bacterium appears to eat through brain tissue quite selectively, leaving primary biological functions intact, such as heart rate and respiration.

'Our main concerns with FURY, and the reason you are

sitting in your bunker right now, are the incubation period and the fatality rate. As far as we have been able to determine, the bacteria will lie dormant for between twenty-four and forty-eight hours before symptoms even begin to show. In addition to that, we have failed to find a single instance of an infected patient actually dying from the plague. It appears that after the late illness stage, the patient's vital signs regulate themselves, and the fever will drop off, but the damage to the brain is done. This makes the likelihood of a wait-it-out strategy very limited in its chances for success. It does not look like the plague will burn itself out, but will likely go pandemic if initial attempts to contain it fail.'

The red dots around the four largest airports began to trickle outward. Dots appeared at the locations of other, smaller international airports throughout the country and spread from there. The map looked like a piece of paper soaking through with blood.

'According to calculations, if initial attempts to contain the plague fail, the probability of containing all infected persons is essentially zero, as they are infected for up to two days without showing symptoms. During this asymptomatic time period, they are extremely contagious. We must assume that we will be unable to stop this threat before it affects the entire population.'

Lee leaned forward in his chair and cupped his hands around his face. He found himself breathing heavily and his heart beating a step faster.

Probability of containment: zero.

'Operating as always under the assumption that we will be dealing with the Worst-Case Scenario, we set the survival rate at 9 percent, at least within the Continental United States. In addition to the lives taken by FURY, there will be widespread rioting and looting, which will lead to more casualties. WCS, we are looking at a complete governmental collapse due to the plague. The power vacuum created by the fall of the institutional United States government will be huge, and there are many crazy people inside our borders who will be more than willing to take control and kill anyone who opposes, should they survive the plague. If WCS occurs, you will be fighting a war on several fronts. You will need to protect yourself and your group from infection, you will need to protect them also from the violent tendencies of those who have already been infected, and you will need to outmaneuver the warlords who will be popping up across the country.

'Tactically speaking, you will need to keep yourself on constant quarantine. No physical contact with anyone at any time. Immediately decontaminate if you are exposed to physical contact with anyone. Prepare your own food and do not share others' food or water. Wear PPE at all times when in the presence of others, particularly if you have reason to believe they are infected. There is no known cure at this time, so attempting aid to the infected will be a fruitless endeavor.

'Again, be aware that due to decreased mental functioning, some infected persons will be unable to speak, and most will not be able to reason. Do not attempt to speak with infected persons. If an infected person attacks you, attempt to gain distance. Use firearms to dispatch hostile infected persons and avoid hand-to-hand combat if at all possible. When engaging infected persons, you will find that due to brain impairment, they don't go down easily. We have many reports from police departments and municipal authorities around the country describing the infected individuals as overcoming apparently mortal bullet wounds and continuing to attack. Bring plenty of ammunition that packs a stopping punch.

'Also keep in mind that even though they have impaired mental functioning, the infected subjects are still human and still have some vestiges of basic predatory instinct. They can even prove to be clever, especially in the early stages of infection before it begins to affect their motor skills.'

Lee's stomach soured. Was he being told to kill United States citizens because they were sick? Why not hospitalize them and attempt to find a cure? Yes, they were violent, but so were millions of mental patients around the country, and we didn't go around shooting them in the head.

'This concludes the brief for Project Hometown regarding Febrile Urocanic Reactive Yersinia. Gentlemen, you are all that is left of the United States government. Good luck.'

Frank's voice was rote. Just reading a script that some scientists had put together.

At the time he'd recorded this message, just prior to Lee's restriction in his bunker, Frank clearly hadn't believed it himself. Just more nonsense from the Washington Worrywarts. They always believed the Worst-Case Scenario was right around the corner.

'Fuck . . . ' Lee whispered. The screen once again faded to the seal of the United States Army. Lee stared at the screen. He sat motionless, except for the rapid pulsing of his carotid artery. In his mind, he had an image of himself taking out the thumb drive and throwing it against the wall, then stomping it into pieces. Losing control.

But instead, he leaned forward and removed the thumb drive from his computer, moving as though stuck in a tar pit. He placed the thumb drive back in the black box it had come from. He didn't close the lid. He wanted something to remind him that forty-eight hours had gone by, that he had already opened the mission packet and watched the briefing.

A part of him hoped that perhaps he would wake up the next morning and find the box closed again. Then he would realize none of this had ever happened.

A fleeting, pathetic thought.

He stood up from his computer chair and looked at the sealed hatch to the outside world and the plaque that hung above it.

THE ONLY EASY DAY WAS YESTERDAY.

Thank you, Navy SEALs. One of his instructors had been a Navy SEAL, as the Coordinators received cross-instruction from several different Special Ops communities. They never received a Ranger tab, or a trident, or any other marker that designated them as Special Forces. But what they received was a vast knowledge of tactics and strategies and, most of all, a drive that never quit. Master Chief Reynolds had successfully beaten every ounce of quit out of the entire group of Coordinators and that was his favorite phrase: *The only easy day was yesterday.*

He thought about the other Coordinators stationed across the country. The last he'd seen any of them was in late January when they had their annual get-together to catch up and drink too much.

Standing orders included that they never communicate with one another while on restriction inside their bunkers. Lee had never tried, but as far as he could tell, there was nothing to stop him. He looked at the bottom of the computer screen and saw that the Internet connection appeared to still be in good working order. Surely one of the others could tell him that this was all a mistake and that Frank had contacted them and there was no violent insanity pandemic sweeping the nation.

He sat back down and opened his email account and found

that it appeared to be working fine. He typed in the email address of his closest friend, Captain Abe Darabie. His message was short:

You hear anything from Frank?

He left out the fact that he had already passed the forty-eight-hour mark and had opened the mission packet. He considered the message for a moment. If this was all a big mistake, he would be written up for violating directives. If it wasn't a big mistake, who gave a shit about directives? And Lee had to know. He needed someone else to tell him this was real, because sitting by himself made it seem like he was just going crazy.

He clicked send. It almost solidified in his mind the concept that all of this was real. Almost. It was too big to just accept. He needed something more than a forty-eight-hour lapse in communication to make him believe that the United States of America had ceased to exist in the matter of three weeks. He waited at his computer for a long moment, then realized that Abe was probably not sitting at *his* computer, waiting for emails. He stood up and walked to the kitchen. He eyed the contents of his refrigerator, paying close attention to the case of Coors Light bottles. He decided now was as good a time as any to have a beer. After all, it was the Fourth of July.

As he twisted off the cap, he heard a tone from his computer.

He sprinted across the den area to his computer and sat in his chair, the beer forgotten. He put it down on the desk so hard it fizzed and overflowed, but he barely took notice.

Abe apparently had been waiting for emails.

Neg on coms with Frank. I'm at forty-eight hours ... did you open your box?

Lee thought about it for a moment. There was no harm in admitting that he had. In fact, all the Coordinators probably had. He responded:

Yeah, I opened mine. Is this for real?

He clicked send, then waited. He took a nervous sip from his beer after the head had gone down. Cold drips fell from the bottle onto his bare chest. He ignored them. The reply came after about a minute.

I hope not ... proly shouldn't be talking ... just keep your head down and wait for them to cancel us ... I'm sure they will.

Lee read the message three times. Abe's confidence that it would all blow over eased the jittery feeling in Lee's gut. Although they were equal rank, Abe had more time on and more combat experience than Lee. Though Lee had done time as a Ranger in Iraq in '03 and '04, Abe had served as a Delta operative for five years in Afghanistan before being looped into Project Hometown. Most of the Coordinators regarded him as their de facto leader.

Lee didn't respond to the message. He took his beer and left the computer.

Lee spent the remainder of the day watching a couple movies because he didn't know what else to do. He went through several beers and carefully lined the bottles in a row on the end table. At 1650 hours the second movie ended and he realized he was hungry.

It was the Fourth of July, so he opened another beer and decided to grill up two porterhouse steaks that he had defrosted in anticipation of being locked in The Hole on Independence Day. He couldn't grill them outside, so he cooked them in a pan. He cut the bone off one and gave it to Tango, who was waiting ever so patiently at Lee's side. Tango made quick work of twenty-two ounces of meat while Lee took his time enjoying it.

At 1815 hours Lee was on beer ten and, in a rush of alcohol-fueled energy, decided more push-ups, sit-ups, and pull-ups were in order. After these he felt better in general. He felt pumped up and ready.

At 2000 hours Lee attempted to log on to redtube.com but found the server was down. He cursed himself for not bringing adult DVDs with him.

At 2030 hours he was on beer twelve and staring at the computer, willing Frank to call and tell him it was over. He would look like shit, unshaven, half dressed, and obviously drunk, but who cared? He was in a damn bunker.

At 2100 hours he decided to switch to water to avoid a bad headache. He moved to the couch and decided to try his hand at the video game console he had purchased but never played. He fumbled with the controls for a few hours before passing out on the couch, the game still running. On the screen, his video game warrior stood stoically in one spot while he was assaulted from all angles by a horde of enemies.

Eventually, the warrior collapsed and died.

THREE

THIRTY DAYS

LEE SPENT THE NEXT FEW DAYS doggedly learning how to play the video games. Tango seemed to be feeling left out and spent his time on the floor, looking at Lee and whining when he needed to use the bathroom. Lee would pause the game, then take him into the back room where he had absorbent pads laid out for Tango to do his business. Lee would gather up the soiled pads and flush them. The toilet was like an airplane toilet and would flush almost anything.

The video games were a good distraction.

So distracting that Lee forgot to exercise for two days in a row. He found himself only occasionally glancing at the computer screen to see if Frank was there, trying to communicate with him.

He never was. Lee felt horrible for a few seconds after each time he checked the computer, and then he would refocus on the video game and push everything else out of his mind. Was this denial? Or maybe he was just being reasonable and avoiding panic. If he started to worry about things, then when it all blew over and turned out to be nothing, he would feel awfully stupid.

Eventually he stopped looking at the computer. He beat the first video game on July 10. For the next two days he punished himself for skipping his workouts. He did push-ups, sit-ups, and pull-ups every hour on the hour from the time he woke up to the time he went to bed. The time in between he spent reading a book or exercising Tango.

Tango was a good working dog and had been Schutzhund trained since Lee had bought him four years ago from a breeder in Germany. He was trained mainly to defend Lee or attack a specific person upon Lee's command. Recently, Lee had been training Tango to protect an item or a different person on command. Though children and Schutzhund-trained dogs weren't usually a great mix, Lee had found that Tango was protective of children and was noticeably gentler around them.

Lee wondered whether, if Tango attacked a person infected with FURY, he would become infected. How contagious was the plague? If it were a bacterium, it could presumably transfer from person to person from something as simple as a touch.

How many people had already been infected?

What was going on up there?

Lee had no family to worry about. His father had died from a heart attack when he was in high school, and his mother had died in an automobile accident while he was in Iraq in 2004. He had girlfriends off and on, but never anything serious.

He thought at length about his last girlfriend, Deana. He wondered if she was still alive or whether she had found her way to a shelter. It wasn't that he planned on finding her during the end of the world, but she had been a genuinely good person, and he hoped she was okay, wherever she was. They had split on good terms in March. Since then, aside from casual encounters, Lee hadn't been with anybody meaningful.

He pushed her out of his mind. There was nothing he could do for her now.

Was this acceptance?

It was July 15 when Lee woke up and finally admitted to himself that Frank was not going to call. There was no conceivable technical problem that could last for nearly a week and a half and not be repaired. If Frank needed to contact them, he would have been able to do it by now. He would have told them to stand down by now if they were not needed.

After realizing this, Lee stayed in his bed for the first half of the day. He didn't get up to take a leak or to eat or drink until almost 1500 hours, when Tango was restlessly growling at the side of the bed. Although Tango could have easily walked into the other room and relieved himself, a good Schutzhund-trained dog did nothing without the consent of his master.

Lee accompanied him to the back room to do his business and realized he had to use the restroom himself. He threw Tango's soiled pads in the toilet and relieved himself before flushing the entire package.

The only easy day was yesterday, because yesterday was done. Time to man up. Lee exercised. He wasn't excited about being thrust into a dying world and watching civilization crumble – God, that sounded crazy – but he did feel a sense of urgency now. He didn't know what lay beyond the sealed doors of his bunker. He wanted to be in the best shape of his life. He wanted to give himself the best chance at survival.

Yes, this was really happening.

How bad it had become topside was anyone's guess, but

the fact that he had not received any sort of communication meant only one very bad thing: The United States government no longer existed.

It was July 18, fifteen days until he was on the move.

Lee could no longer stand it. He had had enough of lounging around and entertaining himself. He had gone through almost every film, wasn't interested in any of the books that remained, and had beaten all of the video games (except one that was based in a post-apocalyptic world, which Lee found too disconcerting to play).

He needed to do something. He opened the door to a large closet behind his couch and flipped on the light. The fluorescent bulb flickered then glowed brightly, illuminating several wire racks of equipment. Lee always thought he could have spent the rest of his career as the quartermaster of a base – there was nothing he loved more than the sight of neat racks of equipment.

From the bottom of the closet he yanked out a very large coyote-tan backpack and tossed it on the floor. The pack would hold everything he would need. Fully stuffed, it would weigh more than a hundred pounds. There was a smaller pack that he also removed and tossed next to the large one. It was also coyote tan, as Lee was a firm believer in light colors being the best camouflage. Dark colors attracted the eye. Even in woodland or swamp environments, desert colors were still good. And since Lee would potentially need to work in several different types of terrain, most of his gear was coyote tan.

The Coordinators had spent the largest amount of their full year and a half of training with the Green Berets, due to the similarity of their missions. The large and small backpacks were a by-product of his association with the Green Berets.

The large pack, or main pack, would hold most of the items he would need on the trip. Various medical supplies, computer equipment, equipment for the maintenance of weapons, food, water, clothing, his sleeping bag and bivy sack, etc. The smaller pack was known as the 'go-to-hell pack' and would never leave his side. Because the main pack would be so heavy, it was not realistic to become involved in any sort of tactical engagement while wearing it. If shit hit the fan, the main pack was dropped and Lee would finish the engagement wearing only his go-to-hell pack, which contained the basics: food and water for a few days, extra magazines for his weapons, very basic first-aid supplies, and a single change of clothes.

Lee pulled out an M4 assault rifle with an M203 grenade launcher attached to the Picatinny rails under the barrel. He had DuraCoated the entire rifle in splotchy tans and light greens. He laid this on the ground. Underneath it he placed thirteen empty thirty-round magazines. The magazines were polymer rather than the usual aluminum 'box magazines.' The advantage was that the polymer magazines fed more reliably and were 'true thirty-round magazines.' Aluminum box magazines could be loaded with thirty rounds, but it was not advisable, as they often jammed when fully loaded, but the polymer magazines could hold all thirty rounds with a little room to spare.

Next to the M4 and his magazines, he placed a green ammo can containing a thousand rounds of 5.56mm ammunition. He also had a case of 40mm grenades. He pulled out another smaller ammo can that contained a thousand rounds of .45 pistol ammunition. He pulled out a Heckler & Koch

MK23 USSOCOM and placed it next to the smaller ammo can.

While he personally preferred the Glock platform for pistols, Lee chose the H&K MK23 for the combination of its detachable suppressor and the stopping power of its .45 caliber round.

Bring plenty of ammunition that packs a stopping punch, Frank had said.

He would also carry the smaller Glock 19 as a backup, which was a 9mm. He had a box of a hundred cartridges for the 9mm, as he intended to only load the three magazines that went with it. The 9mm was smaller and less powerful, but it was excellent as an urban survival weapon, because 9mm ammunition could be found everywhere and in significant quantities.

Left on the shelf was a wooden case containing fragmentation grenades. He would leave those until he was ready to load up and move out. From the racks he pulled down a pair of satellite phones, large things that looked like cell phones did in the early nineties. He was unsure how long these satellite-reliant items would last, as it was likely that the satellites they used would fall out of orbit without human intervention. He would take them anyway.

He also had a handheld GPS device for land navigation. This he set aside next to his go-to-hell pack. That device was his bread and butter, the lifeblood of his mission. Without that GPS device, he was just another survivor.

He pulled out a folded pair of MultiCam combat pants and shirt. He liked the shirt and pants for the built-in elbow- and kneepads, and for the zippered flap on the ass of the pants for taking a shit without having to be caught, literally, with his pants down. He preferred MultiCam as a pattern. Though other more modern camouflages had been touted as superior, he found that MultiCam was effective in almost any environment, while the others stood out in certain places or were generally too dark.

He set these off to the side. He would wear them when he left.

He had two extra sets of each that he would pack, one in his main bag and one in his go-to-hell pack. He would also carry some civilian clothing: a pair of khakis, a pair of jeans, a few polo shirts, and a fleece for colder weather. For extreme cold he had a tan Gore-Tex jacket that was rated for −32 degrees. Overkill for North Carolina, but better slightly warm than freezing cold.

The civilian clothing was for integration with 'Indigenous Personnel,' which in this case would be American citizens. Should he ever need to hide in plain sight, he would be wearing his civvies.

Inside the closet he pulled out a large charging board with four slots for a radio to be locked in and recharged. He plugged this into an outlet in the closet. He slapped rechargeable batteries in four VHF radios and filled the slots on the charging board. Even without the use of repeaters, the VHF radios had a range of several miles over most terrain. He would pack all four, along with the charging board. He set aside a prepackaged medical aid kit that had everything one would need for minor surgery and lifesaving efforts on himself or a third party. Lee was a trained combat medic, as were all of the Coordinators. The medical kit would be attached with clips to the webbing on the back of his main pack.

The remainder of the closet space was taken up by cases of water and Meals, Ready-to-Eat. He would leave those until he needed to pack them when he was preparing to leave.

He stood back from his array of gear. He didn't feel good looking at it anymore. Every day for the last two weeks, he had woken up and thought to himself that none of it was real. He would not believe it until he looked at the calendar and saw that it was, in fact, far past July 3.

Though he had long since abandoned the thought that Frank would call, he allowed himself to believe that it could not possibly be that bad outside, that his mission would not be difficult, that there must be some remnant of the US government still operating but unable to make contact with him or – quite possibly – unaware that he and his teammates even existed. He clung to the belief that everything would be made right in the end.

Solitude began to take its toll.

One of the burning questions for all of the Coordinators during their training phases was *why only one Coordinator per bunker?* Wouldn't it make more sense to have a team in each bunker at the very least? They mumbled about it amongst themselves, and eventually their handlers got wind of it.

The answer that they received was an old saying, smarmily quoted.

Three can keep a secret if two are dead.

In their private discussions, the newly christened members of Project Hometown suspected that the motivations for having only one per bunker were probably more politically and fiscally motivated. State-of-the-art bunkers didn't just appear out of nowhere. Top-of-the-line hardware was not simply donated by defense contractors. Everything cost money, and if it cost money, it had to be approved. And there wasn't a soul in the US government who was going to stand in front of Congress and declare that they had a plan for the eventual downfall of the country.

But somewhere along the line, someone decided it needed to happen anyway. So how do you get money without having to explain it? You 'reallocate resources' from other earmarked budget items, and you funnel them into your special project. And you never take enough to raise a red flag.

And apparently that magic number was enough to pay for forty-eight of them.

After arranging his gear outside of the closet, he wandered around his bunker, thinking calm thoughts. He thought a lot about Deana. He knew he was idealizing her, remembering her as someone more perfect than she was. It was his loneliness, being stuck in The Hole for so long that was causing him to think this way, to cling to memories of the last, most meaningful human interaction he'd had.

He stood for a long moment, leaning his head against the wall, and tried to remember details about her. Pretended for a moment she was in the room with him. He wanted her to be there. He thought of how her pillow smelled after she'd slept next to him, how the small of her back felt through the fabric of the dress she'd worn on New Year's Eve. He couldn't even remember the color of the dress, but he could remember how she'd felt in it. And her kiss tasted like cherry lip gloss and champagne.

He pulled himself off the wall and knelt down to his array of gear. He grabbed one of the M4 magazines and opened the green ammo can containing the 5.56mm ammunition. The smell of gun oil, brass, and the musty metal container ripped thoughts of Deana far away. He loaded the magazine with thirty rounds, then the next, and the next, until all thirteen were filled. Then he started on the pistol magazines.

Later that night, he woke up with tears in his eyes and a sinking feeling in his stomach, though he couldn't remember what he had dreamed to make him feel that way. He rolled over and went back to sleep.

On July 19 he packed everything. His magazines were stashed in his chest rig, his MK23 was snug in a drop-leg holster, the Glock 19 cradled in a hidden compartment of his go-to-hell pack. He had enough water and food in his main pack to last a week. He estimated his main pack at about eighty pounds, his go-to-hell pack at about thirty pounds. It was a lot of weight for one man to carry, but he was trained to do it over rough terrain for miles on end.

He was 100 percent ready. He paced his bunker, thinking everything through.

Eventually, Lee returned to the closet and unpacked everything.

He was listening to music a lot. It helped him cope with the sense of loneliness. Often he thought he was the last person in the world. He wondered if he would find a soul still alive outside. He thought that by the time he got to the surface, everyone would be dead, and he would be the only human being left. Alone for the rest of his miserable life.

Sometimes he would think he heard a noise somewhere in the bunker. The noises appeared furtive in nature and made the hairs on the back of his neck stand up. Lee got in the habit of keeping his MK23 strapped to his leg ... just in case. Theoretically, there was no way anyone or anything could get inside his bunker. He knew that if he was hearing anything at all, it was a perfectly explainable sound.

More likely, his mind was playing tricks. Solitary confinement. That's what this was beginning to feel like. For a length of time he considered the possibility that he was the subject of a secret government experiment and that his bunker was bristling with cameras and microphones. Somewhere nearby, a team of scientists watched him with intense interest and catalogued how often he brushed his teeth.

He began talking to Tango at length. About Deana, about the deaths of his mother and father, which were both long before Tango was born, so obviously he wouldn't remember. Sometimes they would talk about pop culture or politics. Tango never replied, of course, but between the music in the background and his own voice, Lee sometimes felt like he wasn't alone.

He was a survivor in a life raft, adrift in a world covered by endless oceans.

It was July 23. A week and a half out.

Lee sat on the couch with the chessboard before him on the coffee table, the pieces in frozen battle, scattered about the board, an invisible strategy forming. Dead soldiers were set to the side of the board, white on the left, black on the right. Across from Lee, Tango sat and panted on his black chess pieces. Lee had been thinking for a few minutes now, but Tango was a patient adversary.

'You think you got me, but I'm only luring you into my trap.' Lee looked at Tango as though he expected a pithy response. Finally he sighed. 'You know, the whole sphinx routine is getting old. Not talking shit doesn't make you the better man; it just makes you a quiet loser.'

Lee shuffled his knight in its L-shaped move and pushed a black bishop out of the way with it. He removed the bishop from the board and set it to the right with the rest of its fallen comrades.

'Yeah.' Lee nodded. 'What do you think about that?'

Tango sniffed at his king, still safely ensconced behind a row of pawns, then licked it.

'A ballsy move on your part, Tango. But I don't know if it's going to pay off in the long run.' Lee eyed the board for a moment and then moved a black rook into a position that forced Lee's white knight to run back from whence he came. After he moved the piece, Lee hissed through his teeth. 'Ouch. You got me. No, seriously. You're getting better at this. I mean, what's the score? Two to three? Two to two? I know I've won twice. You might be smarter than me.'

Tango rested his chops on the table and huffed, obviously bored with chess. The force of the huff knocked the black king over.

'Oh.' Lee sat back on the couch. 'It's like that, is it? I'm not a worthy opponent, so you're just not going to bother with playing me? God, you can be so conceited sometimes.'

He reached forward and rubbed Tango on the head to let him know it was all in good fun. Tango looked pleased and banged his tail on the ground. Lee sat back on the couch and fiddled with the retention strap on his drop-leg holster. His eyes wandered the room and finally came to rest on the door.

The locked and sealed door to the outside world. Well, actually to the basement of his house. But still . . . it was freedom. He wanted to open that door.

Strange.

He hadn't thought of that before. After so many hours trapped down here, he had never even considered violating the protocols and leaving his bunker early. After all, if there was no US government, then there was no one to give a shit if he broke some protocols. If there was a US government, then there was no reason for him to be shut up down here for the next week and a half. It made sense.

'That' – he pointed at Tango, garnering a look of confusion – 'is dangerous thinking.'

He stood up and walked to the door, mumbling to himself. 'Protocols are meant to protect you. The rules are there to guide you when you are not thinking clearly, such as if you have been in a sunless underground bunker for the past month. Like me. I am not thinking clearly.'

He put his hand on the wheel of the hatch but didn't spin it. Slowly he leaned in and put his ear to the metal. The steel door was cold to the touch and smelled faintly like the inside of a warship – metallic and oily. The sound from the other side was complete, tomb-like silence.

Lee withdrew his ear.

He looked at Tango, who was watching him with what looked like suspicion.

'Well, what do you think?'

Tango smiled, wagged once, and sauntered forward so that he was standing at the door, facing it. Lee wondered if it was as tough for a dog to be indoors this long as it was for a human. He thought that it was probably worse, considering how excited dogs got about going outside. He supposed the dog truly missed being outdoors more than Lee did. To his credit, Tango was handling his misery very well.

'Can't hurt, I guess.' Lee rested his hand on the butt of his pistol. 'Well, actually it can hurt a lot. We don't really know what's out there.'

Somehow the concept of waiting to leave at the thirty-day mark, and then being snuffed out within hours of exiting the bunker seemed sickeningly ironic. It would be marginally better, then, if he were going to die upon exiting the bunker, that he should do it now, rather than wait another week in misery and loneliness.

Maybe there are people outside. Maybe they're good and maybe they're bad. Maybe they need my help. Lee turned away from the door and walked back to the closet where all of his gear was still organized on the floor. At the moment he was wearing a pair of cargo pants and an old T-shirt. If he were to go outside, he would want to be wearing full PPE, in case things were worse than he expected.

He dove into the closet and retrieved a duffel containing a fresh MOPP 4 suit. It was supposedly rated to protect against most biological, chemical, or nuclear agents. He was familiar with the getup from his time in Iraq. During the invasion of Iraq, anytime intel was received that hinted at WMDs being used, command would have everyone go to MOPP 4. He had spent many, many hours in that thing.

Luckily, this one was new, unlike the one from Baghdad that smelled of old sweat and body odor. The smell never came out of those things. It was Lee's theory that the charcoal lining sucked it up and kept it in there. Lee opened the duffel and pulled out the MOPP suit. Then he stood up. He grimaced. 'You know what? This isn't a good idea.' Tango tilted his head, ears forward. 'You're not gonna go anyway.' Lee waved him off.

He thought for a long moment. Pros and cons of opening the bunker.

First of all, he wasn't leaving.

Just opening the door, taking a quick peek out into the world. Recon. That's all it was. And like any good special operations soldier, he needed recon in order to plan his mission effectively. Recon equals intelligence, equals good plans, equals victory.

It was all very simple.

He wasn't even going to violate the protocol. Protocol stated not to leave the bunker until thirty days after his last transmission from command. He would not be leaving. He would be scouting out his area of insertion. Possibly clear it of any threats. Make sure that when he did leave the bunker at the appropriate time, it was smooth sailing. There was no directive that stated he couldn't recon the area.

Yeah ... recon.

'Okay.' Lee nodded to himself, then pointed at Tango. 'But you have to stay here.'

Tango couldn't register the words, but he must have heard Lee's tone and seen him point. He lowered himself to the ground, lying with his head up, curiously observing Lee as he readied himself. Boots went on first, a pair of Bates M-6 Desert Assault boots, which Lee swore by. After tying them snugly, he removed the thigh holster and set it on the back of the couch. He kicked his legs into the MOPP suit and then pulled his arms into it and zipped it up. He pulled on his gas mask and checked the seal. He put on his pistol belt, then attached his drop-leg to it and pulled the hood up over his head, making sure no skin was showing. Last on were his gloves.

He breathed a couple of times with the gas mask on, got used to the feel of it. Then he walked to the hatch. He reached for the wheel, then thought better of it and returned to the closet, mumbling again to himself. 'Can't be too prepared . . .'

He grabbed his go-to-hell pack and slung it over his shoulders. He snapped on the chest belt and pivoted his torso several times, then tightened the shoulder straps, then repeated the pivoting. Satisfied that the pack was secure on his person, he walked back to the door and grabbed the wheel with both hands.

He looked at Tango, as though seeking approval.

'Fuck it. I'm doin' it.' He cranked the wheel hard to the left and broke the seal.

FOUR

BREAK OUT

LEE PUSHED THE DOOR OUT and it swung open on well-oiled hinges, not making a sound. He stood to the side of the doorway, half of his head peering into the gloomy tunnel beyond. In any case, he wanted to avoid backlighting himself in the doorframe if there were any hostiles. This was known as 'avoiding the fatal funnel.'

He doubted any hostiles had made it through his house, into the basement, and down into the tunnel that led underground to his bunker. His house was secured with steel doors and steel frames, and all of the windows were hurricane-rated glass, made to withstand severe impacts.

Still, if someone were determined enough or saw the strategic value in his house, he or she could put the work in and find a way not only into the house but into the tunnel to his bunker. Part of him didn't believe that it could be so bad out in the world that people would be looting houses, especially ones as fortified as his.

But as he had once told a new lieutenant, fresh out of Officer Candidacy School and deployed to Iraq, *Complacency kills. Paranoia is the reason I'm still alive.*

The tunnel before him was high enough to walk upright but lower than a normal ceiling. Dim emergency lights glowed at regular intervals on the walls, bathing the length of it in a dull red. The width of the tunnel was a few feet wider than the frame of the door. Just enough for two people to walk abreast of each other. The tunnel floor was at a visible incline for about fifty yards, at which point the incline grew steeper and the remainder of the tunnel was hidden from view.

Lee visually inspected what he could of the tunnel and listened for almost a full minute before he was satisfied that there was no movement in the tunnel.

He still proceeded with caution.

He wasn't sure at what point he had drawn it, but he realized that on reflex he had un-holstered the MK23. He held it in a relaxed grip and kept it tucked close to his body. Moving quickly, he scooted through the doorframe and sidestepped to the left. Out of habit, he avoided the center of the tunnel but didn't hug the wall. He moved heel to toe down the cement corridor. The heavy fabric of the MOPP suit swish-swashed with each step and Lee could have sworn the sound was echoing down the tunnel. The concept of stealth was canceled out when wearing the damn thing.

With each step down the tunnel, a little more of its incline came into view. In the dim red light ahead, as he neared the point where the floor took its steep incline, he thought something moved.

He stopped. There was no cover or even concealment in the long tunnel. He suddenly felt very exposed. If he wanted cover he would have to run back to his bunker. He wanted to look behind him to gauge the distance back to the bunker door but didn't want to take his eyes off the tunnel ahead.

Lee clenched his teeth and shot a quick look behind him. Down the tunnel he could see the oblong oval shape of the door to his bunker. The inside of his bunker was well lit compared to the tunnel and he could see the light pouring out, silhouetting the frame of Tango, still sitting obediently but attentively at the door.

Tango was most definitely in the fatal funnel, but he didn't seem to care. Lee faced forward again. The cold cement tunnel stretched out in front of him. Silent and still. The movement had been a trick of his eyes. Probably.

He proceeded on.

The tunnel ended in a set of short steel stairs that led up to a circular hatch with a locking wheel, similar to the one on the door to his bunker. The hatch appeared to be secure and could not be opened from the outside without significant efforts. Lee relaxed for a moment, taking the time to blink rapidly, testing the acuity of his natural night vision. It was nearly 1200 hours and would be broad daylight outside; however, the hatch was in the bottom of his basement, which he had left unlit and assumed was still dark. He didn't want to use the light attached to the underside of his MK23 for fear it would draw attention. Recon was about stealth.

He holstered his sidearm but didn't clip the retention strap. He then climbed the five stairs to the hatch. He cranked the wheel to the left. The locks disengaged with only the slightest of metallic clanks, but the noise still made Lee cringe.

He reached down and pulled his pistol out again as he slowly pushed the hatch open, clearing a few inches of space – just enough for him to peek out. Even with his eyes adjusted, the basement was too dark to see anything in detail. He took a long moment to listen for shuffling feet or rustling clothing.

Anything that would tip him off to someone inside his basement.

After another minute of listening, he felt satisfied and pushed the hatch all the way open. He swiveled and gave his surroundings a quick scan with the light on his MK23. He identified the usual occupants of his basement: the water heater, the freezer where he kept venison during deer-hunting season, the tool cabinet, the pile of boxes with Christmas decorations in them.

Everything was quiet and undisturbed.

He flicked off the light.

Lee felt a wash of relief, his body relaxed from tension he hadn't been aware he was holding. The sight of his belongings, all those normal, everyday things still sitting right where he left them, made it feel as though the world was the same one he had left more than a month ago. Whatever had happened could not be that bad if his light-up Santa statue was still lying in the basement, unharmed and collecting dust until next holiday season.

Feeling more confident, Lee stepped out of the tunnel. He reached to close it behind him, paused, then pulled his hand back. The hatch lock was disengaged from the exterior by punching a code into a numbered keypad. While he didn't want anyone slipping in behind him while he was out reconning, he also didn't want to be screwing around with the keypad if he needed to beat a hasty retreat.

If anyone slipped into the tunnel behind Lee's back, Tango would discourage them from getting into the bunker.

From where he knelt he could see up the basement stairs to the main portion of his house. The door at the top was closed, but he could see daylight illuminating the cracks, making it look like a large, glowing white frame hovering in midair.

He made his way to the bottom of the stairs, keeping the pistol at low ready and keeping a sharp eye on the frame of light around the door, waiting for a flash of shadow to indicate movement on the other side.

At the top of the stairs he repeated his stop-and-listen technique until he felt certain the house was empty. He opened the door and stepped through, quickly this time, checking right, then left . . . nothing.

The basement door opened into the kitchen area. In front of him was a granite countertop that turned ninety degrees into a cooking area. Pans hung from the wall, cabinets were stacked with glasses and plates. The brown dishtowel with the white stripes still hung on the handle of the stainless oven. Everything was exactly where he had left it.

Through the windows that surrounded the kitchen, he looked out into the wooded area around his house. The light from the outside world was so bright after a month in the bunker that it nearly sapped the color out of the greenery, making the leaves appear silver in the flashing sun. It was a shock not only to his eyes but to his mind. He realized that he had half expected some post-apocalyptic world, where the trees were charred stumps jutting from the ground and the air was filled with soot.

But this was simply his backyard.

Lee hesitated for a moment. He could continue to clear his house and property, possibly get a better idea of what was going on, or he could return to his bunker and wait out the remaining days. Prudence told him he had pushed far enough and should go back . . . but now curiosity had taken hold and spurred him on.

He turned left, facing the entryway to his living room. Over the top of the couch he could see through the windows that faced the front of his house and the yard beyond. His grass had grown surprisingly long and looked almost waist high. Large weeds had taken root in the cracks of his driveway and had grown to the height of small sapling trees. Amazing what nature could do if you left it alone for a month.

Past the overgrown yard, Lee could barely see the tops of the split-log fence he'd installed along the front of his property the previous summer. A bit past the fence, Lee could just make out the two-lane blacktop of Morrison Street, shimmering in the noonday heat. He wasn't in a neighborhood and the nearest house to his was about a tenth of a mile down the road.

The Petersons.

Jason Peterson was a cop and a good neighbor, as well as a friend to Lee. He'd helped Lee regrade his backyard when water began building up after rainstorms and had displayed some prowess with a Bobcat. He hunted with Lee on occasion, and when Lee couldn't make it out to bag a deer, Jason always made sure to bring him several pounds of venison and some scraps for Tango.

Lee clenched his jaw.

There was a footpath that connected his backyard to the Petersons'. It would only take five minutes to skirt the edge of the property and take a look at his neighbors' house to see how they had fared. He figured it would be a decent litmus test of how things were overall.

Plus, it was the right thing to do. Even just gaining a vantage point on the Petersons' house would allow him to gauge how bad things truly were. Obviously his own yard would be overgrown, since he had been living in The Hole for the past month. It was not necessarily indicative of how the rest of the world was going. If he saw the Petersons' yard clean cut, then obviously things couldn't be that bad.

Lee stepped into the living room and swept left and right as he had in the kitchen. All was clear. His front door was still secured and none of his windows appeared broken or tampered with. He moved through the living room to the front door. The door was steel, but he had installed sidelights with the impact-resistant glass he'd used everywhere else in the house. He liked to be able to see who was knocking on his front door.

This made him think about receiving packages from UPS and he wondered if that would ever occur again.

He cupped a hand against the sidelight glass and peered through. Everything seemed very still. The blacktop in the distance shimmered in the July heat, and the waist-high stalks of grass in his front yard lilted motionless in the baking sun. Not a breeze to stir a blade of grass.

Lee twisted the deadbolt and heard the cylinder disengage with a *clack*, making him flinch. It sounded like the loudest noise he'd heard in ages. He turned the doorknob, felt it catch and release from the doorframe. The weather stripping crackled as the long-sealed door finally separated and swung open.

The heat of summer hit him in the face like steam from a boiling pot. It smelled like grass and pollen and baking concrete. The calls of cicadas, rising and falling, seemed overwhelmingly loud. The air seemed full of flying insects, flitting back and forth across his overgrown lawn. It felt as though nature was completely unaware of his existence, or the existence of any man.

He stepped out onto the front porch and felt the heat and humidity blanket him. Without looking, he pulled the door quietly shut behind him. He walked to the edge of the three wooden steps from his porch to the concrete walkway that led to his driveway. The grass around his front porch appeared flat. Trampled.

He took the steps, looking to his left, toward the footpath to the Petersons'. The next thing he knew he was falling, landing hard on the ground. He felt the concrete bounce the side of his face and the breath came out of him with a *whoosh*.

He heard something shrill, like a woman shrieking. Something had him by the leg. He tried to roll onto his back but felt an iron grip on his ankle, pulling his leg through the stairs into the shadows underneath. He flailed, kicking with his free leg, then bringing his heel down hard on whatever held him. He felt his boot hit something and then his ankle was free.

He rolled onto his back, holding the pistol between his knees. Two pale, bony arms reached through the stairs, trying to grab at his feet. In the hand of one was a small knife, slashing the air repeatedly in an X pattern. He tried to kick the knife, but the arms retreated under the stairs again. He scooted backward and pulled his legs underneath him, trying to gain his feet. Something came out from behind the stairs, scuttling toward him on hands and knees, making noises that he couldn't distinguish as words. Instinct told him to launch with his legs and he thrust himself backward, landing again on his back. His attacker seemed small but was moving fast.

In the half second before it tried to stab him to death, he had the impression of a young girl wearing a smock or a loose white dress, with long, wild hair hanging down around her face.

She reared up and swung down hard, planting the small knife in Lee's left thigh. Lee let out a noise like a cough or a bark and shoved his pistol against the top of the girl's chest and pulled the trigger.

He felt the pressure of the blast on his face and watched the back of her gown burst out. He swung hard with his right knee, catching her in the jaw. She fell to the side, pulling the knife out of Lee's thigh as she went. He was on his feet fast, despite the wound to his leg. He breathed rapidly, his chest burning as the gas mask restricted his airflow. Each inhale and exhale rattled the filter. He pointed his pistol straight out in front of him, finger on the trigger, and backpedaled toward the porch.

The girl – fifteen years old was his best guess – was down but getting up. Even over the rattle of his own breath, Lee could hear the gurgling of her chest wound. 'Stay the fuck down!' Lee yelled.

The girl was standing now, hunched over, strange-looking eyes staring from under a hood of tangled hair. She pointed the bloody knife at him. 'You!' It was a wheezing whisper.

'Drop that knife!'

'You!' She started forward.

He pulled the trigger, instinctively aiming center mass. Three shots in quick succession at near point-blank range spattered her chest in red. She stumbled back but didn't go down. Her breath came out again like she was trying to say something but couldn't form the words. She put one foot in front of the other, and Lee turned and took the three wooden stairs to the porch in one bound. He planted his shoulder into his front door, noticing as he went that there was a piece of paper taped to the door. He didn't have time to grab it. He spun in the doorway, slammed the front door and locked it, then sprinted for the basement door.

He nearly tripped going down the stairs, feeling the pain in his thigh now. His footfalls were a rapid tumble. He hit the basement floor, blind in the dark, and groped around for the hatch. His hand touched cold metal.

He heard something banging on the front door upstairs. 'Slow down,' he told himself but didn't take his own advice. He nearly dove in, hitting his elbow and the top of his fore-head on the frame as he scrambled in. He slammed the hatch behind him, twisted it to lock it in place, then skipped the metal stairs and jumped straight to the ground.

Pain shot up his leg and his knees buckled, crashing him to the floor. He got up and ran for a few steps, then slowed to a jog, knowing that it was panic driving him and trying to battle it off. He breathed deep and tried not to think about the girl running swiftly and silently up behind him to slit his throat.

The door to the bunker came into view and Tango stood up, his head lowered, sensing something was wrong.

'Move,' Lee snapped as he lurched through the door, push-ing Tango out of the way with his wounded leg, then wincing as he realized it was a bad choice. Tango's attention was fix-ated down the tunnel.

Lee swore as he slammed the hatch closed and whipped the wheel into the locked position. He ripped the gas mask off his face, tasted fresh air. He moved quickly to the kitchen sink, pulling open the cabinet doors and grabbing a bottle of bleach from underneath. He spun the cap off and started dousing himself right there in the middle of the kitchen.

He rubbed the bleach all over the exterior of the MOPP suit as he marched into the bathroom with the bottle of bleach and cranked on the hot water. He waited for the water to start steaming and then stepped in, still fully dressed. He doused himself two more times with bleach, working it over every inch of the MOPP suit. The water seeped in and stung his skin. He started pulling the suit off, swearing under his breath through clenched teeth as the scalding hot water sprayed over him. Rivulets of hot water snaked down his body and found his fresh leg wound. He cried out in pain and punched the wall of the shower.

'So fucking stupid!' he yelled.

He doused himself three times head to toe with the bleach, rubbing it everywhere, including the open knife wound, which brought tears to his eyes. He rinsed with the scalding water and stepped out of the shower. He skipped drying and dressing and went straight to his closet where his medical pack lay, grabbing a hand towel off the bathroom sink as he went.

'There's no way I got myself infected. No fucking way.' Lee didn't believe himself.

He riffled through the pack, pulling out a bottle of hydrogen peroxide, yanking off the cap, and pouring it over the wound. He watched as the clear liquid cascaded over the wound, then stung and started to bubble. The more bubbles, the dirtier the wound. There was no telling what the hell was on that knife or if she had used it to stab or cut someone else who was infected. Lee could see the bacteria as microscopic ants racing through his bloodstream, already beginning to pick away at his frontal lobe.

As the hydrogen peroxide did its work, he inspected the wound and thought about the consequences of his ill-fated recon mission. He estimated the knife was about three inches long – he thought it was a kitchen paring knife. Though the blade was only a half inch wide, when she stabbed him she'd pulled it down, slicing open an extra inch of flesh. There was definite muscle damage, but nothing so severe that it would inhibit his movement.

He pulled out a sterile-packaged syringe and held it between his teeth, then found a bottle of lidocaine, an iodine wipe, a pack of triple antibiotic ointment, two medium-size gauze pads, and a pack of suturing needles with a length of nylon thread.

He used the first gauze pad and pressed it down on his wound, kicking his leg up onto the back of his couch to keep it elevated and to reduce the blood flow that had already created red streams that crisscrossed his lower leg down to his ankle and had begun dripping on the floor. While holding the gauze firmly on the wound and grinding his teeth against the sharp pain, he mopped up the blood on the floor and on his leg with the hand towel he'd grabbed on the way out of the shower.

After a few moments of firm, stinging pressure on the wound, he pulled the gauze away and checked the blood flow. The wound filled slowly with blood and trickled over again onto his leg, but the blood wasn't pulsing, which meant no arterial damage, and the flow seemed to be abating with the elevation and pressure. Luckily – if you could call it that – the wound was a clean cut, so he didn't need to use a scalpel to remove any 'nonviable' tissue or smooth out the edges as you would with a ripping or tearing wound. That would save Lee a significant amount of pain.

He put the gauze back down and held it in place with his elbow while both hands worked open the sterile syringe package and used it to draw a few CCs of lidocaine. He cleared the syringe of air and clamped it back in his teeth, then opened the iodine wipe. He pulled off the bloody gauze pad and tossed it on the ground, then swabbed the area around the wound with the iodine wipe, staining his skin a yellowish brown.

He injected small doses of lidocaine into several areas around his wound, creating the effect of a local anesthetic. When the few CCs of lidocaine were done, he put the cap back on the syringe and dropped it with the bloody gauze. Lee waited a few breaths until the stinging sensation in his leg began to numb, then strung a curved suture needle with the nylon thread. He fished out a pair of hemostats and some small shears to cut the nylon thread and began stitching the wound closed. It took five stitches and about ten minutes to close the wound.

He salved it with the triple antibiotic ointment and slapped on a fresh gauze pad, then held it in place with surgical tape.

Patched up, he went back to his bathroom and retrieved the MK23 from its holster, buried in the wet, bleachy jumble of his ruined MOPP suit. He ejected the magazine and cleared the chamber. The thing was still dripping with water and bleach. He inspected the muzzle for any foreign substance – hair, skin, or blood – that might have blown back from the chest of the girl and still be clinging to the weapon.

His hand abruptly began to shake violently as he tried to focus on the weapon. He felt his breath catch in his throat, and for a moment he watched her, chest poked full of .45-caliber holes, still standing, still coming toward him. He remembered the iron pressure of her grip, holding onto his ankle. What teenage girl had that type of strength?

Unable to hold the pistol still, he dismantled it with fumbling fingers and laid the parts out on his bathroom counter to dry.

He needed to get dressed.

FIVE

THE PETERSONS

LEE PULLED ON A NEW PAIR of MultiCam combat pants. His boots were drying in the shower stall, still soaking wet from his hasty decontamination. Wet boots were a curse, and he wasn't going to be putting in any miles in the outside world until they were dry.

That was his excuse, anyway.

He kept replaying the image of the girl coming out from behind the stairs. The spidery way she scuttled toward him on all fours, the thin arms, only skin and bones but shockingly powerful. It reminded him of how a person on drugs or who was mentally deranged could display extreme amounts of physical strength and stamina. He figured that it might have something to do with her frontal lobe looking like Swiss cheese.

Was she just an example of how the rest of the world had become?

He pictured crowds, riotous mobs entirely peopled by sick, violent, and superhumanly strong mental patients waving sharp kitchen implements, lead pipes, and other weapons of opportunity.

He tried to remember what the girl's face looked like, but all he could remember was her wild, tangled hair and those strange, demented eyes. He wondered if he knew the girl. Surely she had to live around here somewhere. Were her parents still alive and sane?

And he kept thinking about the Petersons. Jason and his wife, Marla, and their four-year-old girl, Stephanie. Jason was a smart guy and tough as nails, but Lee didn't know if he would've been ready for something like this. Toughness only went so far. He hoped that people had been able to get help from the FEMA camps. He hoped the Petersons were safe somewhere.

Lee made up his mind then and there to check on the Petersons. Tomorrow. Holing up in his bunker had become counterproductive. It was no longer an option. In another two weeks, things could only be worse. If the Petersons had secured their residence and were waiting for rescue, Lee might be their only chance.

Besides, rendering aid was his primary objective.

I am Captain Lee Harden of the United States Army. The US government has sent me to help you.

That was the script Lee was required to say when rescuing people. Project Hometown existed so people would know that no matter how bad things got, the United States government was still there, still fighting for them. In the front pocket of Lee's go-to-hell pack he had a laminated card that read those very same words in five different languages.

After that, the Petersons were all Lee could think about.

Lee slept poorly that night.

After cleaning his MK23 and topping off the magazine, he drank a few bottles of water and cooked a freeze-dried meal of spaghetti and meat sauce, since all the fresh food had been used. He barely tasted the food and didn't feel like eating it, but he crammed it down anyway because he knew he needed to eat something.

The knife wound began to feel itchy, which immediately made Lee think of infection, though it was unlikely that infection would have set in so fast. Every time he thought of the plague spreading through his brain, his stomach curdled with anxiety.

What a shitty way to go.

Late into the evening he lay on his bed, felt his forehead for a fever, and cleared his throat to see if he were developing a cough. He had no appetite, but that was not surprising given what he'd done to the girl.

Frank had said infected subjects were asymptomatic for up to seventy-two hours, but that didn't mean it couldn't happen faster. Catching through saliva would always take longer to metastasize than being direct-injected into his bloodstream from a filthy, plague-infected knife.

He slept in his combat pants, on top of the covers, with his M4 locked and loaded and tucked in close to his body. Tango lay on the floor to the side of the bed. Lee woke several times in the night to find Tango staring at the bunker door with his ears fully erect. Occasionally, he would emit a low growl, deep in his throat. The dog's attention to the door made the hairs stand up on the back of Lee's neck.

Each time it happened, Lee's pulse would pound in his head so hard it seemed to make the room shake, and he would think to himself that there was no way he was going to be able to fall back asleep. But each time, he would stare at the door, and find his thoughts wandering and his heart rate cooling down, and then his eyes would grow heavy once more.

*

By 0500 hours he decided to get up.

He'd been awake, hugging his M4 and staring at the clock, for the past half hour and when it turned, he immediately sat up. He didn't switch on the lights because it would still be dark outside and he didn't want to ruin his natural night vision. He went to the bathroom and leaned the rifle against the bathroom counter while he relieved himself. While he had his pants undone, he pulled them down far enough to inspect the bandage on his wound. There was only a small spot of blood that had soaked through, but he changed the bandage anyway and applied a fresh coat of ointment. The wound wasn't red, swollen, or itchy. If it were going to get infected, it would have most likely begun to show signs.

After pulling his pants back up, he threw on his combat shirt, pistol belt, and drop-leg holster. He checked that the magazine of his MK23 was topped off, seated securely in the magazine well, and that there was a round in the chamber, then holstered the weapon. His boots were still a little damp on the inside, but he felt like a few hours of body heat would take care of it.

He pulled on his chest rig, which held six double-magazine pouches (twelve magazines total) for his M4. The thirteenth magazine was already loaded in his rifle. He adjusted the straps on the rig until he was comfortable with the weight distribution, then double-checked each of the magazines to ensure they were all fully loaded.

He doubted he would need this much ammunition for his incursion to the Petersons' house, but then again, he had doubted yesterday that a crazed fifteen-year-old girl would jump out from underneath his front steps and stab him in the leg. He realized that his complacency had nearly killed him, just as he had warned that young lieutenant in Iraq. His attitude had transformed overnight, from skeptical to vigilant. He was going to expect and prepare for the absolute worst. His mind had been full of doubts yesterday. He didn't want to believe that the world was spiraling out of control or that it was already in ruins. The extent of the damage to American civilization was as yet unknown. What he did know was that he would have to err on the side of caution. If it had been a full-grown man who had attacked him yesterday, he wasn't sure he would be alive. Mistakes in this new reality would be far more costly than Lee could afford.

On a positive note, he was still asymptomatic.

He didn't feel like bothering with dehydrated scrambled eggs, so he grabbed a handful of PowerBars, shoving one into his mouth and the remaining three into his pack. He washed it down with a hastily mixed 'Orange beverage' that came in a small single-serving packet. It had plenty of vitamin C and carbohydrates for immediate energy. Like energy for running and fighting. Energy he hoped he wouldn't need but had the jumpy feeling that he would.

After his quick breakfast, he shouldered his go-to-hell pack, then slipped on his single-point sling and connected it to his M4. He was going out without the MOPP suit, as he felt that its noise and encumbrance outweighed the benefit of the very little good it would do to protect against a bacterial infection. He was, however, going to wear his gas mask. He just wished he'd received more information from Frank about the plague. Perhaps Abe would know. He would email him about it when he got back.

After masking up and checking the seal, he pulled the charging handle of his M4 back halfway, noted the glint of brass waiting in the chamber, and let it slide forward and lock. He flipped the safety off. That was what trigger fingers were for.

'Tango.' Lee pointed to a spot next to his foot. 'Heel.'

Tango's ears perked and he came running over, excited. It was time to work, which, for him, meant fun, fun, fun. He had no idea what was going on in the world, and that was excellent. Dogs never realized the horrible situations they were in. That's why police K9s wag their tails while attacking armed gunmen. Even one traumatic incident resulting in a negative experience for the dog doing what he was trained to do could ruin it.

It was good that Tango was happy to go outside. But Lee sure as hell wasn't. He looked at his dog, standing by his right side and looking up at his master expectantly. 'Tango, sneak.'

This wasn't a normal command, but Lee had taught Tango a few tricks outside of the usual Schutzhund training. Tango immediately pulled in his lolling tongue and his head lowered ever so slightly, his shoulders hunching a bit, giving him the appearance of a wolf stalking its prey. As long as Lee kept reminding Tango to 'sneak,' the dog would keep low to the ground and wouldn't make a sound. It was almost unnerving for Lee to watch his canine friend revert back to his feral roots.

Lee reached forward and opened the bunker door.

The red-bathed tunnel stretched out before him. It looked empty. He felt a bit of relief and supposed he had been expecting the crazed girl from yesterday to be standing there, waiting for him.

Surely she was dead. No one could survive that many shots to the chest.

Lee and Tango made their way down the tunnel, both moving silently. While moving, Lee quietly but with an excited tone told Tango 'Good,' earning a wag of the tail. He reminded the dog to 'sneak,' and Tango went back to sneaking. Lee did this without even thinking. The cycle of command, obedience, and reinforcement was second nature to Lee, and when possible, he would reward the dog with something. He kept an old chewed-up rope in his cargo pocket, a toy that Tango was particularly fond of. It was Tango's treat for a job well done.

At the stairs, Lee went up first to unlock the hatch. He pushed it open and surveyed the basement, much as he had done the previous day. All clear. He clicked his tongue and Tango quickly climbed the stairs and edged around his legs and into the basement. Lee pushed the hatch closed behind him and punched in the code to lock it. He waited until he heard the *click*, then turned toward the stairs.

In his flight the previous day, he had left the door from the basement into the kitchen standing open. The ambient light coming from upstairs was enough for Lee's adjusted eyes to see the staircase clearly, and that no one stood in the doorway to the kitchen.

He kept the M4 at a low ready as he moved toward the stairs, with his non-trigger hand patting Tango. 'Stay.' Tango sat, ears forward, eyes locked on the doorway up the stairs.

Normally the dog would go first and seek out the threats to prevent harm to the human counterpart. In this situation, with Tango as his only partner and not knowing whether the virus was transmittable from humans to animals, Lee did not want Tango biting any infected people unnecessarily.

Lee made his way up the stairs and cleared the house, the knot in his gut that was always there before shit hit the fan starting to abate as he went through the motions. Each time he prepared to enter a room, the anxiety would flare, then dissipate as he moved. It reminded him of Fallujah, fighting house to house. At the beginning of those long nights he would be sick to his stomach and his hands would be shaking.

Then after they breached the first door, the nerves would begin to fade. By the time they were on their third house of the night, he would feel relatively normal.

On edge, as he was now, but normal. After clearing the house, he went to the kitchen and found that Tango's curiosity had gotten the best of him and he'd made his way to the top of the stairs and was peering into the kitchen, his nose working the air. Lee held back admonition. Good working dogs were sometimes hard to control.

'Come on.' Lee tapped his thigh and Tango padded into the room. 'Sneak,' he reminded Tango.

He made his way to the front door. It still stood intact. The sick feeling made a comeback. He edged over to the sidelight and angled his vision around the front porch. A pale foot lay there, stretched out away from the front door, toes pointed down. The foot was small, petite, even. The girl from yesterday, he knew, and fought acid rising in the back of his throat. He stared, though he couldn't see anything above the calf. The skin was gray and waxy-looking. It was covered in scrapes and harsh bruising, as though she'd run recklessly through a patch of briars.

The logical part of Lee's brain told him that she had to be dead. But something else inside of him cringed, expecting the worst. Lee angled his body and pointed his rifle in the approximate location that he felt her head would be. For a moment, the gun felt heavy and awkward in his hands. For someone who had grown up around firearms, Lee felt that brief feeling crumpling his already shaky confidence. He could taste his half-digested PowerBar creeping up into his mouth. He didn't want to shoot this girl again. He reached forward and touched the cool metal of the doorknob. The door swung open.

Her hand came down, still holding that small knife.

Lee jumped back and only just kept himself from firing a round. The girl lay dead, but her arm had been propped against the door and had fallen when he'd opened it. She was no longer a threat.

Tango rushed in, fascinated and wanting to stick his nose in it. Lee shoved the dog away with his leg and stated in a stern voice, 'No! Leave it . . . Leave it.'

Tango pressed at his leg until Lee gave him a good jab in the ribs with his knee and repeated the command. Finally Tango stood back, but he let out a pitiful whine and stared at the dead girl, transfixed.

The door was covered in smeared blood and pocked with tiny dents made with the point of her knife. She had somehow managed to crawl onto his porch after being shot several times in the chest with a .45-caliber bullet, and had obviously spent some time pounding on the door, whether in rage, or desperation, or perhaps a bit of both.

The front mat was entirely soaked in blood. The sight of blood in large quantities never ceased to turn Lee's stomach. There was something so . . . not Hollywood about it. Artificial blood looked artful and pretty. The splatters were perfect, the pools were all one homogenous color. Paint by Numbers gore. In reality, the aftermath of a traumatic wound was chaotic and disgusting. There was always some strange chunk of anatomy that came out with the blood flow that made you lean in closer and say to yourself, *What the fuck is that?*

These images also had a cumulative effect. Lee found them harder to bear now than when he'd been a younger man. Looking from the dead girl to the pockmarks on the door, he noticed the piece of paper he had not had time to read the day before. It was lined and clearly torn from a spiral notebook. It was held to the door with a single bit of clear tape. The words were handwritten and short.

Lee reached up and plucked it off the door, eyeing the dead girl while he did it. Her failure to die when most others would have made him highly uneasy and he kept thinking about her getting up, even now, and cutting into him with that knife. Before diverting his attention to the note, he kicked the knife away from her hand. Tango tracked it with his eyes as it skittered across the foyer, but he didn't make a move for it.

The note was from Marla Peterson.

Lee,
Jason did not come home from work today and didn't call. We thought maybe he was with you. If you find this note, FEMA is evacuating us at 1 PM today to a camp in Sanford. Please tell Jason to find us as soon as he can and tell him I love him. We will wait for him in Sanford as long as we can.

Marla

The note was dated 7/05.

Lee felt somehow responsible for this, though he couldn't tell why. Sanford was a small city about fifty miles southwest of Raleigh. It seemed like an unlikely and out-of-the-way place to put a FEMA camp, but then again, in a viral outbreak, you would want the safe zones to be a significant distance from major population centers.

Where Lee stood now was about thirty miles directly east of Sanford, outside the small town of Angier. He could make the trip in two days, three at the most. Of course his pickup truck was parked in his garage with a full tank and would theoretically get him there within an hour, but in a social collapse, without the threat of force from police officers and highway patrol, thugs and psychopaths reclaimed the streets and made them the most dangerous place to be.

Driving was out of the question for now. He would stick to cross-country hiking. And then there was the question of Jason and his whereabouts.

Obviously, he had not been with Lee. As a police officer, he was probably one of the last to be able to run with his family. Lee saw four likely possibilities. Either Jason was already with his family, was trying to make his way to his family, was holed up in his house waiting for help, or he was dead.

In any case, Lee's objective remained the same. He folded the note carefully and placed it in his pants pocket. Attention back on the girl splayed out on the welcome mat, Lee gingerly poked the body with the toe of his boot, not sure why he still felt that he would garner a response. They say the less distance there is between you and the person you kill, the more traumatizing it can be. In Iraq, he knew he'd killed people, but mostly it was shooting at muzzle flashes in windows. Only once did he gun a man down while clearing a house. In that instance, the man had been about twenty feet away, reaching for the AK next to him. Through the night-vision device Lee had been wearing, the man had appeared expressionless, emotionless. Just a green specter.

Barely even human.

In the girl's case he had looked her in the eye, as demented as those eyes might have been, and shot her at point-blank range. Then he'd stood up and shot her again. Finally, he'd left her to wallow in a crazy rage as she tried to stab his door and eventually bled to death.

He prayed to God for forgiveness and refused to think about it anymore.

When he was satisfied that the girl was dead, he stepped over her body and, with gloved hands, pulled her by the ankles off of his welcome mat to clear the doorway. He had first intended to pull her off the porch completely, but after yesterday's surprise attack, he didn't feel comfortable backing his way down the stairs. Besides that, it was still dark, and Lee wanted to check his perimeter before he left for the Petersons' house.

He pulled the girl as quietly as he could to the left of the door so she was out of the way. He would dispose of the body when it was light out and he knew his perimeter was secure. While dragging her he noticed rather detachedly that she'd defecated on herself, though he wasn't sure whether this was during her death or whether the infected insane were unaware of their bowel movements.

Loss of muscle control was a symptom of late-stage infection; however, she'd seemed quite in control of her muscles the previous day and had even talked, though it was only one word. He felt that most likely, she was in the early stages of infection and that self-defecation was a by-product of her loss of sanity.

Once he had her moved, he patted his leg, getting Tango's attention. 'Come on. Sneak.'

They left the porch, taking the stairs very carefully this time. Every shadow held a ghost and every grass blade that blew in the soft breeze drew his attention. They made a circle around the house, checking all the nooks and crannies, and found everything secure. Whoever the girl was, she had been there alone.

Died alone. Covered in blood and shit.

By the time Lee had checked the perimeter of his house, the horizon to the east was getting gray, and the cacophony of early morning birds had begun. He also found himself sweating, and noted that it was already warm and humid out. Today was going to be a scorching North Carolina summer day. One of those 'jungle days,' where you got more moisture than air in each breath.

They'd completed a clockwise circle around the house, checking the garage and the crawl spaces underneath the house. Tango never alerted or growled. Just kept his head down and stalked along Lee's side. Lee felt more secure with the dog there, and with his keen nose and guarding instincts, he would serve as an early warning of any human activity in the area – good or bad.

Back where they started, at the northeastern corner of the house, Lee veered off toward the edge of his yard, where his once-manicured lawn turned abruptly into woods. Heading directly north for a little less than two hundred yards would land him in the Petersons' backyard.

He moved slowly through the woods. The light of dawn on the gray trees gave everything a monochromatic look. Each new section of woods looked exactly like the last. The damp air and the dew covering the forest floor made movement quiet and limited the crunch of the leaves he stepped on. Aside from his own breath rattling in the gas mask, the woods were silent.

Finally, the woods opened up into a clearing.

He was at the bottom of a steep hill, over the top of which he could just make out the roofline of the Petersons' house. To his left was a shallow gully with a stream passing through it. Making his way through the woods, he felt that it was less and less likely that he would find anyone in the house. There was no reason for Jason to be there if his family was gone. He was a good guy and a family man, and he wouldn't let Marla and

Stephanie sit in some FEMA camp alone. If he hadn't made the evacuation, he'd be making his way across country to them.

Still . . .

He wanted to know that the Petersons had made it out. The thought of them in safety gave him a bit of hope, a positive feeling.

He and Tango made their way up the hill. More of the house came into view as they gained elevation. Unsure who – or what – might be in or around the house, Lee approached with caution, using trees as cover and concealment as he got closer to the house. Between stands of trees, he ran at a half crouch, keeping his eyes on the shadows.

He noted only one thing as he got closer: An upstairs light was on, causing a single window to glow with muted yellow light.

This meant a few things to Lee. He knew that the Petersons, not being survival-minded people, had not rigged their house for off-grid electricity as he had. If there was a light burning in the house, it meant that the grid was still up. He only assumed that with all the evacuations in the surrounding area, the power plant employees would have also left, but perhaps the National Guard had replaced them or perhaps the power plants were on an automated system.

It wasn't long into this thought that he noticed the light flicker. It was a candle. This told him something completely different. A candle did not burn indefinitely. If a candle was burning inside the house it meant that someone was there now or had been there very recently. Jason? Or a squatter.

Lee still held firm to his opinion that Jason would not stick around when his family was elsewhere. Which meant someone was in the house who didn't belong there. Lee considered how he would approach this situation.

On the one hand, breaking and entering became less of a criminal act and more of a necessity during times of social collapse, when finding shelter was tantamount to surviving the night.

On the other hand, it was his friends' house and he felt a responsibility to keep it secure until they returned. Who knew when the crisis would be over and people would be returning home? He wouldn't want the Petersons finding their home and belongings ransacked and stolen in the name of some hobo's 'survival.'

It was a gray area.

He would have to feel out the situation. The squatters could be shitbags, using the house as a base to set up roadblocks or store whatever they stole. Or it could be a family traveling on foot, trying to find a safe place to spend the night.

Lee moved to the back of the house, Tango following at a trot. He kept his rifle trained on the windows, in case a lookout spotted them. The Aimpoint sight mounted on his M4 was dialed low so the red dot was not overpowering in the dim morning light.

At the back of the house, he moved left toward a set of wooden stairs leading to a large back deck, lifted up on stilts. The house was built into the hill so that the ground floor when looking at the front was the second floor when looking at the back.

The stairs creaked treacherously as Lee made his way up to the deck. He kept his eyes locked on the dark patio doors. They were sliding glass with no curtain covering them. Anyone inside was shrouded in the darkness and would see Lee long before he could see them. He moved quickly across the fatal funnel and posted on the left side of the sliding glass doors. Closer to the glass he could see inside.

The doors led into the living room, which appeared mostly undisturbed. There was a TV, a coffee table with some magazines on it, two couches, and a leather recliner that Lee could picture Jason sitting on every Sunday, watching football with a cold one in his hand. To the left of the room was a long hallway that led to the front door.

He tested the patio doors and found them locked. Shit.

He thought about his options. He could break the glass or try to find another entry point. Both had their risks. Whoever was in the house would almost definitely hear the glass break. Depending on how many were inside, and if they were armed or not, it could be a problem.

Lee was about to move away from the doors when he noticed someone was lying on the couch. It was a girl, young. He saw the dark, curly hair. He had missed her at first because she was lying with her back to the door, and in the half light, she blended in with all the pillows lying there.

Stephanie.

Lee wanted to get her attention, but he knew she would be scared and not recognize him in his gas mask. He made a quick decision and pulled off the mask, clipping one of the straps to a carabiner on his chest rig. He thumped the window with a gloved knuckle and whispered: 'Steph! Steph!'

She didn't respond.

He was about to knock again when he saw a dark figure standing in the hallway, watching him.

'Fuck,' he whispered and backed up a bit, leveling his rifle.

The figure wasn't concerned with his rifle. It hobbled forward with an awkward gait. It seemed like its legs and arms were stiff. Twice it almost fell, but recovered. Clutched in its right hand was what Lee thought might be a meat cleaver.

Stephanie still hadn't moved. The concept hit him like a

punch in the gut. Stephanie wasn't sleeping. She was dead. And the lunatic with the meat cleaver was the one who had killed her. Lee stepped back another foot as the man inside hobbled around the kitchen counter and raised the meat cleaver as though he didn't realize the glass door was between them. Who the fuck was this guy and why was he in the Petersons' house? Lee had never killed anyone in anger before, but now it seemed like an easy thing to do.

He lifted the rifle and put the red dot on the man's chest, then pulled the trigger. The stillness of the morning was shattered, the bark of rifle fire jabbing fiercely at Lee's eardrums. The glass exploded inward, and through the shower of glittering shards, he saw the man still coming forward, meat cleaver raised.

Lee's brain sent the signal to his finger: *Don't stop!*

As Lee pulled the trigger repeatedly, watching the man's chest lurch with each recoil, he saw the man's demented eyes, saw his face, and, for a split second, thought he knew him. Then a round caught the man's jaw and ripped it off, and the following round caved in the front of his skull.

The body dropped face-first into the broken glass but was still twitching erratically. Then Lee realized he was still firing and pulled his finger off the trigger.

Lee didn't even look at Stephanie. In the back of his mind, he registered that she had not moved through the gunfire. He knew she was dead. Instead, his eyes were locked on the body lying before him. Something was wrong but in the moment he couldn't think of it. He wanted to take the time to inspect the body, knew he had recognized that person, but also knew there could be other hostiles in the house.

Lee moved quickly into the living room and surveyed the scene as detachedly as possible. After giving Stephanie a cursory glance, he saw that her throat had been cut and that she had been dead for some time. The stench of decay in the room was suddenly overwhelming. In the kitchen, which he could see from where he stood in the living room, he observed another body. He immediately knew it was Marla. He moved in closer and looked at her face, confirming his fear. Though bloating and decay had robbed her of her kind and caring face, he knew it was her. Someone had hacked away most of her midsection. The kitchen was covered in blood spatter, obscenely reminding Lee of a Jackson Pollock painting.

The wrongness of the man with the meat cleaver finally swam to the surface of his mind. The duty belt. He was wearing a patent leather duty belt.

Lee stepped over to the body, keeping himself angled toward the hallway that led to the rest of the house, in case any other attacker came at him. He pushed hard with his foot, rolling the body onto its back.

Jason stared up at him with blank, dead eyes. Deep cuts scoured his face. Had he done that to himself? His hair had either fallen out in chunks or he had ripped it out. What was left of his face to recognize him by was sunken and sallow. The whole bottom half of his face and neck was covered in dried bloodstains. Like he had been eating the others.

Lee knelt down and sat back on his heels. He waited for emotion to overcome him, but it didn't. He knew this was just how his brain worked. He would feel it later, in the cold quiet of the night, as he was trying to sleep. The bad memories always waited until the water was calm before they floated back to the surface.

He whispered into his closed fist, 'What did you do, Jason?' Jason would never answer. Nor would his family. Tango stood at the door and chuffed, as though trying to get Lee's attention. Lee gave Jason one last look and then stood. 'Stay, Tango.' He didn't want the dog walking through the broken glass. Chances were he'd be fine, but Lee didn't have access to a vet or vet supplies if Tango got injured. Lee grabbed a throw blanket from over the top of the leather recliner that Jason would never use again. He tossed the blanket over the broken glass. 'Come on.' He clicked his tongue.

Lee didn't want to search the house. He didn't want to be anywhere near it anymore. He wanted nothing more at that moment than to leave. But he pressed on, feeling dazed. He still had a job to do. He had to clear this place. Marla and Stephanie deserved to be laid to rest. He could do that much for them.

Tango walked carefully over the blanket. Lee led the way through the kitchen to the hallway. Tango was less interested in these bodies than he was in the girl lying on their front porch, but Lee told him to 'leave it' anyway. He wasn't sure whether Stephanie and Marla had been infected prior to being killed.

He made his way down the hall, the morning light just illuminating family photos that hung on the walls. Lee took down a recent one. All three of them close together, smiling. He didn't hang the picture back up but laid it on the ground, propped against the wall.

He checked the living room, which was clear, and then headed up the stairs. At the top of the stairs, in the master bedroom, Lee found where Jason had been hiding, rotting in his insanity, his brain eaten away to only the most basic life functions. The candle Lee had seen flickering from outside still sat on a nightstand, burning with barely two inches of candle left jutting out of a pool of melted and rehardened wax.

The bedsheets were smeared in blood. Lee wasn't sure whether it was from one of the girls or from the apparent self-inflicted wounds to Jason's face. Lee steered clear of it.

In the master bathroom, he discovered something else.

On the large mirror over the double sinks, I'M SORRY was written in blood, over and over. It was also written on the walls and on the countertops. Lee thought that perhaps Jason had managed a moment of clarity amongst all the violent, insane urges that took the lives of his family and had realized what he had done. Lee pictured him there, staring at his reflection in hatred, cutting his face with the meat cleaver and using the blood that seeped out to write his message on the walls. He wondered how long that moment of understanding had lasted before he slipped back into madness and was merely writing the words out of repetition, not comprehending what they meant or what he'd done.

Lee left the bedroom, feeling light-headed. He checked on the bodies to make sure none had moved, which, of course, they hadn't. Then he made his way to the basement, and from there to the garage. He took a shovel and tossed it out the garage door into the backyard. He then put the gas mask on and went back upstairs. He took Stephanie first, cradling her very carefully in his arms, as though he didn't want to wake her. If he held the head up so the chin nearly touched the chest, he could barely see the gaping neck wound.

Even through the gas mask, the stench made him retch several times. He laid her down in a flat spot in the backyard, just before the yard sloped off. He then took Marla's body out, dragging this one by hooking his fingers under her arms. He laid her down next to her daughter.

Then he stood there and thought for several long moments about whether or not to bury Jason with them. He must have come home before they left for the FEMA camp. It wouldn't make sense for them to stick around once he'd come home, so he would've had to be already infected and symptomatic. He knew Jason worked twelve-hour shifts, but perhaps, in the emergency, they had kept everyone on for twenty-four hours. He had either become infected a few days before somehow finding his way home, or he had been grossly exposed, causing the plague to metastasize faster and mentally crippling him far sooner than he had thought it would.

Lee decided the plague was to blame, not the man.

If there was a heaven, Jason was in it for the things he'd done in his life, not for the things he had done while his brain was half eaten away. He deserved to be buried next to his family. He had loved them both immensely, and Jason the man would not have been capable of harming them.

Lee made his way back up to the house and knelt over the body of the man who had once been Jason. He noted that he was still in full uniform. Jason would have known he was infected, either through trauma resulting in gross exposure or due to the presence of symptoms. In either case, Lee felt that Jason had returned to see his family one last time before dying, not realizing that FURY was about to turn him against them.

Lee went through the two front uniform pockets, finding a crumpled note. The handwriting was shaky at best, scrawled in black ink.

If I am dead, please give this note to Marla and Stephanie Peterson at 110 Morrison Street. Steph and Marla, I was bitten in the arm by someone infected with the plague. This was earlier today and already I am showing symptoms. I tried to get home to see you both one last time, but I guess I didn't make it. Please know that I love you both and if I knew that I would end up leaving you forever, I would have never left the house to go to work. I'm so sorry.

                              Your husband and father

Lee rolled up Jason's sleeve. The right arm seemed fine, but there was a thick bandage on the left. He peeled it back and revealed a deep bite mark in the forearm, just above the wrist.

In his death, Jason had proven himself useful again, providing Lee with an invaluable piece of information: Gross exposure would result in becoming symptomatic within hours, and 'turning' presumably soon after that. In a way, Lee felt relieved. If FURY bacteria had been on the knife the girl had used to stab him with the previous day, he would have been grossly exposed and already showing symptoms.

After folding the note and putting it back in Jason's shirt pocket, he grabbed him by the feet because it was the least bloody part, and then dragged him outside. What was left of Jason's head unceremoniously bounced down the stairs. Lee would have liked to give him more dignity, but under the circumstances, he felt that burying the bodies was the most dignity he could provide.

SIX

SAM

IT TOOK HIM TWO HOURS to dig a hole wide enough for all three of the bodies to lie shoulder to shoulder. The depth was short of six feet but deep enough to cover them for quite a while. The soil in the backyard wasn't bad, but after a few feet he'd hit the base of southern red clay that was near impossible to dig through without power tools. Despite the difficulty, he continued digging for another foot before he had exhausted himself.

Now it was almost 0900 hours.

The sun was already blazing, as he had predicted. His go-to-hell pack, chest rig, and M4 were propped in the dirt, next to the bodies. His combat shirt was dirty and soaked with sweat. Tango was lying beside Lee's equipment, completely ignoring the dead bodies, panting and watching Lee work.

Lee tossed the shovel out of the hole and climbed out. He broke open a bottle of water, drank half, and gave half to Tango. The dog lapped eagerly at the mouth of the bottle as Lee slowly dribbled the water out.

He laid Marla in the ground first, then Jason. Then, between them both, he set Stephanie down. The three of them together made him think of the family portrait inside the house.

Before shoveling in the dirt, Lee decided to take Jason's duty firearm and the two spare magazines from his belt. It was a Smith & Wesson M&P .40 caliber. A decent round, right between 9mm and .45 caliber on the power scale. He put these items in his go-to-hell pack, then got to shoveling.

When he had shoveled the hole full and tamped down the dirt, he went inside and retrieved the family photograph he'd looked at earlier. He thought about removing the photo and keeping it as a reminder of the good times but decided it should remain with the Petersons. He placed it on the ground to mark their graves.

He was in the process of gearing up again when Tango suddenly stood, his ears erect. He looked around, then pivoted in the direction of Morrison Street and let out a low growl.

Lee froze in place, ceasing all movement and listening hard for whatever it was that had Tango all perked up. After a moment of hearing nothing out of the ordinary, Lee quickly clipped his chest rig in place, then slung into his M4. He knew better than to dismiss a warning from Tango. He grabbed his go-to-hell pack by a shoulder strap and sprinted as quietly as he could for the Petersons' house.

He flew fast up the stairs and into the living room, wishing there was a way to secure the shattered sliding glass door. He went down the hall to the front door, checked to ensure it was locked, then peered out a nearby window. Beside him Tango whined and pranced around, sensing Lee's tension.

Lee took the moment he was at the window to pull his pack on and tighten up the straps. He watched for another minute, not seeing anything. 'What did you hear?' Lee broke away from the window and quickly ascended the stairs to the second level. He turned left, away from the master bedroom and into Stephanie's bedroom. Everything was pink and flowers and princesses. If Lee had a moment to let his heart break, he was sure it would have.

The blinds were open, revealing an elevated vantage point of Morrison Street. Now he heard something. An engine? Definitely the sound of someone yelling . . . or screaming. It sounded like a man . . . make that men. Like catcalls. What Jason might have called 'hootin' and hollerin'.' And the engine was definitely there. A revving engine, something powerful, like a V-8.

The view of Morrison Street was narrow. Between the Petersons' house and Lee's house was a thick strand of forest that blocked any view of the road to the south. And Lee simply could not get a decent angle on the road to the north, though he knew there were no trees blocking it in that direction.

Coming from the south, on Morrison Street, Lee could see a red vehicle flash through the trees, and then finally come into view. It was a red pickup truck, a big dually with large off-road tires. In the back were two men armed with long guns, though he couldn't tell whether they were rifles or shotguns. Lee couldn't see through the windows of the vehicle and couldn't tell how many more were inside. The pickup truck slowed. The men appeared to be looking for something.

Lee felt his heart pounding his entire body.

The men in the back began pointing wildly toward the wood line. The pickup truck revved and lurched forward, lumbering off the road, causing one of the men in the bed to nearly fall out. Lee looked into the southern wood line. Bursting out of the trees were two figures, a man and a boy.

Lee swore and pressed himself against the pink bedroom wall, keeping an eye on the two figures running. They were running in the distinct way that a rabbit runs from a pack of hounds. He leaned forward and saw the pickup truck skidding to a stop, kicking up dirt and grass. They were about a hundred yards from the two fleeing figures. The doors to the pickup truck opened and the two men in the back hopped out. Three more men exited the vehicle, all armed with what appeared to be shotguns and hunting rifles.

The man and boy had been making for the house but clearly knew they wouldn't make it. They had stopped running and the man stood, chest out, facing the five armed men from the pickup. The boy, barely in his teens, huddled behind the man who Lee presumed was his father.

The armed men slowed their walk to a strut and began talking loudly and laughing. Taunting. They fanned out as if preparing to flank the man and his boy. Lee couldn't make out the details of the conversation but heard the words *fuck* and *pretty little boy* and that was enough.

'Tango, come.' Lee bolted out of the bedroom, down the stairs, and out the back door. Tango followed him eagerly.

Lee told Tango to stay a few feet back, then took the southwest corner of the house and peered around the brick and mortar base. Beyond the overgrown grass, Lee could see the father still shielding his son but sidestepping toward the house. The man appeared to be fumbling in his pocket for something and finally produced what looked like a small silver revolver.

'Don't . . .' Lee whispered, fishing through a pocket in his chest rig and retrieving a 3x magnifier that he quickly attached to his M4, directly behind his scope.

The man pointed the revolver at the approaching gunmen

and yelled, 'Get the fuck back! I will shoot you!' The man spoke with a thick accent that Lee pegged immediately as Arabic.

One of the men from the pickup, presumably the leader, spoke. 'If there were any bullets in that thing, you would have shot us already.'

Lee found the man's cold logic bore the ring of truth. He figured the revolver was empty, carried for show, or possibly in the hopes of eventually finding ammunition for it.

The leader raised a hunting rifle and pointed it at the man. 'And we don't want you anyway, you Hadji fuck.'

The Arabic man's head snapped back, and a red mist spewed out. He toppled backward. The boy reached out for his father, then withdrew his hand and turned in Lee's direction, running at full sprint. Close behind the boy, the five men all started laughing and jogging after him.

Lee had very little time to work.

As the boy cleared the corner, Lee grabbed him up, lightning quick, and clamped a hand over his mouth before he could scream. He pulled the boy in close – he could not have weighed more than a hundred pounds – and whispered harshly in his ear. 'It's okay. It's okay. I'm here to help you.' That was all he had time for. The boy went limp, and Lee hauled him up, wondering if he'd fainted.

Holding him with one arm, Lee sprinted for the trees with everything he had. His best bet was to be at the bottom of that hill before the men from the pickup cleared the corner. The horizon of the hill would hide them and the attackers would naturally assume the boy had gone into the house and would waste time searching it while Lee found them a better spot to hide.

His lungs heaving and legs burning, Lee made it to the hill

and let his downward momentum take over. Tango ran beside him, looking up curiously at the boy. Lee listened past the pounding of his own heart in his ears for a surprised yell or anything that would tell him he had been discovered.

He made it to the bottom of the hill but didn't stop. He made for the shallow gully and the stream. If he hit the stream he could use that like a highway and take the boy to a point of relative safety, though he kept thinking about the fat fuck who had shot this boy's father.

Reestablish law and order.

Another mission objective.

He remembered the sociology professor who had taught the Coordinators about different theories of how the world would be after a social collapse. 'Swift and brutal justice will be the only way to break through the chaos. You will have to strike terror into not only those who have done wrong, but also into those who are even thinking of doing wrong. You have to be the bogeyman they check for underneath their beds. What I'm talking about isn't arrest and trial by jury. Those techniques are only applicable in a civilized world. I am talking about merciless execution. Putting a bullet in the back of someone's head for something you'd receive a citation for nowadays. I hope you are all ready to do this, because in the post-collapse world, anything less is weakness.'

Fine by me, Professor Thompson.

Lee made it to the creek bed and knelt down on his knees. He propped up the boy, who looked a little dazed, and shook him. 'Hey! Wake up, kid!'

The kid looked at him, still confused.

'You understand me? You speak English?' The kid nodded. 'Okay, come on. We have to run a little farther.' Lee grabbed the kid by the hand while Tango stuck his wet nose in the kid's face to see what smells Lee had been keeping from him. Lee swatted his nose away. 'Leave it, Tango. Come on.'

Lee ran hunched over to keep his upper body under the edge of the gully and out of sight. They ran for perhaps another hundred yards, until Lee could not see the house anymore. He found a fallen tree just over the top of the gully. The root system created a natural cave of dirt. Perfect to hide the boy.

Lee rolled over the side of the gully, then hauled the boy up. Tango followed with a swift jump and sniffed around the area. The boy was out of breath. Lee slung the go-to-hell pack off and set it on the ground in the little dirt cave. He patted the top of the bag. 'Come here, kid. Sit down.'

The boy shuffled over, obviously scared. Either the water from the stream had splashed up on him or he had wet his pants. Lee didn't blame him if he had. He'd seen grown men piss their pants in less harrowing situations.

When the boy had sat down on the pack, Lee knelt down again so they were at eye level. He checked the boy over to make sure he wasn't wounded anywhere. 'What's your name, buddy?'

'Sameer,' he said between breaths. 'Everyone calls me Sam.'

'Okay, Sam.' Lee finished checking him over. No apparent injuries. 'Are you thirsty?'

Sam nodded.

'Here . . . ' Lee motioned for him to stand, which he did. Lee fished out a couple of water bottles, giving one to Sam and keeping the other. He uncapped it, drank two long gulps, then splashed some of it on his face. He dove back into the pack and pulled out the M&P .40 he'd taken from Jason.

Sam seemed nervous about the weapon. 'How old are you, Sam?' Lee checked the weapon to make sure a round was loaded.

'I'm almost thirteen.' Sam seemed to do a few calculations in his head. 'Next month.'

'Really?' Lee smiled and hoped it was convincing. 'I thought you were sixteen. You look pretty old.'

Sam smiled weakly.

'Listen, Sam. As far as I'm concerned, you handled yourself like a man back there.' He put a hand on the kid's shoulder and squeezed. 'You're a man in my book.'

Sam nodded by way of acknowledgment, then took a long gulp from his bottle of water.

Lee held the pistol toward him. 'Have you ever used one of these?' Sam stared at it. Eventually he shook his head. 'Okay. Listen really closely. You have to pay attention.' Sam looked from the pistol to Lee. 'I'm going to put this on the ground right next to you. This is not a toy and you do not play with it. In fact, I don't even want you to touch it. The only time it's okay for you to touch it is if you see one of those guys that was chasing you, okay? Then all I want you to do is pick it up, hold it just like this, point it at them, and I want you to pull the trigger three times.' Lee held up three fingers. 'Three times, Sam. If he's not down after that, pull the trigger three more times. Okay? Did you get all of that?'

'Don't touch it.' Sam nodded. 'If I see a bad guy, shoot him three times. If he doesn't die, shoot him three more times.'

Lee smiled. Kids grew up fast these days. Even faster during social collapse. 'That's right.' Lee set down the pistol. 'You ever play *Call of Duty*?'

'Yeah.'

Lee nodded. 'It's just like in *Call of Duty*. Just remember that.'

'Just like in *Call of Duty*.' The kid looked briefly terrified. 'Okay.'

Lee stood up and patted his leg. 'Tango! Come!' To Sam he said, 'You like dogs?'

'Sure,' Sam nodded.

'This is Tango. He's gonna help keep you safe.' Lee rubbed Tango behind the ears, then pulled him toward Sam. 'Let him smell you.' Sam offered his hand for Tango to smell and lick. Lee snapped his fingers to get Tango's attention, then pointed to the ground at Sam's feet. 'Tango, guard it, boy. Guard it!'

Tango sat down in front of Sam. The kid was already small for his age, but next to the big dog he looked shrunken.

'Alright. I gotta go back up there for a little bit. No matter what you hear, don't move from this spot. Stay right here with Tango until I get back.'

Sam nodded and Lee turned to leave. 'Mister . . . '

Lee turned and looked at him.

'Are you gonna kill those men?'

No need for baby talk. Lee nodded. 'Yes.'

Sam just looked at him, but he didn't respond. Lee turned and dipped back into the gully and was gone.

Nearly ten minutes had elapsed since they shot Sam's father.

Lee's mind was hot and cold. He was a pressure cooker, building heat each time he replayed the image of Sam's father and the bloody cloud exploding out of his head. Sam's eyes, trying to make sense of it all. The men's faces as they laughed. But through the anger, his hands were still, his heart steady, and his mind a blank slate. He had no words, only images of death. With no remorse, he was going to kill everyone.

He crept quietly but speedily through the creek bed, then up over the lip and into the lower part of the Petersons' back-yard. He took cover behind a tree with a thick trunk and listened for a moment. Over the background noise of birds and insects, Lee could hear voices and what sounded like moving furniture.

They were ripping the house apart looking for Sam.

Lee darted from his point of cover, diagonally across the southwestern corner of the property and back into the wood line of the forest between his house and the Petersons'.

Then he stalked, low to the ground, just inside the shadows of the trees, moving parallel to the wood line toward the house. With each step he carefully avoided twigs and dry patches of leaves. His feet rolled slowly heel to toe, his movements noticeable only to his own attuned ears. To anyone else, they made no more sound than the movements of a cat.

He stopped and knelt to the ground, keeping everything slow and deliberate now that he was in view of the house. Quick movements drew the eyes.

He smelled cigarette smoke.

From his perch about fifty yards out from the house, Lee spotted the smoker. He stood on the back deck with a hunting rifle slung over his shoulder, looking out into the woods while he enjoyed his smoke. Cigarettes were a sign that the enemy felt safe, relaxed, and in control.

Lee had the advantage. He already knew how many men there were. With one on the deck, four more remained inside. Including Fat Boy, the man who had shot Sam's dad. From where Lee sat inside the woods, he could just barely make out the bed of the red pickup truck. He only had to slither a few more yards through the brush to get an angle on the truck that allowed him to see inside. One of the occupants had left a back door open, and the way the truck was parked, it provided Lee with a perfect view of the inside.

There was no one inside the truck. Lee thanked God for the first stroke of luck all day. A man in a red hat joined Smoker on the deck and they started talking. The conversation was lighthearted, and it included much backslapping and laughing. These boys were raucous and it made Lee think of drunken rednecks. They stood around grab-assing while their buddies tried to find a thirteen-year-old boy, as that boy's father lay dead in the dirt.

Lee wanted to pull Red Hat into the shadows and slide his KA-BAR knife deep into his guts, working it around until he hit the heart and lungs. He wanted to hold his hand over Red Hat's mouth and watch as the life fled from his eyes. He wanted to know that the last image Red Hat would ever see would be Lee's smiling face.

That would be satisfying in the moment, but it had little chance of success.

A half-dozen different plans ran through Lee's mind. But sometimes the best plan was no plan at all. What Lee had was initiative. He knew that he could take out both Red Hat and Smoker before they had a chance to react. That left Fat Boy and two others inside the house. The only question remaining was, would they fight or flee?

Lee felt confident they would die either way.

Lee settled down into a prone position, most of his body hidden behind a thick tree, just his head and rifle visible, though it was difficult for someone in the bright sunshine to see inside the shaded woods. They probably wouldn't see him, even if he was standing up and wearing hunter orange.

He took a few deep breaths and pulled the trigger on the exhale. He took out Smoker first with a single shot to the temple. Red Hat watched his buddy fall over, his own face splattered with brains, blood, and skull fragments. His mouth opened in terror, but he never had a chance to yell. Lee put two in his chest and tried for The Mozambique, but the target was already falling back and the third shot went a few inches high.

Lee eased back into a kneeling position and waited. He could hear shouting from inside the house. 'Kenny? What the fuck was that?' Lee waited for them to find out. 'Fuck! JC, they're both dead!'

'What?'

'I think someone shot 'em!'

'Get back!'

The rest of it was muffled, as the remaining three men retreated into the house. They would either try to peer out the windows and find Lee – which would cost them their lives – or they would make a run for the pickup truck and try to escape.

The sound of the front door slamming and footsteps across the front porch answered Lee's question.

Slow is smooth, smooth is fast.

Moving with controlled urgency, Lee pushed the barrel of his M203 grenade launcher forward, then extracted a 40mm grenade, which resembled a giant bullet; shoved it into the barrel; and locked the barrel back into place. He elevated the weapon and pulled the trigger on the launcher. The grenade flew out with a heavy *thump*. Lee was worried that his timing might have been off, but it was spot-on. Just as the three men came into view, sprinting for the pickup truck and closing at about thirty feet, the 40mm grenade arced out of the sky and the cab of the pickup went up in a white flash and a billow of smoke.

All three men lifted their hands to shield their faces and fell flat on their backs.

Lee came out of the wood line with his M4 leveled and firing. The first man tried to get up and grab his gun, so Lee put two in him, one ripping into his shoulder and the other punching a neat hole in his neck. The man fell back, choking on his own blood.

Fat Boy and a man in a plaid shirt were still sitting on the ground, and both threw their rifles away and held up their hands.

Lee put one in Plaid's chest at about fifteen feet out. The man grabbed his chest and started rolling around, wheezing and letting out pathetic sounds. What right did he have to plead for mercy or scream in pain? The man they'd killed only a short time ago had died defending his son and he'd done it in silence.

Fat Boy stared at Plaid with his mouth hanging open. He was paralyzed with shock. He looked at Lee and snapped back into the moment. If he had been a fighting man he would have known that it was over anyway and made a break for his rifle so that he would go out swinging.

But Fat Boy was just a fat boy, just an out-of-shape hillbilly with a taste for teenage boys. His heart wasn't made of tough stuff and his mind had never been combat hardened. He only knew fear – how to induce it and how to feel it.

Lee was standing now within a few feet of both men. Plaid continued to moan loudly and roll on the ground. Lee felt that two men to dig a grave was one too many. Still holding

Fat Boy's gaze, Lee finished Plaid off with two more rounds. He didn't watch where they hit, but Plaid was silent after that.

'Please don't fucking kill me! Please!' The fat man started to cry.

Lee shook his head. 'Stop crying.'

Fat Boy whimpered and sobbed.

'Seriously. Stop crying.' Lee kicked his legs. 'Get up. Come on.'

Fat Boy stumbled to his feet, hunched over and cowering. He'd been so bold and brash just a short time ago. Now he was reduced to groveling and . . . pissing himself. A dark stain was growing on his crotch and spreading down the length of his right leg.

Lee motioned the man forward, which the man complied with hesitantly, like a beaten dog. As he got within arm's reach, Lee punched him in the throat, then planted his fist deep in the man's jiggling gut, doubling him over. The man fell sideways onto the ground, hacking and coughing.

Lee wanted to do more, but he also wanted the man alive a little longer. 'Relax and breathe. You're not injured, you're just hurt. Give it a minute.'

Fat Boy rolled onto his hands and knees and wheezed for a few moments before regaining his wind.

'Up.' Lee poked him in the back of the neck with the barrel of his M4. 'You have some work to do.'

Fat Boy dug like his life depended on it. Which it did.

He told the man that if he looked like he was taking his time with the digging or being disrespectful toward the body of Sam's father, that Lee was going to gut shoot him and leave him to die, then finish the digging himself. Fat Boy had four dead friends who bore witness to the fact that Lee was willing and able to carry out that level of violence.

It took the man about a half hour to dig a grave that Lee felt was of suitable depth to bury Sam's father in. He then escorted Fat Boy at gunpoint to collect the body and carry it to the grave. Before taking the body, Lee searched it and saw the man was wearing a gold watch. He took it off his wrist for Sam. Fat Boy struggled at first, then finally was able to pick up the body and carry it over his shoulder.

After Sam's father had been laid to rest, Lee ordered Fat Boy to remove the shoelaces on his right boot. Fat Boy complied and provided Lee with a two-foot length of cordage that Lee used to bind Fat Boy's hands behind his back.

At gunpoint, Lee marched Fat Boy down the hill and into the woods.

'Where are you taking me?'

Lee felt no reason to lie to the man any longer. 'To the boy whose father you killed. The boy you were gonna rape.'

Fat Boy stopped in his tracks and looked at Lee, terrified. 'Why you doin' that?'

'Because I'm going to let him kill you if he wants to.'

Fat Boy's eyes erupted in tears again. 'No! Please, mister!' He got down on his knees. 'I wasn't gonna rape him! Why you gonna let him kill me over nothing? I ain't done nothing wrong!'

Lee looked at the man with indifference. 'You've done a lot wrong.' Lee could actually see Fat Boy trying to think of something, anything to argue his case. But Lee cut him off before he could continue arguing. 'You murdered a man today. You know it and I know it. And I watched you do it with a smile on your face, which makes me think that maybe this isn't the first time you've done it. So for the boy's father and anyone else you've murdered, I would dearly like to put a bullet in your brain. But I'm going to let the boy decide what to do with you. So you can either keep walking and have a chance – however slim – of the boy sparing your life, or you can stop right here and I will gladly do the job myself.'

Fat Boy looked Lee in the eye and tried to match his cold determination, but couldn't muster the stones and looked down at his feet. Then he stood up, turned, and continued walking in the creek bed.

It was only a short distance before Lee saw the top of the root system where Sam and Tango were hiding. He pushed Fat Boy down to his knees and looked up over the top of the gully. 'Sam?'

Sam's head poked up as well as Tango's.

Lee motioned with his head for Sam to come over. The boy moved to Lee, but hesitantly, all the while nervously peeling the bark from a small twig that he clutched in his hands. Lee felt conflicted about what he was going to ask the kid, but it somehow felt more just than simply killing the man after he'd finished digging the grave. It was Sam's father the man killed. It should be Sam's decision what happened to him.

As Sam made his way over, Lee knelt down and whispered quietly in Fat Boy's ear, 'Don't say a word. I promise you'll regret it.'

Sam slid down into the gully, his khaki pants now smudged with mud. He stood a safe distance away and stared at Fat Boy where he knelt. His expression was unreadable to Lee, and again he second-guessed his decision to bring the man to Sam.

But it was a fucked-up world and this day would always be a dark blotch in this young man's mind. Sometimes revenge heals, sometimes it makes things hurt worse. It wasn't for Lee to decide how Sam dealt with this.

Lee stepped between Sam and Fat Boy but angled himself so that Fat Boy was still in his field of vision. He put his hand on Sam's shoulder and spoke in low tones.

'You know who that is, right?'

Sam's eyes drifted to Fat Boy and he nodded after a moment.

'And you know what he did?'

'He killed my dad.'

'Yes. Whatever you decide to do with him, he'll deserve it.' Lee dipped his head down to the kid's level so that their eyes made contact. 'Look at me, Sam. You know the world is very different than it was a little while ago. You know how things have changed. We don't have police and courtrooms to take care of people like him anymore, so now we have to do it our-selves. And it's ugly, and sometimes it hurts, but it has to be done. You understand me?'

Sam nodded slowly, looking at the crying man on his knees. His eyes were cold, which put a chill down the back of Lee's neck. He didn't look so small now. 'Yeah, I understand.'

'It was you that he hurt, so it's up to you what you do with him, okay?'

Sam's jaw muscles bunched, his lips becoming a tight line. His was a face built for smiling, not for scowling, and when the expression came on his face, it was disconcerting. He glanced at Jason's M&P .40, still on the ground where Lee had left it. 'Can I borrow your gun?'

The way he said it was as if he was asking Lee to loan him a dollar. Lee didn't think about it too long. He shook his head. 'I'll do it. You just decide.'

'Okay . . .' Sam seemed partially relieved.

Sam walked forward and looked at Fat Boy, who must have known he was about to die and was weeping uncontrollably now. The man had not an ounce of courage to stay his tears at least for the moment of his death. Instead he blabbered on, snot running down his upper lip and bubbling with each mumbled syllable.

The young man looked at Fat Boy for a very long time, then leaned in close and whispered to the man something that Lee could not hear. Then he turned and walked back to Lee. 'Let him go,' he said calmly.

Lee watched him climb the side of the gully and sit back down with Tango, who stuck his nose into Sam's neck and licked him happily. Looking back at Fat Boy, Lee saw the man's eyes were heavy-lidded and his mouth hung agape. He looked numb.

Lee slid his pistol back into its place and walked over to him. He tapped him on the shoulder, which did not seem to break into his daze. 'Come on.'

The man on the ground turned his head slowly, visibly trembling, and looked up at Lee. 'Are you really going to let me go?'

Lee shrugged. 'The kid doesn't want to kill you.'

Fat Boy stumbled to his feet, eager to be released. 'I swear I won't come back!'

'Mmm-hmm.' Lee smiled humorlessly. 'Start walking.'

They walked in silence back through the streambed, Fat Boy stumbling along with his hands still tied behind his back and Lee following. They reached the back edge of the Petersons' property and Lee instructed Fat Boy to stop. The man stopped, then looked back toward Lee.

Fat Boy took a shaky breath. 'I promise. You'll never see me again.'

Lee nodded and withdrew his KA-BAR from its sheath on his chest rig. 'I know.'

Then he reached around and gripped Fat Boy by the forehead, applying rearward pressure, and inserted the KA-BAR into the base of his skull, just above vertebrae C1, severing his spinal column. Fat Boy's body became a 250-pound sack of concrete and immediately collapsed. Lee wiped the blade off on his pants, then slid it back into its sheath and walked toward Sam and Tango, leaving Fat Boy where he fell.

SEVEN

GUARDIAN

LEE FOUND SAM SITTING ON his go-to-hell pack with his arms wrapped around his knees and his head hanging down. As he got closer, Lee realized the kid was crying. He stopped where he was, wondering if he should give him a minute. He swore under his breath, directing his anger at himself. He should not have brought Fat Boy down there, should not have put that decision on Sam. That was too much for a twelve-year-old to handle. Aside from all of that, the kid was still processing the death of his father. Once the adrenaline subsides, the mind has a chance to start replaying what has happened, and that's when the emotions start to break through.

Lee was quite familiar with that phenomenon, having lost men in his unit while in Iraq. One to sniper fire and two others to a roadside bomb that took out their Humvee. In both cases, he hadn't felt much during the incidents except for fear and some panic, a feeling of helplessness, like there was something he could be doing to help them but could never figure out what it was. Later, off patrol and back behind the wire, he would lie in his bed and stare at the ceiling, overcome with a heavy sadness that felt like being trapped in a strange dream with no way to wake up.

Lee remembered the terrible emptiness, and along with it, the loneliness.

He walked up quietly to Sam. The kid jumped when he heard a twig snap and looked up to find Lee kneeling down beside him. Sam wiped his eyes quickly, then set his chin on his arms and regarded the forest floor.

Lee took a long, deep breath and stared at the ground along with him. 'You made a good choice. Don't ever feel bad about showing someone mercy.'

'I don't,' Sam mumbled, his voice thick with tears.

They sat in the quiet of the forest for a long moment. Lee listened to the sounds of the forest, hearing the occasional small branch falling and the incessant chatter of birds, lost in conversations shouted from one end of the woods to the other. Finally, Lee spoke. 'What was your dad's name?'

'Labib.' Sam gave Lee a sidelong glance. 'What's your name?'

'Lee Harden.' He extended his hand, which Sam shook once. 'I'm a captain with the US Army.'

'The army?' Sam looked incredulous. 'I thought the army was gone.'

Lee suddenly felt like the breath had been knocked out of him. He knew the government would not be at work in the chaos of a post-collapse world, but hearing it come from a kid's mouth as common knowledge that there was no US Army still hit him hard. He didn't let the effects show and smiled with a confidence he didn't feel.

'Oh, we're not gone. We're just working a little more quietly than normal.'

'Where are all your guys? Don't you guys work in teams?' Sam looked behind Lee as though perhaps there were others he had missed.

'Not me, kiddo. I'm trained to work alone.'

Sam nodded. 'You did just kill a bunch of guys all by your-self.' Lee wasn't sure what to say. Sam continued. 'Is my dad still up there?'

Lee placed the butt of his M4 on the ground and leaned on it. 'Yeah, but he's buried now.'

'You mean I can't see him?' Sam's lip tensed as he tried to hold back more tears.

Lee thought about telling the boy that he didn't want to see his father like that, considered telling him that it wasn't his father, it was just a body, but it all seemed so trite, so he didn't say anything at all. He just shook his head so the boy knew that he couldn't see his father. He reached into the cargo pocket of his combat pants and withdrew the gold watch he'd removed from Labib before burying him. He looked at the watch face, wiped a smudge of dirt off with his thumb, then extended it toward Sam. 'Here.'

Sam took the watch and looked at it, unable to hold the tears back.

'I'm sorry you can't see him.'

Sam nodded and held the watch in a tight grip as he cried again. Lee wasn't accustomed to dealing with people in crisis, let alone teenagers. He sat down on the ground and let Sam cry for a moment longer. Lee had become acutely aware of the amount of time they had spent outdoors and the amount of noise and fire and smoke he had created during the firefight. He wasn't sure what kind of attention it would bring, but he was sure he wanted to be inside when it came.

He still had a viable safe house, and he intended to use it.

As if to reiterate what Lee was thinking, somewhere in the woods, a very human voice screamed out with very inhuman anger. Lee immediately remembered the crazed girl from under his front steps and the sound she'd made when she'd seen him. It was the same insane, rage-filled screech. And it wasn't too far away.

Lee shouldered his rifle and scanned the woods. 'Come on, Sam – we should get indoors.'

The trio moved through the woods without speaking. Sam had put away his grief for the moment. His eyes were clear and focused. He scanned from right to left in a constant arc, as cautious as any good soldier on patrol. At first, this impressed Lee, as he wondered how Sam had learned to scan and move so quietly through the woods. Then he realized that, though he himself was new to this world, it was the harsh reality that Sam had lived in the past month. Necessity and survival were brutal tutors, and they only gave pass or fail.

The screeching from the woods began to sound less like rage to Lee and more like a beckoning call. Like the howl of a wolf on the scent of game. The similarity made him pick up the pace a bit – they were still a hundred yards from the house. After a few minutes, Lee could swear he heard an answer to the screeching, coming from the opposite side of the woods.

Boxing them in.

Lee reached behind him and grabbed Sam by the arm, pulling him closer as they walked. He spoke in a low voice. 'You ever hear that before?'

Sam nodded vigorously. 'They heard the shooting.'

'Are they always attracted to loud noises?'

'Yes.'

'Have you ever seen them . . . team up?'

'Not in the beginning, but lately me and Dad have seen them in groups.'

'How big?'

Sam shrugged. 'Four? Five? Once we saw about ten of them.'

'Why aren't they killing each other?'

'They do kill each other.' Sam scanned the woods again, then spoke more quietly. 'Dad says they're like wild dogs – sometimes they get along, other times they fight and kill each other, but they're never friendly toward us.'

Lee didn't ask any more questions and Sam didn't elaborate any further. They came to the tree line of Lee's yard but didn't exit the woods. Lee stood for a moment and took a good look to make sure there wasn't anyone around, normal or infected. The noon sun was hot and sticky and even the birds were silent, unwilling to spend energy making their usual racket in this heat. Just the insects chirped now, loud and insistent, the junglelike air a natural habitat for them.

Satisfied that it was clear, Lee wiped sweat from his eyebrows and stepped out into the open, hunched over and moving quickly to limit his time exposed. He made straight for the front porch, Sam following and Tango bringing up the rear.

Lee kept an eye on the body of the dead girl lying on the front porch as he opened his front door and motioned Sam and Tango to go inside. Sam stared sideways at the body as he moved slowly past it, hypnotized by death. Lee wondered how much of it the kid had seen in the past month, how indelibly screwed up he would be for the rest of his life, or whether he was constructed of the type of soul that shrugs things off and keeps moving on.

Once Sam and Tango were inside the house, Lee slipped

in behind them and closed and bolted the door. The air-conditioning was glorious, and it felt almost arctic on his sweat-soaked body. He'd done his time in the brutal heat and even in places with high humidity, but there was something uniquely cloying and irritating about a North Carolina summer. Of course, the presence of central air made all of that better.

Sam sounded astonished when he spoke. 'Is this your house? You have air-conditioning?'

'Yeah, it's mine. Feels good, doesn't it?'

Sam immediately sat on Lee's couch and leaned back with his arms out. 'How do you have air-conditioning? I thought nobody had electricity anymore.'

Lee dropped his go-to-hell pack and fished out two more bottles of water. 'It's running on solar power and battery cells. We have lights, air-conditioning, and I even have a computer and TV downstairs.' Lee passed one of the bottles to Sam. 'We'll go down into my bunker in a minute, but I need to ask you some questions.'

Lee sat himself down on a lounge chair across from the couch. Normally, sweaty, dirty clothes would not be allowed in his living room, but he supposed it really didn't matter now. He took a long drink from his own water bottle, then looked at Sam. 'Tell me about you and your dad.'

Sam seemed to sink back into the couch, somber again. 'We used to live in a big house in Apex with my mom and my sister. Then the plague came and everyone died.'

Lee realized Sam wasn't going to spill a lot of information. He would have to ask the questions to get the answers. 'What did your dad do for work?'

'He worked for a computer security company. Protected computers from hackers and stuff. He was really good at it.

Other companies were always trying to get him to move and offering him more money, but he liked Apex. Plus my mom was a schoolteacher and didn't want to leave.' Sam looked up at the ceiling and Lee could see his eyes glistening. 'We had a pool in our backyard. A big pool with lights inside of it that changed colors. Dad spent a lot of money to have it built last summer. By the time it was done, it was too cold to swim. We barely got to use it before all this happened.'

Lee leaned forward a bit. 'And do you know what happened?'

'Not really. Dad says someone attacked America with a plague and it was making people crazy. Said it was like rabies and made people attack each other. Mom got sick and Dad told me to hide in the basement. After that I didn't see Mom or my sister again. This was about a month ago.' Sam paused for a long moment, staring at the tiny ripples in his bottle of water. 'I think he had to kill Mom. I don't know whether Farah was sick too and Dad had to kill her, or whether Mom went crazy and killed her before Dad could stop her.'

Lee could not believe how much loss Sam had endured in such a short time. In the span of a month, this boy had lost everyone he knew and loved. 'When your mom and sister were gone, did you guys stay in the house or did you move out?'

'No, we stayed for another week. Then these buses came, and there were soldiers inside, and they said they were taking us to someplace safe. They had nurses that were taking our temperatures before we could get on the bus. Everyone had to wear masks. One of the guys wasn't allowed to get on after they took his temperature and he started yelling and shouting, then these two soldiers with gas masks came up and grabbed him and carried him into this big tent and he got really quiet. I think they gave him a shot, like the kind you give a dog when you have to put it down.'

Though the story obviously came with some pain, Lee needed to hear more about the camps and why Sam and his father weren't there, and had been on the road. 'So did you go to the camp?'

Sam shook his head. 'We were in line, but then there was a lot of shooting, and some helicopters came in. I think there was a big crowd of infected people coming for us, and the buses left without us. Dad and I only had time to grab a few things out of our luggage and then some guy let us get in the back of his pickup truck and drive with them.'

'Was it the guys from earlier today?'

'No. Those are different guys. This was . . . two weeks ago?' Sam motioned with his hand to display his uncertainty about the time frame. 'Anyway, we drove out into the country where this family had a cabin. They were really nice to drive us, and they even gave us some water, but they told us that they didn't have enough supplies to take care of us and that we should start heading toward the FEMA camp in Sanford. It was supposed to be safe; no one there was sick.'

'Is that where you guys were headed?'

'Yeah. We've been on the road for ten days. Last night, we came up on the guys in the red pickup truck. They made us take off our backpacks and searched them. Dad asked them to leave us some water. They said they would leave us water if he would give me to them. Dad said, "Fuck you, sons of bitches," and then grabbed me and took off running. We hid in the woods all night long. They were searching for us too, and they found us, so we started running again. We came to this house first, but you weren't home when we knocked, so we ran through the woods and came to the other house. And that's when they caught us.' Sam took a tentative sip from his water. 'You were there. You saw what happened.'

Lee nodded. 'I saw.'

There was a long silence as Lee tried to think of other questions he had. Sam broke the silence first. 'Why didn't you shoot them before they shot my dad?' Sam looked directly at Lee when he asked it and Lee couldn't tell what the kid was thinking about him. It was the same expressionless gaze he'd given Fat Boy when deciding whether to kill him or not.

Lee felt defenseless for a moment as he contemplated his answer. 'Sam . . .' Lee thought for a bit longer. 'You're going to find that there are situations in this world where you can't do what you want to do. If there was a way to bring you and your dad out of that alive, I would have done it. But if there was a way to do that, I'm not sure what it was. If I had started shooting when I realized they were bad guys, you and your dad would have both died, and probably me too. I had to wait, to make sure I had an advantage, and my advantage came too late. I'm sorry, Sam. I wanted to save both of you. But sometimes you just can't do what you want.'

Sam continued to stare at Lee, unspeaking, with no obvious emotion on his face. Finally, after several long and awkward moments of Lee staring at the floor, Sam spoke. 'When we were on the road, we saw this house, out in the distance. Dad stopped walking because he said he heard someone yelling. I tried to look around, but I couldn't see anything but a house, way in the distance, across this huge open field. I used a pair of binoculars to look, and I could

see three people on the roof. They were looking at me and
Dad with binoculars too, and they were waving a white
towel at us and shouting. I couldn't hear what they were
saying, but I could tell they were asking for help. I told my
dad what I was seeing, and he grabbed the binoculars from
me and looked through them. I said to him, "Dad, we have
to go help them!" After a really long time, he gave the binoculars back to me and kept walking down the road, telling
me to "Come on."

'I got mad and started yelling at my dad. I couldn't believe
he would leave those people up on the roof. I told him, "How
can we expect others to help us if we don't help them?" But
he never gave me an answer. He just kept walking. I told him
that it wasn't right. I even said I hated him, but I was only
trying to get him to stop and listen. When I said that, he
turned around and smacked me, then told me to look
through the binoculars again.

'I did, and when I looked again I could see almost ten of
them, walking around in the yard below. They were in the
house, running around, trying to climb the gutters to get at
the people on the roof, throwing big rocks at them. One of
them ran into the house and came out with a bunch of knives
and started throwing them at the people on the roof.

'Then my dad took the binoculars away from me again. He
said, "If we try to help them, we will die. And then the people
on the roof will die anyway. The only difference will be that
we wasted our lives for nothing." Then he told me,
"Sometimes, the only way to win is to not fight."

'Then we just kept walking. And those people on the roof –
it was a man, a woman, and a little girl – they watched us look
right at them and then walk away. We couldn't help them, no
matter how much we wanted to.'

Lee chose not to say anything further to defend his actions earlier in the day. He felt that there was an understanding between him and Sam, and that to speak more on the matter would only be scratching at the wound. The decision had been made, and there was no way to change it. Sam recognized that Lee had made the best decision he was capable of making at the time, and that it was not Sam's place to second-guess him. After a pause, Lee said, 'How long ago was that?'

Sam thought for a moment. 'Two days ago.'

Lee nodded slowly, thoughtfully. 'Do you remember where the house was?'

Sam gave Lee a hard look. 'Are you going to go help them?' The insinuation was obvious. *Are you better than my dad? He couldn't save them, but you can?*

'Sam, this has nothing to do with your father. He was one man with a revolver and no bullets and he had you to think about. Saving people is my job. That's what I'm here to do. It's what the US government trained me to do, and I have a lot of guns to do it with. Your dad made the right choice. Going in against ten infected people would have been suicide. But I'm sure if your dad had all the equipment I have, he would have been able to do it, just like I can.'

Sam looked down, somewhat sheepish. 'It was on this same road. I don't know how far back it was. We saw them just before it got dark. Then we kept walking for maybe another hour, and then we slept in the woods. When we got up the next morning we walked until it was about to get dark again, and that's when we came up on the guys in the red pickup.'

Lee did some mental calculations. The average person could cover upward of twenty miles in a day in the local terrain. That would put the house with the stranded people anywhere within a thirty- to forty-mile range. Morrison Street was a long road that changed names several times as it cut through different cities and counties, but Lee wasn't sure it was that long. Perhaps they had stopped frequently to rest or to investigate abandoned houses for supplies.

'Did you pass any other survivors?'

'We passed a house with a pile of burning bodies. We couldn't see anyone inside, but the bodies were still on fire and we couldn't tell if they were infected people or normal, so Dad and I ran away from the house. We didn't know if the people who lit the bodies on fire were friendly or not.'

Burning bodies sounded like something one would do to get rid of infected people, but Sam and his dad had been right to give the place a wide berth. People who could kill enough infected to be considered a 'pile' would seem to be packing some heavy firepower. That could make them the type of people to stay the fuck away from, or it could make them great allies. Lee made a mental note to approach that house with caution.

'And where was that house?' Lee asked.

'We saw that one right before we ran into the guys in the red pickup. It has to be close by.'

'Do you remember what the house looked like?'

'Not really. I remember it looked weird . . . like a barn, but it was a house.'

Lee knew exactly which house he was talking about. He didn't know the man who lived there. He knew he drove a black Ford Ranger and had seen him at the local supermarket on occasion. He was a gray-haired guy pushing fifty. Lee wasn't sure if he lived with anyone else. What he did remember was a black sticker on the bumper of the Ford Ranger that said, GOD BLESS OUR TROOPS . . . ESPECIALLY OUR SNIPERS. This seemed to coincide with the pile of bodies. One gun or many, the guy was likely military or law enforcement, and provided he wasn't a raging psychopath, he could lend some much-needed muscle to the team.

Just as Lee was about to ask another question, three things happened in the same instant: Sam's eyes went wide and his mouth opened in a silent scream, there was a loud bang behind him, and Tango started barking ferociously and lunged for the window.

Lee bolted upright and brought his rifle to his shoulder, looking for the threat. He saw a bloody face pressed against the shatterproof window, the eyes wide and crazy, the tongue licking obscenely at the glass and leaving a bloody trail wherever it went. Tango was at the window snarling and barking, the hair along his spine standing straight up like a Mohawk.

Finally Sam found his voice and screamed. Lee almost pulled the trigger, but he knew it would only weaken the shatterproof glass.

As of right now, no one was getting into the house without monumental effort or explosives.

Lee stayed his trigger finger and backed away from the window.

After emptying his lungs in one giant scream, Sam was silent, plastered against the couch as though he was attempting to meld himself into the fabric.

Another bump on the side of the house and a rapid banging on the glass in the kitchen. Lee pivoted and looked into the kitchen. The back patio doors, also steel-framed and shatterproof, were being assaulted by another infected who was holding a hammer and beating the glass ferociously.

Tango didn't notice the new intruder and was still barking at the first.

'Tango, heel! Come on! Leave it!' Tango backed a few feet away but kept barking. Lee grabbed Sam by the shirt and hauled him off the couch. 'Follow me.'

Lee shoved the kid into the kitchen, which Sam resisted, since it was toward the other infected with the hammer. As he was opening the door to the basement, he could swear he heard the one with the hammer scream, 'Open the fucking door!'

He flipped on the basement lights so Sam wouldn't be afraid and pointed down into the basement. 'Go.'

'No!'

'Sam!' Lee shouted. 'Get the fuck in the basement!'

Sam turned and went four steps down, then froze and looked back.

'Tango,' Lee called over his shoulder, keeping an eye on the infected with the hammer. The blows were creating little white scratches in the window but not breaking or cracking it. The big dog came running through the kitchen in a brown-and-black flash and headed straight to the back patio door, locked onto another target. Lee reached out and grabbed his collar. 'No! Go downstairs!' He hauled the dog back, then pushed him onto the basement stairs.

The dog looked back, still barking and wagging his tail. Fun, fun, fun.

Lee closed the door and went back into the living room. The infected on his front porch went nuts when he saw Lee and started punching at the window as hard as he could, then started trying to kick it in. Lee got a better look at the guy. He was dressed in slacks and a polo shirt and was wearing golf shoes. It was difficult to tell the age because his skin was so covered in crusted blood, but Lee could see the creature was balding and guessed mid-forties.

He grabbed his go-to-hell pack. *There's no golf course within miles*, Lee thought. *He must have been running around for days.*

He opened up the door to the basement and found Tango right there, ready to get back in the fight, and Sam, halfway down the stairs, crouched in a ball, unwilling to go back upstairs and unwilling to descend any farther into the creepy basement.

'Come on, Sam.' Lee took the stairs slowly. 'That's shatter-proof glass, okay? Those guys aren't getting in here for a long time. And if they do, I'll take care of them. You believe me, right?'

Sam shook his head.

Lee felt bad for the kid, but there was nothing he could do about it now. He walked down the stairs and heard Sam and Tango fall in behind him. He punched in the code for the hatch, heard it click, then turned the wheel and opened it up. 'It's safe down there. No one can get in.'

Sam peered down the hole hesitantly, saw that it was dark, and shook his head.

Lee knelt down beside him. 'I know you've been through a lot, but you have got to trust me now. I will never tell you to do something unsafe. You got that? If I tell you to do something, it is because that is your best chance at not getting hurt. You have got to listen to me. I promise you there is nothing bad down there. Me and Tango go down there all the time.'

Sam still looked unsure.

'You can't be afraid anymore, Sam. You gotta be brave.'

Sam finally budged and swung his legs into the shaft. Lee wasn't sure if it was anything he had said or whether the kid just made up his own mind to go, but he was happy that they were moving. After Sam got to the bottom, Lee grabbed Tango around the chest, for the first time becoming annoyed that he hadn't insisted on a more pet-friendly entry to his bunker. He knelt down and hoisted Tango into the hatch. The dog scrabbled around, still excited, and Lee lost his grip.

Tango hit the ground with a yelp.

Lee swore loudly and stood frozen as he watched Tango stand up on all fours and walk around. Tango seemed a bit loopy for the first few seconds, but then he looked fine. Lee cursed the dog under his breath and swung down onto the ladder, closing the hatch behind him.

'Is he okay?' Sam asked.

'He's fine. Just stupid.' Lee walked with Sam down the cement tunnel, Tango leading the way eagerly. He was probably hungry and thirsty, though he'd had his fill of pissing on everything he could find after being outdoors for half the day.

'Are you mad at me?' Sam asked, crestfallen.

'No, kid, I'm not mad at you.' *Way to go, Lee. Kid loses his entire family and you snap at him because he gets a little scared.* 'I know it's tough, and you don't really know me, but you have to trust me now, okay? I'm your friend. Friends have to trust each other.'

Sam looked at the hatch to Lee's bunker. 'Alright.'

Lee pushed the hatch open and gestured for Sam to enter. 'Welcome to Château du Harden.'

'What?' Sam looked confused.

Lee didn't feel like explaining. 'This is where I've been staying the last month or so.'

Sam looked around, locking on the big-screen TV. 'Oh my God! You do have a TV! It's *huge*!'

'Yup.' Lee was always amazed at the resiliency of the younger generation. They bounced back better than adults, could go from tragedy to triumph seamlessly, and never thought twice about it. It could also be a sign that Sam was becoming emotionally disconnected. A defense mechanism.

Lee looked at his watch.

It was 1230 hours. He had almost eight hours of light left and two locations of potential survivors. The older man in the barn house could obviously take care of himself and was therefore a lower priority for rescue. The family on the rooftop was the higher priority, though they were an unknown distance away. In this heat, on the top of a roof, they were unlikely to make it much longer without supplies. The survival of the family on the roof was very time sensitive, which meant Lee needed to move to their location ASAP.

The only problem was that he could not realistically make the trip before it got dark out, and certainly not the trip back. He toyed with the idea of making the trek to their house on foot, eliminating all hostiles, and sleeping in the house with the family, then moving out in the morning.

Then came the issue of Sam. He did not want to take Sam with him and expose the kid to needless danger. Lee felt confident he could handle the infected in the yard, but he didn't need to be worrying about Sam while he did it. Or Tango, for that matter. They would both have to stay here. And Lee didn't want to leave Sam and Tango unattended for too long. Two days would be too much.

He didn't like it because it went against his training, but sometimes you had to improvise and adapt your tactics to the situation. Lee would have to use his truck. That meant a few things. First, he had to get to it, which meant taking out the two unwanted guests attempting to beat their way into the house. Second, it meant he would have to take roads to get there, which meant the possibility of another gang like the men in the red pickup truck. While he'd handled them fairly easily, he'd had the advantage of surprise and there were only five of them, none armed with anything more potent than a bolt-action rifle. Should a better equipped or more numerous group ambush him, his chances of survival were greatly decreased.

But the cold facts were that there was a family of three on a roof, likely suffering – if not already dead – from dehydration and heat stroke. Not to mention the complete and utter despair of their situation. He could not imagine the crushing feeling of hopelessness after seeing Sam and his dad, probably the first people they'd seen for a while, and then just watching them walk away.

He had to rescue them. Out of personal conviction, and because it was his job to do so. As a Coordinator, it was his primary duty, and one he'd sworn to uphold, just as he'd sworn to uphold the country and the Constitution.

And the only way to rescue them was by truck. On the positive side, he would be back before nightfall. Lee walked over to his closet and called Sam to join him. The kid was going to be in the house alone. Lee was not going to forbid Sam from opening the closet full of weapons and ammo because there was nothing that would make a kid want to play with the shit more than being forbidden to do so.

Instead, he chose the approach of hoping that some knowledge and instruction on these pieces of equipment would alleviate the kid's fascination with them and hopefully keep him from killing himself.

He opened the closet and saw Sam's eyes go wide. 'Wow. You've got a lot of stuff.'

Lee knelt down and pulled out his 5.56mm ammo can, then extracted the magazine from his M4 and started topping it off. 'These are all tools, Sam. Just like a screwdriver or a hammer. They are here so that I can do my job. And you need to learn about them too, since you're going to be helping me do my job.'

Lee spent the next twenty minutes telling Sam all about the equipment in the closet and some of the equipment on his person. He answered most of Sam's questions and did his best to let the kid handle most of it so he wouldn't be sneaking around behind Lee's back, pulling grenade pins out of curiosity. After a comprehensive crash course on pistols, rifles, grenades, GPS devices, and how to load a magazine, Lee was finished topping off his rifle and pistol and replacing the 40mm grenade he'd used to blow the truck. He closed the door and stood up.

'Now listen to me.' Lee waited until he had eye contact. 'We're friends, like I said, and friends trust each other. That means I trust you. You remember when I said you were a man in my book?'

Sam nodded.

'Nothing's different. You are still a man in my book. And men don't take their friends' tools unless they have permission, or if they really need it. Like in an emergency.' Lee felt his explaining-things-to-kids ability flagging. 'Just don't do anything stupid, okay? Remember, if you pull the pin on one of those grenades, you're going to die. No matter where you throw it in here, the pressure will pop your head open. Got it?'

Sam looked a little apprehensive of the closet now. Good. Lee stood and double-checked his equipment.

'Where are you going?' Sam seemed worried.

Lee wondered if abandoning the kid was the best thing right now, but he decided he couldn't let this one child affect his decision-making when it came to fulfilling his mission. If there were people out there who needed help, he had to rescue them and bring them together.

Subvenire Refectus.

To rescue and rebuild.

'I'm going to go try to help the people on the roof. I should be back in a few hours.'

'But what about the people outside?' Sam almost shouted.

'Sam . . .' Lee gave him a warning look and kept his own voice low. *Lead by example.* 'I have to try to help those people, because that's my job. I will be fine, just like I'm fine now after helping you. And you let me worry about the two people upstairs.' Lee wasn't as sure as he sounded. If the girl from yesterday had taught him one thing, it was to not underestimate the strength or tenacity of infected individuals. 'I'll be fine.'

Sam clenched his jaw, not looking happy about being left alone. 'What do you want me to do while you're gone?'

'Here.' Lee walked over to the remote and flipped on the TV. He was not above bribing the kid into submission. 'Play *Call of Duty*. You better have it beat by the time I come back.'

'That's impossible,' Sam mumbled.

'Whatever.' Lee tossed him the controller and turned on the gaming system. 'I beat it in five hours, but if you think it's too hard . . .'

'I can beat it,' Sam announced and grabbed the controller.

Lee smiled. The kid had a competitive streak. A good thing for someone living in a world like this. Noncompetitive people tended to give up more easily. Competitive people just kept going, even when there was no competition.

Lee opened the hatch and told Tango to stay. Just before he closed it, he looked back at Sam and caught the kid staring at Lee with unguarded fear for what might happen. He gave the kid a brave smile and a thumbs-up, and in his best Arnold voice said, 'I'll be back.'

Lee saw a weak smile before closing the hatch and locking it behind him.

EIGHT

DOWN THE ROAD

HE MADE HIS WAY QUIETLY out of the bunker and up to his basement.

Without Tango there to be his early-warning system, he spent more time listening and waiting. Before opening the hatch to his basement, he hung on the ladder with his ear pressed to the steel but didn't hear any movement from inside. He thought he could still hear the banging from the infected he had begun to mentally refer to as Hammer Guy. The sound was so faint, he entertained the possibility that he could just be imagining it.

When he did open the hatch, he did it slowly and quietly. Once it was open, he crept out, careful to control his M4 and other attached gear so it would not bang on the walls or the hatch and make noise.

Now in the basement, he listened and realized he was not hearing Hammer Guy or Caddy Shack. The basement was silent, and the upstairs along with it. This set Lee off his pace even more than hearing the two goons still trying to break in. Because if he heard them trying to break in, that meant they were still outside. Now, in the silence, he was not so sure.

He checked his chamber to ensure he was locked and loaded. Up the stairs.

SERE (Survival, Evasion, Resistance, and Escape) training taught him to compartmentalize so his life didn't seem so impossible. When you are surrounded by enemy forces and fear drives you to ground and makes you think you are incapable of moving to your objective, you simply compartmentalize. Instead of moving to your objective, you focus on just crawling to that fallen log, and then from there, slithering down into the swamp. You divide it up into manageable tasks that don't seem so life-or-death.

Right now, though fear told him Hammer Guy and Caddy Shack were sniffing around the house for him, making it to the top of the stairs seemed feasible. So he put one foot in front of the other, rifle trained at the door, and quietly eased his way up.

He stopped and listened again.

Hearing nothing, he opened the door just an inch so that he could catch a glimpse of the patio doors where Hammer Guy had been. As he cracked the door, he could see Hammer Guy, squatted down on the ground, facing away from the house, carving something into the dirt of Lee's backyard with the claw of the hammer. The air seemed warmer than it had been when he'd first entered the house, but he'd been in his bunker, which he kept at a cool seventy degrees. He supposed his body had acclimated to the cooler temperature and felt the difference in the slightly warmer house.

Lee watched Hammer Guy work, disturbed by the infected man's raw intensity and aggression. After a few moments, Lee edged farther out of the doorway and looked to the front of the house to see if Caddy Shack was still hanging around. His angle wasn't very good, but that also meant Caddy Shack couldn't see him. He wanted the two infected calm and quiet so he could get a better position of attack on them. And he wanted to kill them silently so he wouldn't attract any more attention.

Lee was beginning to think that the strange howling noise the infected made was some vestige of predatory instinct left over in human DNA from the days of hunting in packs. To Lee, it sounded like the call of a wolf on game, and Lee got the distinct feeling that when one infected made the howl, more infected would come running, out of some primal, knee-jerk response to the call of prey.

He slipped through the doorway, then down a hallway that led to the main portion of his house and the stairs to the second level. He slid quickly around the banister and took the stairs two at a time. He turned left at the top, facing the front of the house where the still-unaccounted-for Caddy Shack had last been seen.

In the guest bedroom decorated in nautical style, Lee squatted down and duck-walked to the window overlooking the front porch and front lawn. The porch was covered, but if Caddy Shack moved out into the yard, Lee would have a good bead on him. Wood blinds covered the windows and were pulled closed. Lee used a single finger to lift one of the slats and gain a view of his front yard.

The view was too narrow. He couldn't see Caddy Shack.

'Sonofabitch ...' Lee dropped his go-to-hell pack with a little less caution than normal. Something hard on the bottom of the pack made a heavy *thump* on the hardwood floors. Lee cringed.

Somewhere in one of the second-floor bedrooms, something glass shattered.

Lee swept the rifle up to his shoulder, thinking, *What the fuck was that?* but not daring to breathe a word. He knew damn well what it was. Something was fucking around in one of the bathrooms up here and had heard him drop his pack. The warmth in the house wasn't because the thermostat was set a few degrees higher – it was because someone had done enough kicking to break in his front door. Now the heat and humidity – and whoever had kicked down the door – were inside his house.

Lee kept an eye on the far end of the hallway through the bedroom door and reached with his free hand into his pack to withdraw a suppressor from a side pocket. He repositioned himself so that he had quick access to the MK23 on his leg should something come into view while he was attaching the suppressor, then turned the M4 skyward and started threading the suppressor.

Something crashed down the hall.

Lee tried to focus on finding the thread but found himself staring back down the hallway. He didn't want to shoot this fucker without a suppressor on his gun. The noise would be loud enough to not only draw attention from other infected in the area, but it would draw them right into his house through the open front door.

He heard the sound of something regurgitating, then the splash of fluid on hardwood floors.

He found the thread and started twisting, fast.

There was a gasp from down the hallway and then pounding feet. Scratching with each footstep. Like cleats. Or golf shoes.

Come on . . .

Lee twisted as fast as his hands could manage. Footsteps were at the door. Done. Something loomed into the bedroom.

Lee brought up the rifle and fought the panicked instinct to just start shooting. He put the red dot center mass on the approaching figure and pulled the trigger twice in rapid succession. Both rounds punched neat holes in Caddy Shack's chest, staggering him back into the door. Strangely, the suppressed M4 sounded to Lee like the snap of someone driving a golf ball down the fairway.

Caddy Shack seemed to recover from the blows after only a second. He looked at Lee and opened his mouth. Thick red blood dribbled out. He reached out with both hands, the fingers twisted into claws, and lurched toward him.

This time Lee did shoot reflexively, pulling the trigger three times. Caddy Shack didn't stop coming. Lee backpedaled fast, pushing his back against the wall and shooting from the hip.

It didn't take long for Caddy Shack to cross the bedroom, and when he was within arm's length, Lee stopped shooting and kicked out like he was kicking a door in Iraq, connecting with Caddy Shack's chest and sending him to the ground. Lee stumbled, recovered his balance, and shoved the suppressor against Caddy Shack's head. The muzzle blast did more damage than the bullet, nearly inverting Caddy Shack's face.

Lee fell backward once he was sure the man was dead and scooted away from the body until his back was against the wall again. 'Fuck me ...' Lee breathed hard, his chest thumping like a kick drum. He could feel the adrenaline pumping through his body and knew if he wasn't holding his M4 in an iron grip, his hands would be shaking.

He pulled himself up and stepped over to a bedroom mirror, checking his face for blood spatter, but couldn't find any.

The shakiness reached its peak and then the relief flooded his system, his body dumping endorphins into his bloodstream.

'Woo.' Lee huffed a few more times, then decided to get moving.

He shouldered his pack and moved down the stairs again, leaving Caddy Shack for later. He didn't want the body stinking up his house, but he didn't have the time or protective equipment to remove it. He found the front door open, as he'd suspected. Little circular star marks were dented all over the door. The tiny cleats from his golf shoes. He'd kicked the door God knew how many times to get the latch to give. After a quick inspection, Lee realized his error. Distracted by getting Sam into the house, he had not engaged the deadbolt.

Lee swore to himself and closed the door, this time turning the deadbolt. Since the frame was steel, it barely showed any damage, and neither did the door. It was simply the latching mechanism that had given way to hundreds of kicks.

Since Caddy Shack was no longer an issue, Lee felt no need to use stealth on Hammer Guy. He opened the back patio door and put a bullet in his head. Quick and easy. He took a moment to look at what he'd been carving in the dirt.

HELLP

Lee looked back and forth between the dead body and the word it had written in the earth. This misspelling seemed to imply both the state of the world and what everyone in it wanted. But Lee knew the infected weren't able to reason to the point of cleverness.

Could they?

Lee continued on to his detached garage and went inside, watching his back as he entered and closed the door behind him. His Chevy 1500 still sat where he'd left it, apparently untouched and still with a full tank. He tossed his pack in first, then climbed in and set his M4 on the passenger seat. He buckled in, cranked it up, and only then did he hit the garage door opener.

The door rattled and cranked its way open. Anyone within a quarter mile could have heard it. Lee backed out and surveyed his yard. There appeared to be nothing there, except the dead body of the man who had been crying out for help. Or saying that the world had gone to hell.

Either or. Lee looked at the body for a long time as he sat at idle. Should he have dispatched the person so coldly? It was a person, after all. These were all American citizens, sick or not. Was it his place to wipe them out wholesale and without warning? The girl had attacked him, and Caddy Shack definitely seemed to be making a run for it, but thinking back to Hammer Guy, pounding on the glass with his hammer and saying 'Open the fucking door,' then carving 'HELLP' into the dirt ... perhaps the person was just looking for help. Looking for a place of refuge. In Lee's fear of the infected, had he mistaken a cry for help as aggression?

Lee shuttered those thoughts away in a dark corner of his mind. Things to think about later. Right now, there were three potential survivors stuck on a roof. People who could be saved. Uninfected. Those were his priority; those were the people he was responsible for saving. Not the dead and dying.

Lee continued backing out of the driveway and onto Morrison Street. He headed south and did the only thing he could do: He hoped for the best.

Morrison Street stretched on through miles of farming country. To either side of the two-lane blacktop, fields would sprawl out, framed by thin stands of forest. Mainly, Lee saw tobacco, but some of the fields were tilled dirt and a few were corn. Every so often he passed a farmhouse, sometimes close to the road, sometimes out in the distance. He drove slowly, and when he saw a house, he would stop and look at it for a long moment, trying to determine if the previous residents were still using it.

They all appeared empty. The windows were dark or boarded up, the driveways overgrown with weeds. No sign of movement inside or on the neighboring fields. He would slowly drive on after giving each house a look-over, constantly scanning the fields around him for signs of trouble. He did not like driving on these roads. Though Morrison Street was only a small back road, and raiders would likely stick to higher-traffic and more target-rich environments, he still felt as though there were eyes in the trees, watching him and waiting for a moment of vulnerability.

He came upon a curve that opened into a long, straight stretch of road. He stepped on the brakes, harder than normal, and came to a stop in the roadway. A large green combine hulked in the middle of the roadway, blocking the southbound lane and most of the northbound lane. From the tire marks in the dirt, it appeared to have come from the field to Lee's right.

Lee immediately put a hand out to his M4, where it was sitting in the passenger seat. The road blockage was a typical ambush point. The raiders could be inside the combine, on the other side, or waiting in a nearby hide. Or it could just be a combine sitting in the roadway. He grabbed the 3x scope from his M4 and brought it to his eyes, surveying the field to his right, where a wide swath had been cut through the massive hay field, all the way up to the road. Using the magnifier, he noticed lumps scattered around the hay field, lying in the path cut by the combine. Lee wasn't positive, but they looked like bodies.

He pictured some old farmer in blue-jean overalls and a straw hat, trapped in his little farmhouse, surrounded by unending acres of chest-high hay fields and a horde of infected wandering through, like alligators in a moat. If Lee had been in that situation, the combine would have been the most likely ticket out. It showed a violent resourcefulness that Lee could appreciate, and again he pictured the old farmer, laughing around a wad of Red Man as he mowed down both the grass and his captors.

Lee took a moment to count the bodies lying in the path. Seventeen. Possibly more he couldn't see. Assuming they were infected, that was a big group. Much more than the 'five or ten' Sam had claimed to see. Did they have enough mental functioning to attack in organized groups, or did they just amble around, grouping themselves together out of some latent social instinct? And why did they not attack each other?

According to Sam, he had witnessed them killing each other. And his father compared them to a pack of wild dogs. Lee considered the pack instinct, as prevalent in human beings as it was in dogs, but more well-controlled in modern society. Social controls or not, humans sought to be in groups. It was not a stretch of the imagination to believe that this would continue despite massive damage to the frontal lobe because of the bacterium. In fact, Lee believed that without reasoning abilities, many of mankind's ingrained instincts would become more pronounced.

It was a lot of hypothesizing on not much evidence.

Lee eased the pickup forward, still keeping an eye on the combine and the surrounding fields, but less concerned with a raider ambush and more concerned with the possibility that the escaping farmer hadn't gotten all the infected that were between him and freedom, leaving a few stragglers behind to attack travelers like Lee.

He drove the pickup around the combine, thinking that at any moment it would roar to life and a crazed old man in blue-jean overalls would run him over in the massive piece of farm equipment, shredding the pickup truck and Lee along with it. But the combine remained still as he passed, like a stuffed lion in a museum that you feel might come back to life and pounce on you as you walk by. Lee accelerated once past, uncomfortable with having the thing lurking behind him.

Not a mile down the road, Lee saw something else that made him stop.

Approximately fifty yards from the roadway, in a tilled-dirt field to Lee's left, a female figure was hunched over. Whoever it was, she had long blond hair that stirred slightly in the breeze as it swept across the field. Her back was to Lee and her head was bowed, but she appeared to hold something that captured her interest, though Lee could not see what it was. She wore a white camisole with blue jeans and no shoes.

She knelt so motionless that Lee would have driven past her had her white camisole not stood out, though as Lee looked more closely, it appeared to be smudged with dirt and grime.

His first instinct told him that she was alive. Dead bodies did not remain in kneeling positions.

His second, more paranoid thought was that it was a trap. It was not unheard of for an ambush party to use a female who appeared to be lost or in distress as bait in a trap. He looked at her for a moment, then surveyed the area around her. It was an odd place for an ambush, not a bottleneck that would force a victim to come to her. Not much nearby cover for ambushers to hide behind.

Lee put the pickup truck in park and grabbed the M4 from

the passenger seat. He gave his surroundings a good second look-over for any threats and then opened his door. The vehicle dinged, reminding him that his keys were still in the ignition and the pickup truck was running. After a moment's consideration, Lee turned off the pickup and shoved the keys in his pants pocket before exiting the vehicle.

Immediately, he brought the rifle to his shoulder and scanned the area through the 3x magnifier. Now out of the car, he could hear the soft sound of crying lilting over the field. He looked at the woman's back and watched her shoulders rise and fall in shudders.

He kept looking around, feeling like someone was creeping up behind him. He didn't want to leave the pickup truck for fear that it was a trap and he would be too far to make it back, or that someone was waiting in the ditch to rob him of his only form of transportation.

He walked toward the woman, as far as the edge of the asphalt, then stopped. 'Ma'am!' He called it out loud and commandingly, his voice a cannon blast in the stillness.

The figure of the woman stiffened and the head turned partially, as though she was regarding him out of the corner of her eye. He still could not see her face, as her hair hung in front of it.

Something was wrong. 'Ma'am, I'm Captain Lee Harden of the United States Army and I'm here to help you.'

That invisible, sidelong stare held for another long moment. Then the woman turned her attention back to whatever was in front of her. Lee wanted to leave but knew it was not an option. He stepped off the road and walked very slowly toward the woman, angling to her left, attempting to get a better read on her face and what she was holding. He kept his rifle at his shoulder and at low-ready.

'Ma'am . . .' he repeated several times as he drew closer to her, now within twenty feet. He wanted the woman to know he was walking up to her. 'I'm coming to you, okay? Can you talk to me? Can you say something to let me know you're still with me?'

He never received a response.

About fifteen feet from her, he stopped. He was directly to her left and could see her face in profile. She'd been pretty once and was still young, though all recognition and intelligence were drained from her eyes. Her mouth was hanging open and a frothy buildup shimmered at the corners of her mouth. Glistening trails of snot ran from her nostrils across the side of her dirty face.

'Oh God . . .' Lee swallowed against the hard fist clenching at his throat and pulled the rifle in a bit tighter, dropping his finger to the trigger.

The woman stared down at a small figure in her arms, pale and sallow. The eyes were sunken in and the lips puckered. The skin looked limp and leathery and the ribs were visible. The baby had been dead for some time.

Somehow his voice cut through to the woman and she turned her head. Lee noticed that she also was mere skin and bones, probably very near a death of malnutrition and dehydration. Her vacant eyes wandered across the field to Lee's boots, then up, slowly, to his face. For a moment, Lee thought there was some sanity there, perhaps some hope. The woman shifted her weight slightly, causing Lee to take a step back, but she did not get up. She lifted her arms, the tiny corpse still cradled in her hands, and she extended the body toward Lee.

Can you help? Can you fix my baby?

The woman, or what was left of her, let out a soft moan.

Lee wanted to shoot her right there. Put her out of her sad

existence. But he could not bring himself to do it. This was one of the rare infected who was not violent. Lee wondered what this woman had been like before the plague had destroyed her brain, if even when her reasoning centers had been rotted away, she could not be brought to violence. Lee thought she must have been a very kind person.

She did not deserve this. No one deserved this. Slowly, her hands and the emaciated figure they bore sunk to the ground. Another sound, like a soft sigh, escaped her throat. Her eyes followed her dead child to the dirt, where it lay motionless, and once again she knelt, staring, unmoving except for the strands of her hair caught in the breeze.

Lee stepped away from the woman, leaving her to fade in her grief, her mind lost and wandering an endless plain of primitive, instinctual memories – the sensation of life from life and flesh from flesh, of nurturing and love, but also of the empty loneliness of death, the desolation of loss.

When he was far enough away, he turned and ran back to the truck.

He got in and closed the door hurriedly, afraid that she had followed him, but when he looked back across the field, she still sat there. Strangely, he thought of Deana again, though he didn't know why. Some small portion of him wished he'd had a family, but the larger part of him was thankful that he had survived alone. The loneliness was nothing compared to the pain of separation.

He started the pickup and kept driving.

He'd been on the road for nearly a half hour when he finally came to a stop and looked out across a field, to a house in the distance. He'd passed so many open fields with no houses attached, he was starting to think he had missed it and that

Sam's eyes were sharper than his. But here was a farmhouse set up on a hill, about six hundred yards out from the road. He just couldn't see anyone on the roof.

He pulled the magnifier off his rifle again and scoped the house. The magnifier was not as powerful as binoculars, but it gave Lee a slightly better image than the naked eye, and through it he could just make out what looked like two figures lying down on the roof. Their dark clothes blended in with the roofing shingles. Though he couldn't see them clearly, they did not look like they were moving.

In the yard below them, Lee could not see any infected. The front door to the house was hanging open, and it was possible that the ten infected Sam had reported were taking shelter from the heat inside, while the house's original occupants baked on the roof.

Now came the question: Should he traverse the distance to the house, putting himself at risk and leaving his vehicle behind, only to discover that the figures on the roof were no longer alive? Or should he honk the horn to attempt to gain their attention, confirming that they were alive but ruining all chances for stealth and making their rescue that much harder?

Lee knew himself better than to labor long over the dilemma. If the two on the roof failed to respond when he honked his horn, that would not be enough for Lee to leave them to rot on the rooftop. He would need to see them, look at them, and check them for pulses before he abandoned them.

Which simplified the situation.

There was a deep drainage ditch on the side of the road, separating him from the field that stretched out to the house. Traversing the ditch in the pickup truck was out of the question. It was possible that he could make it, but Lee preferred to be sure that his getaway vehicle would be ready for him if things went bad and he had to get lost. However, he did pull the vehicle as far off the roadway as he felt comfortable with, then exited, closing and locking the door quietly.

He hitched up his go-to-hell pack and dipped down into the drainage culvert. If he could get within a few hundred yards of the house he might be able to communicate with the two figures on the roof and hopefully plan an exit for them, if the threat of infected still remained.

Lee held out hope that the infected that had tried to kill the family earlier would have lost interest and left the area. Lee had absolute confidence in his ability to take on a threat, but there was no denying that the warped and destroyed minds of the people infected with the FURY plague didn't go down easily. And taking on ten of them at a time was going to be that much harder.

He climbed up out of the ditch and headed toward the house, skirting along a small clump of trees that bordered the field. He moved at a trot, stopping every few moments to survey the area and check behind him. Each time he checked, he looked back at his vehicle. He didn't like the way it was sitting there, all alone and painfully conspicuous on the side of the road. It was begging for attention.

He also took the time to look at the house and see what he could through the windows and the open front door, but he was either too far to see the movement or there was simply no one inside. The thought meandered across his mind that, if the house was empty, what was the family still doing on the roof?

Unless they were already dead.

After several circuits of scooting along the edge of the woods and stopping and looking around, he was about two hundred yards from the house. That was close enough. He took another good look through his magnifier at the two individuals on the roof. It was two females, one about mid-thirties, the other a child, maybe five or six. Still, neither moved. From this distance, Lee could not see the rise and fall of their chests to determine if they were breathing.

Or maybe he was close enough and they just weren't.

He bear-crawled a few yards forward to a stand of thick brush that gave him good concealment. There, he dropped his go-to-hell pack and slipped a hand into one of the side pockets. He rooted around a bit, then came out with a compact of camouflage face paint. He didn't want to camouflage himself right then, but he did want the mirror inside.

He opened the compact and angled it toward the sun until he saw a dull square of light flash over the front of the house. He wiggled it around, finally centering it on the adult female and flicking it over her eyes. He did this several times but garnered no response. He turned the mirror slightly so that reflection washed over the younger female's face and repeated the flicking.

This time the head came up.

Lee could see the girl sit up slightly, shield her eyes, and then peer out into the woods where the flashing light was coming from. The girl had curly blond hair that whipped around in the breeze. She looked concerned and obviously did not see the flashing light as anything friendly. It had probably been so long since anything friendly came by that she wouldn't believe it even if she knew.

Lee kept flashing her with the mirror, then dropped it and came out of his concealment just long enough to wave a quick arm.

This time the look on the girl's face changed from

suspicion to urgency. She rolled toward her mother and shook her arm. The mother, her face sunburned and grimed, looked up, appearing out of sorts or possibly woozy in the afternoon heat. The girl began silently pointing toward Lee, who took the moment to step out of cover again and wave once more.

The mother sat bolt upright and began wildly waving both arms. Then she shouted. '*Help! Please help!*'

Lee swore under his breath and motioned to her, palms to the earth with both hands – *Calm down!*

But it was too late. From somewhere inside the house came that horrid screech.

Lee pointed at the house, counted with his fingers – 1, 2, 3 – then raised his hands in question, attempting to communicate: *How many are inside?* The woman looked down below her feet as though she would see through the roof with X-ray vision, then looked back up at Lee and shrugged. Lee wasn't sure whether the shrug meant she didn't know how many were inside or she didn't understand the question.

He motioned for her to calm down once more, then fell back into his concealment.

Not a second after he did this, a figure burst through the front door. It was a male, tall and very skinny. His left leg appeared injured and he dragged it behind him, though he moved fast, despite the handicap. He was wearing only a pair of briefs and some dress socks. He dragged a garden rake behind him.

The infected craned his neck up to see the two survivors on the roof and began making chuffing noises that sounded like an anxious dog. He came down the front steps, the steel head of the rake clattering after him.

The two females on the roof heard him coming out into

the yard and flattened themselves onto the roof. Lee didn't know whether Slim had already seen them or not, but the shout was enough to rev his engine. He grabbed the rake with both hands and started swinging it overhead like an ax. The tines smacked the rain gutter and he pulled, ripping a section down.

From around the other side of the house, drawn by the commotion, two more infected appeared. They ran to where Slim was standing and started pacing around, looking up at the roof like they knew someone was up there. Neither of the new-comers had a weapon in hand, but both seemed agile and, so far, uninhibited by the plague's effect on motor skills.

Lee waited, breathing hard now. No others came out of the house or from around the back. There were only three left. Lee wondered where the others had gone. Then he wondered why these ones were still here. Were they really that persistent? How long did it take for them to lose interest in something? And did they ever get exhausted, or would they continue trying to get to their victims for hours on end?

Lee quietly pulled on his go-to-hell pack. Then he shoul-dered his rifle and stood behind the brush with one knee on the ground, peering through the leaves at the scene before him. The rake was broken, and now all three infected were making strange noises and staring up at the roof. One was still pacing back and forth, but the other two stood in place, hands clenched by their sides as though ready to fight. On the roof, the woman held the girl in her arms, and both stared fearfully below the edge of the roof, where unseen threats waited to tear them apart.

'Head shots this time ...' Lee slowed his breathing, in through the nose, out through the mouth, then stepped out of his hiding place.

He moved forward, wanting to cover as much distance as

possible to make his head shots more accurate. He figured that a shot to the head would almost always put someone down, no matter how persistent he was, and if all three bum-rushed him, he would need them to drop fast.

He walked at a steady pace, heel to toe, rifle to his shoul-der, red dot trained on the pacer. He seemed most likely to notice Lee's approach, since the other two had their backs to Lee and were still staring up at the roof.

He closed to about one hundred and fifty yards, and they still had not noticed him.

He pictured himself tripping and falling as he traversed the uneven ground, the three infected descending on him as he attempted to right himself. He looked down at the ground to inspect his footing. When he looked back up, the pacer was sprinting at him.

'Shit—' was all Lee could get out of his mouth. He planted one foot behind him as the infected closed the distance with surprising speed. All in that same second he told himself to be still, be calm, and to take a good shot, then he thought about the infected girl, sitting in the field, mourning her infant's death, and wondered if he should give warning before shoot-ing this unarmed infected, the same warning he would give any other person.

Hesitation.

He put the red dot on the infected's head – closing about a hundred yards – and breathed out slowly. The 3x magnifier gave the infected the appearance of being much closer, and Lee's instincts screamed to take the shot, but he waited. Another breath in . . . getting closer . . . breath out . . .

Lee pulled the trigger once, watched the shot clip the infected's shoulder and spin him, fired again, and saw the neat hole punched right above his left ear. The figure dropped.

Lee lowered the scope to see the big picture, which was two other infected, hauling ass toward him and screeching wildly. Lee chose the faster one without the damaged leg and fired quickly. The head shot was perfection and the body dropped. Lee pivoted to the third infected, so close now that his snarling face and skin-and-bones torso filled up Lee's scope. Three shots brought him to the ground, but he didn't want to die and kept crawling on all fours until Lee finished him with a round to the top of the head. Slim died about twenty feet from Lee.

It wasn't until after Slim stopped moving that he heard the screaming.

Lee looked up and saw both survivors standing at the edge of the roof, the woman holding her daughter as she reached out, tears in her eyes and her face clenched in grief and anger. She was screaming at Lee, but he couldn't tell what she was saying; all of her words were contorted with emotion. Lee looked at the mother and saw the look in her eyes, and then he looked down at the body twenty feet from him and heard the little girl cry out for Daddy.

It wasn't Daddy anymore, but this five-year-old didn't know that.

'Fuck.' Lee felt that pressing coldness in the pit of his stomach like he had just massively screwed something up. But what was he supposed to have done? Let the man tear into him because he was afraid to make a five-year-old cry? Lee shook his head and moved toward the house.

When he was close enough to talk, the little girl had turned away from him and buried her face in her mother's chest. He opened his mouth to tell them his customary script, but the words caught in his mouth. He felt ashamed, though he knew there was nothing that could have been done differently. Even so, he didn't want to introduce himself as the conquering hero of the United States Army one minute after gunning down this girl's father.

He went with a simple, 'I'm sorry, there's nothing I could do to save him. I'm here to help you. How did you get up there?'

The woman blinked away tears, obviously upset but also rational enough to understand that her husband had been rendered insane by the plague and would have killed any of them had Lee not put him down. She pointed to the backside of the roof.

'There's a ladder on the ground in the backyard.' Her voice was hoarse and cracked. Lee could not see any supplies on the roof and assumed they were both parched dry from lack of water.

He jogged around the house, taking the corners slowly and panning to see what threats lay beyond. When he saw the backyard was clear, he walked, searching the overgrown grass and weeds for a ladder.

He found a painter's ladder lying in the knee-high grass, angled away from the house, and Lee reasonably inferred that it had been propped against the house, then kicked off to prevent their attackers from following.

Lee picked up the ladder with one hand and heaved it back into place, leaning against the roof. The woman and her daughter appeared over the crest of the roof and worked their way carefully down the incline to the ladder.

The woman pointed to the ladder. 'Abby, go down first.'

The little girl shook her head violently, her blond curls flying. 'I don't wanna go down with him!'

Lee felt stung. 'It's okay, sweetie. I promise I won't hurt you.'

Abby wasn't having it and screamed in an ear-splitting shriek, 'You killed my daddy!'

'Abby.' The woman's voice was shaking but stern. 'You will not talk to him like that.'

The little girl was still sobbing but didn't say anything else. The woman turned and made her way down the ladder. She moved slowly and a bit clumsily, making Lee concerned about the level of dehydration. When she finally reached the bottom, she held out her arms and motioned for the girl to come down. Finally Abby swung her tiny legs out and began climbing down, her mother hovering underneath her, arms outstretched, waiting to catch her if she fell.

When both of them were on the ground, Lee placed a hand gently on the woman's shoulder and pointed toward the brick wall of the house. The angle of the sun cast this side of the house in shade, which was what both of them needed. He noticed that despite the heat, the woman wasn't sweating, which only meant that her body didn't have the fluids to spare.

'Come over here.' Lee held her by the arm as she walked slowly into the shade. 'Cool down for a minute. I have water.'

The mention of water made both of the survivors' eyes go wide. The woman nodded as she sat down against the brick wall. 'Please. We haven't had water in days.'

Lee unhooked his rifle and leaned it against the wall, still close by. Then he took off his pack and set it on the ground. From the main portion, he withdrew four bottles of water, setting two on the ground and handing one to each of the females.

'They're not cold,' Lee advised. 'Drink it slow at first or you might vomit.'

While the two survivors undid the caps on their bottles of

water and sipped at them, obviously using significant self-restraint to keep from gulping them down, Lee scanned the perimeter of the property but saw no threats. Satisfied, he closed the main portion of his pack and opened a smaller section where he kept a stash of medical supplies. From inside he pulled out two packs of electrolyte tablets and two ice packs.

He handed the packs of electrolyte tablets to the mother. 'When you get done with the bottle of water, put both tablets in the next bottle and shake it up. They'll help rehydrate you.' As he said this he crushed the ice packs, breaking the chemical bags inside and turning the contents to a frozen slush.

With an ice pack in hand, he approached Abby cautiously, as you would a dog you were unsure of. The little girl looked at him with fearful blue eyes but didn't react, so he put on a disarming smile and held out the ice pack. 'This is gonna help you feel better, okay?'

Happy to be drinking water, though still obviously distraught, the girl nodded and allowed him to place the ice pack against her head.

After a second she pulled away. 'It's cold.'

'Honey,' the mother said, sounding tired and out of it. 'It's gonna cool you down so the heat's not so bad. Just let him do it.'

Abby relaxed and Lee put the ice pack back on her head, then worked it down to the base of her neck and held it there. After a few moments, he took her hand and put it where his was. 'Hold that there, okay? Even if it starts to feel uncomfortable.'

Then he turned and put the ice pack on the mother's head. Her eyes were closed and tears were coming out, gathering grime as they ran down her face. Lee spoke soothingly.

'It's gonna be all right. I'm gonna get you guys someplace safe.'

The woman opened her eyes, now red-rimmed with tears. Her voice was a soft whisper. 'Thank you.'

Lee nodded in response. 'What's your name?'

'Angela ...' She thought for a moment, like she couldn't remember. 'Mooring.'

'Angela, I'm Lee Harden.' He still decided not to introduce his rank and purpose.

Later, he thought. *Now's not the time.*

While Lee held the ice pack to the base of her neck, Angela finished the first bottle of water and opened the second, dropping in the contents of one of the packs of electrolytes – two tablets. They immediately began to dissolve and turn the water an orangey yellow. She shook the bottle, though her movements were sluggish.

'How long were you on the roof?'

'I think ... three days?'

'Have you had any water at all?'

'We brought up a gallon. That was all we could grab on our way out. They were already breaking through the front windows.'

'Was it just you three?'

She nodded.

Lee looked at both of them. 'You guys did really well. You're both going to be very dehydrated, but hopefully the few bottles and electrolytes will get you out of the danger zone until I can get you back to my safe house.'

'You have a safe house?' Angela said it with some awe, as though she could not fathom the concept of a secure location.

'It's several miles from here.'

'Did you walk?'

'No, I drove my truck—' No sooner had the words left Lee's mouth than he heard the distant slam of a car door. A very distinct sound in the quiet of nature. He immediately froze and looked around. Angela and Abby sat unmoving, staring at him while his eyes scanned.

He grabbed up his M4 and stood. Angela's hand shot out, the quickest she'd moved yet, and held his arm. 'Please ... don't go.'

Lee looked down, pitying her. 'I'm not going far. And I'll be right back.'

She released his arm and he stepped to the corner of the house, then peered around. He could see the land laid out in front of him and his truck on the road. No ... not his truck. Someone else's, parked facing the opposite direction. A dark blue Dodge Ram. Lee leaned out a little farther, gaining a better angle and seeing the rest of the scene.

His own pickup truck was boxed in by the Ram in front and an olive drab Humvee to the rear. Outside of the vehicles, two figures were inspecting his truck, while three others approached the house from the road. A remnant of the US military? More likely just pirated US military equipment. Lee brought up his rifle, using his scope to look at the three men approaching. Two of them – one bald-headed – wore ACUs but lacked any identifying marks, and neither was wearing Kevlar, which made them look like civilians who had raided an army-navy store. The third wore an old woodland camouflage jacket and jeans. All three carried M4s. They walked with the rifles across their chests, not addressed toward the house. Lackadaisical.

If they were military, they were most likely an inactive unit or reservists. They were not equipped and they did not act like an active military unit. Whether their intentions were good or bad, Lee didn't know, and now was not the time to find out. He racked his brain for any readily available plan to snatch back his truck, but none of them was possible with the two survivors to look after.

Lee lowered the scope and estimated the distance.

The three approaching men were about four hundred yards out and walking at a slow but steady pace. That gave Lee and his two survivors only a few short minutes to get the hell out of the area.

He pulled himself back around the corner. Angela and Abby were staring up at him with wide, expectant eyes. 'We gotta move.'

'What?' Angela stood and Abby followed suit.

Lee grabbed her by the shoulder and gave her a gentle push away from the house. 'Head for the woods. There are people coming. I don't know if they are friendly, and we're not finding out.'

'They could be here to help.' Angela argued over her shoulder, stumbling along with Lee. 'They could be friendly.'

'There's five of them and they're all armed.' Lee said, lowering his voice despite the urgency spurring his feet. 'If they don't have our best interests in mind, we're fucked ... Excuse me.'

Angela craned her neck behind her, trying to catch a glimpse of the newcomers. Lee kept a hand on her shoulder and a hand on Abby's and kept steering them toward the woods. 'Come on,' he said. 'I know you guys are tired, but we gotta pick up the pace.'

'What about your truck?' Abby whined loudly. 'How are we gonna get back to your safe place?'

'Shhh!' Lee hissed, looking behind him as though he expected a barrage of shots in response. 'Speak quietly! They have my truck now. We have to walk.'

They hit the wood line and Lee dropped to one knee, tugging on their shoulders and gesturing for them to do likewise. Angela and Abby crowded in close and traded concerned looks, back and forth from their house to Lee.

His speech was a rapid whisper. 'You guys keep going straight through the woods until you can't see the house anymore. I'm going to bring up the rear. When you can't see the house anymore, lie down and hide. I'll find you.'

'How will you find us if we're hiding?' Abby asked.

'Because I'm good at that kind of thing.' Lee looked sternly at both of them. 'You both need to start trusting me. If you want to stay alive until I can get you to safety, you will do exactly as I tell you. Don't question me and don't try to outthink me. Now go.'

Angela nodded quickly and fiercely, though Abby still looked confused. Her mother grabbed her hand and silently headed deeper into the woods without looking back. They moved quickly and loudly, each footfall like an earthquake to Lee. He just hoped the incoming personnel didn't notice.

Lee waited for a moment, then swiveled and duck-walked over a few feet to a large tree and peered around it, his rifle raised. He angled himself slowly, until he got a good view of the house through the brush, and then looked through his scope. Nothing yet. With a few quick mental calculations, he decided he had some time to get a little more distance.

He stood and quietly sidestepped his way farther into the woods and away from the house, keeping as much concealing brush and trees as possible between him and the corners of the house. He kept looking where he was stepping, then back at the house. About twenty yards behind him, the woods sloped down. If he could make it to that slope . . .

Too late.

The three men cleared the corner of the house. One of them moved like a professional – the bald-headed one who wore ACUs – his rifle shouldered at low-ready and his body pivoted like a tank turret. Everywhere his eyes went, his rifle went, and he cleared the corner quickly and smoothly, gaining an angle on the back of the house. Then he motioned his two comrades forward.

The other one wearing ACUs had longer-than-regulation dark hair. The kind of long, slicked-back hair seen on the front of a bottle of Rogaine. He still held his rifle like an amateur – butt-stock under his armpit, muzzle pointed at the sky – and he walked without urgency. The third one wearing the woodland top and the jeans held his weapon ported, the barrel cradled in his left arm.

One possibly military, the other two . . . not so much.

Without Angela and Abby to weigh him down, he could probably take out these three goons and have a good chance at using the house as a defensible location to take out the rest of the squad. But without knowing their intentions, he did not want to be the first to open fire. He wasn't willing to take the gamble on whether they were good or bad guys, but the possibility still remained that they could be partially made up of US Army personnel on a benevolent mission.

Lee had slowly moved his way to another large tree and sank down onto one knee, surveying the scene with only his left eye, peering out from behind the thick trunk.

Bald ACU moved toward the back door of the house, scanning the yard as he did. Rogaine ACU and Woodland followed after him. Bald ACU waited at the back door until Rogaine tapped him on the shoulder, and then all three filed into the house.

That was Lee's cue to leave.

He pushed off the tree and made a dash for the down slope, then took the hill head-on and flew down at breakneck speed, maximizing the opportunity of having all three unidentified persons distracted by clearing the house. He continued his sprint until he felt he'd lost enough altitude that they would not be able to see him over the hillcrest. He stopped and turned, looking back, and could not see the house.

A brief moment to catch his breath from the sprint and then he took in his surroundings, trying to get his bearings. For a split second, he felt out of his depth, one of those crippling and paralyzing moments where one realizes that people are relying on you and that you cannot fail them. The responsibility of Angela and Abby, and Sam, who was probably wondering what the hell was taking Lee so long, felt like a rope around his chest, tightening steadily.

Then he took another breath, shook his head, and the feeling was gone.

He needed to find Angela and Abby, make a plan that would keep everyone safe and not require too much strenuous activity from the dehydrated and undernourished mother and daughter, and get everyone back to the house before Sam lost it and wandered off, believing Lee was dead.

But the first thing was simply to start looking for Angela and Abby. Compartmentalize. So Lee started walking, looking for signs of human foot traffic through the woods.

The presence of survivors had not gone unnoticed by the unidentified personnel who had cleared the house. After securing the premises and calling in the rest of the guys, the bald man in the ACUs took a good long look at the back of the house, where the overgrown grass was matted down. Like people had been lying in it. And the couple of empty water bottles, and the two empty packets of electrolyte tablets that were still lying in the grass. There were also two ice packs, still cold and sweating in the heat. It looked to him like two people had been rescued, which meant there had to be at least one rescuer.

At least three people unaccounted for.

And one of them had medical supplies.

NINE

... ESPECIALLY OUR SNIPERS

AFTER A SHORT SEARCH, LEE found some leaves that were disturbed, revealing the forest floor beneath and a nice half-moon shoe print in the dirt. On the trail, he followed the spoor to a little ravine about fifty yards farther into the woods where he found two frazzled blond heads and two fearful sets of blue eyes peering at him from behind a fallen tree.

'Thank God it's you.' Angela stood and Lee could see she was holding a thick branch like a club. The thing was rotted out and probably would have done nothing but powder an attacker in wood particles, but Lee could appreciate her spunk. Most people would just lie down and wait for fate to deal them their hands. At least this one was willing to fight it out.

Lee took another look behind him to make sure he had no followers, then slid over the fallen log and rested his pack against the log, splaying his legs out in front of him. He took the moment to drink a bit from his CamelBak, then motioned for the two girls to join him on the ground. They both got low.

This time Lee spoke in a normal tone. 'I'm going to get you guys back to my house, but the truck is not an option right now. We have to assume that whoever that was at the house knows we were there and is following us.'

'Will they be?' Angela sounded worried.

Lee shrugged. 'I don't know. But we will assume they are so we aren't surprised when they show up looking for us.' Lee pointed due east. 'There's another farmhouse a few miles that way. An old man lives there. I think he's ex-military. We're going to head that way and hope for the best.'

'I think that's Mr. Burnsides.' Angela gave Lee a look that communicated it was only a guess. 'He's the only ex-military guy I know around here.'

'You know what he drives?' Lee asked.

'No idea. Haven't really talked to him. Seen him in the market once or twice. Older guy with gray hair. Don't know him other than that.'

Lee nodded. That was essentially useless information, but Angela was only trying to be helpful. He looked at his watch. It was already nearly 1700 hours. It would be dark at about 2100 hours.

'Alright, we have about four hours of daylight left.' Lee rolled himself onto his feet. 'If we move quickly, we should be able to make it to Burnsides's house before dark.'

Abby pointed to Lee's pack. 'Do you have any food?'

Angela put an arm on her daughter's shoulder. 'Please, if you have any food ... we haven't eaten in days.'

Lee didn't really want them eating on dehydrated stomachs. It could cause them to vomit and become even more dehydrated. But they also needed something to perk them up.

'Yeah.' Lee dropped his pack and pulled out two MREs. He tore both of them open and fished through the contents. He extracted the PopTart and the fruit cocktail from one and the pound cake and Smarties from the other. He handed the candy to Abby and the fruit cocktail to Angela. 'Eat those slowly for some carbs while we walk. If you hold it down okay, I'll give you the PopTart and pound cake. And keep drinking that water.'

Lee shouldered his pack again and started walking without any further instructions. The two girls followed after a moment of wrestling open their individual packages. They ate eagerly and quietly as they walked in Lee's wake.

Lee peered through thick summer foliage at the farmhouse that sat alone and dark, set back on a long dirt road. The forest came to a point, jutting out across the surrounding land and pointing directly at the farmhouse. From the edge of the woods to the farmhouse was about fifty yards, and Lee made sure he stayed well back in the trees. All around him, flat farmland stretched, planted with half-grown tobacco crops.

It was still light but would be getting dark soon. They'd made the trip in a little less than three hours. In the waning sunlight, Lee could see a large chicken coop in the backyard with several hens and a rooster patrolling the chicken wire. They seemed to still be well taken care of.

The house was dark, but the upstairs windows were open. The interior looked black. If Mr. Burnsides were a true sniper, he would not be sticking his muzzle out the window but hiding far back in the darkness of the room, away from light and prying eyes. Lee wondered if he was being watched right then through the scope of a high-power rifle and the thought made him very uncomfortable. He wanted cover, but there was only concealment in the form of bushes and thin trees. Nothing that could stop a bullet.

In the front yard of the farmhouse was the pile of bodies Sam had spoken of. They were no longer smoldering and were mostly ash, but Lee could see some bits of charred skeleton, even some items of clothing, and a single boot. Again, he wondered if these were infected or just the bodies of everyone who had come looking for help and didn't find it.

Lee looked behind him, keeping his movements very slow so as to not attract any attention he didn't already have. From where he was lying, he could not see Angela or Abby in their hiding place about fifty yards back in the woods. They were to wait for Lee to give them the signal before they came out. No sense in everyone dying if Mr. Burnsides turned out to be a nut job. Lee wasn't thrilled about being the guinea pig, but he couldn't very well make Angela or Abby do it.

Lee took a few deep breaths to calm his nerves, perversely wondered what it felt like to have a high-power bullet punch a hole in your chest, and then stood. He kept his M4 slung but both his hands in the air. He walked slowly to the edge of the woods, and then stepped out into the open.

Please don't be a crazy motherfucker ...

No shot rang out.

A white curtain in one of the dark windows stirred as a breeze kicked up and then died down.

He kept his hands up, fingers splayed as though showing someone the number ten. He stepped a few feet closer to the house and was stopped by a barked command.

'That's far enough!'

Lee stretched his hands up a little farther and couldn't help but cringe, waiting for the shot. He didn't like putting his life in another person's hands, but this was one of those situations where he just had to bite the proverbial bullet and do it. The voice came from the house again. 'Put your hands on top of your head and interlace your fingers.'

Lee complied.

'Now get down on your knees.'

Again, Lee did as he was told, but he decided to try talking. 'I have two civilians with me who need help.'

'Shut the fuck up!'

Lee clamped his mouth shut, his palms feeling a bit cold and sweaty.

'Look down at the ground and don't look back up until I tell you. If you disobey me, you will be shot.'

This was a bad idea.

Lee looked down at the ground. Several long moments passed and Lee heard quiet footsteps approach from his right side, then they swung wide around him and came up from behind. He felt a firm hand grip his interlaced fingers, holding them on the top of his head, while another hand patted him down. Lee's sidearm was liberated from its holster, and his M4 was unclasped from its sling and removed. The hands explored his pockets and inside the tongue of his boots, checking – Lee presumed – for any hidden weapons.

'Don't move,' said the voice, very close now. Lee heard the soft footsteps retreat a few paces behind him and then stopped. 'Moving slowly, turn and face me.'

Lee kept his movements exaggeratedly slow, just to make sure. It was obvious that Mr. Burnsides, if that was whom Lee was dealing with, was not to be fucked with. When Lee turned he found a man, probably in his mid-forties, standing and pointing a Remington Model 700 rifle at him, topped with a very nice Leupold scope. Lee immediately noticed the man was tall and extremely thin. His long-sleeve denim shirt and khaki pants fit him snugly, so Lee assumed the man's scare-crow figure was not a recent development and hadn't been caused by food deprivation. He wore a dirty old ball cap and Lee could see short gray hair peeking out from underneath. Though the man's skin looked taut over his skeletal features, his face was scoured with deep wrinkles that gave him a weath-ered look. Dark, narrowed eyes glared at Lee from underneath wild-looking eyebrows.

This was not the man Lee knew from the market. The man spoke first. 'Who are you?'

'My name is Captain Lee Harden of the United States Army. I have two civilians in my care and we are only seeking to move through here and mean you no harm.'

'Bullshit ...' the man spat.

Lee didn't know whether he meant it about the United States Army thing or about the mean-you-no-harm thing.

'Haven't seen regular army for weeks,' the man clarified. 'All we got left now are some POG reservists out pillaging everything they find in the name of reestablishing law and order.' He said POG like *pogue*. 'You a POG reservist?'

Lee shook his head and spoke in a calm, level tone. 'No, sir. I am active duty. The United States Army has sent me to help.'

'Help with what?' The man snorted.

'My ID is in my pack. Please, see for yourself.'

Still pointing the rifle at him, the man knelt over the pack he had taken from Lee and hesitated at the pockets. Lee told him which pocket to go into and he delved in, retrieving Lee's military ID card. He looked at it for a long moment, then put it back.

'Still not convinced,' he declared.

Lee nodded. 'I understand your hesitancy. However,

whether you are convinced or not of my occupation, I am not here to harm you, and I am only trying to find a way to get two civilians to a safe zone.'

'Ain't no safe zone around here. And what two civilians you keep talking about?'

'They are hiding.'

The man rolled his eyes. 'I ain't tryin' to hurt nobody.'

'Neither am I. And I have a safe zone. If you will promise not to harm me or the two civilians, I will be glad to explain everything to you ... indoors.' The man considered this for a long moment. While he considered, Lee spoke again. 'By the way, you aren't Mr. Burnsides, are you?'

He looked at Lee with suspicion in his eyes. 'I am.'

'Because I knew the man who lived here.' Lee didn't elaborate but left the unsaid question hanging in the air.

'Don Burnsides. Yeah.' The man looked at the pile of ash that had once been a burning tangle of corpses. 'Don was my father.'

Lee could see the pain in the man's face, a face that didn't usually display those types of feelings. There was a story there that Lee could tell the younger Burnsides didn't want to talk about. As quickly as the look of pain came, it passed by, like a cloud casting a quick shadow and then rolling away in the wind.

The younger Burnsides continued. 'I'm Jack Burnsides. And I'm a Marine, so don't try and bullshit me about no military crap. I'll know if you're lying.'

Lee didn't pursue it. 'Well, Jack, can we get indoors?'

Jack shifted his position so that he could see Lee and the woods at the same time. 'Call to your civilian friends. Have them come out. Unarmed.'

Neither had a weapon, so Lee wasn't worried about that.

He yelled their names loudly into the woods and told them it was safe to come out. Lee and Jack waited in an awkward silence for several long moments before the sound of the two untrained woodland movers crashing through the forest reached them. After a few more seconds, the two of them emerged, Abby clinging tightly to Angela's leg and staring at Jack with apprehension.

Jack regarded the duo with some suspicion – he was quite the hard-ass – but did them the mercy of not pointing his rifle in their faces. He stared at them as though trying to figure out whether they were dangerous or not. Lee was not sure what conclusion he finally came to, but he motioned toward the house with his rifle. 'It's about time to get indoors, anyway ... night's a bad time to come across one of them nut jobs.'

Jack ushered the threesome into the house through the back door that led into the living room. He instructed them all to sit on the couch there while he barricaded the door. He had nailed three-quarter-inch plywood into the door to cover the glass portion. On either side of the door he had constructed sturdy-looking wooden arms that held a two-by-four in place across the door, like an old castle, locked down against the barbarian hordes.

After locking down the door, he went and checked the few ground-floor windows that were not completely boarded over. In a few of them he had cut murder holes into the plywood. Through these small openings the waning light from outside cast a dim glow on the interior of the house. With the windows boarded and the doors locked down, it felt more like a tomb than a house.

After he had checked the downstairs for security, Jack

walked back into the center of the living room, casting Lee's weapons into the corner of the room farthest from his reach. Jack then grabbed a gas lantern, cranked on the fuel, and sparked it. The room filled with the cold light of the propane lantern.

With all three of his guests – or prisoners – occupying the couch, Jack chose a wingback chair and situated it to face the trio. He laid the bolt-action rifle across his lap and regarded each of the newcomers for a long moment before speaking.

'I'm truly sorry if this seems harsh to you folks, but you have to understand my situation here. I've had everyone from the crazy ones to rogue military try to come and take my shit . . . Pardon the language.'

Lee nodded. 'You never can be too careful.'

Jack looked at him. 'You say you're army. I seen your ID, but I'm havin' some trouble believing this story of yours. Explain.'

Lee took a deep breath. 'My explanation might seem far-fetched to you, but it's the truth.' He looked at Angela and Abby as he spoke, since he had yet to explain the situation to them. 'Without wasting time with too many details, I am a part of a government initiative, headed by the US Army, called Project Hometown. Myself and forty-seven others just like me are stationed in every one of the lower forty-eight states. Our houses were built by the government and come with a heavy-duty underground bomb shelter . . . more like a vault. We refer to it as "The Hole." Anytime something happens that the government believes could cause a serious threat to the stability of the nation, they sequester us, each in our individual vault. They maintain constant contact with us until the crisis is over and then release us from the vaults. If the crisis does not resolve itself, our orders are to wait thirty days and then begin our mission.'

'It's barely been over a month since this started,' Angela interjected. 'Did they have you sequestered that early? Did they know this was going to happen?'

'They didn't know it was going to happen.' Lee shook his head. 'But they plan for the worst-case scenario. I've been sequestered many times, and it has never developed into anything worse than a bad news story. I'm sure they thought this was going to be the same thing – I know I did.'

'You mentioned a mission,' Jack said, bringing the conversation back. 'What exactly is your "mission"?'

'Rebuild a stable, centralized government in the event of total collapse.'

His words were met with silence. Abby wasn't terribly in tune with the conversation, but the two adults stared right at Lee for a long time. Finally the silence grew stale and Jack voiced what Angela must have also been thinking.

'So ... if what you say is true, you wouldn't be here if the government still existed.'

'The government is completely gone ...' Angela echoed, her voice carrying with it a sense of flat dejection, as though Lee had taken her last shred of hope.

Lee leaned forward. 'In all likelihood, the government is wiped out – at least the government as we knew it a month ago. It certainly seems that way to me. My mission doesn't start until I stop receiving communications from them. The last communication I received was on July 2.'

'What day is it now?' Angela sounded lost.

'July 24.' Jack leaned forward on his rifle.

'Don't you have some information for us?' Angela asked. 'Is there some way we can cure this thing?'

He shrugged. 'The information I received from the government was what they knew when they put me in The Hole. That was June 15. At this point in time, your own individual experiences with the infected probably surpass the limited information I received from my briefing.'

Angela's eyes narrowed. 'I'm not minimizing what you've done for Abby and me ... but if we know more than you do, what good are you going to be in rebuilding the government?'

Lee nodded to concede that it was a fair question, but Jack jumped in before he could speak.

'Because that's what he's trained to do.' Jack stood from his chair, and for the first time, set his rifle down. 'He's trained to organize pockets of people into big groups and get them to work toward a common goal. And he's obviously better equipped than us, or anyone I've seen so far.' Jack pulled a pack of cigarettes out of his shirt pocket and stuck one in his mouth. Then he looked at Angela. 'You mind?'

She shrugged. 'Your house.'

'Thanks.' He lit the cigarette. 'If I heard it from anyone else, Lee, I'd think it was horseshit – excuse me – but for some reason I believe you. Or maybe I'm just depressed and grasping at anything that can bring me some hope.'

Lee watched the lanky man with a guarded look. Behind his expressionless face, Lee was thinking that he was growing tired of convincing this asshole, and he wanted to get moving. Unfortunately, his job wasn't to rescue people and then drop them as soon as it was inconvenient. His job was to begin gathering people into a workable unit, and here were two adults who could help.

'Listen.' Lee stood. 'I understand what both of you are feeling. I'm not asking for your help. I'm asking both of you if you would like my help.' Lee let that sink in for a moment. When neither Jack nor Angela responded, he continued. 'If you choose to accept my help, then we should get going now. If you don't want it, that's fine. I would simply ask that you, Jack, give me my equipment back and I'll be gone for good.'

Angela immediately stood. 'We're going with you.'

Lee was surprised how quickly she made that decision, but he supposed that desperation and survival limited one's options. Now that the two females were decided, all eyes turned to Jack, who was still casually smoking his cigarette.

'What?' Jack stared right back at them. 'You want me to join your merry band?'

'There's no band,' Lee said. 'Just Angela, Abby, and me. Back in my bunker, there's a twelve-year-old kid who watched his father get shot to death earlier today, and my dog's with him. That's it.'

Jack folded his arms across his chest and pursed his lips. 'Why do you want me to come?'

'Because it's my job to gather people. Because I could use you. Because you're a Marine, and – correct me if I'm wrong – you've got combat experience.'

'Iraq in '03 and Afghanistan in '07 and '08.'

Lee smiled. 'Same year in Iraq as me. But I'm not forcing you to do anything. You do what you think is best. But you don't have a lot of time to decide.'

'Yeah.' Jack stepped forward. 'About you leaving . . . I don't suggest moving around at night.'

Lee was about to respond when Jack put up a finger to hush him. For a brief second, Lee thought Jack was just being an asshole, but then he realized that he was listening. In the same moment he heard what Jack was hearing.

'What?' Angela whispered. 'What's wrong?'

Jack snatched up his rifle and Lee dove for the lantern, turning the gas as low as it would go. In the dim light Lee stared up at Jack and whispered, 'I'm going to get my weapon.'

Jack only nodded.

'What's happening?' Angela whispered again, this time her voice sounding like she was on the verge of tears. Abby picked up on the tension brewing and began to whimper.

Lee stepped quietly to the corner of the room where Jack had stowed his things and began strapping on his gear. Jack moved to Angela and put an arm around her shoulder. He spoke while moving them toward the back of the room, behind some large pieces of furniture.

'Someone's coming. There's not a whole lot of friendlies around here, hence the warm welcome that I gave you. They might not be bad, but we gotta play it safe.'

Lee was geared up in a matter of seconds. 'It was us.'

'They either tracked you through the woods . . .' Jack must have been thinking the same thing. 'Or they just came to my house because it was the next logical place you'd be.' It was not an accusation but a simple fact. 'Are they good or bad?'

'I dunno.' Lee knelt down and peered through one of the murder holes. 'I got a hinky feeling about them, but I get a hinky feeling off a lot of shit these days.' Lee was looking at the side of the house facing the woods where they'd come from. 'Side's clear.'

Jack approached the front door and peered out the murder hole to the left of it. 'Eyes on . . . one Humvee . . . two pickup trucks . . . five armed personnel approaching the house in a skirmish line . . . three armed personnel remaining with the trucks.' Jack spread his feet apart and rested the muzzle of his rifle into the murder hole. It was just big enough to allow him to sight through with his scope. The dim outside light coming through the murder hole created a pale square across his face.

Lee pointed upward. 'Jack, take the upstairs. You've got a better vantage point with your rifle.'

'Negative.' Jack just kept sighting through the scope. 'I'm good where I'm at. Five approaching are about a hundred yards out.' He spoke louder. 'Angela, push the couch you're behind. Underneath it there is a big black shotgun. It's loaded – just point and shoot, okay? Anyone comes in the back door, you let 'em have it.'

'I . . . b-but . . .' Angela stammered.

Lee looked toward her. 'Angela, just do it.'

She nodded and pushed the couch out of the way. She leaned down out of view and came back up with the nastiest pistol grip shotgun Lee had ever seen. Angela stared at it with wide eyes, like she was holding a rabid dog.

'Do I have to cock it every time I shoot it?'

'Negative,' Jack responded, still not looking back. 'Semiauto and idiot proof. Like I said, just point and shoot.'

'Jack' – Lee leaned against the wall and rested the barrel of his rifle in the murder hole – 'we gonna challenge them or just open up?'

'Don't feel like it'd be right not to give 'em a chance . . .' Jack obviously wasn't concerned with Lee's opinion on the matter because he immediately yelled to the men outside: 'You men approaching the house! Stop where you are! Lay down your weapons and put your hands up!'

Lee took his eyes away from the murder hole for a moment. He looked at Jack for the brief second after he had issued his challenge. He opened his mouth to ask a question.

'Shit!' Jack hit the deck.

Neat beams of light speared the darkness, one appearing rapidly after the other, tracing a line from one side of the house to the other. The visual was spectacular, but the sound hit Lee's ears a second later. The sound of automatic gunfire punching holes through the plywood-covered windows and Angela and Abby screaming in unison.

Lee followed Jack's lead and flattened himself to the ground.

'Motherfucker!' Jack yelled over the gunfire.

'He's got a fuckin' SAW!' Lee referred to the M249 Squad Automatic Weapon, a 5.56mm belt-fed light machine gun issued to military personnel. The sound of it chattering away at them was unmistakable.

Jack turned his head to look at Lee. His face was still pressed to the ground, trying to be as small as possible, and all Lee could see were his eyes peering over the top of his left shoulder. Lee thought the man must be insane, because, though he couldn't see the rest of his face, Lee could swear Jack was grinning.

'Guess they're not friendly after all!' Jack yelled. Then the house exploded. From where Lee was plastered to the floor, he could see up the staircase to the second level. Out of the corner of his eye he saw a flash, then a billow of smoke as shreds of curtains, chunks of wood, and pieces of plaster went flying in. A heavy cloud of dust and smoke billowed down the staircase and covered him with white powder. He hadn't even registered the explosion, but his ears were ringing.

'—the fuck was that?' Jack yelled.

'RPG!' Running on autopilot, Lee hauled himself up off

the floor before his brain had even registered that the gunfire had ceased. He was on his hands quickly, but it felt like it took him forever to find his feet.

Jack seemed to suddenly realize the gunfire had stopped, and he rolled away from the door. 'We need to get the fuck out of here!'

'Yeah. Let's go.' Lee stumbled to his feet, realizing the concussion of the blast had made him a little unsteady. Perhaps his inner ear was damaged. He shambled over to where Angela and Abby were hugging each other, both curled in the fetal position in the corner of the room. Lee felt angry with them that they hadn't followed Lee's and Jack's examples and flattened themselves on the ground. All around them on the wall were bullet holes. It was a damn miracle that they weren't both shot to shit. In fact ...

Lee knelt down beside them as Jack went to the back door and peered out the murder hole. 'Back side's clear.' Jack announced. 'We need to move *now*.'

Lee shook Abby and Angela. 'Come on. We gotta get up!' As he spoke he was checking them for bullet holes. Sometimes the adrenaline masked the pain and someone could go several minutes without realizing he or she had a wound. They both appeared to be unharmed. Lee grabbed Angela by the arm and pulled her up off the ground – perhaps a little hard, but he didn't have time to be a gentleman about it. 'We need to fucking move!'

He shoved them toward the back door. Abby had her hands pressed over her ears and her mother looked shell-shocked and was still holding her daughter like a teddy bear. Jack stepped in for Lee and grabbed Angela by the shoulder, giving her a hard shake. 'Look at me,' he said. She just kept staring at her daughter.

Jack smacked her across the face.

The look she gave him was utter shock, but he had her full attention. 'I'll apologize later,' he said and put his hand on the doorknob. 'When I open this door, we're going out first, then you and Abby come out and start running. Run straight back for the woods. Lee, you take the right corner; I'll take the left. Ready?'

'Ready.' Those words always made Lee's stomach tighten.

Jack wrenched open the door. Lee moved through first and cut to the right with his rifle up and ready. He didn't see what the others did behind him. There was an old piece of advice that Lee had received many years ago during infantry training at Sand Hill. That advice was to 'watch your lane,' referring to each member of a squad's individual lane of fire. It also corresponded to all individual responsibilities. When you were focused on whether everyone else was doing their job correctly, you were least likely to be focused on doing your own job correctly.

Lee was focused on the corner of the house. In that instant, the corner of the house was his whole world. He kept moving to it, rifle at the ready, walking heel to toe, ready to toast anyone who came around the corner.

About ten feet before he reached it, Lee kicked out a few yards and 'pied the corner.' He leaned to his left and pied a few degrees of angle, then a few more, then a few more, slicing up 'the pie' into tiny pieces that gave him more and more angle on the side of the house ...

Man with a gun.

He was closer than Lee expected. Lee pulled the trigger twice, instinctively. Both shots ripped through the man's chest. The intruder's body jerked, and he lurched toward the house. Lee's angle was too shallow and the man disappeared from sight. Lee immediately pied off a bigger angle, bringing the entire side of the house into view. The man he'd just shot was leaning against the side of the house on his knees, hunched over and doing his best to bring his rifle up to bear. Lee registered that he was wearing jeans and a black shirt and was carrying an AK-47. Lee popped him two more times and he crumpled to the ground, ass up in the air like he was bowing.

There was a dark shape behind the dead man, moving up fast.

The side of the house exploded, spraying his face with chips and splinters. Lee cried out, more in surprise than pain, and ducked back behind the corner. A gunfight was a game of chess that happened in the span of a few short seconds. You didn't have time to think, so you made your moves and hoped your training and instincts were better than the other guy's. At that brief second in time, Lee knew the initiative and the advantage had gone to his attacker and that if he waited too long, he wouldn't be able to get either back.

A gunfight was constant motion.

When you move fast and nonstop, you deprive the enemy of the ability to reason. You put them in mid-brain, and that's where Lee's better training could win.

Lee went down to one knee, then hit the ground on his left side, 'urban prone,' so the top of his head and his rifle were just barely around the corner. The dead man lying ass-up blocked most of Lee's field of view, but his untrained opponent came running up to his downed buddy, hugging the wall of the house like an amateur. Lee gave him two, then two more, just to be sure. He fell right on top of his buddy, and Lee thought the position was darkly comical.

Rising to his knees, Lee spared a look behind him. Out of

the corner of his eye, he could see Angela and Abby sprinting for the woods. Jack was on one knee, leaning out
around the corner and covering the opposite side of the
house.

'You ready?' Lee yelled.

'You call it,' was Jack's response.

Lee briefly glanced at the terrain behind the house. It was
about fifty yards of unkempt grass, and then another hundred
yards of plowed field before the woods. 'Tactical retreat! I'll
cover you from the field!'

'Whatever!' Jack shouted and took a shot. The .308 made
Lee's 5.56 sound like a tack gun. The Marine cranked another
round into his chamber and sighted down the scope.

Lee reached into his chest rig and extracted a grenade. He
peered around the corner and saw the muzzle of a rifle peeking out from the far end of the house. Looked like a few guys
mustering up a stack to take the back of the house. If they
were smart, they'd take the inside and bust through. Lee
would give them a little something to think about.

He pulled the pin and stepped into full view for a brief
moment, tossing the grenade underhand. It flew low and
rolled just beyond the corner of the house where the enemies
were stacking up.

Lee didn't wait for the blast.

He turned and started sprinting for the field. He heard a
few screams and shouts as someone recognized what had just
been tossed at them. Then there was a *BOOM*, followed by
relative silence.

Lee felt like he was running faster than he'd ever run. He
felt like the ground was moving underneath him faster than
his feet could keep up, like the whole world was a giant
treadmill turned up as high as it could go. He reached the

end of the grass and the beginning of plowed field and wasn't sure whether he dove or tripped, but he landed face-first in the soft dirt, recovered quickly, and came back up to his knees.

He immediately brought up his rifle.

'Jack! Move!'

The man with the bolt-action jumped up and left his corner, heading straight for Lee. Though the grass in the backyard was overgrown, he could just see enough over the top of it from his kneeling position to cover Jack effectively as he beat his retreat. Lee would have preferred to be prone, but the battlefield was a dynamic environment where you made the best out of what you had. At least the tall grass provided him some concealment, though it did nothing to protect him.

Jack hit the field and ran straight past Lee, continuing on to the trees. Lee kept the side of the house in sight. Around the corner Jack had been covering came two men, both wearing ACUs and carrying AR-15s. They both moved and looked like professionals. They took the back of the house fast, then scanned for threats. They didn't appear to notice him poking out from the tall weeds, but they trained their rifles on the figure of Jack, still heading for the wood line.

Lee didn't wait for them to take the first shot. He opened fire, feeling very odd that he so readily was shooting at what appeared to be American troops. Perhaps he subconsciously didn't want to kill them, because his shots went very high and both guys immediately went prone.

'Shit.' Lee turned toward the wood line and was already sprinting when he heard Jack call out to him, 'Gotcha covered! Move!'

The soft plowed ground was difficult to run across, like

running in sand, and Lee nearly ate it twice before he finally hit the wood line. Just before he reached it, he saw Jack, leaning up against a small tree, taking aim through his scope and firing one solid round right over Lee's shoulder.

Lee flinched, felt the shock wave smack him in the face, and kept running. Behind him, he heard Jack keeping pace.

TEN

NIGHT

IT WAS DARK BEFORE Lee knew it.

He and Jack had hightailed it into the woods, leaving their attackers behind and themselves with a lot of unanswered questions. When they were deeper into the woods, Lee realized it was dark enough that he was straining to make his way through the woods. The two military men were keeping up a good clip in what Lee figured was a westerly direction. They weren't being overly loud, but they weren't exercising much noise discipline either. They were both still focused on putting as much distance as possible between them and the house.

Houses were fast becoming a big negative for Lee. It was the second time he'd had to escape out the back during a frontal assault. Modern houses were not very defensible locations. A decent rifle round, even one as small as a 5.56mm, could punch a hole clean through the average house, as Lee had seen so recently with the enemy SAW. As the group moved silently, Lee's thoughts were overcrowded. His thoughts first went to the enemy force that had just attacked him. Well-equipped looters or ill-equipped reserve forces? There was an argument to be made for both. The way Lee saw it, there were three options: they were a jumpy reserve unit that got scared and started firing before they should have but were overall benign, they were a reserve unit that had gone completely rogue, or they were regular citizens who had raided an armory and made out with some goodies.

The other pressing issue was where the hell Angela and Abby had gotten to. If Angela viewed Lee and Jack as having less than her best interest in mind, she might have seen that as an opportunity to escape. He supposed Jack slapping her hadn't helped if that was the case; however, she had seemed comfortable with Lee prior to that. And best interest or not, they were without any food or water and had no place to go.

'Hey,' someone whispered.

Lee stopped and looked at Jack. The Marine was standing stock-still, slightly hunched, rifle up, and scanning. Lee waited for a moment.

'What?' he whispered back.

Jack turned and looked at him. 'I didn't say anything.'

They both reacted the same, turning outward and going to their knees, scanning the dark woods for a threat.

Then a familiar voice said, 'Guys, it's me.'

Lee felt relieved. 'Angela?'

'Yeah.' The blond woman stepped out from behind a large tree and waved. She was still holding the shotgun from Jack's house. Abby peered cautiously around the tree, as though she thought her mother might be mistaken.

'Jesus Christ, woman,' Jack grumbled. Angela gave Jack a what's-your-problem look.

Lee let his rifle rest on his sling and walked over to her. 'You and Abby all right?'

The woman looked down at her daughter. 'Yeah. We're fine.'

Abby stepped out and presented her arm with a somber look on her face. 'I got scratched, but I'm okay.'

'We ran through a briar patch,' Angela clarified.

Lee couldn't help but smile at the girl. He knelt down and took her arm gently. 'Let me see how bad it is.' He couldn't really see the scratches in the dark, but he pretended to give them a solid looking-over. 'Those are some pretty good scratches, Abby. You're a pretty tough girl. But I think you're gonna be okay. I think we'll clean them up and they'll be just fine.'

Abby nodded, still very serious about her wounds.

Jack bent down so that he was closer to Lee and spoke in a low voice. 'We should go ahead and make camp.'

Lee looked at him like he was crazy. 'Right here?'

Jack was already unslinging his rifle. 'Yeah. Those boys won't be tracking us in the dark. They know what's up. And us moving around at night is a very, very bad idea.'

Lee just stared. He didn't want to contradict the man, as he felt he was speaking from experience, but Lee did not want to stop. He wanted to get home to his bunker where he could batten down the hatches and sleep in relative safety. And he was worried about Sam and Tango. Sam would probably be scared shitless right now, thinking that Lee was dead. He'd told the kid he would be back in a few hours. Lee was way overdue.

Jack realized Lee wasn't thrilled with the idea of stopping and knelt down. He motioned for Angela and Abby to join him. 'I don't know how much movin' around you folks done, but I got here cross-country from Lejeune, tryin' to link up with my dad. These people – the infected ones – they go nuts at night. They just run around in packs and I don't know what it is, but they can hear as well as any animal. You move around at night, you'll have those fuckers all over you in a heartbeat.' He looked at Lee. 'Now, I can see you seem like a shit-hot hard charger, but I only got a few rounds left for my rifle and didn't have time to grab none of my other gear. And I've seen these infected in groups as large as fifty. You ain't takin' 'em down all by yourself.'

Fifty . . . Lee thought.

That was much larger than Sam had seen. The eyewitness accounts of these groups seemed to be getting bigger and bigger. Was it the tale getting bigger, or were the infected herding together out of instinct, the separate groups absorbing into one another as they met, creating larger and larger hordes?

'I have this gun . . .' Angela offered.

'Ma'am, no offense, but you don't know the first thing about that gun.'

Angela looked indignant. 'I can pull the trigger.'

'What type of gun is it?' Jack smiled.

Angela looked at it. 'A . . . rifle?'

'No. It's a shotgun. How many rounds does it hold?'

'Ten.'

'Five. You know how fast you go through five rounds? You have extra ammunition I don't know about? Do you even know how to reload it? Listen, sweetheart, I'm not tryin' to be mean here, but this isn't the time for politically correct women's rights bullshit. I'll be happy to show you how to use that weapon when I have time, but right now you need to admit that you don't know what the fuck you're doing.'

Angela glared at him. 'I'm not trying to be a feminist Nazi. I'm just trying to help. And don't call me *sweetheart* . . . asshole.'

Jack just grinned. Lee decided to settle the matter before it got more heated. 'Fine. We camp here.'

'Can we make a fire?' Abby asked.

'No, sweetie.' Jack got down on his knees. 'And we have to be real, real quiet, okay? We don't want anyone to hear us.'

'Okay . . .' Abby's voice was an exaggerated whisper.

Lee took off his backpack and opened it. He had enough water left to give everyone a bottle but they needed to make them last until tomorrow when they reached his bunker. He gave Angela and Abby the MREs he'd already opened for them earlier in the day. He'd only packed two MREs, so he gave Jack a PowerBar and took one for himself. Jack thanked him and offered to take first watch. They would switch at 0200 hours.

They all made quick work of their food, eating hungrily in silence. When they were finished, the girls huddled together against a tree, and Jack crept away with his rifle to find a good perch from which to watch the camp. Lee felt strange about having the man he barely knew watching over them while they slept, but options were limited.

From his pack he pulled out his poncho liner and offered it to Angela. She looked at the folded square, seeming unsure of what it was. 'It's a poncho liner,' he explained. 'But it makes a pretty good blanket if you get cold during the night.'

She accepted it with a smile and spread it over herself and her daughter.

Lee settled back, using his go-to-hell pack as a pillow. He crossed his legs and hugged his M4 to his chest. This was his favored position for falling asleep in the field. He'd learned it after many nights in the shallow holes they called 'Ranger graves.' It was the same position he might lie in if he were lying in a hammock, enjoying a warm summer evening, and perhaps that was what made it so comforting to him.

He was surprisingly tired and found himself drifting off after only a few moments. Just as he was about to fall asleep, a single thought made his stomach sink and kept him awake for a few more minutes. He thought that he might never again be able to sit in a hammock and enjoy a cold beer.

Lee woke up to realize something had just hit him in the face. He opened his eyes and saw that it was still dark. Whatever had hit him was small, possibly an acorn dropping from the tree they were under. He looked up at the forest canopy above him. The moon was very bright and cast the leaves of the trees with a silver lining. The night, though much cooler than the day, was still quite humid, and Lee felt his entire body was covered in a thin layer of sweat and his clothes were sticking to him.

He thought again about Sam and Tango. He was sure the kid was worried. He had witnessed his father murdered, and then the guy who had saved him runs off and doesn't come back. Lee had no way of contacting him and letting him know they were okay – relatively – and on the way back. He could see the kid's imagination getting the best of him. He just hoped Sam didn't do anything stupid.

Off to his left he heard a soft breeze working its way through the forest. He closed his eyes again and waited for the breeze to flow over him and hopefully dry up some of his sweat.

Something hit him again.

This time, Lee could have sworn it was more forceful than just something dropping from a tree. He leaned up onto his elbows and looked around, just as another object bounced off his chest. Lee was about to stand up and ask what the fuck was going on, but then focused and saw Jack staring at him in the moonlight. The guy's skeletal features looked creepy in the moonlight; his eyes were just sunken, glittering shadows and his cheekbones stood out like he was grinning at Lee.

What the hell was he doing?

Then Lee realized that Jack had a finger in front of his lips, signifying the need for silence. Lee also simultaneously realized that nothing in the forest was stirring from the breeze, and that the 'breeze' was not a breeze at all but the sound of several people moving stealthily through the woods.

Lee clicked the safety off his M4 and pulled it snug into his shoulder. Then he slowly turned and looked at Angela and Abby. They were both still asleep, but he didn't want them to wake up and make noise. Angela had scooted down and was lying more on her back than leaning against the tree now, and her foot was only inches from Lee's. He sidled very carefully and quietly until his boot touched her shoe and gave it a good nudge.

She woke instantly and stared straight at him with wide eyes. She was about to open her mouth to speak when he brought his finger to his lips, then motioned with his eyes to where the sound of movement was coming from.

Both of them looked out into the darkness.

In the moonlight the shapes were hard to make out among all the trees, but Lee could see the movement, distinctly human and distinctly predatory. They were moving in a pack of seven or eight, maybe fifty yards from the camp and parallel to where Lee imagined the road was. None was armed, and Lee knew without thinking about it that these were not the people they'd gotten into a firefight with.

These were all infected.

His reaction to them was twofold. Physically he felt the adrenaline pumping hard through his veins. There was nothing he hated more than hiding and waiting. His mouth was dry, his tense muscles were beginning to quiver, and he felt like he was about to piss his pants. Mentally, he was detachedly surprised at how quietly they moved through the woods and how they obviously moved as one unit. It confirmed what Sam had told him about them banding together like dogs. In addition to that, their stealth could only mean one thing: They were hunting for prey. Lee wondered if this was something that would eventually go away as the FURY bacteria ate through its victims' brains or whether the plague only did so much damage, turning people into ghouls and then leaving them that way.

Lee glanced over at Angela. Abby was still asleep in her arms, but the woman had her hand clamped over her own mouth and her eyes were squeezed shut as though she was trying not to scream or to cry. She opened her eyes momentarily and Lee watched tears spill out, leaving glistening streaks on her face. He didn't know what he could do to comfort her. Speaking was out of the question. He put his hand out and motioned very slowly with a be-calm gesture.

He mouthed the words, *It's okay.*

She closed her eyes again: if I can't see them, they can't see me. Childhood fears come to life, making you want to hide under the blanket and wish to wake up.

Lee looked back at Jack. The man was sitting against a fallen stump, just his head peeking over. He was looking out at the moving figures, his rifle tucked neatly into his shoulder but somewhat relaxed across his chest. Actually, Jack himself looked fairly relaxed. His face appeared unimpressed by what he was seeing.

Lee wondered about the man and his mental stability. He appreciated having another military man, especially one as cool-headed as Jack appeared to be. But the devil-may-care attitude made Lee concerned that he might be a little off his rocker. Or he might just have brass balls. Only time would tell.

It was several minutes before the pack of infected had passed by into the darkness and could no longer be heard. It was several minutes after that before anyone moved an inch. Finally, Jack looked back toward the group and arched his eyebrows, though he was still unwilling to speak. He got up very slowly and quietly and made his way over to Lee.

'Guess what?' he whispered.

Lee looked at him. 'It's 0200?'

Jack just grinned.

Lee rolled away from his warm spot on the ground and took a moment to work out a few kinks. Angela watched the two men with tears in her eyes but still said nothing. Jack took off his plaid shirt, under which he wore a gray T-shirt. He balled the plaid shirt up and stuck it under his head. He rolled onto his side, hugging his rifle like Lee had hugged his.

Before standing, Lee gave Angela a reassuring pat on the leg and his best confident smile. 'Relax and try to get some sleep. Twelve hours from now, we'll be back at my bunker and you can clean up and sleep in a real bed.'

She smiled bravely and Lee stood and walked to his post.

He hoped those words were true and that nothing unfortunate would befall them before they managed to get back home.

By the time he settled into position at the stump, he could already hear Jack breathing steadily, asleep.

ELEVEN

COMPANY

THE DAY WAS GOING TO be a scorcher.

By 0530 hours it was already humid, and by the time everyone was awake and moving, it was getting uncomfortably warm. Lee had no more food left in his go-to-hell pack, but Abby was the only one who complained of being hungry. Lee was sure that Angela and Jack were hungry as well, but they knew he didn't have any food left and that, hopefully, they would be at his bunker in several hours. Lee himself was hungry, but he'd experienced worse hunger in the past.

The group drank what water they had left and broke camp. Angela and Abby simply stood up and brushed the leaves off of themselves. Angela folded the poncho liner neatly and handed it back to Lee with a smile and a thank-you. Lee stuffed it away, then shouldered his pack and slung into his rifle.

They stood around in silence, looking out into the woods. The morning birds were all singing loudly, but the hum of insects hadn't quite begun. The woods weren't what you would call foggy, but there was a definite haze as the heat began to boil the water out of the moist forest floor.

'Everyone ready?' Lee asked. He received three silent nods. 'Jack, take point?'

'Sure.'

'I'll catch up in a second.'

Jack ported his rifle and led Angela and Abby out of the small campsite.

Lee grabbed a branch and gave the campsite a good sweeping to fluff the matted leaves and dirt and disguise that they had slept there. He was more concerned with the threat of infected than he was with anyone attempting to track them. But the party from yesterday was still something he had to think about.

When the site was sufficiently 'cleaned,' Lee tossed the branch into the woods and headed out after the group. When he caught up with them he walked next to Angela for a moment.

'How are you guys feeling?'

She gave him a grim smile. 'Hungry, thirsty, tired ... everything hurts ... but I'm glad to be off the roof.' The look of her smile changed to one of sincere appreciation. 'Thank you for everything. You've been very kind.'

Lee waved it off. He looked at Abby and wanted to ask Angela how her daughter was handling the death of her father, but he wasn't sure either of them was ready to talk about it. Though she obviously was no commando, she'd been through the ringer and held up quite well. Lee could appreciate the amount of self-control and understanding it must take for her to be able to trust the man who had shot her husband, even if her husband had been out of his mind when it happened. He wondered briefly if there were other circumstances unbeknownst to him that made the death of her husband and Abby's father less emotionally devastating. Perhaps the marriage had been in trouble.

Or maybe Angela was simply as tough as she appeared to be.

He supposed that if she decided to stick around, she would be ready to talk about these things in her own time. And Lee had weightier matters to focus his attention on than Angela's former home life.

He took a few long strides and walked next to Jack.

'Captain Harden,' Jack said with a shit-eating grin. 'And how's life treating you this fine morning?'

Lee regarded the older man with a blank look. It struck him that Jack might take a while to figure out, but Lee's immediate take on him was that he was the type of guy who loved being a Marine, loved being in danger, and loved, most of all, a reason to carry a high-powered rifle. None of which were bad things at all, especially given the circumstances they found themselves in. People like that might be borderline sociopaths, but they did very well for themselves in crisis situations because they thought independently and functioned well in circumstances where others would assume the fetal position.

'I'm doing okay,' Lee eventually answered. 'I'm not positive how far out we are, but if we keep parallel to the road and head east, I think we should make it by early afternoon.'

'Which side of the road is your place on?'

'The other side.'

'We'll need to cross.'

'Yeah . . .' Lee trailed off. 'So, Jack, what was your MOS in the Marines?'

'Scout sniper. Just like my pops.' Jack's eyes scanned the woods as he walked. 'Planned on bein' a lifer, but God and the Hadjis had different plans.'

Lee decided he'd bite. 'How's that?'

Jack removed his dirty old baseball cap for the first time and turned so Lee could see the left side of his head. There was a thick scar that ran from his temple all the way back to his crown, then curved down toward his ear.

'Ouch,' was all Lee could think to say.

Jack replaced his ball cap. 'Just got done with one of the most dangerous missions I ever been on. Drivin' in a Humvee from the rally point back to base, and an IED goes off right underneath us. Well' – Jack grimaced – 'right underneath the driver, anyway. They didn't find much of him. I was in a coma for two weeks. Had brain damage. They did surgery and now I can't see too well out my left eye. They said they don't know whether it was the brain surgery or the trauma that caused me to lose my vision, but in either case, I got my papers about a week after they found out I couldn't see no more. "Thanks for everything and all, but we can't use you anymore."' Jack turned and smiled. 'Guess I'm just lucky.'

Lee found it hard to smile at the story. 'At least you have a sense of humor about it.'

'Nope.' Jack wiped a bead of sweat from his nose. 'I really was lucky. It was a coordinated attack. We were in the lead Humvee and the IED they used on me was supposed to be for the guys in the rear of the convoy. About a mile down the road, they find a guy sitting in a pickup loaded with enough explosives to turn us all into jelly. The guy in charge of setting off the IED fucked everything up. If he hadn't blown the IED early, the guy in the pickup truck would have pretty much incinerated us. So now, I thank my lucky stars that God's merciful and the Hadjis are incompetent.'

Lee actually chuckled for the first time in a while. It felt good.

'What about you, Captain? How'd you do your time?'

'Well, my butter bar years were spent in Iraq in a Humvee, patrolling Baghdad.'

Lee downplayed his own history, because swapping war stories wasn't the reason he wanted to talk to Jack. 'I did that for two tours, and then they gave me captain and offered to build me a house and a bunker and all I had to do was be prepared to rebuild civilization at the drop of a hat.' Lee's voice was good-humored but sarcastic.

Jack nodded. 'All in a day's work, my friend.'

They walked for a long moment, at which point Lee asked, 'So how long has it been like this?'

'Like what?' Jack looked around. 'Hot and humid?'

Lee reworded the question. 'When's the last time you saw a cop? Anyone from FEMA? Any members of the military still working for the government?'

'Ahh ...' Jack gave him a weird look, like he was picturing something else while staring at Lee. 'Last cop I saw was when I was makin' my way through Clinton, about two weeks ago. Him and about thirty infected chasin' him. He ran around a corner. Don't know what happened after that.'

Lee walked in silence for a moment, wondering if the cop had made it. Probably not. Jack continued. 'Then I saw three helicopters comin' outta the Raleigh area about two days later. Flyin' low and fast. One was smoking pretty bad, but I never saw if it went down. After that, all I seen are infected and bands o' thugs like yesterday.'

Angela had made her way up to the men. 'I saw a cop about a week ago when we tried to go to the store and buy some food. He had his shotgun. I remember him because I've never seen a police officer look scared. He was pulling out as we were pulling in. Stopped and told us that the store was closed. Then he drove off real fast.' She paused for a long moment. Her voice became quieter. 'We could hear screaming from inside, though, but all the doors were boarded shut.

We think they locked a bunch of infected inside. We went home after that.' Angela tried to put on a smile that didn't fit. 'Ate canned green beans and corn by candlelight because the power was out ... We joked around that it took the power going out for us to have a candlelight dinner together ...'

Lee and Jack exchanged a glance. 'How long has the power been out?'

Angela seemed to realize he was talking to her and snapped out of her memory. 'Um ... maybe a week and a half ago? It's hard to tell. The days kind of run together.'

Jack's eyebrows narrowed at Lee. 'Wait – do you have power?'

Lee looked at the two expectant faces staring at him. 'Yes. My house and my bunker are wired to a battery bank. It's trickle-charged by solar panels throughout the day.'

'So ...' Angela looked like she was thinking it was too good to be true. 'When do the batteries run out?'

'They don't. The solar panels recharge them.'

'So you have power indefinitely?'

'Pretty much.'

The look on Angela's face could almost be called wonder. 'Like ... air-conditioning and everything?'

'Air-conditioning, hot water, you name it.' Lee smiled at Angela and Jack, who were looking at him like he was Saint Peter taking them into Heaven. 'Being down there, it's almost like the old world.'

'I'm taking a hot shower,' Angela declared, as though checking something off of her bucket list.

Jack smiled wistfully. 'I'm gonna have a big ol' glass of cold water.' He looked at Lee. 'Assuming you have a fridge.'

'Yup.' Lee switched topics. 'I really need to talk to you both about what's been going on. Keep in mind that, while I have some nice supplies, you guys are the ones with all the knowledge. I need you both to bring me up to speed.'

'Sure.' Angela shrugged. 'What do you want to know?'

'Either of you seen that group of guys from yesterday?'

Angela shook her head, but Jack just sneered. 'You mean the cocksuckers who stole all that military equipment? Yeah ... I seen 'em before.'

'I guess that answers my next question.' Lee shifted his pack. 'Obviously you think they're civilians who raided an armory.'

'Or took out a guard unit and stole their shit. National Guard was all over this place about a week and a half ago. Had choppers flying everywhere and Humvees escorting busloads of evacuees to FEMA camps.'

Angela spoke up, but quietly, like she didn't want to piss off Jack. 'They seemed like military to me.'

Jack screwed up his face. 'Listen, honey—'

Lee decided to interrupt before another argument erupted. 'I think she has a point, Jack. I agree that the majority of them look like they don't know what they're doing, but there were a few that moved like soldiers.'

Jack was silent.

Lee continued. 'Have you heard of any units going rogue?'

The older Marine was quiet for a long moment as they trudged along. 'I s'pose it's possible, but I haven't heard nothin' 'bout any particular unit going rogue. Maybe we should ask them next time.'

Lee patted him on the shoulder once. 'I'll leave that to you. Whatever they are, what have you heard about them?'

'Well.' Jack shifted the strap of his rifle. 'I've heard all kinds of things from people I come across while gettin' here. Some folks say they're out rapin' and murderin'. Others are saying

they're going around looking for people that will offer them
supplies so they can continue their mission, which is to osten-
sibly eliminate everyone that's infected. I suspect the truth lies
somewhere in the middle. I think they probably have it in
their heads that they're going to put a dent in this epidemic
by wiping out the infected population, and so they're going
around "requesting" donations from people. Maybe they get
a little heavy-handed if donations aren't made. Maybe they get
a little jumpy with the trigger sometimes.'

Lee snorted.

'Like a protection racket,' Angela spoke up. 'That's sick
how people take advantage of situations like this.'

'There's a power vacuum,' Lee stated. 'Every yahoo with a
gun and something to prove is going to be trying to fill that
void. Some are going to be worse than others.'

Angela looked right at Lee. 'But you're not one of them?'

Lee tried not to take offense. He smiled instead. 'I'm not
a "yahoo with a gun." I'm a member of the United States military. And I'm not looking for power either. Just trying to
help.'

Jack stopped walking.

Angela stopped close behind him, and Lee immediately
brought his rifle to a low-ready and scanned the trees. 'What's
up?'

Jack's head was lifted skyward just slightly, and Lee thought
he heard him take a deep breath through his nose. 'You smell
that?' he asked.

Lee took a moment to sniff the air and caught it. 'Smells
like something's burning.'

Jack nodded. 'Wind's blowing from the east a bit. Doesn't
smell good . . . not like wood smoke.'

Lee knew the scent quite well. He'd smelled it several times during the Iraq invasion. It was the smell of artificial products burning, like plastic on fire. It was a rank, noxious smell from up close, but now it only tinged the air. When he smelled it again he thought of dusty streets, everything in sandy desert tones, walls close in and high up, dark windows staring down, everything tainted with the residue of smoke and pockmarked with bullet holes.

Everyone was silent for a long minute, considering what this meant, like they were all seers watching a hawk fly by, determining the secret omen it bore.

Lee turned slightly to the left and pointed. 'The road should be that way.' He began walking in that direction. 'We should cross now.'

Without argument, the other three followed.

TWELVE

HOME AGAIN

IT DIDN'T TAKE LONG FOR them to reach the road.

In more normal times, Lee had walked these woods for pleasure and exercise. He'd always found his way back to the road by the sound of cars passing by, like the sound of a river. Now the road was empty and silent and Lee almost stepped out onto the asphalt before he realized he was there.

The party stopped just inside the wood line. Past the trees, the shoulder of the road rose slightly to the asphalt. Jack offered to check it out, and Lee deferred. He knelt down, Angela and Abby hovering close behind him, while Jack low-crawled up to the road to survey in both directions.

'How far is your house, mister?' Abby whispered.

Lee looked both directions down the road, but being in the woods had disoriented him to what section of the road this was. He could be a mile from his house or ten. Luckily, he'd been keeping steady track of the amount of time they'd been walking, and he ran some quick numbers in his head.

'Rough guesstimate . . . maybe two miles?'

Abby didn't answer. The kid was being a trouper hanging in there, but when a kid didn't complain, you had to wonder what was wrong. Lee's best guess was that she was so tired and dehydrated that she didn't have the energy to complain. Her body and her mind were in survival mode.

He turned and looked at the mother and daughter.

Both of them looked rough, to say the least. The few bottles of water he'd been able to give them would have barely hydrated them in the state they were in when they came off the roof, and certainly not now after a day of hiking. He noticed that Angela was massaging her thigh and he suspected muscle cramps.

He needed to get IVs in both of them. They couldn't go on like this forever. He was pretty sure they could make it to the house, though. And then he could rehydrate them and get them back into working shape.

A quiet whistle drew his attention back to the road.

Jack was still on his belly on the shoulder of the road. He looked back at Lee and gave a thumbs-up.

Lee turned back to Angela 'You guys ready? We're almost there.'

She and her daughter both stood slowly and Lee motioned them forward. Angela jogged with her little girl across the road and disappeared into the woods on the other side. Lee waited until they were safe, then crossed quickly, Jack following closely behind. They continued into the woods until they could just barely make out the blacktop, and then turned due east, heading once again in the direction of Lee's house.

As they walked, Lee noticed that the acrid smell of burning materials had grown slightly stronger. There was a haze hanging in the forest, but he could not tell if it was light smoke or the last bit of dew burning off in the warming sun. He kept his observations to himself, as he did not believe they would serve any purpose but to worry the others. They had hiked approximately another two hundred yards when Lee heard what he initially thought was someone shouting, but then immediately recognized as barking. Specifically, Tango's barking.

'Whoa.' He held up a hand and everyone stopped walking. They all stood in the middle of the forest, straining eyes and ears for any signs of danger. 'That's my dog.'

'How can you tell?' Angela asked.

'I know Tango's bark.'

'Thought he was in your bunker.' Jack spoke almost under his breath, as though he was pointing something out that would anger or embarrass Lee.

'He was.' Lee nodded. 'If he's out, the kid's out.'

No one spoke. Tango barked three more times, and Lee realized he was getting closer. They were upwind and Tango had sniffed out his master. That was all well and good, but why the fuck was he outside to begin with?

The dog burst through a tangle of thick brush and came running full speed for Lee, tail circling wildly behind him like a propeller. Lee was glad to see Tango unharmed but he couldn't help having a greasy feeling of dread. Where was Sam? And what had happened?

He held up a hand and bent down to one knee as Tango approached, slowing to a trot, then coming to a halt before his master, tail sweeping an arc of leaves from the forest floor behind him. Just happy to see Lee.

Lee gave him a quick scratch on the head and then looked up to the woods. He didn't have to wait for long before he saw a small, skinny figure running toward the group in that awkward prepubescent manner. Sam saw them, waved once, but then kept looking behind him, as though he were being pursued.

'Fuck . . . ' Lee held his rifle at a low-ready. 'Something's wrong.'

'Yep.' Apparently Jack had come to the same conclusion.

Lee didn't know what to expect from Sam, but the kid ran up and latched onto Lee, clinging around his waist, and it broke Lee's heart. He wasn't this kid's father. He couldn't be that person for him, and he didn't have the time even if he wanted to. This was survival, not a Social Services visit.

'Sam, what happened?' Lee asked sternly.

The kid was out of breath. He kept glancing back into the woods. He spoke between gulps of air. 'I'm sorry. I'm sorry. We thought you were dead.' Sam's voice broke as he said the last part.

Dammit ... Lee was trying not to be angry. 'Why aren't you in the bunker?'

'I took Tango outside so he could go to the bathroom. Then some army men came. I was scared. They didn't look nice. We hid in the woods, and they went into your house. They took everything out. Then they set it on fire.'

Lee stared down at this pathetic kid clinging to him like a life raft.

'Are you fucking kidding me?' Lee mumbled without thinking.

'Captain!' Angela hissed behind him.

Tears sprang into Sam's eyes and Lee immediately regretted letting the words slip out of his mouth.

'I said I was sorry.'

There were other choice words that Lee wanted to say – not directed at Sam in particular, but at the situation that he now found himself. But for the sake of the kid, he kept it to himself this time. He removed Sam from his leg – perhaps a little roughly – and pushed him into Angela's arms. 'Watch him for me?'

She nodded once.

He looked at Jack. 'You're with me.'

Then Jack and Lee took off at a run.

The haze in the trees was thickening and above the forest canopy Lee could see a dark column of smoke rising into the sky. The smoke was dark tendrils and light-gray mixing together like cloudy boiling water. Strange memories from old science classrooms: black smoke from petroleum products, white smoke from plant products.

'Captain . . .' Jack slapped him on the shoulder to get his attention.

Lee slowed and stopped behind a cluster of trees. 'What?'

Jack wiped sweat from his eyebrows. 'What if they're still there?'

Lee considered the odds. 'If we take them by surprise and hit them hard, we can probably take out about six or seven.'

Jack didn't look convinced.

'If you can get a good hide, I can start taking out any heavy weapons or vehicles they have.' Lee indicated his 40mm grenades, of which he had three left. 'Attention's on me; you take out the survivors.'

'If your house is burned down, there's no point in attacking them. It's all risk and no reward.'

Lee knew Jack was right. 'Fine. I'm comfortable saying we can take out five. If there's more than five, we'll leave it.'

Jack seemed to chew it over. 'Alright. But give me some time to scout it out.'

'Agreed.'

They started moving again, this time slower, watching their footsteps and gliding through the woods nearly without noise. When they had drawn closer to the house and the smoke was palpable, Jack motioned Lee to remain while he crept quietly forward. Lee took cover behind a large tree and settled down at the base of its trunk, watching Jack move forward like a big cat prowling.

The skeletal man slid easily through the woods, nearly to the point that Lee could not see him. Lee could tell that the woods opened up just ahead of Jack's location, and at certain angles Lee thought he could see his house.

He watched Jack stand very still for several moments, then settled slowly to the earth, propping his rifle on a fallen log and scanning the area through his scope. Jack made four very careful, very slow arcs across Lee's field of view. Lee watched impatiently, wondering how long the sniper was going to take.

After what was probably close to five minutes of complete silence, watching Jack reconnoiter the area, the sniper looked back in Lee's direction and motioned very slowly with his hand to move forward, then patted the air just above the ground, indicating Lee should move stealthily.

Lee moved out of his cover smoothly and made his way toward Jack at a steady glide. When he got within about ten feet of Jack, he lowered his body to the ground and low-crawled up shoulder-to-shoulder with Jack. From his new vantage point, much closer to the edge of the woods, Lee could see his house.

Or what was left of it.

It was still on fire, although it was beginning to smolder. It had obviously been lit on fire several hours ago, as the fire had completely eaten the structure and the upstairs had completely collapsed in on itself. What little remained of the house jutted up out of the ground – burned and uneven walls sagging and torn down. Like the ribcage of a recently gutted animal.

For a moment, Lee couldn't speak. It wasn't the house that he was attached to. In fact, it wasn't anything that he was attached to. It was purely the worry of survival that he now felt like a vise grip being ratcheted down on his stomach. His house was superfluous, but now his bunker was covered in what looked like five feet of burning rubble, and it could take days before that much burning material cooled enough for him to get through. Inside were supplies that meant the difference between life and death. Desperately needed food and water were now inaccessible, if they were even still down there. In all likelihood, whatever raiding party had come along and burned his house had cleaned it out of anything useful prior to lighting the match. The guns and ammo would be gone, without a doubt. Some of the more sensitive equipment they may have left alone – not knowing what it was or how it could help them just meant it was extra weight.

The second immediate concern was the medical supplies. He hadn't truly concerned himself with the condition that Angela and Abby were in. The truth was, while he'd stabilized their malnutrition and dehydration as best he could with the supplies he'd had in his go-to-hell pack, they were both still in a bad state and getting worse by the hour. He had been relying on the ability to get them to his bunker and stick them both with IVs to rehydrate and stuff them with MREs for a few days to get their strength back up. Without that possibility, their chances looked bleaker by the minute.

And Lee didn't have any food or water left in his pack. Without those essential supplies, he had to put a timeline on each of their lives. Lee and Jack were both fairly well fed and hydrated as of yesterday, which meant they could probably go without water for the next two days, given the heat and their stress levels. He gave Angela and Abby until the following night.

Without a word, Lee dropped his pack and knelt down on

one knee. He unzipped one of the front pockets and thrust his hand in, rooting around for a second before withdrawing the GPS device. He knew it was in there, knew it was safe and still in his possession, but in that moment he needed to look at it and touch it. It was hope made tangible.

'What's that?' Jack asked.

Lee just breathed a sigh of momentary relief and shoved the device back in the pack. 'Let's just say it's an insurance policy.'

Lee hauled the pack onto his shoulders again. *Focus. Compartmentalize.* The bunker was no longer an option for shelter, but he had to get Angela, Abby, and Sam into some sort of safe place. In order to accomplish this, he needed to know what, if anything, Jack had seen.

In a tone as calm as he could muster, Lee spoke. 'You see anyone?'

'Not a soul.' Jack looked at Lee. 'I'm pretty sure they burned the house just to fuck with you. They must've gotten your address from your truck.'

'My registration,' Lee nodded. The general two-man consensus was that the rogue army unit had done this. 'I need to check out my neighbor's house. We're going to need to get our group indoors. Hopefully they didn't burn that house down, too.'

Jack just shook his head. 'Hoping is a bad habit these days.'

THIRTEEN

HORDE

THE PAIR MOVED SWIFTLY across Lee's property. Lee fought to keep his eyes scanning for threats and not to simply stare at the burning wreckage of his home. He was scared now. His attitude had been somewhat lax, removed from the reality of his situation. He'd felt safe sitting on top of all his readily available supplies. Now, he had four more people following him, and his supplies were gone. The dire circumstances were becoming real to him. Real in the form of thirst, hunger, and diminishing ammunition.

The issue was time. He had less than forty-eight hours by his own estimation to get water to Angela and Abby. Food was less urgent, but Lee was still concerned about the amount of calories they were putting out with all this hiking. Even Jack seemed to be suffering, though he didn't voice it. Lee's own body was stronger and not as malnourished as the others. Lack of food was not a priority for him as it was for the others.

Ammunition depended on how much trouble they ran into before he could get the group to a point of relative safety. Best-case scenario, they didn't get into anything before he could find a place for the group to sit tight for a while. Worst-case scenario, they were attacked, ran out of ammunition, and were killed.

The smoke in the air cleared a bit as they moved farther away from Lee's burning house. They were moving into the wind blowing steadily from the west, and it seemed to be pushing away most of the smoke. They neared the edge of the woods and stopped, surveilling the Petersons' house. Nothing appeared out of place. The graves in the backyard were still mounded high with freshly upturned soil. Lee noticed Jack giving them a hard look, but Jack didn't ask about them, and Lee didn't really feel like talking about it.

After a few moments of watching, Lee decided to break the wood line. Jack fell in behind him and they moved at a walking pace toward the back of the house. Everything still appeared as he had left it. Jack mentioned quietly that there was a burning pickup truck in the front lawn that looked like it had been blown apart.

Lee nodded. 'Yeah. That was from earlier.'

Jack didn't prod further. They entered through the back door and cleared the house. After it was clear, Jack walked into one of the upstairs bedrooms, Stephanie's old room. 'I'll hole up here and keep watch while you go get everyone else.'

'Okay ... If you get attacked ...'

Jack smiled. 'You'll hear me shooting.'

Lee fished into his pack and retrieved the Smith & Wesson pistol he'd taken from Jason Peterson's body, handing it butt first to Jack. 'It's got a full mag. It'll give you a little more time, at least.'

Jack took the pistol and stuck it in the back of his waistband.

Lee flicked him a quick salute. 'Be back in a few.'

As Lee exited the house, he checked his corners to make sure there were no surprises, and then began moving with less caution. He covered the terrain at a jog, stopping if anything piqued his curiosity or didn't sound right, but never for more than a few seconds before he continued on. He crossed the open lot of his house at a run, then fell to a jog when he was back in the safety of the woods. A few hundred yards east, he found the three rescues crouched down near a large tree. Tango watched his master approach with a wagging tail.

Lee caught Angela's eyes and jerked his head to the side. She rose from her crouch with the two children, telling them to stay there. Then she walked a few paces away and conferred quietly with Lee.

'What did you find?'

As she spoke, Lee noticed her unsteadiness on her feet and the crusted salt deposits around her eyes, nose, and mouth. Her dehydration was worse than Abby's. Lee figured she'd given her daughter most of the water when they were on the rooftop. He had several diagnostic questions pop into his head to clarify the extent of her dehydration, but he thought it better to wait until they were indoors.

'My house is gone, but my neighbor's house is still there. We're gonna hole up in there.'

Angela looked heartbroken. 'What about ... the medical supplies? What about Abby? How are you gonna help her?'

Lee shook his head. 'I don't have any medical supplies right now.'

Angela's worn face contorted like she was about to start crying. Or maybe her body simply didn't have the moisture to spare for tears.

'Look, we have some time ... it's just not much.' Lee put his hand on Angela's shoulder. It felt frail and bony. 'We're going to get you guys indoors, and we'll figure it out from there.'

'What if she doesn't make it?' Angela croaked. 'I can't do it. I can't lose her ... I can't lose anyone else.'

Her voice was low enough that the kids couldn't understand her, but they must have understood the tone of her voice and looked up in that way children do when they know something is wrong.

'Angela, she's going to make it.' Lee had no way to back up that promise. 'We'll do whatever we have to. But right now we need to go.'

Lee didn't wait for an answer. He turned Angela so she was facing the correct direction, then beckoned for the kids to join them. They both shuffled to their feet. Lee led the group through the woods, taking the same way he'd traveled the previous two times. Urgency spurred him on, but he forced himself to maintain a slow pace so the kids could keep up.

For the first time he noticed his own body showing the signs of fatigue through hunger and dehydration. Besides the hunger, which he'd learned to ignore long ago, his hands felt shaky, and his mouth was getting dry. Every once in a while, despite the heat of the day, he felt a chill work its way through his body.

They made the walk to the Petersons' house in about twice the time it had taken Lee to get to the group. He listened the entire time for the telltale sound of Jack's rifle, but all was silent. They approached the house, and Lee saw Jack peer at them from an upstairs window, then gave the okay symbol with his fingers.

Once inside, Abby stared at the splashes of blood across the living room carpet and in the kitchen while Angela tried to act like she didn't notice anything. Lee guided them past the gore marks, through the hallway, and into the dining room at the front of the house. From where they were, Jack could be seen leaning over the top of the stairs to the second floor.

'Everyone okay?' he asked.

'Yeah . . . ' Lee looked up. 'I need you to keep watch while I try to get some water for the girls.'

Sam spoke up. 'I'm thirsty, too.'

'Buddy.' Lee tried to keep his voice lighthearted, tried to disguise the severity of the situation. 'We're all thirsty, but the girls need the water more than we do, alright?'

Sam hung his head.

Lee felt guilty and exasperated at the same time. He was doing his best with this kid, but having no parental experience, he didn't know what was appropriate to say to kids and what was not. Sam would just have to deal with it for now. He hoped that when things calmed down a bit, Jack and Angela could take over being the parents. He sure as hell didn't feel ready for it.

Lee pulled out a few chairs from around the dining table. 'Angela, Abby, go ahead and sit down. I'm going to try to find you guys some water.'

Leaving them in the dining room, he went into the kitchen. The bloody mess left behind by Marla's butchered body had crusted over, but it still managed to stick to his boots. The whole house was starting to stink. He riffled through the cupboards and cabinets and came up with a plastic pitcher and a coffee mug. Taking these, he went to the sink and put the coffee mug under the faucet. He hoped there was enough pressure in the pipes to give a little bit of water.

Turning on the faucet yielded a pathetic groan from the pipes and a tiny squirt of water that filled the coffee mug about halfway. Without humor, Lee thought that this was definitely a case of the glass being half empty.

Nevertheless, he deposited the bit he had into the pitcher and headed for the downstairs bathroom, which was near to the front door. The smell from the bathroom was obvious and not a good sign. He went to the toilet and removed the top to the reservoir tank. Again, he was disappointed with a bone-dry tank. It was obvious the toilet was filled with feces and the Petersons had apparently continued attempting to flush until all the water was gone from their pipes. With no water from pipes, it was impossible for the reservoir to refill itself.

Swearing, Lee left the bathroom and ran up the stairs to the second-floor bathroom only to find the same situation in this one. This presented another, less pressing issue. Latrines where feces and urine had collected and not been flushed were horrible for accumulating bacteria and disease. If they were forced to stay in the Petersons' house for any length of time, they would have to set up latrines somewhere else. As it was, he didn't want anyone going into either of the bathrooms.

His last-ditch effort was in the garage. He went down to the first floor and exited into the garage via the door in the kitchen. He was greeted with a positive among all the negatives: The Petersons' Ford F-150 was still sitting in the garage. Lee hoped that he could find the keys, and that the Petersons had left him a little fuel. The roads weren't the safest routes to travel in these circumstances – in fact, they were decidedly deadly – but Lee was trying to count the little things. If they needed emergency transportation, they had it . . . maybe.

Off to the side of the garage, Lee opened the utility closet and found the hot water heater. Dropping his go-to-hell pack, he extracted his knife from inside and tapped the side of the water heater. The sound was the best he had heard all day.

'Thank you, Jesus,' he mumbled.

He'd tapped the tank low to the ground. He estimated that there were at least a few gallons from the point he'd tapped. Just to test, he tapped a little higher. This time he heard a hollow clank. So there wasn't much water in the tank, but a few gallons were better than nothing.

He crammed the pitcher under the drain spout for the water heater and cranked the ball valve. Clear water flowed out and Lee thought it looked beautiful. With the angle he had to tilt the pitcher, he was only able to fill it about halfway. He brought the pitcher of water back into the house, carrying it like it was liquid gold. He grabbed another cup from the kitchen cabinets and took everything into the dining room.

The look on Angela's face was one of immense relief.

Lee poured glasses of water for both of them, speaking as he handed them out. 'Drink it very slowly. You're both extremely dehydrated and if you drink it too fast you're going to throw it up. Take a sip, then wait a minute before taking another one. Keep doing it until the pitcher's gone.' Lee looked at Angela. 'There's another gallon or two in that tank outside, so don't give it all to Abby. You need it more anyway.'

Neither Angela nor Abby answered, as they were busy sipping.

'Captain . . .'

Lee turned and found Jack leaning over the stairs and waving to him. Jack jerked his head upstairs. 'Bad news,' he said.

Lee's fingertips tingled. He left the living room and flew up the stairs, close behind Jack. Jack made for Stephanie's old room that overlooked the road, but he stopped short of the door, with his hand held up to caution Lee. He bent down and walked at a half crouch over to the bedroom window. He took care not to touch the curtains but carefully peered around them.

'Middle of the road,' Jack whispered.

Lee mimicked the Marine's caution and stood back from the windows, where he knew the shadowed room would keep him in darkness, invisible to the outside, as it was obvious Jack felt there was someone or something outside that might notice their movement.

Lee heard it before he saw it. The metallic rasp of steel being drawn across concrete. It was a long, eerie note with no beginning and no end, stuttered and interrupted every so often with a soft *clank-clank*.

Even in the waning sun, the image shimmered from the heat coming off the road. In the back of his mind, he noted that the mirage did not flow in any direction – no wind, and an easy shot at two hundred yards – but every other part of him vibrated like a gong and his pulse picked up speed.

A big man, maybe 6' 4" and 240 pounds, without a stitch of clothing on his body, walking slowly along the road. With his left hand he dragged a shovel behind him, the steel head scraping steadily across the road, sometimes striking a loose bit of concrete or a small rock and making the shovel head bounce off the ground: *clank-clank*.

He was focused intensely on the house, the way a man dying of thirst might stare at the mirage of an oasis in the distance. Lee got the uncomfortable feeling that the man was staring right at him.

'Infected or not?' Jack said quietly.

'No idea,' Lee admitted. 'He looks fucked up, though.'

'You want me to take him out?'

'Not yet.' Lee pictured the crushed and bloody heads of all the people the man had smashed with his shovel. 'Let's see what he does.'

'Roger.'

The two men were huddled between the window and the small bed. The floor was strewn with all things Stephanie: jeans with flowery pink stitching on the pockets, a pink 'princess dress' she'd worn for the previous Halloween, a stuffed panda. For a brief moment he fixated on the panda, imagining it under the arm of Stephanie while she slept.

Jack slowly pushed his back against the side of the bed and brought his knees up to his chest, resting his rifle on them, pointed out toward the road. He squinted into the scope. He craned slightly to see over the top of the window-sill.

He made a sucking noise with his teeth. 'He's not the only one.'

Lee sat up a little higher and looked for himself. Coming from farther down the road, a few more were meandering out from behind the trees that obscured the southern section of the road. At first there were only one or two, spaced out by several yards. But like a stream swelling from ice-melt in the spring, they seemed to multiply. Every time Lee started counting, the number doubled, the crowd of them getting thicker. Some of them walked steadily forward, while others ran in erratic circles, but as a group they seemed to be following the leader: the man with the shovel.

'Pack instinct,' Jack said coolly, as though he were watching a nature documentary. 'They're gonna do whatever Shovel Guy does.'

So Shovel Guy was the dominant one, established by

whatever primal firing of synapses had occurred inside their brain stems. Finding safety in numbers. Was it the FURY bacteria eating them away to their very base instincts, or were they adapting to overcome? Was this devolution or evolution?

Lee didn't like it, however it was sliced.

And Shovel Guy was now standing at the end of the driveway, still staring at the house but not yet approaching it.

'If we shoot him they'll hear the noise and come running,' Lee thought aloud.

Jack's eyes remained on whatever he saw through the scope. 'It may not make much difference.'

'What do you mean?'

'I mean he's going to come over here.' Jack spoke as if it were a bad joke he'd heard before. 'You should get the girls up here.'

'Yeah.' Lee squirmed off the ground into a squatting position. With each passing second the possibilities of how this was going to go were dropping off. There were only a few scenarios now, and all of them ended with the house being overrun. He voiced his opinion: 'We can't keep them out.'

'Nope. Patio door's smashed open ... bunch of ground-floor windows ... front door didn't look that sturdy to me. I give it ten minutes max before they're inside.'

Lee craned his neck and tried to count again. 'Fuckin' A, there's a lot.'

'Probably about eighty.'

Running was out of the question. Angela and Abby couldn't go on. For that matter, Lee wasn't sure how much longer he and Jack could go on without water. Fighting was the only option, and that option looked grim. Lee couldn't count on anyone but Jack to be combat effective, which made it a two-against-eighty fight. With limited ammunition and dehydration and fatigue setting in, their odds weren't something a betting man would take.

Lee felt like he should speak with Jack more, formulate some sort of grand plan that would allow them to escape this situation or at least give them the upper hand in the fight. But there was no situation to plan around. It was a basic fight for survival. Kill as many of them as possible. Pray to God there's a tomorrow in store.

Lee stood up when he was clear of the window. 'I'll get the girls.'

FOURTEEN

SIEGE

LEE FLEW QUICKLY DOWN the stairs and scooped up his rifle and pack. He told Angela and Abby to go upstairs. They grabbed the meager bit of water left and went upstairs without asking questions. Abby looked numb, but Angela was clearly terrified, clinging with a white-knuckled grip to the big black shotgun in her hands. Lee didn't know if she'd heard the conversation or if she could just tell from Lee's face that something was wrong. Sam followed and Tango tagged along with him.

Lee was about to follow them up when, as an afterthought, he stepped back into the dining room. Two at a time, he dragged all the wooden chairs from around the dining table and began laying them over on their sides at the base of the stairs, their legs pointing out. Crude mantraps. The stairs were a natural choke point and the only entrance to the second floor of the house.

He vaulted the banister and ran up the stairs. Angela waited at the top, looking down at him with wide eyes while Abby and Sam peered around her. Lee pointed to the bedrooms. 'Guys, grab everything you can out of these rooms and throw it down these stairs. Make the biggest trash pile you can.'

'Okay!' Sam said eagerly and ran into the master bedroom.

Angela and Abby were more reserved. Angela nodded and guided her daughter into the room across from Stephanie's old room.

'Cap'n, they're headin' this way,' Jack called from his lookout.

'Jack, set up over here.'

There was a crash from the master bedroom and Sam came out lugging a nightstand half his size. 'Is this good?'

'That's great, buddy!' Lee gave him a thumbs-up and Sam tossed the nightstand down the stairs where it clattered into the chairs. Lee was dismayed to watch the tiny wall of chairs shuffle as the object hit them. His wall might look big, but bricks with no mortar didn't stand very strong.

Sam ran back into the bedroom. Angela and Abby came out simultaneously and started throwing things down the stairs. They were tossing them so fast, Lee couldn't catch what they were. Slowly, the pile of junk at the bottom of the stairs grew. Clothes and pillows were thrown, books and DVDs, small pieces of furniture. Lee and Jack grabbed the mattress and box spring from Stephanie's bed and shoved them down. It was a tight fit, but they would force someone to stop and negotiate over them.

Jack had run back into Stephanie's room to glance out the window again. 'Shovel Guy's pretty much making a beeline for us.'

Angela spoke up. 'How many of them are there?'

Lee didn't specify. 'Lots.'

Jack looked back at Lee. 'You got any more forty mike-mikes?'

Lee nodded and held up two fingers. Jack didn't need to

explain anything. Lee shucked the two 40mm grenades out of their pouches, held one in his hand, and shoved the other into the M203 receiver. He locked back and armed the weapon as he slid quickly over to the window overlooking the front yard.

Glancing around the curtains, his stomach dropped. The image of the mass of bodies, squirming toward the house like a single entity with Shovel Guy at the lead, made Lee's stomach churn. He felt it now – the adrenaline dump. He thought about dying, about being torn to pieces by a mob of crazies. He thought that it was the most likely outcome, and his body coursed with the nearly overwhelming desire to survive. Flee and live to fight another day. Leave all these stupid civilians behind. Save yourself.

Almost against his will, he looked at Jack and spoke. 'Any chance they might pass us by?'

The words were hollow.

Jack shook his head. 'They're fixated, Cap'n. They ain't goin' nowhere. Hit 'em now, while they're still all bunched together.'

Lee didn't have to explain his concern to Jack. It was still within the realm of possibility that Shovel Guy, with the horde in tow, might poke around the house a bit, then get distracted with something else and leave, taking the group with him. But if Lee opened fire, it would send the infected into an aggressive frenzy and it would be a fight to the death.

It was clear that Jack felt their path had already been chosen for them. Now it was just time to make what they could out of it. Lee stuffed his desire for life behind his conscious decision that he wasn't going to leave these people. Live or die, they were his problem now. He flipped up the M203 sights and jabbed the window hard with the muzzle of his weapon.

The glass shattered.

As though they were of a single mind, linked by an invisible neural connection, every head in the mob of infected simultaneously snapped up to look at the window. Lee wasn't sure what came first, the scream of rage or the guttural *THUNK* of the barrel spitting out a grenade, but he watched the first round hit right in the middle of ten infected. It shredded the closest ones into body parts and meat fragments and threw the others a few yards away. Lee was quick with the reload, but the horde had already begun to run for the house, spacing out their ranks and making the blast less effective.

Lee had barely retreated from the window when he felt the house shake violently as the mob of infected hit the front door. Glass shattered downstairs and Abby started screaming. What looked like a hatchet crashed through the window and glanced off the side of Jack's rifle just as he steadied to take aim. The two men exchanged a glance that said, *Way too close*.

'Lee!' Angela's voice slipped through Abby's piercing wail. 'They're coming through the windows!'

'Let's go!' Lee slapped Jack on the shoulder as he turned and ran for the top of the stairs. He took a quick glance down. Daylight around the edges of the front door. It rattled on its hinges, pounded mercilessly from the other side. Flecks of wood and drywall flew off the doorframe. An arm reached through the broken sidelight and groped around for anything it could lay a hand on.

Lee grabbed Angela and the two kids in a bear hug and pushed them into the master bedroom. Before closing the door and backing into the hall, Lee caught Angela's gaze. He pointed to the shotgun in her hands. 'You take the safety off?'

Angela nodded fiercely, her hair flying in her face.

'Don't open this door until I say it's okay.' Lee slammed the door closed behind him. From downstairs, he heard the distinct sound of the front door giving way.

Footsteps cluttered the landing and Lee registered the hissing, moaning, screeching sounds that echoed up the walls. It made his stomach turn over. Jack looked at him and Lee thought he looked pale and scared.

He was sure he looked the same.

He dropped his pack and kicked it over to Jack as he shouldered his M4 and flipped on his red dot sight. 'Get the other pistol out of there and every bullet you can find.'

Lee took a knee at the top of the stairs and pointed his rifle down. At least twenty faces stared up at him. Hands caked in dried blood reached for him. Others held makeshift weapons – crowbars, hammers, knives – and jabbed and swung at the air. Bile rose in the back of his throat, and only after the bitter taste hit his tongue did he notice the overpowering stench. Rot and body odor and feces.

The makeshift barricade creaked and moved under the weight of the horde pressing in. Lee picked his target and put the red dot of his scope on the bridge of its nose and pulled the trigger. He didn't wait to see if his target went down. He put the dot on another head and pulled the trigger. Then another. His shots were even and paced, but panic was knocking at the back door of his mind, trying to spur his trigger finger.

He was counting rounds as he sent them downrange. One shot was a triumph. Two shots was a tragedy. It wasn't long before he felt the bolt of his M4 lock back, indicating an empty magazine. He checked the chamber – clear – then flipped the mag out and grabbed another from his vest. How many did he have left?

His mind screamed at him to get his weapon back in the fight.

It happened so fast, Lee didn't get a good look at the attacker. He got the impression of someone young – maybe a teenager, dressed in what he thought looked like a soccer uniform – vaulting clear over the blockage at the bottom of the stairs and landing inside the stairwell with a screech. The creature rolled and squirmed till he was on his feet again and bolted up the stairs, shrieking at Lee.

The boom of Jack's .308 rifle was like being punched in the face.

A chunk of the soccer player's chest went missing and he flew back down the stairs, crashing into the junk pile at the bottom and lying still.

Lee didn't waste the time to thank Jack. He slammed in his fresh magazine, recharged his M4, and went to work. The infected were yanking at the chairs now, pulling them out of the way. Lee tried to identify and focus his fire on anyone who appeared to be messing with his blockade, but he was confronted with a new problem. The pungent sting of cordite was filling the air, and the smoke was obscuring the already-dim hallway, making his targets hard to see. He couldn't tell where his rounds were hitting or whether he was taking anyone down with his shots. For all he knew, he might have just wasted the last ten rounds.

Panic stabbed his gut again and he forced himself to slow down and count his shots.

Fire . . .

And scan . . .

Fire . . .

And scan . . .

Every so often the stairwell would explode as Jack pulled

his trigger again. But with only five rounds, that wouldn't last long. Another mag change. Lee watched the empty magazine tumble down the stairs.

Another, fatter infected was clawing its way over the banister and into the stairwell. Lee put one to the top of its head and the fat creature just hung there, motionless on the banister. Another determined attacker pushed the fat one out of the way and attempted to hurdle the banister. This time it was Jack's rifle that took the shot.

Lee refocused on the ones trying to pull at his trash barricade. Though their brains were damaged by the plague, it was obvious that they were able to recognize an obstacle and formulate some plan around it in order to get to a victim. Almost as though they were following the commands of a single consciousness, one infected would step up and yank at a chair, only to be dispatched by a bark from Lee's rifle. Before the first had even hit the ground, another was replacing the fallen infected and pulling at the chairs again. It was with a sudden scream of rage that an infected the size of a linebacker grabbed a huge mound of trash and furniture in his arms and ripped it out of the way. Despite his size, it still only took one 55-grain bullet to bring him down, but the damage was done.

The infected began pouring through the narrow opening into the stairwell, like water over a collapsing levy. The other portion of the blockade was suddenly enveloped and disappeared in a mass of bodies. Their screams suddenly intensified. The horde rushed up the stairs, too fast for Lee to choose his targets. He began pulling the trigger indiscriminately. Bodies would fall back like weeds cut down by a scythe, and – dead or only injured – they would tumble back into the others, creating a new blockage of human bodies directly in the middle of the stairs. Their progress up the stairs stalled for three of Lee's pounding heartbeats, and then the horde pressed forward again, climbing over the bodies of their dead and injured.

To Lee's right, the boom of Jack's .308 changed to the *pop-pop-pop* of pistol fire. Lee found his back pressed against the wall, the stairs in front of him. His M4 went dry – a quick mag change and he was back in the fight – but even that brief cessation in his suppressive fire gave the infected horde a few more feet in a battle of inches.

Pop-pop-pop and Jack's pistol went silent.

Lee edged to the left, toward the master bedroom, as Jack picked up his rifle and began swinging it like a baseball bat. Standing to the right of the stairs close to Stephanie's room, Jack began smashing the solid buttstock into anything that popped up from the stairs.

Lee could not imagine the mound of dead infected lying at the bottom of the stairs, but the horde kept coming, kept pressing them back. Now Lee and Jack were being divided, and the oncoming attackers were reaching the top of the stairs, filling the gap between the two comrades. Lee held Jack's gaze for a brief moment before he disappeared under a wave of infected.

'Jack!'

Lee kept firing, kept recharging his weapon after every empty magazine, but he found himself backpedaling, now against the closed door of the master bedroom. He no longer saw individuals in the oncoming mob but only a faceless, amorphous mass of sickening human flesh, all gnashing teeth and clawing hands. Lee emptied his last magazine.

He tried to figure how many were left, tried to do the grisly math – it couldn't be many more after he'd used every last rifle magazine that he had strapped to him – and yet, there were more coming at him, though he could not determine their numbers. He could only keep fighting and hope that he had enough to outlast them.

He transitioned as fast as he could to his pistol, but it was too late. Out of the bodies clawing toward him, what looked like it used to be the leg of a large piece of furniture slammed into his left shoulder, knocking him down. For a brief second he couldn't see. But he refused to quit, refused to get taken out like that. By a fucking piece of furniture. He felt his back hit the ground, his head and neck pressed up against the master bedroom door. He tucked his gun arm tight into his body and brought his MK23 to his chest, pointing out.

He felt someone on top of him, but he still couldn't see past the bright sparklers going off all around his eyes. He felt arms, a shoulder, a neck. He grabbed hard around the neck with his left hand, felt his attacker's hands clamp desperately around his own wrist as he shoved outward. It was a rough approximation, but he pushed the muzzle of his pistol into what he thought was his attacker's chin. He shut his eyes and mouth and turned his head away, ready for the fountain, and pulled the trigger.

The writhing body on top of him became dead weight.

He hugged the body close to him, felt a river of warmth running down his neck and chest, smelled the shit and piss and horrid unwashed odor, but clung tight to that body like a drowning man to a raft. Perversely, he felt comforted by the weight. A human blanket. A body shield.

He punched out with his pistol, and in the narrow section of his vision that had cleared, he began picking off targets as they rushed him. He counted rounds as they went out, a death clock on its last seconds.

Two.

Three-four.

Five.

Six-seven-eight.

The bedroom door supporting his head was suddenly gone. He felt the back of his head slap the ground and thought his head had exploded. There was white fire and sparks and a *boom* that he felt in his sinuses. Then another and another.

Hot shotgun shells were falling from the sky, burning his face. Angela was yelling for him to get in the room. Lee shoved the dead body off and rolled onto his hands and knees, then launched himself past Angela's legs and into the bedroom. He was up on one knee when he heard Angela grunt and fly backward into the footboard of the bed.

Lee twisted in time to see a shovel coming down on him like an ax. He jumped forward, felt the shovelhead glance off his ankle, and recovered his position on one knee. He punched out with his pistol and put his sights on the big naked man in front of him. At the same time, Angela let loose with another 12-gauge round that ripped apart Shovel Guy's left shoulder, nearly shearing the arm off.

The big man stumbled back with a groan, but he still held the shovel in his other hand. The shovel was big, but he whipped it around like a toy, even with just one hand. Angela ducked at the foot of the bed, and Shovel Guy waved his weapon back and forth in rapid arcs.

There was a vicious growl, and suddenly Tango was attached to the big man's upper arm. The shovel dropped to the ground. Shovel Guy flailed and screeched, but Tango wasn't letting go.

Lee was quick to his feet, not wanting to take the shot with Tango in the picture – it would have to be a contact shot. He closed the distance and managed to maneuver himself directly behind Shovel Guy. He put the muzzle at the base of the man's skull, pointing upward, and pulled the trigger. The top of his head erupted like a shaken soda can and the body turned heavy and collapsed.

Tango followed the body to the ground and kept growling and ripping at the arm. Lee grabbed the dog's collar with his non-gun hand and yanked the dog back with a sharp 'Leave it!'

It was anything but silent.

Lee heard ringing in his perforated eardrums, the rasp of his own breath, Angela gasping for air, the two kids whimpering in their hiding place somewhere in the room. He could hear the blood rushing through his ears like he was standing under a waterfall. All through the house came the pathetic lilting moans of the dying.

But no one was screeching. No one was running at them. Lee knew it had only been a few short minutes, but time stretches when you're certain you're going to die. Lee moved quickly to the bedroom doorway and looked through, keeping the muzzle of his pistol pointed down the hall and the weapon itself tucked in close to his chest.

He first noted that Stephanie's bedroom door was shut, which gave him hope that Jack had survived the attack by locking himself in the room. The hall that separated them was littered with corpses and those that still clung stubbornly to life. Their desperate situation did not affect their aggression. Lee watched one of the injured infected crawling over the bodies of others, unable to move its legs but still biting and clawing at the air.

He waited another long moment, listening to the sounds of the house, but there was only the constant groan. Lee called out to Jack but got no answer. He felt someone move beside him and turned to find Angela standing to his right, pointing the shotgun at the figure crawling slowly toward them.

Lee reached out a staying hand. 'Don't waste the ammo.'

She looked at him, confused. Lee holstered up and took the shovel from the ground. He turned and put his hand on the doorknob. The others did not need to see the messy cleanup. Angela looked at him with eyes as blank as any professional poker player, and Lee had to appreciate her guts.

Before closing the door, he nodded to her. 'You did really good, Angela. Thank you.'

'Yeah,' was her subdued response.

Lee closed the door and faced the hallway. Dusk had cast the house in a dim gray, but he could still make out the shapes of the bodies and see the movement of the ones still twitching or clawing for him.

Inside the master bedroom, Angela stood like a statue. Her only response to the sickening sound of the steel shovel crushing bone was a blink of her eyelids.

Cleanup was a messy business. It took more than one strike to dispatch most of the crawlers. To be sure he hadn't merely knocked them unconscious, Lee put the point of the shovel to their necks and stomped down, severing the spinal column. The stench was overpowering, and Lee felt sick to his stomach doing the work. These people who littered the ground, they were less than animals to him now. He was killing the wounded with no more thought than he would give to crushing a bug.

Twice he retched but produced nothing. His stomach was

empty. After taking out five of them, he made it to the closed door of Stephanie's bedroom.

He didn't want his head blown off trying to open the door, so he tapped it first and called out to Jack, hoping to God he would answer.

'Jack, you with me? Talk to me, buddy.'

The response was strained. 'Yeah.'

Lee threw open the door and found Jack sitting against the far wall. He was covered in blood from head to toe, but Lee couldn't tell if it was his or from the three dead bodies at his feet. Lee needed to check, but he thought he could guess which it was. Jack looked bad, but he was still holding a big KA-BAR knife that he had produced from somewhere.

Lee stepped over the bodies to get to Jack and knelt down. 'You look shitty, devil dog.'

Jack grimaced and Lee saw blood staining his teeth.

'Where'd they get you?'

'Eh . . .' Jack grunted and leaned forward. 'I'm fine.'

'You're bleeding.'

Jack just gave Lee a look. 'Yeah, I know.'

Lee nodded. 'Where's the blood coming from?'

'One of them was swinging a hammer around and nicked me in the mouth . . . knocked out a few teeth.' The older guy slumped and was silent for a long moment. 'And one of 'em bit me.'

For a perverse moment, Lee thought Jack was kidding. Surely it was a joke. Then Lee scanned Jack's arms for wounds. The older man was holding his right forearm with his left hand. He withdrew the hand and Lee didn't have to ask the question he was thinking: *Did it break the skin?* On Jack's forearm there was a near-perfect circle of teeth marks, gouged well into the skin. It could have just been the trauma to the wound, but Lee thought it already looked red and swollen.

Lee wanted to swear, but he controlled himself.

Jack immediately saw the look on Lee's face. 'You don't gotta pussyfoot around it, Lee. I know I'm fucked.'

Lee noticed it was the first time Jack had called him by his first name. 'Not necessarily ... I mean, even if you are, you won't show symptoms for a while.'

'So what?' Jack snorted. 'You're just gonna keep me around, getting sick and going crazy, 'cause you don't have the stones to do the job?'

Lee gritted his teeth. 'I'm not gonna kill you, Jack.'

'Fuck ... ' Jack was quiet. 'You have to shoot me.'

'No.'

'Shoot me, Lee.' Jack's eyes got fierce. 'Don't play this whole comrades-in-arms, never-leave-a-man-behind bullshit with me! I don't even know you, motherfucker! Put me down! Do it before I start losin' my mind! Fucking shoot me!'

'I'm not—'

Jack cut him off by lunging for Lee's pistol. 'Gimme that!'

Lee swatted his hand down. Jack grabbed for Lee's collar, but Lee slammed him back into the wall and shook him hard. His face was red. 'Fuck you!' he shouted in Jack's face. 'You're not the only person trying to survive here!'

'I'm gonna die anyway!' Jack twisted away.

Lee slammed him against the wall again. 'We're all gonna fucking die!' Jack glared. A few heartbeats passed in intense silence. 'We're all just a step away from it. But right now we are closer than ever and there's a woman and two children and they're on the fucking brink!' Lee took a few deep breaths in silence, then lowered his voice. 'I need every working trigger finger I can find to help me get them out of here and into someplace safe. You wanna die? Do it yourself. But don't ask me or anyone else in this group to lessen our chances of survival.'

Lee stood up and grabbed the shovel.

Before exiting the room, he stopped and turned. 'We need to wash the blood off.'

FIFTEEN

DECISION TIME

LEE DIDN'T BOTHER COUNTING the bodies as he walked downstairs, finishing off the ones that were still moving. The hallway was littered with them, and he fought to keep his footing on the steps. There were even more on the landing, piles of them, often stacked three or four high. With the risk of contagion, it was out of the question to attempt to move the bodies out of the house.

Not to mention the smell was becoming too much to bear.

When he had scoured the lower level of the house for stragglers and come up empty, he returned upstairs. Jack stood at the top of the stairs, looking shell-shocked, staring at the wall. Certain death was a difficult concept to wrap your brain around. Knowing that very soon you would cease to exist. Knowing that, for you, there was no such thing as a future.

Lee left him to his thoughts without speaking and went to the master bedroom. Angela was sitting on the bed, holding the two children. The two kids looked like they'd been crying, while Angela just looked numb.

Lee stood in the doorway, not sure what to say.

Angela broke the silence, her voice soft and cracked. 'Jack got infected?'

Lee didn't answer for a long time. He wanted to rub his

face, but his hands were sticky with blood. His shirt under his combat vest was clinging to his chest and becoming stiff. His whole body felt like it was coagulating. 'Yes.'

Angela's only response was a long, deep breath.

'It's almost dark,' Lee's voice was flat. 'You got blood on you. There's a stream in the backyard we can use to wash it off.'

Lee felt himself brace for some volcanic reaction from Angela, but she only nodded and then slowly stood up. She grabbed the two children by the hands, appearing to take comfort from them as they did from her. Watching it made Lee feel more alone. The trio walked slowly past him, down the hallway, and edged past Jack, who still stood at the top of the stairs.

Lee felt a cold nose nudge his arm. He gave Tango a scratch behind the ear. The dog's fur stuck to the blood on Lee's hands. They left the master bedroom behind. At the top of the stairs, Lee looked at Jack. He thought of different things to say, but they all tasted wrong in his mouth. After a pause, he simply touched Jack lightly on the shoulder and kept moving.

Down the stairs, over the bodies, he followed Angela and the children out of the house. They all walked slowly down the hill, stepping around the freshly dug graves as though they weren't there at all.

Shortly after they walked down the hill, Jack exited the house and followed.

They decided that the pickup truck in the garage was the best place for everyone to hide out for the night. The smell inside the house was too rancid to live with, even for just one night. The truck was a king cab, so the group would fit into the vehicle comfortably, with Tango curled up in the bed. Lee found the keys on the kitchen counter, which was a small miracle in and of itself. The bigger miracle was that the truck turned over and had a quarter tank of fuel left in it.

Lee cracked the windows so it wouldn't get stuffy and turned off the car, but he left the keys in the ignition so he wouldn't have to fumble with them if they needed to drive away quickly. He left the dome light on, as it was the only light in the garage. Angela and Jack sipped slowly on cups of water. Lee had taken the last gallon or so of water out of the hot water heater. He drank enough to take the edge off his own dehydration and gave the rest to the others.

The two children had taken a few cups of water each and had fallen asleep shortly after. Abby looked slightly better, but Angela was still critically dehydrated. Jack had insisted that she take most of the remaining water for herself, as he thought it would be a waste for him to drink too much of it.

'How are you feeling?' Lee asked him.

He pursed his lips. 'Fine.'

'Maybe you're not infected.' Angela sounded hopeful.

Jack smiled wanly but didn't say anything. They all knew that Jack was probably infected. Lee thought about Angela's husband. She must be familiar with the signs and symptoms of infection, as she probably watched her husband succumb to them, all the while hoping he'd break out of it, that the impossible would happen and the infection wouldn't take hold. It would be difficult for her to watch it again.

Lee spoke. 'We need to move.'

They both looked at him.

'In the morning, I mean. We'll sleep here tonight, but we can't stay here. The little bit of water we had is just holding off the dehydration, not curing it. And we have no food at all. We need to find you someplace to stay.'

'What do you mean "find me someplace"?' Angela leaned forward. 'What about you?'

Lee twisted in the driver's seat and looked back at her. 'I'll stay there too. But I'll have to get a resupply. I need to leave you guys in a defensible location that has some food and water.'

Jack leaned back against the headrest and spoke quietly. 'Why don't you tell us about that insurance policy, Captain?'

Lee faced him.

'What are you talking about?' Angela asked.

Jack looked back at him steadily. 'Your GPS device? What's on there?'

Lee stared straight ahead and didn't answer.

'What's he talking about, Lee?' Angela and Jack waited in pregnant silence for a response from Lee, but he wasn't sure how to tell them. The facts were likely to only make them angry. The facts were also very dangerous, not only to Lee but to anyone who knew them. And the more people who knew, the more dangerous the secret got for Lee.

Then again, they deserved some sort of explanation. He couldn't expect two grown adults to simply trust him implicitly with their very survival. He needed to tell them enough that they would trust his decisions but not so much that he was putting them or himself at unnecessary risk.

'Fine.' He nodded slowly. 'Understand that everything I say is going to be the short version. It's not because I don't trust either of you, but it's for your safety. And what I do tell you needs to be kept between us. Agreed?'

Angela and Jack both nodded.

'There are going to be groups out there. Groups of survivors who have banded together for protection. It's these groups that I'm supposed to unite and attempt to rebuild a centralized government with. However, as one man – especially an outsider – I'm of no value to them. They'll never trust me, never listen to me. I have to bring something to the table. Something they can't say no to.

'Think of the GPS as a bargaining chip. It gives me the upper hand when I'm negotiating with these groups of survivors. It will be what brings them together, not me. The only issue is, with that much sway, I also make myself a huge target. Anyone who knows what's on this GPS is going to be a target. There's going to be a lot of people who will believe it will be better to simply take it from me, rather than work with me. Because of that, there are fail-safes in place to keep this bargaining chip out of the wrong hands. The first and most important is that I am the only one with access to it.

'Obviously, if I were to tell you what is on the GPS or where these things are, you would also become a target. So I won't tell you, but I'm sure you can reasonably infer what I'm talking about.'

Angela's eyebrows went up. 'Umm—'

Jack cut her off. 'Guns, ammo, food, water, medicine . . .' He smiled. 'You're holding all the keys to survival. You got everyone by the balls.'

Lee didn't directly confirm Jack's theory. 'Don't read anything Machiavellian into it, Jack. I'm here to help, not conquer the world. The only caveat is that I do have an ulterior motive: If you want to play with my toys, you gotta play nice.'

Jack shrugged. 'I've got no problem with that.'

'So . . .' Angela seemed like she was still trying to wrap her head around it. 'What do we do now?'

Lee looked back at her. 'Tomorrow, we have to find somebody to take us in. They won't want to at first. They'll be suspicious of outsiders. But I'm pretty sure I can convince them. The hard part will be finding them.'

'What are we looking for?' Jack seemed more in tune now.

'A large group of survivors. Could be individuals who banded together out of necessity and are now holding a defensible location, or it could be a group of people who were already a community prior to the collapse and have fortified their position.' Lee rubbed his face and felt thick stubble. 'The most likely places to find these groups will be locations where some sort of security or fortification already exists.'

'What type of security are we talking about?' Angela asked.

'Could be many different things. A factory with a tall fence around it. A gated community. Even just an industrial building with heavy doors on it.'

'I'm not real familiar with this area,' Jack stated. 'You guys know of any places like that around here?'

Lee grimaced. 'I had a map of places fitting that profile, but it was in my bunker.'

'There's a gated community a little closer to town,' Angela offered. 'I can't think of the name of the road it's on, but I know how to get there.'

Lee tapped the steering wheel. 'Do you remember what it was called?'

'Timber Creek,' Angela answered immediately. Her voice got quiet. 'I had a friend who used to live there. Maggie Dunham. She moved to Raleigh last year.'

Lee and Jack both looked at Angela for a brief moment. Lee got back on track. 'We'll want to avoid population centers, but the outskirts should be good. I think I remember Timber Creek being toward the edge of town.'

Angela nodded. 'Yeah. Almost at the city line.'

'How long do you think it would take to get there?'

Angela looked around as though she was disoriented for a moment. 'I don't know. Maybe twenty minutes?'

Lee did mental calculations. Auto manufacturers in the US generally made their gas tanks big enough to carry the vehicle about three hundred miles on a single tank regardless of MPGs. With a fourth of a tank, one could generally look at getting between fifty and seventy-five miles. Lee decided to go with the conservative number. Fifty miles was probably enough to get them to where they were going. A twenty-minute drive on surface streets was usually about fifteen miles. If Timber Creek was a bust, they would hopefully have enough fuel to try for another location.

Hopefully.

This was all barring the possibilities of raiders, rogue military factions, or hordes of infected.

'Alright.' Lee leaned his head back and clicked off the dome light. 'We should get some sleep.'

The exhausted group slept deeply, despite their desperate circumstances. Their dreams were dark and hazy and filled with fear and hope. They slept unaware that fate would not allow all of them to reach Timber Creek alive.

SIXTEEN

ON THE ROAD

LEE AWOKE TO THE SOUND of Tango growling.

In the blackness of the garage, Lee grabbed his pistol from its holster, still half asleep and unsure of what was happening. The three glowing green dots of his pistol's tritium sights looked like a UFO hovering in midair. He fumbled for the door handle and popped it. The dome light came on and Jack startled awake.

Lee turned on the vehicle's parking lights and the garage was bathed in a yellow glow. Tango was still growling, but the garage door was closed, as was the door into the house.

Lee motioned for Jack to remain seated and stepped out of the pickup. He immediately dipped down to one knee and checked underneath the vehicle for any intruders. Finding nothing, he made a slow, cautious circle around the car, Tango all the while still pacing in the bed and growling.

Lee stepped over to the door into the house but thought better before opening it. They needed to leave, not get in another fight. If anything was in the house, their best option was to leave it behind, not waste time and ammunition or risk death trying to kill it.

Lee motioned for Jack to join him.

The lanky man got out of the car slowly. He looked bad.

Dark circles rimmed his eyes and his skin seemed pale and waxy. Lee wasn't sure whether it was the onset of symptoms or the dehydration catching up to him. Lee's own mouth felt like it was full of sand. He kept swallowing, trying to encourage his mouth to make some saliva, but it was bone dry.

Lee's voice was parched and cracked. 'How are you feeling?'

'Under the weather,' Jack said. His voice was hollow. Defeated. 'Feverish.'

The two men shared a long and awkward silence. 'Look . . .' Lee began.

'I should ride in the bed,' Jack said flatly. 'I don't know if it's catching or not, but there's no sense in risking it. Besides, looks like Tango could use some company.'

Lee only nodded.

Jack looked at the dog, who was now silent but still pacing in the truck bed. By now, Angela and the two kids had woken up but were sitting quietly in the cab, watching Jack and Lee. 'What's wrong with him?' Jack asked, nodding toward Tango.

'Smelled something he didn't like?'

Jack smiled. 'I smell something I don't like, too . . . me.'

'We need to get out of here, but there might be something in the yard. Think you can open the garage door and jump in the bed in time for us to tear out of here if we need to?'

Jack shrugged. 'Sounds doable.'

Luckily the pickup truck was backed into the garage. Lee got into the driver's seat and cranked it up. He regretted leaving the house behind without a thorough search for any supplies they could have used, but given Tango's growling, Lee felt this was the safer option. He just prayed they would get to someplace with some food and water soon. Ammunition would be a big plus as well.

'You guys sleep okay?' he asked his passengers.

There was a mumbled chorus of 'yeah' and 'okay.'

He checked his watch. It was just after dawn. They must have been tired. Lee didn't recall waking up at all during the night. During the last two days he'd only slept for a few hours total. His body had felt the effects, even if his mind was too wired to notice.

Jack signaled that he was ready with the garage door. Lee put the pickup truck in drive and prepared to floor it at the first sign of attackers. He nodded back to the Marine standing ready and he lifted the garage door up with one heave.

A lady in a dirty gray business suit, still holding her handbag, was leaning against the door, and she flopped over into the garage when Jack opened it. He jumped backward as what appeared to be a dead body at first raised its head and reached for Jack.

'Motherfucker!' Jack hauled ass into the bed of the truck.

In the fleeting moment before Lee smashed the accelerator, he wondered if she was simply some tired refugee, trying to rest before continuing on her journey. Then the pickup truck ran her over and Lee didn't slow down. He hit the street, taking only a moment to look back at the yard and see the two pockmarks in the dirt where his 40mm grenades had hit the night before. He thought he could see body parts sticking out of the long grass. Maybe one of them moved.

He made a left on Morrison Street and stepped on it, speeding up to sixty and then leveling off. He didn't feel much of anything at all. His heart rate had barely risen. In the rearview mirror, Jack gave him a thumbs-up from the truck bed, while in the backseat Angela held the two kids in her arms with her eyes squeezed shut as though waiting for a nightmare to be over.

They passed more houses as they drove.

Lee didn't dare stop at any of them. Some looked ransacked. A few were boarded up. Others looked like they'd been burned. They left the country road behind and started heading toward town. The single houses set back on huge acreages began to be interspersed with what were once quiet subdivisions and county parks. There were very few abandoned cars on the road. So far, none of them was pushed into the travel lanes to create a roadblock, but Lee took his turns carefully and kept a watchful eye for anything that resembled an ambush. The neighborhoods they passed looked desolate. Curtains billowed out of broken windows. Trash filled the streets.

The kids were surprisingly quiet. Lee had expected them to be whining about hunger and thirst, but they hadn't said a word since leaving the Petersons' house. He thought perhaps the violence and stress of the last few days were beginning to cause the children some emotional breakdown. No one – including Lee – could live through something like this and come out unchanged, but the children would be affected on a much deeper level than he was. He had long ago made peace with the malevolence and tragedy of human existence. Children just didn't know any better.

After another pillaged subdivision, Lee saw a welcome sight. To the left of the road was an old convenience store with a few fuel pumps out front. Lee tempered his hope with realism: Over the course of a month it had most likely been picked clean by looters and passing refugees.

But still, it was worth a look.

Lee slowed down to a crawl and gave the area a good, hard looking-over. He checked for signs of foot travel through the overgrown weeds all around the convenience store. He surveyed the nearby tree lines for anything out of place. As he crept closer he could see that most of the windows were busted out. The sides of the building were vandalized with graffiti that Lee didn't understand. But the place looked abandoned.

He turned the truck around in the parking lot and backed it as far behind the building as he could to hide it from the view of any passersby.

'Is this where we're going, Mommy?' Abby asked.

Angela looked curiously at the gas station. 'No, honey.'

Lee stepped out of the pickup and then leaned back in. 'Give me a second to clear it. Stay here.' He thought for a second. 'Actually, get in the driver's seat. If you hear me yelling, just drive away.'

Angela nodded.

As Lee stepped away from the vehicle, Jack jumped out of the bed, looking sore and tired. Lee left his M4 in the truck, since it was out of ammunition. He cleared his MK23 from its holster. Jack had acquired the shotgun and its remaining round from Angela and held it at a low-ready as they proceeded around the corner to the front of the store.

Their footsteps crunched in the broken glass that littered the parking lot. Lee looked through the broken storefront windows as he walked by. The interior of the convenience store looked like it had been emptied out. Most of the shelves were tipped over, and whatever shelves still stood were empty. The coolers lining the walls were empty as well. Lee pulled on the door and found it unlocked. He stepped through first, Jack following just behind him. The cash register was busted and the cash drawer removed. Little good cash would do anyone now.

The tobacco shelves had been completely wiped out. Someone had even taken all the scratch-off lottery tickets.

Jack stooped down and picked something up off the floor. A few pieces of broken glass glittered to the ground. It was another scratch-off lottery ticket. Jack smiled wistfully. 'I used to play these all the time.' His voice was hoarse. 'Drop a twenty every week on a twelve-pack of beer and scratch-offs. Never won shit.' He laughed.

Lee smiled along with him, more at the sight of seeing him cheered.

'You ever play a scratch-off?' Jack asked.

'No. Never was big into games of chance.'

'Well,' Jack held out the ticket. 'Try it.'

Lee laughed this time but shook his head. 'Nah, I'm good.'

'Come on.' Jack leaned over on the counter and fished a coin out of the give-a-penny/take-a-penny tray in front of the register. 'This might be the last scratch-off lottery ticket you ever see. It's a piece of American history now.'

'Well, you have to preserve it, then.'

Jack made a rude noise. 'Fuck preserving. Scratch this bitch.' He held out the penny.

Lee chuckled. 'Alright. First and last lottery play ever.'

Jack held a grimy hand in front of his mouth in mock anticipation. 'You're lucky. This is gonna be a winner.'

Lee looked around to make himself feel better, then holstered his pistol. He took the penny and scratched away at the little piece of paper. Having never played before, he didn't really know what to look for, but Jack narrated his progress as he went.

'Got a diamond there; that's not worth anything … Thirteen isn't one of the winning numbers … Forty-three, nope …'

Lee finished the scratch-off and blew the shavings away.

'Holy shit.' Jack pointed. 'You won a hundred goddamn bucks, you sonofabitch!'

Lee stared at the paper. 'I did? How can you tell?'

'Twenty-seven is one of the winning numbers, and you got a twenty-seven. The prize is a hundred bucks!'

'Ha!' Lee smiled. 'Too bad it's not worth anything anymore.'

'Bullshit,' Jack folded the ticket and offered it to Lee. 'Hang on to it. It'll be good luck.'

Lee nodded and stuffed the ticket in a pocket on his combat shirt. 'We could use all the luck we can get.'

'Who knows?' Jack began to meander around the store. 'Maybe someday things will get back to normal and you can cash it in.'

'Yeah ... maybe.'

Jack made his way to the back of the store while Lee poked around in the piles of trash for something to eat. Maybe a bag of peanuts or some Cheez-Its. Anything, really. Something big scraped across the floor and Lee jerked up to see Jack pulling a fallen shelf off the wall.

'Oh yeah ... ' Jack turned and smiled. 'Storage cooler?'

Lee abandoned the piles of trash and joined Jack at what appeared to be a door into the cooler section that led behind the shelves of beer and soda. It was padlocked.

'It's like no one has even tried to get in there,' Lee said in amazement.

'Might not be anything back there worth wasting your time on.' He looked around briefly. 'But ... maybe they just weren't as hungry as we are.'

Jack found what he was looking for and pulled up a fire extinguisher. He walked back over to the door and swung the fire extinguisher hard, aiming not for the lock but for the whole door handle. It took him three hits and he had sufficiently mangled it enough that when he and Lee yanked on it together, the door popped open.

The interior of the cooler was dark and not exactly cold, though it was definitely less than room temperature. The two men both simultaneously smelled the air, Lee wondering if anything had spoiled or perhaps died in the cooler. But it just smelled like a cellar. Cool and dank.

'You got a flashlight?' Jack asked.

Lee shook his head. 'Not on me.'

Jack fished his lighter out of his pocket and flipped it on. With the little butane flame burning, he stepped into the dark cooler for a closer look. Lee covered him with his hand hovering over his holstered pistol. His eyes strained to see in the dark. The flickering lighter was barely enough to illuminate the small room, but after a few short moments, Jack found the far wall and the light from the flame cast a fluttering glow over several cases of water, soft drinks, and sports drinks.

'Oh, sweet Jesus!' Jack was ecstatic.

Lee allowed himself to feel a moment of relief. A tension in his gut that he didn't know he'd been holding suddenly let go. Jack was already grabbing a case of water. Lee followed suit.

'Let's grab as much as we can, but I don't want to stay in the same place for too long.'

After a few hurried trips, looking over their shoulders as though this stroke of good luck was about to be stripped from them at any moment, they were able to grab three cases of water and a case of sports drinks. They threw them in the bed of the truck and Lee ripped into a case of water and started handing the bottles out with the same instructions: Drink slowly.

If everyone kept a bottle of water down all right, he would give everyone sports drinks. The electrolytes would help them retain the water they would drink afterward. It wasn't until he grabbed a bottle of water for himself that Lee noticed Tango was not in the truck bed. In the excitement of finding the water that might save their lives, he hadn't noticed Tango's absence.

He looked around for a brief moment before asking Angela and the kids, 'Where's Tango?'

Abby spoke without hesitation. 'He threw up.'

'Tango threw up?' Lee looked to Angela for some adult clarification.

Angela nodded. 'Yeah. He started heaving and hopped down out of the truck bed. He wandered off into the grass over there.' She pointed to the passenger side of the vehicle.

The poor dog was as dehydrated as the rest of them. Got the dry heaves and was trying to find a puddle of water to get something to drink. Lee grabbed another bottle of water and walked around to the passenger side of the vehicle. He didn't want to whistle or yell to Tango for fear of drawing unwanted attention, so he clicked his tongue and called the dog's name in a normal conversational voice.

After a moment of silence, he could hear rustling in the brush at the end of the parking lot. Paranoia grabbed him and he moved to draw his pistol, but then he saw Tango's long, wolflike face poking through the tall weeds. The dog wasn't moving at his usual breakneck speed. He simply walked along, his tail at half-mast and his head lower to the ground. What little resources they'd had, Lee had given to the humans in the group and he felt a pang of guilt for letting Tango's condition worsen.

Lee bent down to one knee and opened one of the bottles of water. 'Come here, boy.'

The dog walked to his master, tongue lolling out of the side of his mouth. The corners of his mouth were strung with that frothy yellow substance that dogs sometimes vomit up. Lee poured water into his cupped hand and offered it to the dog. Tango went straight to Lee and without hesitation planted his muzzle in Lee's hand, lapping up the water. In about two gulps, the water was gone. Lee repeated the process a few more times but didn't want to give Tango too much at one time, as he would likely not hold it down.

Tango kept panting, but at least held his head up.

Lee capped what was left of the dog's water and wiped the slick saliva from his hands. Tango followed him back to the truck and after a moment of staring up at the truck bed like it was an insurmountable obstacle, he jumped in with Jack.

Jack didn't look much better than the dog, though he leaned against the back glass with his eyes closed and a faint smile on his face. The sun was warming the sky and Lee felt for the first time that the air did not feel as dense or humid as the previous few days, and the sky seemed free of the usual summer haze.

Lee didn't interrupt Jack from his reverie. The man had a few miserable days left. He should enjoy the small satisfaction from the sun on his face and a little water in his belly. Lee got into the driver's seat and cranked the truck up again. They pulled out from the back of the convenience store's parking lot and got back onto the road. Inside the vehicle, the mood was lighter than before. A brief moment of levity while Sam and Abby found a reason to giggle at something for the first time in days, possibly weeks.

He wondered how long it would last.

SEVENTEEN

TIMBER CREEK

LEE DROVE ANOTHER HALF MILE before Angela directed him – somewhat unsurely – to take a left onto a two-lane highway that ran east to west, with downtown Angier a few miles to the north. Lee found himself reaching to turn on the blinker and nearly laughed at himself. Perhaps if the circumstances were different it would have been funnier.

He drove with the window down and his arm hanging out. The air smelled like summer, and not at all like the end of the world. The sunlight flashed in and out of the trees as they drove by. Lee felt that if he could just close his eyes for a brief moment, he would wake up, driving down a country road with a beer in his hand and Deana in the passenger seat next to him.

It was then that Jack began screaming.

Lee's first instinct was to accelerate, rather than stop. He looked in the rearview mirror and couldn't see Jack. In the span of a half second, Lee was certain that Jack had turned and was flying into a blind rage. Lee would have to gun him down. And then Jack's hand pounded the back glass and he began screaming Lee's name.

This time Lee slammed on the brakes. There was a tumble from the bed and the yelling choked off. 'Stay in the car!' he said over his shoulder. Lee threw the vehicle in park and was out of the car before it even skidded to a stop.

He drew his pistol and pointed it at the bed, not sure what he would find. There was a flash of bloody arms and legs and Jack threw himself over the side of the bed and landed on his face in the middle of the road.

Following the man overboard, Tango thrust his head over the side and began snapping his jaws. Lee thought it looked like he was barking, but there was no sound. It was like the dog was trying to bite Jack but couldn't reach. Bloody slobber hung in frothy ropes from the dog's mouth, dangling back and forth and sticking to the side of the truck.

The dog's eyes were wild and strange.

'Fuck!' Jack stood up unsteadily and backed away from the truck. He had bleeding marks all over his arms and face. 'Lee ... dog ... bite ... Dog bite! Dog bite!'

Lee lowered his pistol and looked Jack in the face. Behind the blood seeping from several bite marks, Lee could see the man's eyes were confused and frustrated.

Jack must have seen the look of pity on Lee's face and grabbed his hair with both hands, like he was trying to pull it out, his face twisting into a grimace. 'Fuckdammit ... words are hard.'

Confusion. Loss of speech.

Tango let out a hacking bark. Lee turned to his dog and pointed a stern finger at him. 'Tango, leave it!' The dog looked at Jack, then looked at Lee. He sat down, but his eyes were fixed on Lee. The aggressive snapping jaws turned into that stupid smile, with his tongue hanging out of the side of his mouth. His eyes regarded Lee with what looked like relief, as though to say, *Hey, I know you. You're a friend.*

Lee turned back to Jack. 'Slow down and breathe. Think about your words.'

'Ah ... umm ...' Jack kept rubbing his hands over his head, raking his hair back with his fingers. 'I ... I ...'

Lee heard the door of the vehicle open. He turned and watched Angela step out and close the door behind her. 'Oh my God,' she exclaimed. 'Are you okay?'

Jack sat down in a squat, head in his hands. Blood was dripping from his arms onto the ground. Lee and Angela kept their distance from him. 'Something is wrong ...' Jack spoke haltingly. 'With Tango. He ... he ... snapping his jaws ... and bites me. Keeps biting me.'

This time Angela spoke quietly to Lee. 'Maybe Tango can smell Jack turning.'

Lee looked over at his longtime companion, who now paced restlessly in the back of the pickup bed. Growling low, head hanging, tail slightly tucked. Uncharacteristically fearful. Undeniably aggressive. It would be more pleasant for Lee to believe that Tango simply smelled the infection in Jack and attacked on instinct. But Lee wasn't living in a pleasant reality.

He didn't answer Angela as he walked over to the side of the bed.

Tango kept pacing, growling, grumbling to himself. Then he saw Lee and his low-slung tail rose just a bit and wagged two or three times.

'Hey, buddy.' Lee reached into his right cargo pocket and pulled out that old tattered rope toy. The dog wagged his tail and stared at the toy. In his simple canine mind, it was just time for fun, fun, fun.

Inside the Petersons', Tango had defended them by attacking the infected man with the shovel. Probably taken a good chunk out of him when he did it. Lee wanted to blame himself for it, but he knew it would have been impossible to keep Tango from coming in contact with the infected. His only hope had been that interspecies infection was impossible.

Lee walked to the end of the truck and lowered the tailgate. He moved slowly, like his legs were encased in concrete. He felt flushed. Light-headed. He held the rope toy out and Tango made his way to the end of the tailgate, then jumped off. He didn't look as nimble as he had the day before. He looked like a different dog.

Angela spoke softly. 'Lee, we can just leave him here.'

Lee matched her low volume, but his tone left no room for argument. 'I asked you to wait in the truck.'

There was a moment of silence. She tried again. 'I understand that—'

Lee turned to face her. 'I will do what I think is best. Now get in the fucking truck.' Lee turned to Jack. 'You too. Both of you get in the truck. Leave me be for one goddamned minute.'

Lee turned back to Tango and gave him the rope toy. The dog chewed on it. Carefree. Ignorant. Beautiful. Behind him, Lee heard the truck door open and the scuffle of Jack climbing back into the truck bed. Then the door closed and there was just the quiet rumble of the truck's engine at idle.

Lee bent down and took the rope. 'Tango, give.' The dog obediently released it. Lee walked toward the grassy field to the side of the road, still holding the rope toy.

Tango followed, tail wagging. The dog's stride was stiff, but he didn't seem to notice. Lee kept walking, feeling Tango moving diligently next to him, occasionally his flank brushing Lee's leg as they walked, as it had so many times before.

Lee wasn't sure how far he walked, and he didn't care. He knew that everyone in the truck could still see him, but he wanted to be away from them. This was not their business. This was just Lee and his dog, alone again. Like they started. Simpler.

The man stopped, and his dog stopped with him. Lee looked down at Tango. 'You want the toy, buddy?'

Tango wagged his tail. Lee tossed the rope, but not too far. When he would take Tango out into the backyard, when things were normal, he would throw tennis balls as far as he possibly could. Tango was a fast dog and would sometimes catch them before they could bounce twice. This time he hobbled after the rope, his mind excited but his body uncooperative. Lee had always admired the dog's muscular grace. Now he didn't think he could throw the rope again. He didn't think he could watch the dog hobble anymore, ignorant of his own sickness.

Tango returned at a walk, the rope hanging in his mouth. 'You tired already?' He tried to sound cheerful for Tango, but his voice was weak. Lee knelt down to Tango and put his left arm around the dog's chest, felt the dog's ribs and wished the last couple days of Tango's life hadn't been so rough on him. He scratched the dog's neck, leaned in close, and whispered, because he couldn't find his voice. 'You're a good dog, Tango. I can't give it to you, but you deserved a full belly and a soft blanket.'

Tango wasn't listening. He just kept chewing the rope. Fun, fun, fun.

Still holding the dog, Lee pulled out his pistol, put the muzzle against the dog's head, just behind the ear, and killed him with a single shot.

*

They drove on in silence.

Lee's mind pulled him a dozen different directions. His emotional response to losing Tango had dismayed him. Not because he did not have affection for the animal, but because as a handler of a working dog, he knew his dog was there to do a job, not to be a pet, and he understood the danger inherent in that. Lee had not wanted to become emotionally attached to Tango, but it was unavoidable, especially given the long weeks he'd spent in The Hole.

It also struck another sensitive chord inside of him. Everything he knew was being stripped away in one way or another. His house, his dog, everyone he knew – everything was gone. It had all been replaced with this new cold reality that offered no comfort, no familiarity. It was as though he had been borne through a raging furnace and come out the other side with every old thing burned away. In the span of days, he found himself living a completely different life.

Tango had been the last tie to his old life. The last comfortable, familiar thing he knew. Besides the shell-shocked state Lee found his mind in, there were other concerns.

Such as Jack. It had been obvious to everyone – including Jack – that he was becoming symptomatic. The confused speech, the pale skin, the constant sweating. In Lee's briefing, what felt like months ago in the comfort of his bunker, Colonel Reid had established a seventy-two-hour asymptomatic time period. However, that may have been old data based on a less intrusive means of infection than being bitten on the arm.

With no other data available on the plague or how easily it was transmitted, Lee felt increasingly uncomfortable with carting the infected man around. Lee knew he couldn't catch the plague simply by being around Jack, in the same way he knew it took a detonator to set off a nuclear device. But it didn't make it any more comfortable to sit next to one.

And whatever the science might be behind Jack's contagion, the fact of the matter was that he wouldn't be around much longer. He was a time bomb, and Lee didn't know how long the fuse was. He knew he didn't want to abandon him and he didn't want to kill him, especially when Jack could help them get to a safe place. But the longer they waited, the more of a risk Jack became. It was coming to the point where Lee continuously checked the rearview to make sure Jack wasn't frothing at the mouth and trying to beat his way through the back glass to attack them.

From a strictly utilitarian perspective, the only reason Jack wasn't dead was because he could still help in a fight. But how much trust could there be in a combat situation when Lee knew the guy who was watching his back could turn into an instinctive killer at the drop of a hat?

Then there was the mission, which was essentially on hold until Lee could get Angela, Abby, and Sam to a safe location. His mission required that he travel among groups of survivors and continue to make contacts and connections and build bridges between communities. He couldn't do this with parties of survivors slowing him down.

Was his mission even feasible?

In that moment it felt ridiculous, outlandish, and impossible. He'd spent two days on the surface of this shitty place and had come into contact with only four survivors, one of which was about to die. And that wasn't counting Sam's father. To pay for this he'd lost his house, his supplies, his dog, and a generous helping of his positive attitude. What he was left with was a pistol with four rounds left in it, an empty rifle, a symptomatic infected man, and three survivors who were now only slightly further away from terminal dehydration. Not to mention that edible food appeared to be nonexistent. Did he really think he was going to find entire groups of survivors in this wasteland?

'That's it! Right there!'

Lee snapped out of it and saw Angela leaning between the two front seats, pointing out the windshield at the entrance to what looked like it had once been a well-to-do condominium complex to the left of the road. The sign, made of brick and plaster and missing a few vowels, announced it as T MBER CRE K.

Lee slowed down and turned left into the entrance, then rolled to a stop.

The inside of the pickup truck was awkwardly silent, as though no one could think of the right thing to say. In the rearview mirror, Jack stood up and looked over the cab. Lee didn't know whether he felt like laughing or crying. He wasn't quite sure what they'd expected to find, but he knew what they'd *hoped* to find, and this was not it.

The gates to Timber Creek looked like someone had driven a Mack truck through them. One of them lay mangled but still clinging to the lever that once had opened and closed it. The other one was gone completely. The complex itself looked like someone had burned half of it to the ground and looted the other half. Burned-out husks of cars still sat in their designated parking spaces. Trash and broken glass were littered in every corner. The buildings stood like skulls in a catacomb, their broken windows as black as eye sockets, and just as dead and empty.

To keep himself from laughing or crying, Lee took a slow,

deep breath and tried to let it out quietly, though he was sure everyone in the vehicle knew what mood he was in. 'Well . . .' He looked around at the mess in front of him. 'I guess we can look around.'

And that's when the truck slammed into them from behind.

EIGHTEEN

THE PATROL

LEE HEARD THE IMPACT LIKE an explosion and felt himself spinning, like he was strapped into a carnival ride. Jack tumbled over the top of the cab and dented the hood on his way to the ground. When they stopped spinning, they were turned nearly 180 degrees counterclockwise and were now facing their attacker. Lee got the impression of a freight tractor with no trailer attached, its twin exhaust pipes poking up like devil's horns. He didn't wait to see what came out of the truck.

Lee had just enough of an angle to stick his pistol out the driver's side window and still draw a good sight picture on the truck facing them. He pointed for the driver's seat and cranked off his last four rounds. The dark windshield turned into white spiderwebs. Jack staggered to his feet and fired his last round of buckshot, peppering the driver's side door.

As Lee pulled his gun back into his pickup truck and tossed it on the passenger seat, he watched as the driver's side door of the truck opened and a bloody body was shoved out like a bag of garbage. The truck immediately started rolling toward them.

'Jack! Get in!' Lee screamed over the roar of the diesel engine bearing down.

Jack stood in the open, still holding his empty shotgun. He never looked back. The truck hit him so hard, it looked like the old Marine simply disappeared.

Lee tore his eyes off the scene and slammed his pickup's accelerator, steering hard right, trying to maneuver for the wreckage of Timber Creek. With not a bullet among the four of them, Lee felt their only chance of survival was to evade and outflank their attackers inside the condominium complex.

Their vehicle almost made the turn, but the pickup's powerful engine and heavy torque spun the wheels for just a bit too long and, as Lee wrangled the pickup toward the damaged gate, the freight truck T-boned them on Lee's side.

Glass shattered inward like a sharp horizontal rain. The kids were screaming like air raid sirens. Lee heard a popping sound that he thought was the engine malfunctioning and then quickly recognized it as small arms fire. He mashed the accelerator again, but the pickup wouldn't budge. The two vehicles were hooked together.

Lee ducked as two rounds punched clean through the side of his door and missed his midsection by inches. 'Get out!' he yelled at Angela and the kids, who were already opening the rear passenger side door. He launched himself over the center console, leaving his MK23 and his M4 but grabbing his go-to-hell pack as he shoved open the front passenger side door and leaped out, face-first.

He tried to pull his arms in front of him to brace his fall, but the weight of his backpack held them back. He felt his face slam concrete and tasted blood and grit, and he wasn't sure where it was coming from. He was only glad he hadn't blacked out.

He staggered to his feet, feeling like it took him ages to accomplish this simple task, and saw Angela and the kids, already sprinting through the entrance to Timber Creek. Dirt and concrete chunks exploded around him and Lee realized that he was still being shot at.

He sprinted for the complex's entrance, holding the backpack with one hand and digging in the pockets with the other. Rifle and pistol fire continued to track him as he ran, chewing up the ground and pinging off the metal gate. The only thought in his mind cycled in a tight loop: *Get the GPS! Get the GPS! Get the GPS!*

'Lee!'

The scream broke his attention. He looked up and saw that Angela and the kids were now running back toward him. He felt his fingers touch the GPS and grabbed it in an iron grip and simultaneously realized why Angela and the kids were running back toward him.

Drawn by the loud noises, three infected were sprinting straight for them.

Lee didn't have time to plan and didn't have much in the way of weapons, so he simply acted on the first thing that popped into his head. He pulled the GPS out of his backpack and shoved it into his cargo pocket as he charged straight at the approaching infected. Previously fixated on Angela and the two children, the infected shifted their attention to Lee.

The first attacker caught Lee's backpack in the face as Lee swung it like a flail. The hit knocked the infected off its feet, but it grabbed the backpack on the way down and Lee let him have it. As the next infected approached, Lee took two big sprinting steps and jumped, slamming both feet into the creature's chest. The two of them tumbled to the ground, a few feet apart. As Lee tried to get to his feet, he saw Angela and the kids taking advantage of his distraction and flanking around, heading back into the condo complex.

The third infected reached Lee before he could react and threw him back to the ground. The thing was fat and blood was pouring from its mouth. Lee was on his back looking up at it as it screeched at him. He thrust up with one hand, catching the thing around its flabby neck, his only concern to keep it from biting at him. With his other hand he reached down to his boot and yanked out a small thrust dagger he kept there – the only weapon Lee had left.

The fat infected swung wildly at him, grabbing a fistful of Lee's face and sinking in its dirty fingernails. Lee screamed in rage and pain and slammed the thrust dagger into the infected's temple, causing it to instantly go limp.

Lee shoved the dead body off of him. Both of the other infected were now on their feet again. Lee yanked at his dagger, still embedded in the side of the fat infected's skull, but it would not budge. Lee left it and started running in the last direction he'd seen Angela and the kids headed. Breath came to him in ragged gasps, his legs felt numb as they flew across the concrete, and Lee could sense the instability in his sprint and feared his legs might give out before he made it to safety.

He glanced behind him and saw several armed gunmen pouring through the front gate, rifles and pistols flashing, but the noise just sounded like muted thumps to Lee. One of the remaining infected's heads split open and it tumbled to the ground. The other froze in place, unsure whether to pursue Lee or attack the gunmen.

Lee faced back around and found himself running straight for the door of a ground-floor condo. He didn't think about it, though in the back of his mind he knew it wasn't the best decision to go into a confined space when he was being pursued. He hit the door with his shoulder and it shattered open. Lee felt a spiking pain through his right arm as he stumbled into the condo and immediately regretted his decision.

The room he found himself in was completely black. The windows must have been boarded up by a conscientious condo owner, and the light that pushed through the open door only lit up a small square of the room.

But he couldn't go back.

Blindly, he kept moving straight ahead, feeling in front of him with his arms. He found a long, narrow hallway, passed a few bedroom doors, felt his boots step on something soft halfway down the hall, but didn't stop to try and see what it was. He made it to a door at the end of the hall and fumbled for the doorknob.

Behind him, he heard shouts at the front door.

He pushed through the darkness and entered this last room. Again, he was met with pure, inky blackness. He shut the door behind him and locked it. Then he put his hand out to the right wall and started feeling around. There had to be a window in this room. *Please, God, let there be a window.*

Lee pushed over furniture, knocked what he thought were pictures off of the walls, and tipped over a chair before finally finding a window. Without hesitation he reared back and put a boot through the glass. It shattered easily, but the plywood on the other side did not. Lee knew it was his only option. This wasn't a prison. He could get out. It would just take some effort. He would not die, gunned down by some fucking raiders in a dark, dead back bedroom of some looted condominium. Not after all the things he had already survived.

He kicked again at the plywood, this time feeling some slight give. He could hear shouts coming from inside the condo now. Surely they heard him crashing through the darkness and pounding at the window. He had only seconds left before they caught up with him. He kept slamming his foot into the plywood, feeling it rattle just a little more each time until finally he saw a hint of daylight creeping through the lower left-hand corner of the window.

One more kick and the corner of the plywood came loose. For a brief flash as the plywood swung back, Lee saw grass on the other side. This time he put his hands to the plywood and pushed as hard as he could, feeling a few more nails come out of the window frame.

There was a loud boom at the bedroom door. 'He's in here! He's in here!' someone shouted. Lee knew the bedroom door wouldn't last long. He pushed the plywood and saw about a foot of daylight through the jagged teeth of the nails that still poked through the plywood. Lee knew it was going to be painful, but he couldn't wait any longer. Pain was better than death. Lee gave the plywood covering one last shove and put his head through. As soon as his hand let go of the plywood, it swung back into place and Lee felt the nails gouge into his skin. He let out a yell, less because of the immediate pain and more because he knew it was about to hurt so much more.

With the nails already embedded in his skin, Lee thrust his shoulders through the opening, felt the sharp points rip through skin and muscle, clawing down his back. He screamed until his breath ran out and he couldn't draw another. He planted both his hands on the sides of the outside wall and pushed with everything he had.

The nails were caught on his belt.

Through the blinding pain, Lee twisted, each movement he made working the nails deeper into his flesh. He grabbed the very corner of the plywood and yanked it out as hard as he possibly could. His belt came free of the snag and he fell, the plywood slamming the nails into the side of his left leg, but his downward momentum didn't allow him to stop. The metal spikes sheared right through his flesh and Lee landed in a heap on the ground, felt the grass on his face.

Bullets punched through the plywood covering.

Lee didn't think they would follow him through the window. They would go out and around, which gave him a few precious seconds to escape. He tried to haul himself to his feet but found his back in such excruciating pain that he couldn't complete the movement. On hands and knees, he scrambled forward, trying to see where he was going.

Pain blurred his vision and made the sun appear white-hot, and everything touched by it was blindingly bright.

The only easy day was yesterday.

Lee almost laughed at himself. *Get the fuck up, Lee! Get off the fucking ground!*

'There he is!'

Lee brought one leg up, the stretch of his skin spreading the deep lacerations all over his body and causing another wave of intense pain. He managed to get a foot up and knelt on one knee, supporting his body with a hand on the ground. He looked behind him.

Some guy in a black sleeveless T-shirt was running at him, holding an AR-15. 'It's him! It's the guy!' Around the corner of the condominium complex, two more gunmen appeared. Lee knew he couldn't outrun them. He looked around for anything he might use as a weapon. A stick, a sharp piece of glass, maybe a two-by-four if he was lucky. He knew they would kill him if he fought, but he also knew that he wasn't going to let them win. In his current state of mind, his imminent death simply seemed ... regrettable.

Lee couldn't find anything to use, so he focused on the first approaching gunman and decided if the man didn't cap him by the time he got within arm's reach, he would play the wounded captive, then he would seize the man's head and plant his thumbs into both of his eye sockets, rip out the eyes, and, with enough force, gouge through to the brain. Then he would use the man's rifle to take out the remaining gunmen.

But as the man and his comrades approached Lee, a very strange thing happened.

They burst into flames. The blast of heat nearly knocked Lee back onto the ground. The sound of their screaming was even enough to make Lee's stomach turn as they stumbled around madly and collapsed on the ground in writhing heaps of flame. But over their screams, Lee heard someone call out his name, a voice he didn't recognize.

'Lee! Run!'

Lee didn't need any encouragement. The momentary reprieve from certain death boosted him enough to get to his feet and start staggering toward the nearest cover: jagged remains of a condo building, which was now just a few charred brick walls, but hopefully enough to stop a bullet and give Lee a long enough moment to assess his situation and perhaps come up with a plan to get himself out of there.

What about Angela and Abby and Sam? Lee had to survive first before he could worry about the others. And who was it who had called to him? It had been a man's voice. Lee made it to a waist-high brick wall and clambered over. He fell onto his back on the other side, found that too painful, and rolled onto his side. He looked around, didn't see anyone. Who the hell had called to him? And where were Angela and the kids?

He began processing what was happening around him. Nearby to him, he was hearing some sporadic pistol fire. It wasn't rapid, but it was close. It was also a smaller caliber. Farther away, Lee could hear the crack of more powerful weapons, probably rifles. The two appeared to be exchanging gunfire. Lee also noted that none of the gunfire seemed to be directed at his position.

He leaned up and peered over the top of the brick wall.

He was looking down a wide corridor that had once been a parking lot for the condos. On either side of the long parking lot were what remained of the rectangular two-story condos. There was a single condo building between Lee's position and the condo he'd been trapped in. He could see the window he'd snaked out of and it faced the parking lot. In the darkness of the condo, he'd become disoriented and hadn't realized what direction he'd been facing.

At the corner of the condominium building he'd just escaped from, four bodies were still burning, though they'd stopped rolling around. Behind them, Lee could see a group of men huddled behind a burned-out SUV, taking potshots at another building across the parking lot and closer to Lee's position.

Lee followed their fire and saw the muzzle flashes coming from the ground floor of one of the condos facing the parking lot. Then Lee watched as a young man with a red bandanna covering his face leaned out of the front door of the condo and hurled a bottle with a flaming tail. The bottle arced high and landed with a splash of fire, just on top of the SUV the gunmen were using for cover. The splash of flaming liquid rained down on the gunmen taking cover there and they immediately began trying to put themselves out.

The young man screamed something at whoever else was inside the condo and began sprinting for Lee's position. A second later, he was followed by Angela, Abby, Sam, and a second young man, also with a bandanna covering his face, this one blue. They moved together in a mass, undisciplined and panicked. The young man with the blue bandanna held a black revolver in one hand, what looked to Lee like an old .38 or .357 police-issue revolver. He took potshots as he ran, the rounds flying wildly downrange and impacting nowhere near his intended targets.

Red Bandanna vaulted over the wall and pulled Sam and then Abby over. Angela and Blue Bandanna followed.

As soon as they saw him, Sam and Abby both exclaimed in unison, 'Captain! We thought you were dead!'

'No time for reunions!' Red grabbed Lee by the arm and hauled him up to his feet. 'We need to get the fuck out of here!'

Lee craned his neck back at the burning wreckage. 'How many more?'

'We counted ten coming in,' Blue spoke up as he pushed the kids toward the back of the complex. 'I think we got six or seven of 'em.'

The group made quickly for the back of the complex. Lee observed that the entire complex appeared to be enclosed with the same wrought-iron fencing as the front was. It was about ten feet tall with spikes on top and Lee wasn't sure whether these kids expected him to climb it or not, but in his current condition, he thought he might disappoint them.

They hit the fence and started running along it. All six of them were out of breath when Lee saw what they were looking for. A section of the fence had been pulled away and there was an obvious footpath cutting through the brush on the other side. The two men in bandannas didn't bother to explain. They moved the group single file down the footpath, Lee and Red taking point.

Lee moved the best he could, but each step sent raking pain down his back and legs. The deep lacerations covered so much of his skin that he couldn't find a way to move that didn't feel like it was stretching the wounds apart. Everything began to feel alternately hot, then cold. He could feel the back of his shirt and pants beginning to cling to his skin, soaked with his blood. He was pretty sure he hadn't lost enough blood to cause him to pass out, but the pain was making him feel light-headed.

The two young men in bandannas – both perhaps in their early twenties – didn't appear very cautious, and Lee got the impression that they were more or less familiar with this territory and felt comfortable that it contained no threats. This made Lee feel only slightly better. It was obvious to him that the two of them weren't well trained, and their eagerness to put ground between the gunmen and themselves might be making them move faster than was prudent.

The footpath broke from thick brush into moderate woods and the group swung a hard right. The woods almost instantly cleared into what Lee thought was an old service road beneath some power lines. At the edge of the woods, there was a beat-up white pickup truck that Lee thought looked like it belonged in the desert with a couple Iraqi militants sitting in the back.

As soon as the group cleared the woods, an older man stepped out of the driver's side of the pickup with a pump shotgun in one hand. He held up a hand and they stopped moving toward the pickup. Lee got the distinct feeling that this man was in control.

'What the fuck is this?' he demanded.

Red let go of Lee and he and Blue approached the older man, speaking in low tones, though Lee could still hear what they were saying. As he listened, he watched some sparkling spots appear at the corners of his vision and he bent over, trying to keep blood in his brain and keep thinking clearly.

'Milo's guys attacked them. We couldn't just leave them.'

The older guy stared at Lee while he listened.

Red hung his head a bit. 'I mean . . . we don't have to take them back or anything, but we just couldn't leave them out there. You know what Milo does to women and children. And the dude's pretty fucked up, too.'

The old man shook his head and spoke in a harsh whisper. 'This is the third time you've put me in this position. We can't care for these people! We can barely take care of our own!' He stepped forward and addressed Lee and his group. 'Look, folks . . . my boys didn't want to see you guys die, so they risked their lives to save you. However, unfortunately, we can't take you back with us.'

Lee just looked at the older man. His tongue was stiff and dry and his scalp was tingling.

Angela tried to speak up. 'But—'

'Ma'am, we have no room for newcomers. We're over-crowded as it is, and we certainly don't have the supplies to take care of you. We're barely getting by ourselves. I know it sounds harsh, but I have to think of my group first.

Please understand – we would help if we could, but we can't.'

The older man turned back toward the pickup truck and spoke through clenched teeth. 'Give them your canteens and whatever food we brought.'

Lee cleared his throat and fought to think clearly. 'How many people do you have in your group?'

The older man stopped and turned. He eyed Lee up and down, looking unsure. 'That's none of your business.'

'Are you the leader of the group?' Lee countered.

The man crossed his arms. 'I speak for him.'

Lee smiled weakly. 'I'm pretty sure he'll want to meet me.'

NINETEEN

THE SURVIVORS

THE OLDER MAN JUST LAUGHED. 'Yeah, I'm pretty sure he won't.'

Lee laughed along with him, not because anything was funny, but because it was the exact opposite of what the older man was expecting. 'You always send your boys out to tangle with gangs of raiders with nothing but an eighties police-issue revolver and a couple of Molotov cocktails?'

The man's laughing tapered off and he got serious. 'We have plenty of weapons. Don't think we're not well defended.'

'Hmm.' Lee looked thoughtful. He continued to speak, thinking in the back of his mind that he hoped his words were making sense. 'Of course you would say that to me. I'm an outsider and you don't want to let on that ten guys with assault rifles could take over your entire operation. Don't worry, that's not us. But what do you have back at the base? A few shotguns? A few hunting rifles? Mix-and-match ammunition? Maybe a couple hundred rounds total?'

The man was silent now, his face made of stone.

Before the man could interrupt, Lee pressed on. 'You already admitted that you don't have any extra food or water, but I think maybe you don't have any at all, or at least not enough to get you more than a few weeks down the road. I figure you wouldn't be sending two outgunned men into a war zone unless things were pretty desperate.' Lee raised his eyebrows. 'Should I go on? Any medical supplies to speak of? Of course not. Who has medical supplies when you're just trying to find your next meal and not get killed or infected? Any basic communications systems? I think if you had them, your boys would have been using them to speak with you.'

'Just shut the fuck up,' the man said quietly. 'If you try to fuck with us, I will personally find you and rip your fucking heart out.'

Lee held up his hands and blinked to clear his rapidly fading vision. 'I'm not here to hurt anyone. I'm here to help. I can get you access to everything you need. Guns, ammo, food, water, medical supplies. You name it. But whether you accept my help or not is up to you. Me and my group will continue to survive like we have been, and eventually we will encounter a group of survivors that wants our help and they will graciously receive everything I have to offer. Too bad it won't be you guys.'

'Yeah.' The old man shook his head. 'Too bad. Look, I understand the desperate situation you find yourselves in, but I've heard people promise all kinds of things just to get some food and water.'

Lee could tell the older man was waffling on his decision or he wouldn't be defending it. 'Then don't give us anything. Blindfold us, tie us up, and don't even take us into your camp. Just let me speak with whoever is in charge. If he doesn't like what I have to say, you can kick us to the curb, and you didn't lose a thing.'

The man stared at Lee for a long time.

'Come on, Bill ...' Red, who had now removed his face covering, prodded. 'It can't hurt. And he needs to see Doc.'

Bill took another moment, just to make it clear that he had come to his decision on his own and not from the prodding of his underlings. 'Fine.' He pointed a thick finger at Lee. 'But you're all getting blindfolded and tied up until we figure out what's going on.'

Lee maintained consciousness for perhaps another two minutes. Getting blindfolded and tied up and placed in the back of the pickup truck was hazy. After that he was in a dark, nonsensical dreamland. He was on a roller coaster that wouldn't stop going down. It just kept plummeting and everyone on it was trying to get out. One by one, their safety harnesses failed and they went flying out of the coaster, screaming as they floated off into space. Eventually it was only Lee riding that lonely roller coaster to oblivion.

He woke up when the roller coaster slammed into the ground.

The pickup truck had hit a stiff bump and he'd banged his head on the bed of the truck. He could smell the rust and the dried leaves and dirt that caked the truck bed, but none of it made sense to him. Then he quickly lost consciousness again. In the brief moments when he was awake, he desperately tried to twist around to feel and make sure that the GPS device was still in his cargo pocket. He thought it was. But he wanted to put his hands on it. The pain of the cuts in his back made the twisting movement difficult, and he never quite succeeded in getting his hand in his pocket.

After the smell of the truck bed, the next thing Lee remembered was standing up.

He couldn't see anything. It was dark as midnight, but he could feel warm sun on his face. Someone was angry, but he was fairly certain they were not angry with him. He felt strong hands gripping his arms and holding him up. He was glad, because his legs felt rubbery, and he knew that if the hands were not there, he would fall.

He wondered if this was another dream.

'Jesus Christ, Bill!' the angry voice said. 'Did you have to blindfold them? This guy's half dead anyway. Doc! Doc!'

'Where the hell did he go?'

'He was right behind me.'

'Someone get Doc.'

'He's right here; he's right here.'

'Fuckin-A, Bill, did you do this?' It was a new voice, slightly higher than the others, but still a male voice, Lee thought.

'No. I think Milo's guys did it to him.'

Lee opened his mouth but his throat was dry and scratchy.

'What? You gotta speak up, buddy.'

'I just got scraped by nails ... Angela and Abby are ... dehydrated ... Sam too.'

Doc spoke again. 'Mikey, get the chick and the two kids into my triage room. And someone help me with this guy.' To Lee: 'Hey, buddy ... you say you got scratched by nails? Can you tell me how that happened?'

'Window,' Lee responded.

There was a brief moment of silence and Lee felt the hands pulling him forward. He tried to move his feet and found his knees weak. He was thankful for whoever was holding him up.

'Seriously,' Doc said to someone else. 'Can we take the fuckin' blindfold off? Are we done with this Guantanamo shit? Thank you.'

The world was suddenly very bright. Lee squinted. When his blurry vision cleared, he tried to focus on his surroundings for a moment and figure out where the hell he was. He could see that there was gravel under his feet. There were several large vehicles parked around him, a few beat-up old pickups like the one Bill had been in. Behind the vehicles, Lee could see some curious faces staring at him. He looked straight ahead and saw what appeared to be their destination: a steel shipping container. He also noticed that behind the shipping container were several others, and behind them, a large industrial building of some sort.

'So what happened to you?' Doc asked.

Lee turned to the sound of the voice and found a squirrelly-looking man peering up at him. The man was probably no more than 5' 6", and scrawny. He had natty-looking brown hair and, perched on a prominent hook nose, he wore a pair of glasses that bore some evidence of hard times: The lenses were both scratched and the frame was held together with duct tape on one side.

Someone spoke up for Lee. It was Red. 'He was trapped in one of the condos, so he kicked open a boarded window, but he could only get it partially open, so he had to squeeze through and the nails from the board scratched the shit out of him.'

'Ahh.' Doc peered around Lee and whoever was carrying him to view his back. 'Yeah, that's more than "scratched" and I hope to God they weren't rusty because I ain't got shit to give you if you develop tetanus.'

Lee just nodded.

With Doc leading them, Lee and Red, who was supporting him, turned the corner into the open end of the shipping container. Lee could see scant medical supplies, but he figured by the bloodstained sheets and the smell of disinfectant that this was a medical station. Angela, Abby, and Sam were sitting on a few crates and a woman, Lee guessed about college-age, was handing out bottles of water. The bottles were a mismatched collection and obviously had been refilled and used many times.

Red guided him to a bed with a stained sheet on it. 'Lay him on his left side,' Doc said. 'His left side ... his left side, Miller!'

'Workin' on it!' Red – aka Miller – snapped back. They lowered him into the bed on his left side. Lee kept squinting because the pain was now coming in long, fiery bursts that started in his side and lower back then radiated out. As soon as he rested his head on the mattress, he felt Doc pulling the ripped and bloody clothing away from his flesh and snipping through it with a pair of medical shears. The entire time he snipped away, he made disapproving noises. Lee assumed his injuries were worse than Doc had believed.

When Lee realized Doc was in the process of cutting through his pants, his hand shot out and touched his cargo pocket. He felt Doc jerk back. Lee thrust his hand into the pocket and felt the plastic casing of the GPS device. He wrapped his hand around it and removed it. The college-age girl tried to take it, but Lee wouldn't release his grip. 'No one touches this,' he mumbled under his breath.

With his clothes cut through and removed, Lee sat naked on the bed and felt chills coming on. He felt fleetingly embarrassed about being naked in front of strangers, and especially Angela and the kids, but mostly he wondered if Doc had the medical supplies necessary to patch him up. He couldn't imagine that the bleeding was so bad he could die from it, but he supposed infection was a good possibility.

'Jenny, I need you,' Doc called.

Lee opened his eyes long enough to see the college-age girl who had been tending to Angela and the kids come running over. Though she wasn't a real looker, she was just attractive enough for Lee to feel even more embarrassed that he was naked.

Doc spoke to her. 'Get me one of those towels, and I'm going to need some water for him. And when you get done with that I'm going to need my suturing kit.'

'Be right back,' she said, and twirled around to get what Doc requested.

To Lee, he spoke a little softer. 'Alright, here's the situation. Your scratches are more like lacerations. In a couple of places, they've cut into muscle tissue, so I'm kind of surprised you're able to stand upright. The good news is that I have the supplies to suture you up and hopefully keep you from getting infected. The bad news is that I don't have shit in the way of anesthetic, and it's gonna take me about an hour, maybe even two hours, to finish stitching you up. So the next two hours of your life will suck, but maybe you'll be lucky and pass out pretty soon.'

Lee heard Jenny return with the requested items.

'Before you pass out,' Doc continued, 'you should drink as much of this water as you can. You lost a lot of blood. Not enough to be concerned with, but you need to hydrate. I'll see if we can't get you some juice or something ... Jenny! Juice?'

Lee opened his eyes to see if Jenny was there, but she was out of his field of vision.

'Okay ... "no" on the juice. Sorry, buddy. We're just about tapped out of everything.'

Lee nodded and pressed his face into the mattress. 'Do what you gotta do.'

'Good man,' Doc encouraged.

Lee lay on his side while Doc cleaned the wounds. The young physician used a large syringe filled with sterile water to irrigate the wounds and clean out all the pieces of dirt that had been trapped there while Lee had evaded being shot to death. After a thorough cleaning, Doc patted the wounds dry. By then, Lee had finished his second bottle of water.

Lee felt the doctor's hands leave his back. Lee could hear him working with something behind his back, and he concluded it would be the sound of him threading sutures and getting ready to stitch Lee back up. From Lee's medical training, he knew that Doc would have to stitch the severed muscle tissue first, and then the skin. This was double the pain for Lee, but he shared Doc's hope that he would pass out before long.

Doc sighed behind him. 'Okay. You ready?'

Lee nodded once again and grabbed a fistful of white bedsheets.

Doc turned out to be right. Lee passed out in no time.

TWENTY

THE DEAL

WHEN LEE CAME TO, HE DIDN'T recall the details of his dreams, but they left him with an uneasy feeling that clogged his veins and sickened the pit of his stomach. His mind was full of flashed images of violence and gore and inhumanity. He could still feel the GPS device held tightly in his hands. Good. They hadn't taken it from him.

He opened his eyes and saw he was still lying on the bed in Doc's little medical trailer. He felt weak and shaky, but he lifted himself up onto one elbow so he could look around. The movement sent splitting pain across his back. It wasn't until Lee was sitting up that he realized someone was standing at the foot of his bed.

It was a broad man with a dark, bushy beard. He wore a dirty tank top and a pair of old woodland-pattern fatigues. What Lee thought looked like a Colt 1911 pistol hung in a leather shoulder holster under the man's left arm. The man with the beard stared at Lee for a long moment and then nodded.

'Can you stand?'

Lee didn't answer because he hadn't tried. He swung his legs out of the bed and prepared to heave himself up.

The man with the beard smiled. 'Don't get up. Doc said you need to rest. Just curious if you could stand.'

Lee relaxed back onto his elbow, trying not to grimace too much from the pain. 'Thanks for patching me up. I know resources are scarce.'

'They are indeed.' The bearded man grabbed a metal folding chair from a desk with a lit propane lamp burning on it that was the sole source of illumination in the cargo container. It wasn't until that moment that Lee realized it must be dark out. He wondered how long he'd slept. 'Name's long and Greek, so let's just stick with Bus. I'm kinda the de facto leader of this little operation.'

'Okay, Bus. Lee Harden.'

'Mmm-hmm.' Bus relaxed in the chair. 'I understand that the arrangement you had with Bill was that you wouldn't receive any care until you'd sold me on whatever you're trying to peddle. He didn't give me many details. And you and your group have also received the food, water, and medical care that we can offer, meager as it is. We've done more than keep up our end of the deal. So . . . what is it that you claim you can do for us?'

Lee rubbed his eyes and tried to clear his foggy mind so he could speak intelligently. 'Yeah . . . uh . . . '

Bus let out a big sigh. 'It's okay.' He sounded disappointed. 'We get this a lot lately. Food and water are hard to come by, so people will act like they have it just to seek refuge here when they really don't. Just come clean with me and you and your group can leave with our blessing.'

Lee managed a smile. 'Sir, I'm not running any con game on you for some sutures and a few bottles of water. What is it that your people need?'

Bus didn't answer immediately. He spoke slowly. 'I'm going to be frank with you, Mr. Harden. I have no reason to trust you. And explaining to you what we lack also tells you where we are weakest. That isn't information I will readily give out to strangers, and honestly, when you ask those questions, it makes me a little uncomfortable.'

Lee pursed his lips. 'I understand.'

'Perhaps if you can explain to me how you came across these alleged supplies, I would be more inclined to believe you. Because right now the thought of anyone having access to some sort of cache seems like a fairy tale.'

So Lee told him everything. He began by explaining his position as a member of Project Hometown, and what that entailed, and how he came to be in possession of several large caches that could supply a small army with everything from boots to bullets to bandages. He explained in detail that the caches were kept in underground bunkers, similar to the one he had come from, and that the access points for these bunkers were hidden, their hatches sealed and locked so that only someone with the proper clearance could find and access them. He left out the specifics of his GPS and the data it contained.

When he finished, Bus looked at him with eyebrows knit with concentration, arms crossed over his broad chest. Not entirely convinced, but considering the facts. Lee hoped that the details he had given would lend his story the ring of truth necessary to convince Bus to trust him.

Lee continued on. 'Bus, I've got a job to do. I know it's difficult to believe that the United States government still exists, albeit on a very small scale, but we're here to rebuild. I'm not asking anything of you. And you know you can't refuse what I have to offer. I know you don't want to trust a stranger, but you have to understand that this cannot go on. You and your group won't survive the winter, scavenging for scraps. We have to start rebuilding and we have to start now.'

Bus sat without moving, and his expression did not change.

Lee had finished talking. There was nothing further to say.

After a long pause, Bus finally let out a deep breath. 'Okay. How can we work this? What are you proposing?'

'Quid pro quo. I need you to answer some questions for me.'

Bus looked like he was in pain for a brief moment. 'Fine. Ask away.'

'First of all, where are we?'

'We call it Camp Ryder. We're in a Ryder truck factory right now. About three miles southwest of Angier.'

'How many people do you have living here?'

'Fifty-eight by my last count.' Bus sounded like he thought about that number quite often.

Lee considered for a brief moment. 'Okay. How many of those fifty-eight are capable of fighting?'

Bus made a raspberry. 'Twenty, if that.'

'What about guns?'

'A few deer rifles, couple hunting shotguns, and some pistols. Two of the pistols are .22, so they aren't much good for killing anything except small game. We take 'em hunting every once in a while.'

'I'm assuming ammunition is low?'

Bus nodded. 'That would be correct. And we have Molotov cocktails. We got lots of those made up. Found a recyclables truck last week with a shit-ton of glass bottles in it. It also had several gallons of diesel fuel, and none of our vehicles run on diesel, so we made the cocktails.'

Lee closed his eyes, trying to build a mental picture. 'Tell me about the building behind us, defense-wise.'

Bus leaned forward in his chair. 'Big cement building. Best we could find. Only two entry and exit points, besides the cargo bay doors, which we managed to weld shut. There's an electrified fence all around the perimeter of the compound, but our generators aren't big enough to power it. Still, it keeps out the infected.'

'But not a sane human who wants in.'

Bus shook his head. 'We patrol the fence line as often as we can, but we're undermanned, and even if we caught people breaking in, I'm not sure we'd have the firepower to stop them. Our basic plan is to hole ourselves inside the factory building. But even then we only have enough food and water stores to last us two or three days.'

'Has anyone attempted to attack you?'

'Not attack us.' Bus stroked his bushy beard. 'We've had a few curious people drive down the dirt road to our main gate who we've turned away with a few rifle rounds. But if someone was determined to get in, I doubt we could stop him.'

Lee opened his eyes. 'Have you blockaded the driveway?'

Bus looked confused. 'No . . . we use it.'

'You need to find another way in and out of the gate. The driveway's too obvious and you're going to continue to get visitors, and it also makes it easy for an attacking force. Couple trees across the roadway won't stop someone on foot, but it'll stop a vehicle for sure.'

Bus looked thoughtful. 'Bill and his scouts have been using the alley cut through the woods for the power lines to get through to the main road without being seen. I suppose everyone can use that.' Bus aimed his stare back at Lee. 'So where's all this going?'

'Just trying to get a feel for what we'll need.'

'You mean your supplies?' Bus snorted. 'We can worry about extra stuff later. Right now we need food, water, and guns. Medicine is a close fourth, although I'm sure Doc would disagree.'

Lee grimaced. 'Multiple trips at this point in time are a bit more of an endeavor than we should risk. You have to understand that my caches are local, but the way things are out there, a few miles might as well be a few hundred.'

Bus smiled humorlessly. 'You are using a lot of "we" statements. I'm getting the feeling that you're not just going to borrow one of our trucks and come back with a bumper crop of supplies.'

Lee looked Bus straight in the eye. 'With all due respect, my going out alone at this point in time would essentially be suicide. Forty-eight hours ago, you would not have heard those words come out of my mouth, but I've got a little more wisdom and a lot fewer weapons. I'm going to need a team to go with me.'

'Okay.' Bus bridged his fingers in front of his face and leaned forward, resting his elbows on his knees. 'I'm not saying that I'm cool with that, but let's say you get this "team." What happens then?'

'Well.' Lee took a breath. 'We'd need at least three of your vehicles, preferably the ones that can hold the most cargo, and two men for each vehicle at the very least – one to drive and one to gun if things get tight. We can probably pack enough supplies into three vehicles to last us through the winter ... hopefully.'

Bus sighed. 'Three vehicles, huh? Is this including medical supplies and guns and ammunition?'

'Food and water will take up a lot of space.' Lee rubbed his temples. 'So would ammunition. Food and water are number one, but I'm pretty sure I can fit a six-month supply into three vehicles. Then throw in some weapons, ammunition, and maybe a little ordnance, and some medical equipment ... yeah, we should be able to fit it in three. It'll be tight, though.'

'You realize I don't make the decisions all by myself, right?' Bus asked as he stood up.

'I take it you will propose this to a committee, then?' Lee felt a breeze seep into the cargo container and pulled the sheet up a little tighter.

'Pretty much.'

'If it's a committee we're talking about, let's go for five vehicles and three people per.'

Bus actually laughed. 'I thought I knew everyone who lived here, but apparently you've been here longer than I thought.'

Lee smiled and relaxed onto his side. 'You forget, Bus. I'm US Army. I know how things work in committee.'

Bus turned around and walked out. Over his shoulder, he said, 'Rest up, Captain,' and then turned the corner and exited the cargo container. As he left, Jenny and Angela filed in. Jenny was holding a tray with another bottle of water and a plastic bowl. She set the tray down in front of Lee. The bowl contained what looked like rice and black beans.

Jenny smiled. 'Doc's orders: gotta get some food and water in you.'

Lee accepted the tray with a nod. 'Thank you for helping us. You and your group have been more than kind to us already.'

'Well.' Jenny helped Lee sit up in his bed and checked the bandages on his back. 'We keep you alive, you keep us alive ... that's the plan, anyway.'

Angela sat at the edge of Lee's bed. Her bloodstained and filthy clothes were gone and she now wore an old T-shirt and a pair of cargo shorts. Both looked big for her, but they were clean. She also looked like she'd been able to wash up, and she looked much better. It was amazing what simple hygiene could do for morale.

Lee spoke around bites of rice and beans. 'Looks like you got that shower you wanted.'

Angela smiled. 'Bucket of rainwater and a piece of a soap bar: the next best thing.'

Jenny excused herself and reiterated her desire for Lee to rest. Lee promised he would sleep more. To Angela, he asked what time it was and discovered it was about nine thirty PM.

'How are Sam and Abby?' Lee asked.

Angela shrugged noncommittally.

'Did they get food and water?'

'Yes. Jenny gave them plenty of water and a little bit of food. Sam ate fine, but Abby wasn't feeling well.'

Lee could see worry tightening Angela's face. 'I'm sure she's fine.' Angela nodded but Lee could see tears in her eyes and she bit her bottom lip to keep it from trembling. Lee leaned forward and touched her arm. 'It's not uncommon for dehydrated people to feel ill after drinking or eating.'

'It's not that.' Angela shook her head, looking like she was trying to regain her composure with a sigh and a skyward gaze. 'She's just . . . changed so much. If you'd have seen her a month ago, you wouldn't believe it was the same person. She's just gone through so much in such a small amount of time . . . ' She trailed off.

Lee let a long moment of silence pass before speaking. 'We've all changed, Angela. No one comes out the other side of something like this the same as she went into it. We're surviving through something that none of us expected. But we're surviving. And that's what counts.'

Angela didn't respond. She buried her face in her hands, looking ashamed of her tears, but Lee could see her shoulders rock slightly with sobs as they came and went, like waves buffeting a shore. Finally, she wiped her face and looked at Lee with red-rimmed eyes.

'Sorry. You're right. And we have it better than most.'

Lee nodded. 'We'll make it.'

Angela stood up. She turned to leave, but stopped and looked at Lee. 'Honestly, do you think we'll survive?'

Lee met her stare unflinchingly, though he took a second to consider the question before answering. Did he really think they had a chance? The survivability of the plague was almost nil. The projections for human casualties that he'd received in his mission brief were what could only be described as biblical. Did he truly believe that he and some survivors could turn the tide of the infection, could fight back against brutal nature?

He nodded. 'It's going to be a tough road, but we'll make it.'

Angela accepted Lee's foretelling with a weak smile and left him to his meal. Whether she really believed it or accepted it simply because it was more pleasant to believe in, Lee didn't know. For that matter, he had to ask the same question of himself.

He finished his rice and beans and his bottle of water.

The food felt like a brick in his stomach, but the water helped soften it. He was still dehydrated, but at least he was recovering. He switched sides and lay down, careful not to pull at his stitches or mess up his dressings. He stared at the corrugated steel wall across from him and tried to construct plans that would help him and the Camp Ryder group survive, but he was tired and his thinking was muddy.

Eventually he fell into a dark sleep. It was full of sounds but he couldn't see, like he was staring into a black hole but could hear everything around him. He heard the roar of an unstoppable fire and the cries for help of every victim it consumed. The cries were at first distinguishable from one another, but they steadily grew more numerous until they became one single, sustained note of panic and excruciating pain. The maddening sound of screaming turned into the throaty screech of the infected, and Lee thought to his dreamself, *Who are the real victims in all of this? The infected or the survivors?*

Gunfire startled him awake. His dreams had become reality.

extras

An Empty Soul

a Remaining novella

also by D. J. Molles

CHAPTER 1

The soldier behind the megaphone blinked away sweat and took a loud, amplified breath. When he spoke, it was deliberate and slow, the sound of his voice taking on the muffled, squawky quality of any loudspeaker announcement.

'Folks, we cannot fit everyone on the bus with everything they're carrying.' A very thin layer of patience was still intact. 'We only have room for you to take one bag. That's one bag per person. If you can't fit it into that one bag, you have to leave it behind. Also, there're no firearms on the bus. If you have any firearms with you, please hand them over to the soldiers standing next to the big green boxes and we'll try to make sure everything is returned to you at a later date.'

Clyde Bealey stood on hot, cracked concrete, crammed in with everyone else. Hundreds of scared, sweating people. Above them, the sky was bright and cloudless. The sun merciless. All the tiny muscles in his face ached from squinting so long against it. Under its broil, the blacktop shimmered and heated the soles of his dock shoes to the point of discomfort. Wearing them without socks seemed like a bad idea now. His cotton polo shirt hung damp on his shoulders. One stubborn strand of his longish blond hair kept meandering over to the center of his forehead, routing drops of sweat right onto the bridge of his nose, where they caused his thick glasses to slide out of place.

He felt sick to his stomach.

It never happens on a cloudy day, he thought. *Bad things always happen on sunny days.*

He had watched the news. He knew what was out there. As did everyone else standing in that crowded parking lot. They knew it academically, on a small, muted scale. They'd watched the madness in other, poorer countries, and they'd seen it spread. And the whole time they had the attitude of, *That's so tragic for those people over there.*

But then it was stateside. And then it was a few cities away. And now they were standing here, scared to death, thinking of all the videos they had watched on their televisions and laptops, and wondering how the great and mighty United States government could let this happen to them.

The soldier pushed on. 'If you need to rearrange your belongings, please step to the side and make room for others to pass by. You don't have to worry about losing your place. We've got enough buses for everyone. You won't be left behind. Just keep making your way forward in an orderly fashion and comply with the soldiers as they search you and your bags.'

The soldier with the megaphone stood in the bed of a Humvee, painted tan to mismatch every other piece of military equipment around that was painted green. They were gathered in the middle of a high school parking lot. Everything around them had the usual sandy-looking dilapidation that went hand-in-hand with towns along the coast. The wide-open expanse of cement was fissured and potholed. Water stood in large puddles from last night's rain.

There were perhaps three hundred people in the parking lot, and still more were coming in. As the crowd grew, so did the sense that panic was resting just underneath the surface of everyone's minds. When the crowd had been small, there had been the sense that they were only the silly 'paranoid ones.' The sense that everyone else was more levelheaded and didn't believe it was necessary to evacuate to FEMA camps.

Now, as the crowd began to press in, the mood changed. It was clear that they were not the paranoid ones. It was clear that everyone was sharing the same fears. And a shared fear is made real, and can no longer be rationalized away.

The cars that everyone had driven were clustered up around the high school parking lot and completely jammed the surrounding roads. The only path that remained open was one marked by caution tape and guarded zealously by soldiers. It led the buses through the packed-in vehicles and out to the only lane of Highway 55 that remained open. There, they would step on the gas, the engines roaring like they were airliners heading down the tarmac, and they would haul ass to the FEMA camp at New Bern.

Still, people were trickling in, having parked blocks away from the school and hiked in, lugging all their precious things that the sweat-soaked soldiers would soon tell them they couldn't have. There were small hills of personal effects that had been left behind. Soldiers walked among the piles, dressed in their gray and tan digital camouflage, wet rings around their collars and armpits.

Clyde watched them and realized that none of them wore helmets or body armor. Most of them had rifles strapped to their shoulders. But Clyde didn't think they were loaded. He didn't know much about guns, but he thought these ones should have had big clips sticking out of them. And he couldn't see a single rifle that had one. Some of the soldiers who stood at the big green crates full of confiscated weaponry had pistols strapped to them that looked like they were loaded, but that was it.

Strangely, it gave Clyde comfort.

After all, if the US Army didn't think it was serious enough to give their soldiers ammunition, then surely it wasn't that dangerous, right?

A hand gripped Clyde's arm. The heat and sweatiness of it annoyed him briefly. He looked down and found Haley looking up at him, brown hair frizzed on top, matted underneath. Her cheeks flushed with heat. Eyes sharp and clear blue.

The two of them were polar opposites. The kind of relationship that he knew his friends talked about behind his back, secretly betting against them. Clyde and Haley were like people from different countries. He was upper-class Richmond, Virginia. She was lower-class Farmville, North Carolina – she disliked even saying the name of her hometown around Clyde's friends because she knew the name alone made them laugh inwardly. As though only rubes could be produced by a place with such a name.

Clyde's friends were not the only doubters. His family bordered on hostility. His sister had essentially avoided Haley from day one. And when he had announced to them that he was going to propose to Haley, his father had just quirked a single eyebrow, and his mother had cried bitter tears of disappointment.

But his was not the only family that disliked the marriage. Haley's family was blue-collar to the bone. Her dad was a second-generation farmer. One of her brothers was a plumber, and the other couldn't hold a job, because he was in and out of jail.

To these three men, Clyde was a strange little man. It was a mark against him that he knew more about stock portfolios than corn growing. They balked that he had never hunted before. To them, he was an 'upper-cruster,' a 'rich guy,' and sometimes even a 'silver spoon motherfucker.' But most often, they just referred to him with a mumbled, 'Pussy.'

Haley was no country bumpkin. She was not only book smart, but she had street smarts that he lacked. And what she had learned, she had learned of her own desire, and not due to family obligations or stipulations for accessing trust funds. She was beautiful, where Clyde was awkward. She was the princess of her town, and he was some gawky foreigner come to steal her away.

And while she took the snobbery of his family with grace, the disrespect from her father and brothers grated on him immensely. Right off the bat, he had been surprised that they would view him as less than a man. Incapable. Effeminate. And certainly not worthy of Haley – which was the general opinion of most of the Farmville population.

When he was around her family, he acted differently. Like a bird ruffling its feathers, trying to make itself look bigger and stronger. Haley would tell him to quit acting like an asshole, but he couldn't help himself. Silver-spoon upbringing or not, he still felt like he always had something to prove to them.

And to Haley.

And there in that parking lot, smashed in with a bunch of strangers, the feeling of being incapable was stronger than ever before. Strong enough to set his heart racing when he saw how Haley looked at him, her eyebrows up like she was expecting him to answer something. But he wasn't sure what he was supposed to answer. He looked down to her belly, prominently showing all thirty weeks of its growth so far.

'You okay?'

'I'm fine.' Her lips twitched, showing some irritation. 'Did you hear me?'

He dabbed his mouth on the shoulder of his T-shirt. 'Did you say something?'

Haley shoved off of his arm and ran her hands nervously over her midsection as she looked down at their belongings. 'What are we gonna do with all of this shit, Clyde?'

He looked down at his feet.

In addition to the old hiking pack he wore, they had a giant suitcase, plus a smaller duffel that hung on Haley's shoulder. They'd packed these bags full of things they thought they would need. Money, jewelry, the paperwork that made up their life. Their college degrees. Their financial statements. The hard drive from their computer. Even their wedding album. He'd packed like you might for an incoming hurricane, taking all the things that you didn't want washed away.

He rubbed his forehead, feeling overwhelmed. Everything had happened so fast. He hadn't planned on leaving. He'd sat in front of his TV at night, like everyone else, and he'd watched the news about what was going on around the country. He'd pulled up the Internet and read articles and watched terrifying, grainy videos that people had taken with their cell-phone cameras. And it all just seemed like some big opera going on in a place called *elsewhere*. But then it had happened here. Someone got sick. And then someone in another town got sick. And those two turned into ten, and those ten turned into a hundred.

And his response had been to go to work the following morning with a surgical mask over his face. Like all those Japanese people during the SARS outbreak. But then there were big green army vehicles rolling through the streets and soldiers on megaphones just like the one on the back of the Humvee, riding through their neighborhoods and telling them that there was a mandatory 'containment.' And from that point they had four hours to pack their shit and get to Pamlico County High School, where they would be bused to the FEMA camp at New Bern.

Four hours to look at your life and decide what came with you and what was left behind.

How do you do that? How do you decide what you need in four hours?

Not thinking straight under stress – Haley's brothers would roll their eyes and tell him to man up.

The news had reiterated the evacuation order, though they continued to call it a 'containment' rather than an evacuation. Everyone was being moved into FEMA camps that they called 'containment zones,' where experts on virology and epidemiology could make sure no one was catching the plague. Trying to keep it from spreading any farther.

It all smacked of a last-ditch effort.

He shucked off his backpack and dropped it at his feet. He bent over the suitcase and unzipped it. When he opened it, he stared at clothing, sentimental keepsakes, knick-knacks, heirlooms. Stuff like his father's pocket watch. Her mother's ceramic dolls. He stared down at the mess of items, shaking his head.

'We didn't pack any food or water,' he mumbled to himself.

Haley fanned herself. 'Do you think we should have? I mean ... won't they have that stuff at the camp?'

He looked up, saw one of the big yellow buses rolling out, crammed full of passengers so that he couldn't see through one bank of windows and out the other. The tinting of the windows darkened their faces. They stared out at the people who were left, almost with pity. Like theirs was the last bus and everyone else was doomed.

He swallowed. Already felt thirsty. 'Yeah. They'll have food and water there.'

Haley touched his arm again. 'This isn't going to last long, is it?'

'Not long,' he said, but wasn't so sure. 'A month at the most?'

Her eyes widened. 'A month?'

'I don't know. Maybe not even that long.'

Tears were in her eyes. 'Clyde! I am not giving birth in a goddamned FEMA camp!'

'Babe, you're not due until August.'

'What if the baby comes early?' she hissed. She began breathing heavily, looking down at their stuff. 'We can't take all of this shit. We're gonna fucking lose it all! They're not gonna let us take it and we're gonna lose everything. We should have left it at the fucking house!'

Haley's casual foul language had actually been something that he liked about her. A separation from the stodgy, country-club attitudes of his parents and everything he'd grown up around. She was someone who didn't really fit into boating clubs and Ivy League colleges, and he found it endearing, even if his mother did not. But here was the other side of that coin, where her words prickled like desperation and made him uncomfortable.

'You want me to leave it in the car?' he asked.

She wiped her eyes, took a few breaths. 'I'm sorry. I'm sorry.' She plucked at the wet sections of her shirt that were clinging to her. 'I'm not mad at you, honey. I just have a lot going on right now. It's okay.' She closed her eyes. 'I'm sure this will work out. This *will* work out. It's gonna work out. It's gonna be okay.'

He clenched his jaw. He needed to step up here. Figure something out. Take the stress off of Haley. 'Alright. Let's just calm down and think logically here. I'm sure this is just the governor covering his ass. It'll be over in a week or two. We'll have food and water and beds at the FEMA camp. It won't be comfortable, but it's not like we can't come back for our stuff, right?'

She nodded, a little hesitant.

'Alright.' He bent over and started zipping up the suit-case. 'I'm just gonna take this back to the car . . .'

He was drowned out very suddenly by the noise of two helicopters roaring over their heads, flying low. The down-draft of the rotors whipped up dust and debris. Bits and pieces of those abandoned piles of people's belongings tumbled down and blew away like they were caught in tornado winds.

Clyde instinctively ducked and Haley grabbed his arm

again, looking up into the sky as they watched the two heli-copters grow rapidly smaller, the sudden and ear-shattering roar fading fast. Clyde looked around, his mouth hanging open. He found the same expression on nearly everyone else's faces, including the soldiers.

'The fuck was that about?' one of them griped.

Everyone watched the two helicopters disappear behind a wall of trees that blocked their view. They could no longer see them, but they could still hear them. *Still within a mile of the school*, Clyde thought. The sound of the rotors changed, it seemed. Became more staccato. Clyde pictured them pulling up into a hover.

Then there was another noise. One that Clyde had never heard before, but it was still unmistakable. Heavy. Rapid. Percussive.

The civilians stood motionless, as though entranced.

The soldiers began to move quickly, like ants disturbed.

'They're shooting at something,' one of them said. 'Sarge! You hear them shooting?'

The soldier with the megaphone leaned over and spoke rapidly to another. Clyde watched them, feeling his stomach fluttering. That kind of panicked feeling you get when you don't have a clue what's going on, but you know that it's very, very bad.

'Honey.' Haley squeezed his arm so that it hurt. 'What's going on?'

'I don't know,' he said, still watching.

The soldier with the megaphone seemed to be higher-ranking, and Clyde assumed he was giving orders. The soldier who took those orders turned and began waving to the others. 'LT says to load up!' he called.

The crowd began to stir.

A murmur of worried conversation quickly grew to shouting.

Someone made a run for the boxes full of confiscated weaponry and was thrown to the ground by two soldiers. A barrage of yelled questions was directed to the soldier with the megaphone, but he just stood there, wiping sweat from his eyebrows and staring back at everyone like he wished he were anywhere else on Earth.

'Clyde?' Haley said, her voice quaking. 'I don't like this.'

Clyde's own heart was pressing on the inside of his breastbone. He couldn't really figure out what to say back. He wanted to tell her that it was going to be all right, but he didn't know that it was. He didn't know if this was normal. It sure as hell didn't seem normal.

Should he be scared?

Should he still be standing there?

The soldiers at the front of the line weren't searching the bags anymore. They were just pushing people through. Shoving them onto buses. The line was flowing forward, faster now, but there were still probably a hundred people ahead of them. Clyde began shuffling the giant suitcase along with them, unsure of what to do with it.

He looked at Haley. 'You think I have time to take the suitcase back to the car?'

Haley shook her head vehemently. 'No. Just stay here. I don't want to get separated.'

'Honey, it's our entire lives in there.'

'I swear to God, Clyde, if you leave me I will kill you.'

'Alright. I'm right here. Calm down.'

'Don't tell me to calm down!' Haley raked hair out of her face.

Haley sulked and Clyde kept shuffling them forward,

teeth grinding together, shaking his head and feeling the heat welling around him, stuffy and uncomfortable. A few soldiers, rifles loaded now, ran through the crowded parking lot in the same direction that the helicopters had disappeared into.

At the head of the line of civilians, people kept climbing onto the bus until it was as crammed full as the last one, and then it began to roll and was immediately replaced with another, empty bus.

'Shit . . .' Clyde looked at the crowd. They were not so far behind now. He bent over the suitcase and ripped it open, even as he kept scooting it forward across the asphalt. He dove his arms inside and began grabbing things out – wasn't even really paying attention to what they were – and he began stuffing them into his backpack. He got a handful of social security cards and birth certificates and their marriage license. Then he tried to get their wedding album but couldn't quite squeeze it into his backpack.

'It's not gonna fit, Clyde.'

'No, I can get it in there.'

'It's just stuff!'

Clyde let out a frustrated noise and gave up trying to squeeze the wedding album into his pack. He dropped it back into the suitcase. 'There's more important stuff in the suitcase than there is in your duffel. We can just get rid of your duffel.'

'Sir!'

Clyde glanced up, found a soldier standing there shaking his head.

'You can't take that suitcase.'

'No, we were going to drop her duffel and keep the suitcase.'

'You still can't take that suitcase.'

'But the other guy said one bag per person.'

The soldier raised his voice. 'That suitcase is too big.'

Clyde felt the crowd pushing him out of the way as they moved toward the bus, skipping him in line. But he didn't think about it at that moment. Just kept thinking about the suitcase full of things he didn't want to lose. He stared at the soldier in front of him. Clyde could feel his frustration reaching a boiling point. 'They said one bag per person! My bag and this suitcase for the two of us! I can't just throw away everything that's in here!'

Haley grabbed his arm. 'Just leave it, Clyde!'

The soldier just kept shaking his head. 'You can't take the fucking suitcase.'

Clyde stood there, Haley trying to drag him away by his arm. 'This is bullshit!' he proclaimed and felt a wash of adrenaline at confronting the soldier. Maybe he should have just cooperated and stayed in line like the soldier with the megaphone had told them . . .

Someone screamed.

But it sounded wrong. Muffled. Warped. Throaty. Like an animal, but he could tell somehow from the pitch and timbre that it was a person. A dreadful noise. A screech like the sound a madman makes when he has fallen into some excited delirium. And it was not inside the parking lot, but coming from somewhere in the woods.

The soldier no longer seemed concerned with Clyde's suitcase.

'What the hell was that?' Clyde said, trying to keep the tremor out of his voice.

The soldier had unslung his rifle. 'Just get the fuck back, okay?' Then it seemed like Clyde no longer existed, and the soldier began scanning the crowd. 'Sarge! Hey, Sarge! You hear that shit?'

'Clyde, come on!' Haley pulled him toward the bus.

There were three people ahead of them.

Clyde hesitated, unsure what to do.

Grab the suitcase and make a run for it, or comply with the soldier and go without it?

With two people in front of them and Clyde still vacillating, the doors to the bus slammed shut. A soldier smacked the side of the bus, yelling, 'Get 'em the fuck out of here!' Then the bus growled and rolled down the narrow path to Highway 55, and Clyde realized there was not another bus there to take its place.

CHAPTER 2

Clyde stood, dumbfounded. The bus tilted awkwardly as it made the turn onto Highway 55. Clyde and Haley and the other two people ahead of them just stood there, still holding their bags, watching it go.

That was my bus, Clyde thought dumbly.

Another screech, this one coming from a different direction.

'Hey!' Haley yelled at a passing soldier. 'Is there gonna be another bus?'

The soldier didn't even look at her. He had his rifle in his hand and he started jogging to the north side of the high school. The one with the megaphone marched past and Haley tried to reach out and grab him, but he dodged her arm, looked pissed, then glanced over their heads and started shouting orders to someone Clyde couldn't see.

'Get these people inside the gymnasium! Lock the doors and gimme a full three-sixty around it!' Then he was running to the north side of the high school along with all the other soldiers. A Humvee went past, a soldier in the turret, racking back the big heavy bolt on the machine gun.

The crowd started moving. Like a herd. Like frightened cattle. Clyde wasn't even sure if they were moving toward the gymnasium. There were soldiers pointing in different directions, and the crowd seemed to be moving in none of them.

He reached out and took Haley's hand. Her eyes were wide with fear, and he knew his were the same. 'Stay with me,' he said, and he clutched her flesh like any separation would kill them both. 'Stay with me.'

'We should go!' she said. 'We should run!'

The screeching noise again, but this time from several directions. One after the other.

Like wolves calling to each other on the hunt.

He craned his neck and tried to see over the heads and faces of the panicked crowd around him as they surged clumsily on. He could just make out the gray and tan uniforms of the soldiers and their black rifles. When he'd first seen them at the high school, it was so surprising that it seemed like there were dozens of them. Now, looking at them, he realized it was only a small squad. Maybe ten men.

Not enough, he thought. *It's not enough.*

He couldn't keep dragging the suitcase along with him. He let it go. Behind him, someone tripped and fell over it. He didn't stop, and neither did anyone else. The megaphone was blaring now, squelching on its own sounds, and Clyde could hear the soldier's voice cracking: 'Stay back, or you will be fired on!'

And then, gunfire.

Clyde squeezed Haley's hand harder. 'Run! Run!'

The school gymnasium was forgotten, if anyone had even intended to go to it in the first place. The gunfire sent a panic through the crowd. Everyone began running for the road, breaking for the gridlock of cars that surrounded the school. Like maybe they thought they might all hop into their cars and drive away.

Haley dropped the duffel, and he watched it tumble onto the ground, little odds and ends flying out of the side pockets – toiletries and a paperback book. It suddenly seemed ridiculous to him, watching the items that he'd packed. Like they were about to hop on a fucking flight. Like this was an overnight business trip.

He watched his toothbrush skitter across the pavement beside them, like it was trying to keep up. He watched it, and he wondered, and he knew, all at once, that he had been horribly, dreadfully wrong. He had been incapable of grasping the situation. He had not been able to think clearly and now Haley would see it. She would see that he was just lost and scared. That he was out of his depth.

The crowd hit the cars and dissipated like a wave smashing on rocks. They weaved in and out of the cars. None of them was thinking, and Clyde was no exception. He was just running, mind lost in a panicked loop: *You weren't ready. Don't make Haley pay for it.*

They reached their car – maybe that had been his destination all along. They were jammed in on all sides by vehicles, but he fumbled the keys out of his pocket anyway, Haley standing next to him, breath going in and out of her in trembling gasps. Her eyes were stretched and scared and looking north past the school.

His hands were shaking so badly, he could hardly find the car key on his ring.

'Clyde . . .'

'What?'

She tugged at him, and when he looked up, she was staring at the school still, and he followed her gaze. From their vantage point, he could not see the north side of the school, but he could still hear the gunfire. It was less of a fusillade now and more simply sporadic shooting. And among the pops and cracks of gunfire, they could hear the screeching and the barking of *them*, too numerous to distinguish the numbers.

And men screaming in fear and pain.

Haley slapped his shoulder repeatedly. 'Come on, baby! Come on! Unlock the car!'

'I'm trying ... I'm trying ...' He went through the keys twice, like he was blind. He knew he'd passed up the car keys, but he couldn't seem to see them or register when his fingers touched them. He panicked, thinking maybe they had fallen off.

There was the roar of an engine.

He looked up, fingers frozen. A Humvee hauled down the narrow path they'd left open for the buses. There was a soldier in the turret, but he was struggling to get the gun turned around. The big tan vehicle swerved and sideswiped a parked car. The soldier in the turret tumbled out, but the Humvee just kept on going. Clyde couldn't see the soldier amid all the jammed-in vehicles, but he could see the shapes of three people, dressed in civilian clothing. They sprinted after the fleeing Humvee, and the way they ran did not seem normal.

Oh my God oh my God ... it's happening ...

The soldier who had fallen out hobbled unsteadily to his feet. He turned and yelled at the three people who were running at him, but if they even heard him or registered what he was saying, they gave no sign. The first one collided with him – a small, balding man in a tan suit – and the other two followed them to the ground as the mass of struggling limbs fell out of view.

Clyde gulped air. He looked down and found the car keys clutched between his fingers, and he shoved them into the lock and twisted violently. The little knobs just inside the car window popped up and he ripped the door open.

A wave of heat boiled out of the car, causing him to squint

and his rapid breathing to seize in his chest. He took Haley and shoved her into the backseat, knowing damn well they were not going to be able to drive out of there, seeming to realize for the first time how monumentally stupid it had been to run for the car. As Haley clambered in, he looked out over the tops of the cars again and could see more figures sprinting through the tightly packed vehicles. They moved with shocking agility, climbing over the tops of them, making strange hooting and barking sounds.

'Clyde!' Haley screamed. 'Get the fuck in here!'

He dove in, slamming the door behind him as he did, and slapping the locks down.

Between the front seats and out the windshield, Clyde could see glimpses of them drawing rapidly closer. He sprawled himself over Haley and forced her to lie down. 'Put your head down!' he said, and lay flat alongside her, their faces pressed into the seat cushions. 'Don't look up,' he said in a harsh whisper. 'Don't say anything.'

Haley's voice shook. 'Did you lock the doors?'

'Yes! Be quiet!'

The air stifled them like a sauna, hot and heavy. The stink of their sweat. The smell of their huffing, fearful breaths mixing in the air, humidifying it. Clyde dared not close his eyes, though he wanted to shut out the world. He could feel the sweat trickling across his forehead, didn't dare move to wipe it away. It meandered along his eyebrows, dripped into his eyes. He could feel his hands and arms growing slick with it. The backpack was still heavy on his shoulders.

This can't be happening. This can't be happening. This isn't real.

'Baby, what's going on?' Haley whispered.

'Shh.'

A woman ran up to the side of their car and began pounding on the window. Clyde felt fear seize his heart in his chest, but then the woman spoke, yelled at them, horrifyingly loud: 'Please! Open the door! Let me in! Let me in, you motherfucker!'

She stood at the door where Clyde's feet were pressed, and he looked down along the line of his own body and he didn't turn his head, but his eyes latched onto hers and he moved his mouth without sound: *Go away!*

'You sonofabitch! Open the fucking door!'

He mumbled what was perhaps a prayer: 'Please go away. Please go away. Please go away.'

'Help . . . !'

Something hit her. Tackled her to the ground. Clyde flinched and squeezed his eyes shut. Knew that this was a nightmare. Knew that none of this was possible, but for some goddamned reason he couldn't wake up. He kept closing his eyes and opening them, hoping to wake up in his own bed, bathed in sweat, flooded with relief. But every time he opened his eyes it was just the hot, stuffy interior of the Volvo.

Another figure dove onto the ground, just behind the first, and Clyde could feel their car rocking as a struggle occurred against the side of it. The noises of the woman were not screams or shouts anymore but hoarse, breathless sounds of terror. And they were drowned out by something else. By growling. By the muffled pop of breaking bones. By the wet rending of flesh.

And whatever was outside of that door, only inches from Clyde, it spoke strangled, malformed words. And Clyde could hear what it was saying, even as the desperate woman's thrashing died away. 'Where is it?' it shouted, as though it were searching *through* the woman for something. 'Where is it? Where is it?'

Below him, smashed into the backseat, Haley's entire body shook as she sobbed quietly.

Clyde didn't know what to do. His mind was white-hot with panic, and at the same time, almost lost and spaced-out in the otherworldliness of it all. Things that could not possibly be happening were happening to him right now, and it was a horrific sensation that felt like a black hole in his gut. That thin door was all that separated him from being ripped apart, just like he'd seen in blurry images on the news. And he knew it was happening here. It was happening here like it had happened everywhere else, even though he wasn't ready.

It can't happen here, he thought.

But it was.

It was happening whether he was able to wrap his brain around it or not.

The struggle finally died, but the mad creatures outside the door did not move on. It seemed they were caught in a frenzy. And Clyde watched, peeking over his shoulder and feeling his bladder spasming as though he might wet himself. He could see their arms, their hands like gnarled claws, rising and falling and ripping at that poor, stupid woman on the ground, splashing blood and gristle onto the windows so that he looked away and felt faint.

Haley was nearly in hysterics. Her eyes were wider than he'd ever seen them, unblinking. Her chest was hitching rapidly, almost wheezing like she couldn't catch her breath. It seemed incredibly loud to Clyde and he reached up and put a hand over her mouth, trying to stifle the noise. It was like he didn't exist to her in that moment. She just kept staring at the gore on the window, and his hand over her mouth did not seem to register with her.

There was no end to it. The sounds continued, the splashing blood continued. There was no relief from it, and if it lasted a full minute, it may as well have been eternity. Lying there, half on top of his wife, his hand clamped over her mouth to keep her quiet while he waited for those mad things to go away, *please, dear God, go away*!

He could hear other people screaming now. The sounds of it were far away, and he seized on that desperately. Maybe they were moving farther away. Maybe he wouldn't be stuck in this car forever. Maybe the madmen outside of his car would go away and he and Haley would be able to get out of there.

For the first time, he thought more than one step ahead. They would not be able to take the car. If they got out of the car, they would be exposed. They would have to go someplace. But where? Should he try to make a run for the school gym, where the soldiers had told them to go? He couldn't think of a reason why that was a good idea, and the concept of going back toward the school just seemed ridiculous.

Then he thought about their home, maybe six or seven miles north of where they were. They could make it on foot. They could get there before it got dark, no problem. But what was there? The place that he had called home now seemed like some forgotten rock floating out in space. Behind enemy lines. He didn't picture it now with its manicured lawn and well-pruned natural areas, or the colorful little windmills that Haley liked to put out near the azalea bushes. He pictured it surrounded by mobs of madmen. Hostile and comfortless.

But they could not stay in the car. They would bake to death if they stayed inside.

Haley worked her mouth out from under Clyde's hand. 'I think they're gone,' she whispered.

Clyde just lay there for another moment, listening. Still in the background, he could hear the sounds of terror that made his stomach weak and sick. But outside the car, there was silence. The heat baked them, the sun coming in the windows. Every bit of him was sheened in oily sweat but somehow he was still shivering, his body covered in goose-flesh. He leaned up, craned his head toward the window.

Haley covered her eyes with her hands. 'I don't want to see it, Clyde.'

The higher he pushed himself up off the seat, the more he could see of the scene outside the window. The narrow space between the cars was bathed and spackled in it, and his pulse became rapid and weak and he could feel his stomach convulsing, his mouth watering along the sides, the saliva pooling around his tongue. But he couldn't stop looking at it.

It doesn't look real, he thought.

And then he vomited onto the floorboard of the car.

Haley didn't seem to react to this. She just turned away from him and wept.

When he had recovered enough of himself to look around and make sure the coast was clear, he wiped his mouth and leaned over his wife's body, grabbing the door handle on the passenger side, farthest away from the mess of the woman who should have just kept on running. He didn't open the door just yet.

I killed her, Clyde told himself. *I killed her by not letting her in*.

Haley wouldn't look at him. Wouldn't pull her hands away from her face. He reached up and pulled them away for her, forced her face to look at him so that they were inches apart. He could see her nose curl at the smell of the vomit on his breath.

'I'm gonna open this door,' he said, still speaking quietly. 'And then we're going to run. We're going to run for that patch of woods, right there. And when we get there we are going to lie down and we are going to stay quiet.'

Haley looked mystified. 'How long?'

'Until they're gone.'

'What if they come back?'

Clyde had no idea. 'We'll figure it out. But we can't stay in here.'

The stink of his vomit in the hot car began to waft up at them, seeming to side with the man who'd expelled it: They could not stay there. The heat would cook every bit of hydration out of them. They needed to get away from this place. They needed to get someplace cool and quiet, where Clyde could assemble his frazzled thoughts and figure out what the hell they were going to do next.

Maybe none of that made sense.

But it seemed obvious to him at the time. And he needed to go. He needed to run. He needed to get his wife and his unborn child away from this place. Haley shouldn't be in these circumstances when she was so late in the pregnancy. What would happen to the baby?

What had already happened?

He pulled the door handle and pushed it open.

Fresh air blasted in. The humid, ninety-five-degree air outside the car felt cool and refreshing compared to the two-hundred-degree hotbox they'd been in.

Clyde nudged Haley. 'Go!'

They tumbled out of the car, trying to be quiet, but Clyde felt clumsy and obvious. He came out hands first, walking his palms forward until he could get his feet under him. The hot blacktop burned his hands and speckled them with gravel. They stayed low as they darted among the cars, shuffling along and looking this way and that.

Haley moved ahead of him, and he kept his hand on her lower back, hot to the touch and soaked. He realized he still had not taken off his backpack, and his back and his abdominals ached and cramped from holding himself in that half-crouched position. Still he would not take it off.

They reached the end of the cars, perhaps fifty yards away from the woods. There were a few industrial-type steel buildings that sat on road frontage, and a single brick house behind them, seeming out of place. And then there was the woods. Overgrown, and green and solid. Like a force field behind which they could shelter. Inside that thick growth, he was certain they would not be found.

Neither of them spoke as they ran. Haley slowed, breathing harshly and holding her stomach, her face showing some pain. Clyde didn't feel much better himself. He looked around again. There was nothing to see but cars parked in haphazard fashion, people's belongings scattered on the road, and the conspicuous absence of their owners. But he could still hear it, farther away now, so that it echoed off the adjacent buildings at him – screams and screeches.

A single, impotent gunshot.

He took Haley by the hand. 'Come on, baby. We're almost there.'

They reached the woods and disappeared into it, shrouded by greenery. On the inside it was dark with shade, but the humidity was worse and the breeze could not reach them, so it felt stifling and they could not catch their breaths. The mosquitos were thick in the woods and they swarmed them whenever they sat still.

Haley gulped air and looked down at her jeans. They were dark in the crotch.

'Oh my God.' Clyde put a hand to his head. 'Did your water break?'

Haley shook her head tightly and tried to wipe at the darkness. 'I think I peed myself.'

In the distance came a howl. Inhuman. Enraged. Clyde looked off in the direction that he had heard it coming from, but there was only a shroud of trees to meet him. When he turned back around, Haley was staring at him, eyes puffy red slits. Her mouth was seized down into a thin line. He knew the look very well.

'What's wrong?' he said, as though he didn't already know.

'What do you have in your backpack?'

He glanced behind him. Shifted uncomfortably under the burden of it. 'I don't know. Some of our stuff.'

'Some of our stuff,' she said heatedly, shaking her head.

'Haley . . . I don't know what you want.'

She stepped toward him, hitting him in the shoulder with the heel of her palm. 'You don't know what I want?' she hissed. 'You don't fucking know? How about not to be in this fucking situation? How about a clean pair of fucking pants?'

'Haley . . .'

'We should have been on that bus!' she shouted suddenly. 'Do you think I give a shit about all of this *stuff*? About the suitcase? About all the paperwork? It's not important, Clyde!

You're important! *This baby* is important. All that other stuff is just stuff. It doesn't mean anything.'

'You can't blame me for this,' he said lamely.

'You sat there and argued with the guy about the fucking suitcase! While other people took our spots in line! I tried to get you to leave it behind!' She kicked leaves at him. 'You're so goddamned stubborn!'

'Alright!' he suddenly shouted. 'I'm sorry!'

Haley rubbed her belly nervously, nostrils flaring.

Clyde ripped off his backpack and tried to throw it, but it was too heavy and it landed with a dull *thud* just a foot or so from his feet. 'Is that what you want, Haley? You want me to just throw everything away? Fine! Done! There! I threw it away!' He raked his fingers through his hair, feeling bits and pieces of leaves and sticks come out as he did. 'Pardon the fuck outta me for not knowing that this was gonna happen!'

Haley just looked away from him.

'I know we should have been on that bus,' he growled. 'But there's not a whole lot I can do about it right now. I mean . . .' He clenched his teeth. 'What do you want me to do? Just tell me. What should I have done, and what the hell do you want me to do now?'

She turned back around toward him, enunciated her words with sharp motions of her hands. 'I need you to think, Clyde. Please. I need you to help me think. I need you to get us out of this.'

'Get us . . . ?' Clyde stared at her for a long moment, felt the desperation in her eyes bleeding the anger out of him. What was left was just nausea. The gumminess of his dry mouth. The tang of his own vomit still lingering on the back of his tongue. He sank down, sat himself in the leaves. 'Okay . . . okay . . .'

Haley took long breaths and blew them out through pursed lips. Her eyes stayed on her husband for a time, the expression she wore not giving much away except for sadness, though he could not tell whether she was sad at him, or sad at the world, or just sad in general.

He motioned to her. 'C'mere. Sit down.'

She sat down next to him, holding her back and wincing. Clyde's neck stretched and he looked around, surveilling everything, trying to see what was beyond the tree line. As he looked, he spoke, his voice more controlled than it had been before. 'We need a gun.'

'My dad taught you how to shoot, right?'

Clyde's jaw clenched. 'Yeah, he took me shooting.'

A random scream drew their attention, but they couldn't tell where it was coming from.

Someplace far away. And it didn't come again.

Clyde continued, quieter this time. 'We'll sneak up to the school. And ... and I'm pretty sure some of the soldiers, they, uh ...'

'Some of them got killed,' Haley finished for him. 'We could take their guns.'

'Yes. And there might be food and water.'

'Okay.'

'Okay.'

'Clyde.'

'What?'

She touched his arm lightly. 'Where are we going after that?'

'We're gonna go to the FEMA camp we were supposed to be at today.'

She made an uncertain noise. 'That's, like, I don't know how many miles—'

'I'm gonna get you there,' Clyde interrupted, his voice strong, even if the rest of him wasn't. He had conviction, he thought, and maybe Haley believed it and maybe she didn't, but she sat back and seemed to concede. 'I'm gonna get you there,' he repeated.

'Well, let's go.' She started to rise.

He took her arm and pulled her back down. 'No. We're gonna stay down. We're gonna stay right here. Until it's dark. It'll be safer to move at night. Right? Yes. It's gonna be safer at night. We'll wait till then.'

CHAPTER 3

They waited while the day trickled by.

Like waiting for a dripping tap to fill a barrel.

Some time before the sun went down, something crashed through the woods, out of sight of them. By then his heart had slowed to a normal pace, but the sound sent it rocketing again and Clyde and Haley both clung to each other's sweaty forms and burrowed into the leaves to hide. The crashing stopped for a brief moment, followed by the sound of some strange, gargling noise. And then whatever it was ran back off into the woods, away from them.

They did not move, even when the noise was gone. They lay on their backs, the mosquitos hovering around their faces and circling their ears. Their skin and clothes dampened as the sun lowered toward the horizon. Things crawled over their skin as they lay in the leaves. They watched a bit of dappled sunlight that had pierced the forest canopy. It crawled so slowly toward them, like a dying thing seeking help, and then it disappeared just before reaching them.

Birds raced noisily through the woods, busy about their daily business of surviving. The presence of the two humans on the ground mostly went unnoticed. Squirrels shimmied from tree to tree, freezing when Clyde or Haley stirred to swat a mosquito. They would stare and wait for stillness before continuing on. Oblivious.

No matter what happened outside of those woods, they would continue to do what they had done their entire short lives. They would harvest their food, and they would hibernate, and they would procreate, and they would die, and the disaster of humanity would have little effect on them, if any at all. Their instinct would drive them, and they would continue to perform their tasks, and the forest would continue on regardless of anything that happened to Clyde or Haley or their unborn baby or anyone else in the world. Those animals were just a bunch of biological cogs in some giant, organic machine whose purpose Clyde could not fathom. He only knew he was jealous of their single-mindedness. Envious that they could just flippantly go about their days without any care as to what was occurring beyond them.

Just after dusk, when the light was still blue across the sky, Clyde heard an engine.

He turned his head, facing through the edge of the forest and toward the school. He saw headlights flash and glimmer and then lay still, illuminating a row of cars. Though he could not see the vehicle that produced the headlights, he could hear the engine idling. Like the occupants were waiting for something. No sound of opening and closing doors. Just a throaty grumble. *A truck*, Clyde thought.

Almost immediately he was on his feet, pulling Haley up after him. 'C'mon!' he said loudly. 'Let's get them before they leave!'

Haley's voice wavered as he dragged her through the woods toward the school. 'Clyde! We don't even know who they are!'

'They could be more troops, or cops, or firefighters,' he said breathlessly. 'Or maybe we can just catch a ride with them. Maybe they're trying to make it to the FEMA camp. Come on!'

If Haley said anything else, he didn't hear it over the

sound of his own yelling: 'Hey! Wait up! We're friendly!'

They staggered through green grass turned blue in the twilight, then hit the pavement of the road, and over it to the school grounds on the other side. The whole way, Clyde screamed at the top of his lungs, trying to get their attention, while he pulled Haley along behind him, getting the sense that she was resisting just slightly. But he was so focused on the concept that someone might be there who could help him that he barely noticed. He just stared at the glow of those headlights and hoped and prayed to God that they would not drive away before he could reach them.

With no wind left in his lungs, he reached the corner of the school building and saw the headlights. They belonged to an SUV, something like a Suburban, but lifted a few inches and with oversize tires. He also saw dark shapes standing there, and he squinted into the glaring headlights until his eyes could focus on their faces.

'Don't fucking move!' a man's voice yelled.

Clyde stuttered to a halt, Haley stumbling into his back, both of them breathing heavily.

'It's okay,' Clyde said between gulps of air. 'We're friendly.'

'Lemme see your hands!' the voice commanded.

Clyde squinted against the headlights and his eyes adjusted to give him the full picture. There were three people standing before him. A woman and a child, hovering close to the SUV. The woman held a shotgun, and it was pointed at Clyde. The child was a boy of perhaps five. The third person was a man, standing a little farther from the woman and child. He was larger, and it was obvious he was well built, as he was wearing a tank top that showed his arms. Not 'body-builder' big, as Clyde would have called it. But a lean, corded look. Someone who did a lot of physical labor. He wore a tan ball cap with no logo on it and had a goatee, thick and blond. He held a rifle of some make that Clyde was not familiar with, and like the woman and her shotgun, it was pointed at Clyde.

'Whoa, whoa.' Clyde raised his hands.

The man took a half step forward. 'Shut up,' he ordered. 'Do not move or I will shoot you dead, you understand me?'

'Yes. Yes.' Clyde fumbled for words. 'Look, we're not trying—'

'I said to shut up.' The man's voice was still sharp, but it was not raised anymore. He had mechanical eyes that didn't show much of the thoughts behind them, and they seemed to scan Clyde and Haley up and down for a moment. Assessing them. Determining whether they were a threat or not. Finally, he turned his head just slightly, while keeping his eyes locked on Clyde, and spoke to the woman and the child. 'Honey, just stick close to the truck.'

The woman nodded coolly. 'Okay.'

A moment passed with the man still eyeing them and Clyde not quite sure what to do. For Haley's sake, he wanted to do something, to reason with the man, to accomplish something, to show that he was just as capable of fending for his family as this man was. But he could see, even in the dark, how straight the aim of that rifle barrel was – how that little black hole was staring straight at his face.

'I don't know you,' the man said finally, as though deciding something. 'I think it'd be best if you two just turned around and got lost. Leave us be. And don't show your faces again, or I will kill both of you. Don't doubt me on that.'

'What?' Clyde blurted, shocked. 'What do you mean you're gonna kill us?'

The man just stared. 'You heard me.'

Clyde shook his head slowly. 'Listen, we're not here to hurt you or bother you.' He gestured to Haley. 'My wife is pregnant. We need to get to the FEMA camp in New Bern. Are you folks driving out there? Or can you give us a ride to somewhere nearby . . . ?'

'Not givin' you a ride anywhere,' the man said. 'I don't know you. And I don't trust you.'

Clyde could feel frustration boiling up inside of him. 'I need help!' he said with sudden desperation. 'I need some fucking help! Can't we work together on this? I mean, if you're going to the camp, then we can just sit in the back. We won't get in the way.'

'We're not going to the FEMA camp,' the man said.

Clyde looked confused. 'But there was a mandatory evacuation.'

'Yeah, there was a mandatory evacuation in Jacksonville, too. And Atlanta. And that didn't work out too well for them, did it?' The man shook his head, seemed bitter for a moment. 'Jamming everyone into one spot like that . . . just making a bigger target.'

'Okay.' Clyde's shoulders began to ache a bit from holding up his hands. 'Look. Just let us grab a few things. We're hungry and thirsty. And we need a gun. Just one.'

The man was shaking his head before Clyde even finished.

Clyde looked at him questioningly. 'Why are you shaking your head?'

'You're not taking any of this stuff.'

'What? Why not?'

'Because *I'm* taking it.'

Clyde's eyes were wide. 'Are you fucking kidding me? There's plenty of shit lying around here! You can't possibly use it all. You won't even be able to fit it all in your truck!'

'Then we'll make two trips.' The man's voice was starting to sound heated.

Clyde could feel himself losing his temper, like he had with the soldier in line. But the muzzle of the rifle was still pointed at him, and Haley was squeezing his arm. And in a certain aspect, it angered him. Like she didn't think Clyde could handle this man without getting them both shot.

Clyde swallowed, forced himself to be calm. 'Look. Just some food and water. And one gun; that's all we're asking. You won't miss it. And we'll be gone. You'll never see us again.'

'And what if I need it?' the man said. 'What if that bit of food and water I let you take could possibly save my wife and kid? What if a couple weeks from now, that little bit of food and water keeps them alive long enough for me to find some more supplies?' The man did not say it with venom or spite. He said it with sincerity and conviction. 'Do you think that if my family dies of starvation or dehydration, that I'll be okay with the fact that I gave away some of our food and water to strangers? Do you think that I value your family more than my own?'

'No.' Clyde shook his head.

'No,' the man confirmed. 'My family is my responsibility. And your family is yours.'

'This isn't gonna last forever,' Clyde said quietly.

The man's eyebrows went up. 'How long do you think it takes to die during a disaster like this?' He seemed to make the final decision that he would not converse with them anymore. His face fell flat and emotionless, and he motioned away with his rifle out into the darkness. 'Now get lost. Both of you. Find food and water somewhere else.'

Clyde and Haley backed away, as though they feared he might shoot them in the back if they turned. Eventually they did turn, and they went out into the darkness that had grown deeper in the small minutes that had passed. The light of the SUV showed them their path, and they took it hurriedly through the parking lot toward the street.

As they hit the street and made their way through the cars, they passed out of the light of the headlamps. Now the sky was nearly black in the east and a cloudless, deep blue in the west. In the half light, each to the other seemed like a faceless smudge, glossy with sweat, but the features melted away. As they moved through the cars that were parked along the highway, they tried to ignore the carnage around them.

As Clyde walked, the tension and fear of being held at gunpoint began to abate. It was replaced with anger. Indignance. Almost a sense of shame. He refused to look directly at Haley, because he feared he would see in her eyes the same reproach and disappointment that he forced on himself. Like self-flagellation. For not being strong enough. For not being tough enough. For not being prepared to defend his wife.

The words just kept rattling around in his brain, getting sharper as time went by, like chipping at flint: *My family is my responsibility. And your family is yours.*

Like even as he had said it, the man was picturing them already dead.

Like Clyde's failure was a foregone conclusion.

Clyde's eyes kept wandering down, though, to see where he was stepping, and then he would see these poor people. He'd heard that the sick people would cannibalize in their delirious state. But for some reason when he saw the civilians and soldiers, saw the pieces and parts missing from them, he tried to come up with a different explanation.

Clyde stopped and put his hands on his knees, feeling like he might vomit again.

'Honey, you okay?' Haley asked.

He shook his head violently, then spit on the ground, still unable to take his eyes off the forms that were crumpled against the cars all around them. He looked for the pattern of digitally speckled grays and tans that would denote a military uniform in all that dark blood. He found one, leaning against a fender. The jacket had been stripped away and the shirt torn open. His chest and arms had been heavily masticated. His stomach had been opened, his guts piled up next to him. One arm still holding them, like he didn't want them to get away. His mouth hung open, bloody and soundless.

Clyde retched, but nothing came up.

Haley made a gagging noise herself, but he couldn't tell whether it was sympathetic from him or whether she could not handle the sight, either. She pushed at him, attempting to get him to leave this spot and go farther down the road. 'Come on, Clyde! Let's go!'

Clyde wiped saliva from his mouth and stood up fully so he could look back toward the school. It sat perhaps a tenth of a mile away, the SUV still sitting in the parking lot. But Clyde felt they were too distant to be keeping watch on him.

'No,' he croaked. 'We need … We need …' He didn't finish his sentence, but he moved closer to the dead soldier. He tried to see in the growing darkness, but not much was visible to him. He would be forced to find it by touch. He knelt down, his fingers touching the cement, feeling the grit but also the sticky viscosity of coagulated blood. And the stench of it. The metallic, butcher's-shop smell. And the smell of loosened bowels.

He felt around. His fingers brushed cold meat. His stomach felt like it was curling into a ball inside of him, his throat like a gaping hole, widening as it prepared to purge itself again. He closed his eyes as he leaned closer to the dead man, unwilling to stare eye to eye with it.

'What the hell are you doing?' Haley hissed, quiet but urgent. 'We need to get the fuck out of here!'

'We need a fucking gun!' he snapped.

Haley swore, bending down so she could not be seen between the cars and looking back over her shoulders at the school. Clyde could not see her, but he could hear her breathing. The rapid, shallow rhythm and the words that whispered out of her lips: 'What are we doing here? What are we doing? What are we doing?'

It was not a question to him, he understood.

But he answered it anyway, silently.

We are surviving. This is how people survive.

They do what they do not want to do.

Someday when this is over, I will look back and say I did some things I'd rather not talk about, but I'm here. And Haley's here. And we survived it.

Someday when this is over.

When he hefted it out of the darkness beneath the car, he felt proud. Validated. He looked at it, though he could barely discern it, black on black. He could feel it, though. Cold and metal. Lighter than he thought it would be.

Haley had gone silent and she looked at him. 'You sure you remember how to shoot a pistol?'

He didn't, but he refused to admit it. 'Yeah. Of course.'

He had to be the man. His family was his responsibility. He would not pass the pistol over to her and tell her to defend them. And she might not make a big deal about it, but somehow the truth would get back to her father and her brothers. And they would never let him live it down. They would talk about how Clyde the pussy, silver-spoon mother-fucker, had to have Haley defend him because he couldn't figure out how to work a goddamned pistol.

How hard could it be? Just point and click, right?

'Alright,' he said. He held the pistol in his right hand and held onto Haley with his left, and they moved quietly and cautiously down the road. 'We can probably make up most of the distance before dawn.'

'You sure it's safe to travel at night?' she asked.

He felt annoyed by the question. 'Of course it is.'

CHAPTER 4

They walked through the dark. Their eyes remained fixed on the woods and pastures and neighborhoods around them. Clyde couldn't believe how black everything was. A few streetlights still glowed, so he knew that the power grid was not out, but there was not a single light on in any of the houses. Everything was stiff with silence, like someone holding a breath, and it made him uncomfortable and caused his eyes to dart around, little noises making him jump.

'Honey, I need to stop.' Haley put out a hand to stop him, the other clutching her stomach.

Her feet alternated on the pavement, one relieving the other for just a moment. He looked down at her feet and for the first time actually took notice of what she was wearing. A simple pair of flats. Canvas, with a floral pattern. They'd become dingy from the long walk and from hiding in the woods. She wore no socks, and Clyde could only imagine the blisters that had begun to form.

'Okay.' He nodded, then stopped. He looked around, forward and back in the roadway, seeking a place where they could rest, but it seemed like nothing but empty road in either direction. He focused his attention forward and peered through the darkness, as though he could light the way by squinting. Still, he thought he could see a small sign straight ahead. Perhaps a convenience store or a roadside diner or something.

'Can you keep going for a little bit?' he asked. 'I think there's a place ahead we might be able to stop.'

She balanced on one foot, propping the other on her knee and massaging it. She looked at him with narrowed eyes but didn't respond to his question. It wasn't quite a glare, but it wasn't a friendly look, either.

'What?' He spread his arms, feeling the cool breeze wick the sweat from his armpits.

She shook her head. 'What the fuck are we doing, Clyde?'

His teeth locked shut. *What the hell does she want with me?* 'I told you,' he said flatly. 'We're going to the FEMA camp.'

Haley looked away from him. 'What if it's not there by the time we get there? What if they've closed it down, and we miss it?'

Clyde made a beleaguered noise. 'Well, we're never gonna find out if we keep standing around in the middle of the damn road.'

'Clyde, don't be an asshole,' she snapped. 'I'm asking you a serious question.'

Clyde rubbed his face. Exhaustion was suddenly springing up from the balls of his feet. He could feel it like a dull ache. Like he was walking on coals, but rather than burning him, they only imparted weariness.

She sniffed and he could hear the wetness.

He took a deep breath. 'It's not gonna be like that. It's not. It can't.' He thought of the man at the school, the calm confidence he had displayed. And the way his wife and child stood there, trusting him. Knowing he was capable. Not doubting him. Not questioning him.

Clyde tried to make his voice strong, like the man's had been. 'I'm not saying this isn't bad right now, but it will get better. It always gets better.'

Haley's voice caught. 'I don't know.'

'Well, I do. Come on.'

He put his hand on her shoulder and gently pushed her on. They continued, but at a slower pace, and it took them almost five minutes to reach the sign that he'd seen in the distance. It was an old convenience store. A single stand of gas pumps sitting outside. Two for regular unleaded. Two for diesel. One for kerosene, off to the side.

It was dark, as Clyde had suspected. He assumed that it was still in the mandatory evacuation zone – or mandatory *containment*, he supposed – and that the owner and clerks were gone. Either bused off to the FEMA camp or scattered after the attack. And Clyde stood there in the middle of the parking lot of the convenience store, like he'd suddenly been struck dumb, and he thought about what had happened, what he'd witnessed, and he felt a feeling rising in him like the panic of knowing that you are wrong about something.

You are very, very wrong.

He shook it off. Stowed those memories into a little bin in his mind that he would save for later. He would procrastinate thinking about them, processing them, because to do so might be to give credence to the thought that this was not as temporary as he wanted to believe. The thought that maybe the survivalist psycho back at the school had spoken the truth.

Bullshit. Bullshit.

He rejected it.

Ahead of him, the windows of the convenience store were dark. In them hung advertisements and dark neon signs. The king of beers. The North Carolina lottery. Cheap prices for cartons of cigarettes. Ice-cold Coca-Cola. All of that seemed normal. It seemed real. These were things that could not be killed. These were fixtures of modern life. They comforted him and told him, even in their darkened, slumbering state, that everything would be okay in the end. That just like everything bad that had ever happened, it too would come to an end, and soon he would be back at the store, purchasing Budweiser and lottery tickets like any damn freeborn American.

This too shall pass, he told himself, and he felt wise and levelheaded for thinking it.

At the window, he cupped his hands over the glass and peered through the window, trying to see inside. A single streetlight cast an odd glow over everything, not emanating from the parking lot where typically the overhead halogens would drown it out, but coming from a little farther down the road, so everything was cast in shadows of extreme angles, like time was frozen at sunset.

There were a few aisles that sat in deep shadow. A checkout counter over-cluttered by advertisements, lotto tickets, chewing gum, and loose cigarettes and cigars. For the most part, everything looked as pristine as you would expect a dingy convenience store to be. For some reason, Clyde had half expected it to be ransacked.

He tried the door and was not surprised to find it locked.

Haley let out a little moan. 'Well, this was worth it.'

Clyde looked through the window again, then all around the parking lot. His tongue touched his lips and both were dry. Now he was looking into that convenience store, into coolers still filled with cold beverages, and wanting badly to get his hands on them.

'We could . . .' He trailed off, trying to find a less criminal way to say what he was thinking. 'I'm sure we could open the door somehow.'

'You mean break in?'

He didn't respond directly. Instead, he bent down and began looking at where the deadbolt was seated in the door-frame. Checking for weaknesses. 'It's not like we're petty criminals, Haley. I'm sure everyone would understand that we needed someplace to sit and rest for a bit.'

'They're just gonna call us looters!' she hissed. 'What if one of those army units comes by and sees us? Aren't they shooting looters?'

He looked at her with a quirked brow. 'I don't think so, hon. This isn't North Korea.'

He could tell by her expression that she thought he was being difficult.

He raised a placating hand, a gesture that he knew she disliked but which he often used anyway. 'Look, we're just gonna slip in. We're not touching the money in the till. We won't take more than we need. Just a couple damn granola bars and a bottle of water. I'm sure everyone will understand.' He shook his head. 'Besides, I don't know if there are any police around here anyway. Everyone's been evacuated. Or *contained*. Remember?'

Haley mulled it over while Clyde screwed around with the door, trying to figure out if there was a quiet, secret-agent method of getting it open. Eventually, Haley held her belly and winced at the pain in her own feet. She couldn't keep going. And neither of them wanted to sleep out in the open.

'Fine,' she said quietly.

She stood there, staring out at the darkness of the street, as though keeping watch.

Clyde looked over his shoulder and could see her attention was elsewhere. He took the opportunity to pull the pistol from his belt, using his body as a shield to block her from seeing what he was doing. As quietly as he could, he looked the weapon over. Like a savage looking at alien technology.

He disliked how awkward it looked in his untrained hands. He was shamefully uncomfortable with it. Amazing how, despite all his education and his white-collar upbringing, he was no different from every other American male, who somehow expected himself to be an instinctive expert on firearms and was heartily disappointed when this was proven wrong. Like not knowing how to use a gun was essentially like finding out your prick was two sizes too small.

But, like most other American males, what he'd seen on TV and movies was his guide. He knew there was a button on the side that he could depress and make the magazine fall out of the gun. He fumbled around for this but eventually found it. He pressed it with his thumb and, like magic, the magazine fell down into his waiting hand.

He could see gold, or brass, or whatever it was that they used to make bullets. He could see at least two coming out of the top, but below that he couldn't tell. He looked the magazine over quickly, found slots in the back, and he figured they were to show you how many rounds you had in there, though they were not numbered. He could see the glint of the cartridges through the first hole, but not the second or third. So what did that mean? He guesstimated, based on the size of the cartridge he was looking at, that the magazine held somewhere between ten and twenty rounds.

So maybe five in the magazine?

Possibly less.

He thought about taking them out to count, but he feared he wouldn't be able to figure out how to get them back in. On the two occasions that Haley's father had insisted Clyde come shooting with them, he'd never let

Clyde load the magazines, saying that Clyde might do it wrong and 'blow them up.' Clyde was pretty sure it was hyperbole, but it cast enough doubt that now he didn't want to risk it.

He seated the magazine back into the pistol, pressing it in until he felt the click. Then he hefted the thing in his hands a few times, trying to make himself feel more comfortable with it, or at least look like less of an idiot.

'Babe, what are you doing?' Haley asked.

Clyde stuck the pistol back in his pants. 'Nothing. I was just . . . just checking out the door to see if it had an alarm. I don't think it does.'

'Thought you said that it doesn't matter.'

He looked back at her. 'It doesn't.'

'Well, open it, then.'

'Okay.' He looked around on the ground. Found a chunk of loose asphalt near the worn-out-looking ice chests and wrangled it from the ground. It was about the size of his fist. He'd never used a rock to bash something in. Never actually broken a window before. And he wasn't sure whether this would do the trick, but he didn't see why not.

He thought about whether to throw it or use it as a club.

Decided to throw it.

The door was your typical convenience store or gas station door. Just a rectangular frame of metal, this one with a cross-bar going across the middle of the door, dividing the glass into two equal sections on the top and bottom. Clyde aimed for the top section of glass, near the doorframe.

It shattered nicely through, making a fist-sized hole just to the left of the locking mechanism. A well-placed shot that Clyde almost smiled about. They listened to the abruptly loud *pop* of the glass breaking, then the crystalline, trickling sound as all the shards and pieces skittered across the inside of the store. For a moment he stood, almost shocked with himself for committing this crime.

No alarm, he thought with some relief. *Good*.

Then Clyde stepped forward and reached carefully through the hole in the glass. He unlocked the door and pulled it open. He stood there like a doorman, holding it open and waiting for Haley to pass through, but she stood there and looked unsurely between Clyde and the dark interior of the convenience store.

'I don't know,' she said. 'This feels wrong.'

Clyde huffed. 'Would you just get inside the damn door? Nobody is gonna arrest us.'

'How do you know?'

'Because it's ridiculous!' That was Clyde's only defense.

Haley pursed her lips and stepped through the door, shaking her head. Clyde took another glance around the parking lot and then followed her in. Inside, the temperature was slightly cooler, but it was stuffy and he could feel a bit of sweat break out across his head because there was no breeze to dry it. He swung the door closed behind them and locked it again.

'Do you have any cash on you?' Haley asked.

'Why?' He raised his brow.

'So we can leave them money for the things we take. And for the window.'

Clyde fought the desire to brush this off. Instead, he just said, 'My wallet was in the backpack. In the side pocket.'

In the harsh angle of light from the single streetlight outside, Haley's face was half in the light and half in the dark. The shadows were odd. Extreme. They added ten years to her face. He could see the glimmer of emotion hiding just below her skin, but she was trying hard not to show it. She was typically not an overly emotional person, but that had changed during pregnancy. Which he supposed was to be expected.

And then today had happened.

'I need to sit,' she said, and simply sank down onto the floor. She let her hair hang in front of her face, using it as a curtain, trying to hide from her husband.

It baffled him when she did this. Sometimes she would let it out in front of him without any shame or reservation. Other times it was like she felt that her emotion was inappropriate and tried to secret it away, though in truth it made no difference to him. He never criticized her for it, but when and where she decided to show her emotions seemed to have no rhyme or reason. Somehow it was acceptable to break down looking at baby clothes, but not here in the middle of a convenience store they'd just broken into because they were on the run and needed a safe place to sleep.

He turned to the aisles, tried to change the subject or cheer her up. 'You hungry, babe? What do you want? You want me to find you a Milky Way?' Those were her favorite pregnancy food.

'No,' she said miserably.

'C'mon,' he prodded. 'It'll make you feel better.'

'It's gonna make me throw up. I just know it.'

He mulled that over. 'Okay. Anything that you think you can keep down?'

Something clattered. Like empty tin cans hitting pavement.

Clyde stiffened, shot a look to Haley, whose head was up now. Alert.

'What was that?' she whispered. 'Was that outside?'

Clyde barely moved – just raised his hand, the index finger up to indicate silence, and then he waited, frozen like he'd been turned into a stone. The cans rattled again, like something was shuffling them around. The noise bounced around oddly, so that he couldn't quite tell whether it was coming from inside, or perhaps from the back storeroom.

Maybe it's just a raccoon, he told himself desperately. *Or a possum or something*.

'Clyde . . .'

'Shhh!'

Then came a strange noise. A voice. Just a single, wavering note of displeasure: 'Aaaahh . . . Aah!' Like someone was irritated with themselves for knocking over the cans. The sound continued for a bit, and then dissolved into a slurry of consonants. Like a stumbling-drunk homeless man, muttering to himself in a back alley.

Clyde turned toward Haley, stepped very lightly into the center of the shop. He could feel it in his feet, arcing up into his legs and his back. It was a feeling that he'd only felt a few times in his life. The feeling that something bad was hovering close by, and he hoped that he could avoid it. He'd gotten that feeling when he was walking with Haley to their car one night and that shady-looking guy was following them, and Clyde had just been positive they were about to get carjacked.

'Come on,' he whispered, pulling Haley up off the floor. 'Get behind the counter.'

He wasn't sure if it made sense. Part of him thought it might be a better idea just to run, but that would mean leaving the store, and right now these walls and these windows were the only things keeping him separated from whatever was out there. And if they left the store, then he couldn't hide. He'd be out in the open again.

'Is it one of those people?' Haley asked.

'I don't know.' But he was thinking, *Yes. It has to be.*

They both ducked behind the counter. Haley stayed low, eyes to the floor, but Clyde looked up and over the counter-top, through the cups of loose Black & Milds and Fireball candies. The yellow streetlight stared baldly at them from across the street, a dull midnight sun hanging on the horizon. Clyde realized that his breath was coming quickly.

The muttering continued, broken by sudden, sharp barks. *Something's wrong with this person.*

'It's one of them.' Haley's voice was just a tense squeak of air. She reached out and clutched at Clyde. 'Did you lock the door?'

Clyde looked away from the windows and found his wife's eyes searching his face. He felt exposed and naked in front of that stare, and he was certain she was searching him for some sign that he knew what the hell he was doing, that he wouldn't get them killed. Searching for some reason why she should trust him, and not her own instincts.

When he looked back up, there was a man. He stood, slouched at the far corner of the window. Outside, but staring in. His whole body was a silhouette lined in yellow by the streetlight behind him, and his face was a mask of shadows so that Clyde could not see if he were looking at them or not. Beside him, Haley tensed and put a hand over her mouth.

Clyde did not move. With every beat, his heart seemed to be working its way further up his throat, seeming determined to lodge there in his airway and suffocate him. Clyde's knees ached from kneeling, but he didn't register the signals of pain.

All he could feel was his heart, and the breath going in and out of him.

The man at the window stood for a while, and Clyde could see him swaying on his feet. He held something in his hand. Something long and thin. Perhaps a crowbar or a tire iron. As he swayed, the object swung lazily back and forth, his arms loose and dangling.

Slowly, the man leaned forward so that his nose just lightly touched the window. He opened his mouth, and Clyde could see his tongue snake out, and it seemed abnormally long and viscous. It touched the glass, slid slowly about, leaving a trail on the glass that shimmered darkly, and Clyde thought that it was red like blood.

The man began to walk, or sidestep, very slowly, keeping his tongue in contact with the glass, as though trying to taste all of it. There was something about it that made Clyde's stomach feel weak, something disturbingly sexual in the way the silhouetted man traced his bloody tongue along behind him.

The man reached the door and he stopped.

Here, from this perspective, Clyde could see his face. It was blank. Devoid of life. Like a meteor-scarred moonscape. And there was more than blood around his mouth. There were bits of things that Clyde could not identify and did not want to imagine.

At the door the man pulled his head back, retracting his tongue. His eyes fell to the jagged hole in the glass and the handle of the door just beside it.

Clyde could not take his eyes away. He just kept thinking, kept praying, *Please go away! Please go away! Please just go away and leave us alone!*

He had to forcibly extract his arm from Haley, and then

he took the pistol from inside of his waistband, where the slide and sights had been digging uncomfortably into his skin. It was warm with his body heat. Moist from his sweat. It felt like a live thing in his hands, and he was suddenly afraid of it. Like it would decide on its own what happened when Clyde attempted to use it.

The man standing at the door spoke, and his voice sounded like his mouth was full of marbles: 'Ah wan' in.' His hand fell clumsily to the door handle and tugged at it. 'Ah wan' in! Ah *wan'* in!' He tugged more furiously. 'Ahwanin! Ahwanin!' He reared back and swung hard with the object in his hand – a tire iron, just like Clyde had thought. It struck the glass and the rest of the already weakened window came exploding in.

CHAPTER 5

Haley screamed.

It was only a short sound – she choked it off as soon as it left her mouth.

The thing at the door snapped his head toward them, somehow immediately able to triangulate on the sound he had just heard. He stared into the darkness for a moment and Clyde knew that they were no longer hidden.

The thing let out an ungodly noise, incredibly loud in the cramped space of the convenience store. The face, blank and drunken before, was now twisted into wide-eyed rage, and he launched himself at them. The crossbar in the door stayed him, the entire door rattling in its frame.

Haley bolted upright and backpedaled into the wall of cigarettes behind her. Boxes of Marlboros and Newports tumbled down over her shoulders as her hands spastically grabbed about, like she was searching for a doorknob that might open up the wall and allow her to escape.

Clyde tried to speak, but nothing came out of him.

Something in that scream – the primal hunger of it – had ripped every shred of courage out of him. He stood now, panicked and thoughtless in the path of an imminent attack, his mental condition fading to black as his brain pumped overloads of chemicals into him that his body had no idea how to work through.

Adrenaline and noradrenaline shot through his bloodstream. His veins and capillaries constricted, sending his blood pressure skyrocketing. His heart rate and respiration slammed his chest. His eyes dilated, his corneas warping and causing everything outside of the two degrees directly in front of his face to look speckled black. All high-road thought left him. All complicated notions of courage and protective instincts suddenly evaporated into nothingness. Haley was no longer a concept that he was aware of. The only thing his animal brain could comprehend was his own death and survival.

Clyde sank behind the counter again – perhaps because he wanted to hide, or perhaps because his knees were giving out. He never registered when Haley ran around him, trying to escape by running out the back of the store. His eyes remained affixed on the creature in front of them as he pulled himself through the door, over the crossbar.

Jags of glass were still embedded in the weather stripping. They ripped open the man-thing's midsection as he heaved himself into the convenience store, and when he landed in the sea of glass inside, things began to flop out of his gaping stomach, coils of his own guts caught on the glass of the crossbar.

But he did not seem to notice that it was tethered to the door by its own entrails. He stumbled to his feet, his hands sparkling with the chunks of glass still poking out of his skin. The pail rope of his gut came loose of the doorframe and plopped down onto the ground. He kept moving to the back of the store, trailing his own intestines. He did not look at Clyde.

Clyde found himself curled up behind the counter, no longer upright enough to see over the top. He closed his eyes. His hands fumbled uselessly with the pistol. He held it awkwardly, and he was not aware that it was even there, let alone what his hands were attempting to accomplish with it.

In the back, Haley screamed.

And finally, some part of him woke up. Some half-dead portion of his consciousness, like a body washed up on the rocks and only revealed when the tide goes out. *My family is my responsibility*, the man at the school had said. *And your family is yours.*

It's Haley.

It's Haley.

It's Haley and your fucking baby!

He shook so badly that he nearly dropped the pistol. He stared at it as though he were surprised to find it there, still in his grip.

There was a clatter in the back, and the sound of Haley's screams changed pitch.

The screeching of the man-thing overpowered her.

'Oh, God,' Clyde said. He came to his feet with great effort, his vision blurring with tears. 'Oh, no. Oh, no ...'

'Clyde!' Haley screamed for him. 'Clyde!'

She was screaming for him.

For him

For him.

He moved, though he felt poisoned by his own fear, his muscles barely breaking loose of paralysis. His body knew what his mind would not concede – that he was not matched for this fight. That he could not win it. And because his body knew this of itself, it seemed determined to avoid the fight altogether, to lie down and hope all of those bad things would pass him by.

You are a coward, he told himself, but when he pictured the words, they were spoken from the mouths of his father-in-law, and his brothers-in-law, and the man in the tan baseball cap from the school whose family trusted him to get them through.

Haley kept screaming for him, and he kept moving, his shoulder sliding along shelving units, causing whatever they held to fall over and crash to the floor behind him. And when he came to the backroom of the store, soiled and drenched in a cold sweat, trembling so badly that he could barely keep his knees locked, he saw them both on the floor. Haley on her back, legs kicking, arms flailing, punching, clawing. The man-thing crouched over her, his mouth agape, reaching his jaws past Haley's glancing blows, seeking her jugular.

Haley saw her husband standing there, and the look that broke through the panic on her face was one that destroyed everything Clyde had ever believed about himself. One microsecond of an expression, and he knew the truth about himself. Because she was looking at him, and in that instant she was confused. She was wondering why her husband was standing there, doing nothing, when another man was attempting to hurt her. She was wondering why the man who was supposed to love her, to protect her, the man whose baby sat curled in her womb, could only stand there and weep.

'Do something!' she screamed.

Almost reflexively, Clyde fired the pistol. He fired it five times. He pulled the trigger as quickly as he could, and he flinched as the gunshots detonated in the small area. He used every round that was in that pistol, and he did it without aiming. One of the rounds hit the man-thing in the lower back, another punched through his shoulder, and the next managed by sheer chance to strike his head, ending his movements abruptly. The other two rounds were high and wildly off target.

The man-thing was suddenly silent as he collapsed onto

Haley. She struggled underneath his weight and Clyde stared, shocked and ashamed. He felt sick to his stomach, standing there with this man's guts coiled on the floor at his feet, blood and bile and shit mixing on the linoleum. He wanted to pull the body off of Haley, but when he reached down, the thought of touching it suddenly revolted him so badly that he stopped and heaved. Nothing came up.

'Clyde …'

He reached forward, dropping the pistol in the mess at his feet, and he pulled the dead thing from atop his wife, from atop her pregnant belly. Freed of the burden, Haley didn't get up. Her hands flopped around like birds with broken wings. Her chest rose and fell rapidly. Her head was tilted back, eyes on the ceiling, her mouth gaping. Like she was trying to catch her breath.

'Baby?' Clyde's voice was a whimper.

Tears spilled over her face. 'It hurts,' she said, choking on the words. 'It hurts.'

Clyde felt his own tears running. Snot ran over his upper lip. 'What's hurting? What's hurting, baby?' He bent over her, on a single knee, his own hands panning over her body, hovering like a diviner, trying to sense where her injury was. As he got closer to her, he could see everything. The deep bite marks in her arms that oozed blackness. The way the skin along her forearm had been avulsed and now hung white like a fish's belly, while the flesh and muscle below gushed.

And the one little hole. Just below her right collarbone.

Haley wheezed, 'I can't breathe.' Every time she tried to breathe in, it would issue a terrifying sucking noise. And when she tried to speak or breathe out, it would bubble and spit at him. He stared at it, shaking his head as though he could argue with it. As though he could convince it to seal itself up.

'Oh, no no no,' he said. 'What do I do, Haley? What do I do?'

Haley leaned forward with some effort, her eyes skipping past Clyde and going to her stomach. She tried to speak, but coughed instead and blood stained her lips and teeth. 'Is my baby okay? He didn't hurt my baby?'

Clyde looked at the tightly stretched belly. He couldn't see any injury to it. Some of the man-thing's blood had stained Haley's shirt, but there were no tears, and nothing seemed out of place. 'I don't know,' he said. 'I think the baby's okay, Haley. I think the baby's okay.'

She didn't relax. Her eyes shifted to her husband. She said something that he couldn't hear.

'What?'

She struggled against pain for a moment, her eyes closed. She kept trying to get that breath, but it simply wouldn't come for her. Like she was being constricted. When she opened her eyes again, her mouth moved, but her voice did not come. There was not enough air behind it. Clyde wept, a scared, childlike sound, but he shut himself up when he saw her trying to speak, and it was only through the movement of her mouth that he could hear what she was saying. And he knew the words that were coming from her, but he kept shaking his head, because he did not want to comprehend them. He did not want them to be the last truth of his life with Haley. He did not want them to be the final test, because in doing or in failing, he knew that he would be ruined.

'Save my baby.'

*

He would tell his daughter this one day.

Sometimes people do things they don't want to do, so that they can survive. And I loved you so much, even before I knew you, that I did something I really didn't want to do, so that you could live. Because I needed you to live. Do you understand that? I needed you because I knew, right at the moment that I had to do that horrible thing, that you were the only thing I had left in the world.

He would tell her these things.

Someday when all of this was over.

CHAPTER 6

They found him walking along Highway 55, just outside of New Bern. To the two men watching from behind their truck, he seemed to shimmer like a ghost that had not yet taken full form, the heat coming off the road distorting his figure as he moved down the long strip of asphalt, coming toward them. The two men were young and old, one with scars on his face, the other with curiosity and a bit of apprehension.

The older one lifted up a scoped rifle and leaned against the bed of the pickup truck. The younger hovered close, wondering what they would find. The older looked through the riflescope for a time, his brow furrowing. Then he lowered it and pursed his lips.

'Sicky?' the younger one asked.

'Can't tell.' The older wiped sweat from his forehead. 'He was holdin' somethin', though.'

'What was it?'

The older man just shrugged.

They waited for the figure to draw closer. Their pickup truck was on the side of the road, amid several others. For the most part, they were concealed. All around them there were pine forests and farmland. The forests were strange, all the pine trees standing perfectly erect, all of them grown to a uniform height and in perfect rows and columns. The farmland was mostly a sea of wheat stubble, harvested, but the second crop not yet planted.

Almost the same distance behind them as the man was in

front of them, there stood a large white building. Its severe roofline and tall steeples gave no doubt to what it held. And that was their home now. Their reason for being there, for guarding the road. To make sure that no sick people made it past their checkpoint. Make sure nobody with bad intentions found their home.

The man who walked down the road drew closer, and now they could see him clearly with their naked eyes. He was a slight man, tattered and worn. His hair hung in bloody clumps down the sides of his face, and he wore glasses that were filthy and askew on his nose. His mouth hung open, his tongue halfway out. His clothes were rent and dirty and covered in gore. Actually, his entire person seemed to be covered in it. His legs, his arms, his torso, his neck, and up to his face. Like he had bathed in it and now it had crusted over and scabbed and dried to that unmistakable black-brown color.

Perhaps they would have shot him right there, because he looked like another man succumbed to the plague. But they could see that he held something in his arms, something small and dark red, like the rest of him.

As he came within twenty feet of their truck, they stepped out from behind it, brandishing their rifles, and they shouted and yelled at him, ordering him to kneel down. He stopped there in the road, right there on the double yellow line, and he looked at them with nothing on his face. And then he knelt, still holding the thing in his arms.

The older man stood back, aiming for his chest, while the younger one moved cautiously forward. The younger man craned his neck to see what it was in the man's arms, and when he saw, he recoiled and looked back at his older partner. 'Oh, my God!'

'Don't take the Lord's name in vain,' the older man said sternly.

The younger man's face had blanched, and he trembled. 'It's a baby.'

The man kneeling before them shifted just slightly, hugged the form against his chest just a little tighter, as though he thought they would try to take it from him. He looked from the younger man to the older, searching their faces, trying to determine their intent. It was the first time that he showed any thought at all.

The older man took a step forward. 'What happened, son?'

'I need ...' The man's voice was kiln-dried and splintered. 'I need water for my baby girl. She's not ... She's not ...' He looked down at the form in his arms, but didn't actually see it. It was the look of a man who saw only what he wanted and refused to see what was real. 'She's not doing so well. She needs food and water. Do you have any formula? I've checked ... so many places. But I can't find any. Do you have any formula? Or a nursing mother? Please.'

The older man lowered his rifle, but only an inch or two. He stepped forward, looked down into the kneeling man's arms to confirm what he already knew. It was a tiny thing. Just barely fully formed, but not yet grown to any normal birthing weight. 'Son,' he stated, his voice level and honest. 'That baby there's been dead for days.'

'No.' The man shook his head. 'She just needs water. Please. She hasn't had any food since ... since ...'

The older and the younger exchanged glances, and in them were hidden disgust and pity.

'What's your name, son?'

The kneeling man tore his eyes away from the dead thing in his arms and he looked up at the older man, as though he were confused, as though he had to think to recall his name. 'Uh . . . Clyde.'

The older man nodded. 'Drake Chalmers.' He pointed back behind them. 'I'm a deacon at that church right there. Got a lot of good people in there. And I think we do have a nursing mother. Would you be willing to give your baby to her?'

'Is she gonna help my baby girl?'

Chalmers smiled. 'Of course.'

There was a woman in the church, just like Chalmers had said.

They had led him into the vestibule, and there Chalmers left him with the younger man, disappearing through the heavy oak doors of the sanctuary, where just beyond there was the murmur of conversations and many curious eyes looking in at them.

None of that registered with Clyde. He stood swaying on his feet, eyes opening and closing slowly as though he were fighting to keep from passing out. His mouth still hung open, white crust formed on the corners of his lips. If the eyes were the windows to the soul, his looked in on a vacant house.

Chalmers returned a moment later with the woman. She looked confused and a little frightened, and when she saw Clyde and the thing in his arms, she stopped dead in her tracks. Chalmers held her by the upper arm and kept her from retreating. Behind her, the doors to the sanctuary closed, and the faceless people inside were silent.

Clyde looked at her but still gave no expression. 'Can you

feed her?' He extended the form in his arms, the flesh limp with the beginnings of decay. All of it darkly rusted.

The woman squeezed her eyes shut. Tears came out.

Chalmers's grip on her forearm tightened just a bit, and he pulled her forward. 'Sarah,' he said calmly. 'Can you help this man's child?'

She forced her eyes open. She and Chalmers, and the other, younger man, they all stared at Clyde as though gauging or waiting for his reaction, but still none came. He seemed robotic. Devoid of his humanity. Like something had disconnected inside of him.

The woman, Sarah, reached out with shaking hands and took the child. Her face tightened with revulsion and horror as she touched it, but she did not pull away, and she took the child as any careful nurse would – cradling the head, supporting the back.

Her voice cracked and trembled. 'I'll take care of her.'

Chalmers gave her a fractional nod, and she left them. She went through the doors to the sanctuary, and all the eyes of those inside tracked her. And it was not until the doors clunked closed behind her that she let out a single, thin sound of misery and grief that never made it through the thick oak to Clyde's ears.

He slept for a long time. He was not sure how long. They brought him water and small amounts of food. He drank and ate and fell back asleep, in a small side room where children's paintings and pictures in crayon were hung on the walls. Once, he awoke to gunfire, but no one came for him, so he closed his eyes again. He did not speak, and he moved very little. A creature in chrysalis.

When finally he did awaken, it was bright sunshine

outside. It lit up the windows of the small room he was in, and it was harshly white, so that he knew it was the heat of the day, when all the soft golden light had already been burned up. The interior of the room was stifling, and his shirt was moist with his own sweat. Clyde tried to remember if there had been air-conditioning in the room before, but he couldn't say for sure.

He sat up and stared down at the carpet. He knew where he was, like one might know something from reading it and not from firsthand experience. The world felt real enough to him now, but everything that had happened before, his entire life preceding, seemed a displaced montage of snapshots. Just a collection of dreams and imaginings.

He stood up slowly, felt his feet solid underneath him. His hands had been cleaned, but the blood on his arms and clothing remained, so it seemed he wore red sleeves. He did not react when he saw this. The pain he felt when he saw it was muted and faraway. Like an echo of himself bouncing back from the bottom of a deep cave.

He went to the door of the room and opened it. Fresh air flowed past his face, and only then did he detect the foul odor of himself. The air was still warm and humid, but it dried the layer of greasy sweat that already sat on his skin, giving him the impression of being cool.

Clyde looked both ways out of the door. He was in a long hallway. There were doors to either side. To his right, the hallway ended in a door that Clyde believed led outside. To his left, he could hear the sounds of people singing, very quietly. The words came softly as they sang in unison, and Clyde could not determine what they said, only that it was a hymn.

He stepped out of the room and began walking toward

the sounds of the singing. At the end of the hall was another door, and this appeared to lead into the sanctuary. There was a narrow glass window through which he could see a congregation gathered at the front pews. They were knelt, hands clasped in front of them, singing softly as though they did not want to be heard.

Clyde pushed the door open slowly and as quietly as he could. He stepped through and stood in the sanctuary, alone at the back. No one turned or gave notice of him. The sanctuary was a bright thing, painted white, and hot with the sun. There were large windows that stretched floor-to-vaulted-ceiling, but they were only frosted glass. For some reason Clyde had expected stained glass. The lack of them gave the place an institutional feel.

He stood there for a time as the voices rose and fell. He felt his sweat gather at his hairline and meander over the grooves and furrows of his forehead, and they traced an unfamiliar path, as though he did not know his own face. He breathed deeply of the stifling air and his lungs stretched in a strange way, like they had never been used before.

The air tasted different to him.

A hand touched his shoulder. He did not jump, because the touch did not threaten him. Instead he turned and found a man standing by his side. The man was not old, nor was he young. He was perhaps a bit more than middle-aged but had the form of someone who exercised frequently. His hair was graying from its original brown, and a prominent goatee stood out only slightly darker. His expression was slight – a calming one, something that spoke of kindness. But there was the glint of an edge to his eyes.

'You must be Clyde,' the man said. His voice had a tone, a bearing, something that enwrapped you. Made you subconsciously seek his approval and fear his rejection. One of those people who were to everyone a father, and took the role gracefully and effortlessly.

Still, Clyde had to think about it for a moment, though he finally nodded. 'Yeah.'

The other man's face became grave. He nodded, and a slight pressure from his hand convinced Clyde to move, to be guided toward the door he had just entered into the sanctuary from. Quietly, the man said, 'Come with me, Clyde.'

And he went with him. Down the hall and past all the doors, including the one Clyde had come from. They went to the very end of the hall, where bright outside light made its way in. A sign above the door stood out – dark, but it still spelled clearly the word EXIT. They left through this door and were consumed by air that felt more like steam.

Still hotter than the inside of the stifling church.

'How long has the power been out?' Clyde asked.

'A day now,' the man said.

'And how long was I asleep?'

'About a day and a half.'

They continued walking. Around them was the sandy half turf of what passed for grass in the coastal region. Clyde glanced behind them as they walked and saw the bulk of the church. A simple cinder-block construction, painted beige. The roof a dark red, almost brown. *Like dried blood*, he thought. There were two steeples rising out of it, one in the front and one in the back. The front steeple was crested with a cross.

Clyde turned back around and saw their destination ahead of them. Near the woods that ensconced the church, there was a small plot where the dirt was upturned. A pale, sandy loam that looked clumped and cracked on the top where they had recently dug and replaced the dirt. There were three mounds, each with a white cross at the head.

Clyde swallowed thickly as they stopped before the small plot. From the corner of his eye, he could see that the man standing next to him was eyeing him, assessing him. Clyde did not make eye contact with the man, but instead scanned the mounds of dirt, and his eyes fell to the one that was very small, the dirt very fresh.

The man next to him spoke slowly, evenly. 'You know that she was dead, right?'

Clyde was silent as he considered the words.

His neck tingled with the heat of the sunshine. The call of cicadas surrounded them, loud and insistent as it rose and fell. Clyde could feel the truth down deep in him, like the hard-baked residue of a nightmare. And he scrubbed it down into the dark cellars of his mind and he boarded up any place it might get free. This was not denial. He knew the truth. He just refused to face it. He avoided it like a hand avoids a red-hot piece of metal.

He nodded once, because to speak in that moment would be to break himself open.

'We didn't have a name for the cross,' the man said. 'If you wanted to put one on there . . .'

Clyde shook his head.

He had no name for the girl he'd carried in his arms. He had no name for the child he had made with his dead wife. Nothing to call the stillborn thing he'd ripped from her womb, birthed dead in a dead world, swimming in blood. A name would only make it real. A name would bring that nightmare out of the shadows he had pushed it into.

They were quiet for a time.

The man spoke, his words cautious but forthright. 'In the Book of Job, the Lord tested a man. He let the Devil strike the man's wife and children with sickness and disease until they died. He let the Devil bring pests on the man's crops and kill his cattle. He let the Devil take everything from this man until he was just an empty soul. Kind of like you. Like all of us, really.'

The man looked out, squinting against the sun. 'We've all lost something precious. Most of us have lost everything. These are times of tribulation.' He shook his head slowly. 'This country is reaping what it has sown for generations. And now the Lord is calling on us to remain faithful, even in these trying days. Because all this hurt, all this loss' – here he looked at Clyde again – 'all the things that we are forced to do that we don't want to do ... this is what the Lord intended for us. That we prove ourselves faithful to him. And then, just like in the end of the Book of Job, we will reap the blessings of his reward.'

The man faced away from the graves and back toward the church. Clyde turned with him, a question on his lips, but then he stopped, because the man named Chalmers was standing there. He had a rifle slung on his back, and he held another in his hands. And Clyde forgot what he was going to ask.

'Pastor Wiscoe,' Chalmers said, holding up the rifle.

The man that Chalmers had called Pastor Wiscoe looked at Clyde, and in his eyes was pity, but also a depth of under-standing. Pastor Wiscoe knew what was inside of Clyde, and he did not recoil from what he saw.

He took Clyde by the shoulders and stared at him straight on. And his words went into Clyde and dove down deep. 'I know that you think you have failed, Clyde. I know that you think you let your family down, that you weren't strong enough, you weren't brave enough or tough enough. But what happened was according to God's design. He took everything from you in order to lead you here, to this point. Because He needs people with nothing to run to, nothing to fall back on.'

Wiscoe smiled. It was a smile that imparted forgiveness. 'It wasn't your fault that any of this happened. And none of the things that you did were your fault. Because you were pre-ordained, my friend. You were preordained to be one of the faithful. And the only way you can ever truly fail is by giving up now, when your name has been called and you are most needed.'

Clyde felt tears in his eyes, watched them blur his vision. He looked upward into a bright, cloudless sky that seemed different to him from any other sky he had ever seen. Here he was not the man that he was. He was not the coward. He was not inadequate.

Here, he could be whatever he wanted to be.

He could be whomever he *needed* to be.

Clyde felt simultaneously dead and reborn.

He closed his eyes against the brightness of the sky and felt the tears squeeze out of him, the last tears he would ever cry, he knew. And when they had dried on his face, he spoke in a voice that he did not recognize as his own. 'What do I have to do?'

Wiscoe took the rifle from Chalmers's hands and turned to Clyde, the weapon extended toward him. 'You must do the Lord's work, Clyde.'

about the author

D. J. Molles is the bestselling author of The Remaining series. He published his first short story, *Darkness*, while still in high school. Soon after, he won a prize for his short story *Survive*. The Remaining was originally self-published in 2012 and quickly became an Internet bestseller. He lives in the southeast with his wife and children.

Find out more about D. J. Molles and other Orbit authors by registering for the free monthly newsletter at www.orbitbooks.net.

if you enjoyed

THE REMAINING

look out for

THE REMAINING: AFTERMATH

also by

D. J. Molles

CHAPTER 1

CAMP RYDER

Who are the real victims in all of this?
The infected or the survivors?

Gunshots perforated the darkness of Lee's dreams, yanking him violently out of sleep.

He sat upright on a cot in almost complete darkness, his

sleep-blind eyes struggling to focus and make sense of what was going on around him. Half in and half out of sleep, Lee's mind conjured up the nearest memory of darkness and gunfire: the dim stairwell in the Petersons' house, the haze of cordite hanging in the air, the stench of the infected.

His breath caught in his chest. Dread hammered at the back of his mind. Something horrible had happened in the Petersons' house. Something terrible and irreversible . . .

Jack had just been bitten!

But no. That didn't make sense.

Because wasn't Jack already dead?

He had to shake his head to clear the images of the Petersons' house and Jack in the bedroom, covered in blood. He knew they were false. This wasn't the Petersons' house. It was . . . someplace else. *Someplace safe*, he thought. *But maybe not so safe anymore, because there's screaming and gunfire coming from outside*.

Another gunshot rang out, this time very close to him.

Adrenaline pumped like a piston in his guts. His heart rate quickened.

Slow down. Evaluate your situation. Try to remember.

Try to remember what the fuck you're doing here.

He took a moment to look around and work through what he was seeing.

He was not in complete darkness, as he'd first thought: A single gas lantern glowed dimly against dull corrugated-steel walls. He was completely naked, save for a thin white bedsheet that had been spread over him from the waist down. He lay on a cot in what looked like a shipping container and his back was in excruciating pain, though he couldn't remember why. His tongue felt thick and pasty. And he had no weapons.

Where's my damn rifle?

From somewhere outside he heard Tango howl.

Tango! he thought, almost jumping off of the cot, but stopping himself as the sound of it reverberated and echoed. *That's not right. That doesn't sound like Tango.* The howl tapered off into a throaty snarl that didn't sound much like a dog anymore. It was human.

It couldn't be Tango, anyway.

Because he was dead too.

And with that thought, the rest came back with sudden and overpowering force. Tango was dead. Jack was dead. He'd lost his rifle at Timber Creek. Someone named Milo had ambushed them. He remembered crawling through a boarded window, nails carving through the flesh of his back. Red and Blue saving their asses with Molotov cocktails. Angela and Abby and Sam just barely making it to Camp Ryder ...

The survivors. Camp Ryder. Wasn't there a ten-foot-high fence around the compound? How the hell did the infected get inside? It was an infected he'd just heard; he was sure of it. But who was shooting at them? The questions all struck his brain in rapid succession.

I can't just lie here, he thought. *I've got to move.*

He ripped the white sheet off of himself and stood, staggering through a flash of light-headedness. The questions still rolled around in his head, but he couldn't answer them now. Most of his thoughts were still muddled, but two things were coming through with piercing clarity: He needed a weapon – anything would do better than his bare hands – and he needed to get out of the shipping container. Running on instinct, these desires became a white-hot need, as real to him as his need to breathe.

That howl again, this time just outside the shipping container.

A shotgun boomed and the pellets struck the steel walls.

Flashlights from outside played across the wall, casting the wavering shadow of a man running straight for Lee. The movements were unmistakably wild and animalistic.

A short, sinewy form lurched around the corner of the shipping container just in time for another blast of buckshot to scoop its legs out from under it like a rug had been pulled. The infected hit the ground hard on its back and attempted to stand again without any regard to its injuries. Its wide eyes glistened feverishly in the lamplight as its shredded right leg twitched about, pulled in different directions by rearranged muscle fibers. It collapsed with a hissing sound and began to drag itself toward Lee, leaving a thick trail of blood behind.

Like a car with a faulty transmission, Lee's mind finally dropped into gear. He lunged for the table with the medical equipment. He wasn't sure what he was looking for, but if anything was to be a weapon, it would be something on the table. He swept his hands back and forth like a blind man feeling in the dark, knocking over a metal tray with a few scalpels and forceps soaking in alcohol. The tray clattered to the ground and sent the instruments skittering across the floor. He thought about diving for one of the scalpels, but it wouldn't bite deep, and given infected people's penchant for not even registering flesh wounds, he decided he needed something with a little more stopping power.

Lee grabbed the heaviest object he could find – a big microscope that felt like it was solid metal. He spun toward the infected and found it nearly close enough to grasp his legs. Lee shouted in surprise and jumped back, grabbing the microscope by the eyepiece with one hand and smashing it down as hard as he could on the head of the infected. The heavy base of the microscope made a wet cracking noise as it dented the skull.

The crazed man on the floor thrashed and drew in a loud, gasping breath. His eyes turned skyward and he began to convulse violently. The sight of it soured Lee's stomach almost instantly. He stared, frozen, for several of his rapid heartbeats before swinging again. The bludgeon struck his attacker in the temple. His eyeballs bulged and the top of the skull mashed into a strange, cone-like shape.

Lee swallowed hard against gorge in the back of his throat. He dropped the microscope and took a faltering step back, trying to catch his breath while his pulse ran away from him. The pain in his back, all but forgotten for those brief few seconds, suddenly spread over his body like he was soaked in kerosene and playing with matches.

He staggered toward his cot but didn't make it. He lost his feet and planted his hands and knees on the floor as he felt his stomach suddenly reject whatever was inside of it. He felt the splatter on his arms and then hung his head, breathing hard and spitting.

Pounding footsteps behind him.

Still keyed up, Lee turned toward the sound and lashed out with both fists.

'Hey! Whoa!'

Lee focused on the face, kneeling down next to him.

A broad face with a wild man's beard. A Colt 1911 in one hand, the other gripping Lee by the shoulder and shaking him gently. 'Can you stand up?'

Lee wiped vomit from his lips and searched his mind for this man's name. 'Uh . . . Bus?'

'Yeah.'

Lee became suddenly aware that he still had no clothes on. He stood up shakily, with Bus supporting him. 'Can I get some pants?'

The big man pointed toward the foot of the cot where a pile of clothing was folded neatly beside Lee's old Bates M6 boots. 'It was all we could rustle up for now.'

Lee nodded and stepped to the cot, straddling his puddle of vomit – *rice and beans*, he remembered. It was a pair of athletic shorts and a green T-shirt with a yellow smiley face on the chest. It was a far cry from his trusted MultiCam pants and combat shirt, but at least he had his boots back. The harsh reality of his last four days had only strengthened his opinion that these were the best boots ever made.

Inside one of the boots, he noticed someone had stashed his GPS device. Before Doc and Jenny had begun to operate they had tried to take it from his hands, and Lee had refused to give it up. It appeared either that they had succeeded in removing it when he'd fallen asleep or perhaps that Lee had dropped it and they had been kind enough to put it back for him. Either way, finding it snug in his boot immediately increased his trust for these strangers. He'd made clear one simple wish and they'd abided by it.

At the entrance to the cargo container, a younger man appeared holding a big hunting shotgun. He was skinny, but he had a round, childlike face and a patch of blond hair that stood off of his head like a halo. Despite his cherubic features, Lee guessed him to be about twenty years old. As he entered, he looked first at Lee, then to Bus, then to the mess of what once was a human being on the floor.

'Holy shit . . .'

Lee pulled on the athletic shorts and spoke to Bus. 'How'd they get in?'

'I guess they found a hole in the fence. Or made one somehow; that's the only thing I can think of.' Turning to the young man, Bus said, 'Josh, give Captain Harden your pistol.'

Josh pulled a Ruger LCP out of his back pocket and held it out toward Lee. It was a tiny pocket pistol that could fit in the palm of his hand, and essentially worthless on a moving target past a range of about twenty feet. Just as Lee was about to take it, Josh jerked his hand back and looked at him suspiciously, an expression that didn't quite fit on his face. 'I'm gonna get this back, right?'

Lee honestly didn't know, so he just looked to Bus for clarification.

Bus shrugged back at him. 'I'll get you something better when we have time.'

'Then I guess you'll get this back,' Lee said to Josh and accepted the gun. He pulled the magazine out of the well. It was a .380 caliber with only four rounds left in the magazine, plus one in the chamber. He would have to get in close to use the thing effectively. Still, it was better than a microscope. He shoved the magazine back into the gun and stomped his feet into his boots. The GPS device he slipped into the pocket of his athletic shorts.

Josh pointed out to the darkness of Camp Ryder. 'I think we got most of 'em.'

Bus just shook his head. 'We don't know that. Get everyone in the square.'

'A'ight.' Josh spun on his heel and ran off into the night.

Bus looked Lee over. 'You okay? Didn't get bit?'

Lee gave himself a quick once-over before answering. 'Think I'm good.'

'Let's get moving.'

Lee followed the big man out of the cargo container at a jog. 'What's "the square" and why is everyone going there?'

'This ain't the first time we've been attacked,' Bus said cryptically.

Lee found himself just rolling with it, the way you roll with the nonsensical facts in a strange dream, simply accepting the unacceptable because there are no other options. Lee felt like he was about to understand, anyway. He was about to get a crash course in how Camp Ryder dealt with attacks.

In a way, Lee felt strangely at ease being the follower. Over the course of the four days, it hadn't just been about his own survival but the survival of everyone in his little group. Angela, Abby, Sam, and until recently, Jack and Tango, had all depended on him to survive. Now it appeared that Bus was the head honcho, the man with a plan, and the absence of responsibility was like dropping an eighty-pound rucksack off his shoulders. And Lee had to admit, while he didn't know Bus well enough to say he trusted him completely, the man had a rock-steady attitude about him. There was something hard and unbreakable inside of him, and Lee could respect that.

Outside of the shipping container, he could see the stretch of gravel and dirt that made up the center of Camp Ryder, like some Main Street in an old Western movie but much narrower. To either side of the gravel stretch, the survivors had used anything and everything they could find to construct small shelters for themselves and their families. It reminded Lee of the shantytowns he'd seen in third-world countries.

Who am I kidding? Lee thought numbly. *This* is *a shantytown. And America is a third-world country now.*

Lee noticed that the shantytown was beginning to churn

with bodies, like an anthill after you scuff the top layer off. People in raggedy clothes were emerging out of cars and shacks and tents. Everyone carried flashlights or lanterns in one hand and a weapon in the other. A few had firearms, but mostly it was axes, shovels, crowbars, and baseball bats. It felt like a lynch mob. The townspeople heading out to find Frankenstein's monster.

They ran past Lee and Bus, toward the center of Camp Ryder where a large but shallow pit had been dug and lined with bricks and stones. A fire pit, perhaps? It appeared to be full of ash. Lee guessed correctly that this was 'the square.'

Suddenly remembering something, Lee stopped and began craning his neck around, trying to see through the jostling crowd and the darkness. To Bus, he spoke with a measure of urgency: 'Where're Angela and the kids?'

Bus motioned for him to keep walking. 'Josh is telling everyone to gather in the square. They'll be there.'

As they walked, Bus snatched an ax handle from where it was leaning up against a tent. It was thinner toward the base of the handle and thicker at the top where the metal ax-head was missing, which made it perfectly weighted for a striking weapon.

'Harris!' Bus yelled.

A man in the growing crowd of people looked up.

'Captain Harden is borrowing your ax handle.'

The man nodded and gave a thumbs-up.

The ax handle was pushed into Lee's arms. He noticed that someone had written on the handle in Magic Marker: BRAIN BUSTER.

Cute.

Lee cinched the drawstring of his shorts up tight and stuck the little Ruger LCP in his waistband. Bus stepped in front of the crowd and looked like he was hurriedly counting heads. Lee estimated about fifty, which was close to the number Bus had given him last night. As he looked out over the crowd, he could see a tangled mess of blond hair on the other side of the crowd. In the glimmering lamplight, he could see Angela's face, etched in worry. As the crowd shifted, he glimpsed the two children, standing to either side of her.

A fear he hadn't realized he'd been harboring released its vise grip on his stomach. He thought about calling to them but decided against it. They were here with the group. They were relatively safe. For now.

Josh ran up beside him and stopped to catch his breath for a brief second. 'That's everyone.'

'Hopefully,' Bus murmured.

'So . . .' Lee looked around at the gathered mass of people. He noticed that everyone had their backs to the fire pit and had placed their flashlights at their feet, creating a bright, noisy gathering. Lee was about to ask what the plan was but suddenly managed to figure it out on his own. He turned so his back was also to the fire pit and got a solid grip on the ax-handle.

He looked at Bus and shook his head. 'I can't say I like this idea.'

Bus only shrugged and then shouted to the crowd. 'Alright, folks, call 'em when you see 'em!'

Lee saw stony faces, all etched in harsh light and deep shadows. Glimmering and fearful eyes stared out into the darkness. Weathered hands twisted tighter and tighter grips on an assortment of opportunistic weapons. Those with firearms were at the front, pointing their hunting shotguns and deer rifles out at the suspicious stillness.

Circling the wagons.

The quiet of the night felt forced. Like a breath taken and held for fear of someone hearing. Even the night birds and chirping crickets were conspicuously absent.

Lee shifted his weight and tried to focus on anything that lay beyond the ring of light created by the dozens of flash-lights.

The silence stretched uncomfortably.

Someone whispered, 'Why aren't they attacking?'

And another: 'This is weird.'

And still another: 'Are you sure there are more?'

Someone's dog began barking.

Then a shout: 'I see movement!'

The group collectively tensed.

'Over by the trash bins!'

Heads turned, everyone simultaneously spinning in the same direction. Lee followed suit because he didn't know where the 'trash bins' were. He saw a collection of old steel shipping containers, identical to the one that held Doc's medical station. The tops of the containers had been removed so that they looked like big, open sardine cans. Several of them were filled with the monumental amount of trash that came from refugees all jam-packed in and living together.

In the murky shadows of the trash bins, Lee strained to see the movement.

A couple of the stronger flashlights probed the darkness, but didn't reveal anything. The darkness was becoming dis-orienting. He realized he still wasn't thinking clearly, wasn't operating like normal. The injury and the lack of food and water had taken more of a toll on his body than he'd thought, and he was only just beginning to recover. He kept repeating in his mind, *It's time to do work. It's time to do work.* Because that was what he used to tell his squad when they had to focus on completing a mission.

It's time to do work.

'There!' someone shouted.

A flash of movement between two trash bins.

'I see it!' A man with a deer rifle stepped forward a bit, but then hesitated. 'Why isn't it coming at us?'

A chunk of trash suddenly shifted and that strange, unearthly screeching sound echoed out at the band of survivors. Lee couldn't see any details of the figure, but it ran straight at them. Just as it was within twenty-five yards of them it suddenly stopped and veered off. For a moment, it trotted along the edge of their lights, like a wolf probing a herd for weaknesses.

The entire crowd seemed frozen and perplexed, like everyone was trying to figure out what the hell this one was doing.

'Shoot it!' Bus shouted at the man with the deer rifle.

The rifle barked.

Lee watched the dirt at the infected's feet explode. Sympathetic gunfire followed the rifle shot as the tension became too much for some trigger fingers to handle. The night was abruptly engulfed in a volley of shotgun blasts and rifle fire. A scattershot of rounds caught its legs, then ripped into its shoulder, pummeled its chest, and finally split its head open.

It wasn't until that moment when Lee watched the miserable thing collapse to the ground that a small, familiar voice cut into his brain, dissipating the fog of disorientation and reminding him of who he was, and how he had been trained.

Watch your lane.

When learning to operate in a squad, each member would have a designated 'lane of fire' to watch for enemies. If you were constantly checking to make sure that your buddy wasn't missing things in his lane, then you were probably missing things in your own lane. In other words: Stop worrying about everyone else and do what you know you're supposed to be doing.

Squad Tactics 101.

Watch your lane.

Lee spun around just in time to see two clawlike hands latch onto a young teenage girl and yank her backward. Lee watched the girl's dark hair fly up like it was suddenly in zero gravity as she was pulled to the ground. Her eyes locked onto Lee, and he saw a scared indignation, as though she were thinking, *This isn't supposed to happen to me.*

The infected was an older female. It hunched over the younger girl and lunged for the neck. The girl let out a small cry and her hands came up, trying to block the infected's mouth from reaching her jugular. The old woman bit down hard on the girl's wrist and Lee heard tendons snap.

He managed to yell, 'Behind us!' and then swung for the fences. The ax-handle connected just behind the ear and left a deep hollow in the old woman's skull.

It was only then that Lee realized there was a second infected. It lunged out of the darkness and seized hold of the teenage girl and began to backpedal, trying to drag her away from the crowd, looking at the other survivors and hissing aggressively. It pulled her by the shirt collar with one hand and hammered the girl's face with the other, knocking her unconscious after two or three blows.

Lee jumped forward and wound up for the swing. A

gun went off just to the right side of his head. The infected's throat exploded and it collapsed into a writhing ball. Lee instinctively recoiled from the noise of the gunshot so close to him. As Lee clenched his jaw against the ringing in his ears, the crowd swarmed around him, yanking the girl away from the infected and then bludgeoning it to death.

He looked to his right, where the gunshot had just come from, and saw a man drop a small revolver to the ground. His face was ashen. He rushed past Lee and slid to his knees next to the girl and began to wail.

The gathering erupted in confusion.

Everyone was yelling and pressing forward to hover over the girl. A younger man in the crowd turned and looked at Lee with accusatory eyes, as though Lee had done something wrong, as though it was *his* fault that the girl had been attacked. In a flash of anger, Lee thought about using the ax-handle on him too. But in the back of his mind he thought, *Isn't it your fault? Shouldn't you have been paying attention? You're the professional here . . .*

Over it all he heard Bus yelling, 'Steve! Steve!' and the man who had fired the revolver wailing: 'Oh, Jesus! Oh, fuck! Come on, baby! Wake up! I'm so sorry, baby!'

The girl's father?

Bus tried to push past with the rest of them, but Lee was thinking a little bit more clearly now, thinking about how those infected had hid from them and flanked them. There could be more. And if they didn't find where the intruders had come through, there *would* be more. He reached out and caught Bus with a firm hand to his chest. 'Are there any others?'

Seeming to ignore him, the big bearded man craned his

neck to see the girl on the ground, then abruptly realized that Lee was speaking to him. 'What?'

Lee pulled the man closer, speaking low so as not to be overheard and start a panic. 'Are there any other infected?'

'Uh ...' He tapped his Colt 1911 against his thigh and wiped his sweaty brow. 'Shit. God. I don't know.'

The group was already scattering to the wind. Doc and Jenny were pushing people out of the way and Doc's skinny voice was needling at the crowd: 'Everyone get the fuck outta the way! Someone help me lift her!'

More people than necessary to carry a 120-pound girl stepped in. Everyone was trying to get a hand in to help and becoming more of a hindrance. The girl's father cradled her head in his arms as they moved her quickly toward the medical trailer.

Bus was staring at the girl again, so Lee shook him gently to get his attention. 'Grab a couple guys. We need to close whatever hole those fuckers came through and then do a perimeter sweep.'

CHAPTER 2

INVESTIGATION

Bus seemed to gain his senses again. He reached out with a thick arm, coarse with wiry black hair, and grabbed Josh as the young man attempted to run past and join the crowd as they whisked the bitten girl off to Doc's medical trailer.

'You're with us,' Bus said, and when he spoke he had returned to his normal steady tone. 'We gotta find where they're coming through the fence.'

'But what about Kara?' Josh's eyes were wide and concerned.

Bus looked the young man in the eye. 'Let Doc handle that. You can't do anything for her right now. We have other things to take care of. Now let's go.'

Josh didn't argue further. He nodded once and then both men turned toward Lee.

He quickly surveyed his surroundings and made a decision. 'We need a fourth ...' Lee spotted a familiar face. Miller, wasn't it? The man in the red bandanna who had helped them escape Timber Creek with the use of some Molotov cocktails. Lee waved him over. 'Hey! Borrow you for a second?'

Miller took a second to recognize him in the darkness, but

after shining his light a few times in Lee's face, he came running over, hand on his holstered .38 Special to keep it from flopping around on his belt. 'Yeah?'

He was roughly the same age as Josh, but taller, and his features were more gaunt. While Josh gave the impression of someone much younger, everything about Miller was older, from the squint of his eyes to his confident-but-not-cocky stride. There was something else there too. Something in the tilt of his head, in the set of his jaw. Miller liked to fight.

Lee pointed to the fence behind the trash bins, as it was the closest section of fence to their current location. 'We'll both start there. Run the fence line in opposite directions and see if we can find where the infected are getting through. If you find the hole, post up and secure it as best you can until we all meet back up.'

Three heads nodded quickly.

'Bus, you and I will go clockwise. Miller and Josh, you guys go counterclockwise.' Lee and Bus took off for the fence at a trot and began walking briskly along it, inspecting the integrity of the chain links as they went.

Lee had asked for Bus to team up with him because he wanted a chance to talk to him. There were things about their most recent encounter that disturbed him and he wanted to get Bus's thoughts on it.

While they walked, Lee spoke. 'What happens to the girl now?'

'Kara?' Bus mumbled absently. 'Doc will amputate and hope for the best.'

Lee almost stopped in his tracks. 'Amputate? Are you kidding me?'

Bus shook his head, looking briefly run-down. 'No. The faster they cut off Kara's arm, the better chance she has of not contracting FURY. Doc figures it works about half the time, which is better than a hundred-percent chance of infection. Only problem is that most of the time the amputation goes septic. Or they lose too much blood.' Bus swore bitterly. 'We just don't have the medical equipment. It's like the fucking Stone Age again. Like Civil War surgeons just hacking off limbs with saws and crossing their fingers.'

Lee couldn't think of anything else to say. The concept of amputation to prevent bacterial infection through a bite or open wound seemed to be a reckless medical maneuver, but when faced with the certainty of turning into one of *them*, the amputation had a cold practicality.

Lee pressed on. 'Did you notice anything about those last infected?'

Bus didn't answer immediately. He stalked along and painted his flashlight over the length of fence before them but found it to be secure. When he finally spoke, he seemed to be choosing his words carefully. 'I remember how they were a month ago.' He stopped walking and turned to look at Lee. 'They were disjointed and confused. Lost. Insane. They attacked each other just as often as they attacked us. I don't know what the hell is going on or how it's happening so fast, but the groups are changing. Learning. And they're doing it quickly.'

Lee pictured the dark shape darting out of the trash bins and circling the edge of the lamplight while they sat in their encirclement, weapons pointed out. The cold, blood-crusted talons dragging that young girl to the ground and the other trying to carry her off.

'Like a wolf pack,' Lee said, almost more to himself than to Bus. 'Adaptation. Evolution. It doesn't seem like they're mindlessly attacking anymore. It seems like they're hunting us.'

Bus stopped and looked Lee in the eyes. 'Bullshit,' he said.

Lee shrugged. 'Think about it. That's the first time you've ever seen them come from both directions. Usually they're in one solid group and they just charge you. This was different. It was like they were trying to distract us so the other two could get in close.'

Bus didn't answer. He just started walking along the fence line again. The truth was that the words were bitter. It was not an 'aha' moment, it was an 'oh, shit' moment. The infected were bad enough as a mindless herd. The thought of them in small packs, hunting them like prey, was a hard pill to swallow.

But Lee wasn't willing to ignore the situation either.

'This is the first time we've seen them maneuver like that.' He followed along with Bus while he spoke. 'When the situation changes, your tactics need to change along with it. If they're getting smart enough to get past your chain-link fence, we're going to need to think of something else to keep them out.'

Bus shook his head fiercely. 'Even a dog can dig himself under a fence. That doesn't mean anything. They're mindless shells of what once were human beings. They're just running on autopilot now. There's no evolution in this.'

He sounded distraught, as though he were attempting to convince himself. *I reject your reality and substitute my own.* Lee decided not to push it. He just hoped Bus had other things on his mind and wasn't this unreceptive all the time.

Lee had to admit to himself that it was difficult to tell with the infected. Sometimes their actions seemed like the result of logical thought, and other times it just looked like instinct. Most of them appeared to be able to manipulate tools, but they weren't using them properly; they were simply using them as blunt objects to strike out with. Just because a monkey can strike somebody in the head with a wrench doesn't mean it can fix your sink. They all seemed to hold on to some rudimentary intelligence, but it also seemed to vary from individual to individual. Just as some were more aggressive than others, some were more intelligent than others. But then the question arose again, was it intelligence or instinct? Lee kept coming back to the example of a wolf pack. When a pack hunts, singles out the weakest prey, and then flanks it to take it down, is the success of their hunt based on a premeditated plan or ingrained animal instinct?

A voice came hollering across the compound. 'Bus!'

Bus and Lee both looked and saw Miller running up, breathing heavily. 'I think we found where they came in.' He took a big gulp of air. His eyes darted back and forth, carrying grave meaning. 'I think you should take a look at it.'

Miller turned on his heel and started jogging back across the compound. They followed behind him, their flashlights strobing up and down as they ran. Lee took a sidelong glance across the center of the compound and saw the crowd at the medical trailer being pushed out by a man Lee didn't recognize. From inside the trailer Lee could hear screaming, high-pitched and wretched. Doc had begun the amputation.

'Right here.' Miller had stopped and was pointing.

They turned the corner of a shanty made out of aluminum siding and blue tarp. Lee and Bus looked forward as they slowed to a walk and approached what Miller pointed at. Confusion passed over their faces followed by a deep, dreadful uncertainty. They looked at each other and then back at the object of their attention.

An opening had been peeled back from the fence, from top to bottom. The chain links had been pulled away and rolled up like two sides of a scroll. Only they weren't pushed inside, but pulled outward and tucked in so neatly to create the man-size breach in their defenses that it left little room for question about who or what had done this.

It was then that Lee and Bus both noticed a low, husky voice, quietly intoning some strange narrative: '... *but only slowly they neared the foe. As they neared him, the ocean grew still more smooth; seemed drawing a carpet over its waves ...*'

'What the fuck is that?' Bus glared and shot his flashlight toward the sound of the voice. The flashlight played around a bit and then found the culprit. Nestled in a patch of over-grown grass at the corner of the shack was a small black CD player, round and glistening like an insect's head; the two bulbous speakers stared up at them like compound eyes.

'... *the breathless hunter came so nigh his seemingly unsus-pecting prey, that his entire dazzling hump was distinctly visible ...*'

Bus moved swiftly forward, raising his foot as though to stomp the thing out of existence, but Lee's hand shot out and grabbed him by his arm, hauling him backward. Bus looked at him like he was about to turn that foot on Lee, but then understanding dawned.

Lee nodded. 'Might want to check that out real good before you go stomping around it. Depending on who put it there, it could be booby-trapped.'

Bus managed a halfhearted smile. 'That's why I keep you around.' He gestured toward the CD player. 'I'm guessing you have much more experience with booby-traps than I do. You tell me.'

The voice, supremely ignorant of the circumstances, con-tinued its droning: '... *the blue waters interchangeably flowed over into the moving valley of his steady wake ...*'

Lee gave the big man a humorless smirk and leaned forward with extreme caution. He shined the flashlight first around the immediate area of his feet, then lit up the patch of overgrown grass. When he saw nothing to alarm him he stepped forward and peered down into the nest of grass, working the flashlight around at different angles.

' ... *the hunters who namelessly transported and allured by all this serenity, had ventured to assail it; but had fatally found that quietude* ...'

Lee let out a long breath and relaxed a bit. Then he knelt down and stabbed the top of the CD player with his finger. The black cover popped open and the disembodied voice went silent. Underneath, a white disk spun madly at first, and then came to a gradual stop. Lee reached his hand in and plucked the CD from the tray, looking at the title and reading aloud: '*Moby-Dick* by Herman Melville. It's an audiobook.'

Bus's face was made of granite. 'Hilarious.'

Lee shook his head. 'I don't think it was a joke.'

Miller chimed in, pointing to the neatly clipped ends of the chain links. 'Pretty sure someone cut his way through this ... looks like bolt cutters.' Bus regarded Miller with a dubious look, to which Miller responded drably, 'I wasn't always the upstanding citizen I am now.'

'Milo?' Lee suggested.

Bus crossed his arms. 'I don't see who else would be interested in fucking with us, and given our recent tiff, I think that's a pretty good deduction.'

'Why not just attack us?' Josh finally spoke.

Lee offered a possible answer. 'Because a day attack is too easily defended and they know they can't be out in the woods at night because of the infected. So they use the infected. Cut a hole in the fence. Put a CD player with just enough volume to attract the infected but not get noticed by us.'

'Kind of clever if you think about it.' Bus stared grimly out at the dark woods. 'Audiobook just sounds like some guy talking. Music would have caught our attention.'

Everyone who had survived up to this point seemed to know that the infected had nearly superhuman hearing at night when they became more active. Lee had to assume that because of this, Camp Ryder enforced noise discipline at night. Even at the low volume it had been set at, the CD player had probably been the loudest noise coming out of the camp, though it probably would have gone unnoticed by regular ears or dismissed as a quiet family discussion.

Lee stood up and stepped to Bus's side. 'I think maybe you should tell me about Milo.'

Bus nodded, then pointed to Miller and Josh. 'You two patch up that fence. Only one of you working at a time; the other keep watch. Don't let anyone else sneak in. I'll send someone else down to help you.' Bus turned to Lee. 'Walk with me.'

The two men walked through the darkness, their flashlights casting a dull glow off the ground before them and just barely illuminating their tired faces. Most everyone had gone back to their makeshift homes, but a few stragglers still made their way through the dark. Unlike the deep silence of early morning, there was still a whisper of excitement – quiet voices echoing out of wood and tin shacks, holding furtive conversations. Lee had to wonder: How many other infected were in the area to hear those barely audible whispers?

Lee looked up at the sky and saw the faint glimmer of

dawn to the east, or perhaps it was his imagination. It wasn't until you spent time outside of the comfort of civilization that you began to realize why people in ages past feared the night. The night was long, it was uncomfortable, and it was dangerous. The dawn marked the end of the dark misery and the return of warmth and safety.

'You know what time it is?' Lee looked briefly at Bus.

'About four in the morning.'

Lee felt his heart sink. The light to the east was just his imagination after all. Dawn was two long hours away and there would be no sleeping after this. The pain in Lee's back was beginning to catch up to him.

A dark figure strode up to them as they crossed the center of camp. All Lee could see was the figure's right side, illuminated by the cold blue light of an LED lantern. As the figure approached, it raised the lantern up to eye level and Lee recognized the pursed face and the balding dome of his head, washed out and pale in the glow. The angle of the light cast shadows that made his face look weirdly severe.

Lee thought he remembered Miller calling the man Bill.

He was the one who had resisted bringing them back to camp, only to be convinced by Lee's arguments and Miller's pleading to give them a chance. He was of average height, and probably average weight before he had been forced to ratchet down on his belt during these lean times. He was probably in his forties and going bald on top, with a ring of wiry gray-brown hair. Overall, his body language and his facial expression communicated to Lee that he was not a pleasant person to be around.

'Bus.' He nodded to his superior with respect then turned a somewhat disdainful eye on Lee. 'Are you supposed to be up? I thought Doc wanted you recuperating.'

Lee was about to respond, but Bus cut him off, and Lee was grateful. He was too tired to argue. With a dismissing wave of one meaty hand, Bus said, 'Harper, we have a problem. Captain Harden is just helping me out, and then I will let him go straight back to bed.'

The man's cold silence said enough.

Lee quirked his eyebrows. 'So is it Bill or Harper?'

'Bill Harper,' he said with a grumble. 'Miller's the only one who calls me Bill. Everyone else calls me Harper.'

Lee nodded. 'Harper it is.'

Bus led the trio toward the Ryder building. The larger structure towered over the shantytown like a castle amongst the villagers' mud huts. It was a two-story cement structure with very few windows that Lee could see. Purely industrial, with very little to beautify it. Lee wasn't sure what it had been used for prior to the arrival of its current occupants, but he immediately began looking for its strong points, its weak points, and how it could be improved as a defensive location. If a firefight occurred, the thin walls of the shanties would provide very little protection. This building would have to be their defense.

It had a lot going for it. In addition to no windows and concrete walls, Lee could only see one entrance, which was two steel doors flanked by narrow sidelights – too narrow for a man to squeeze through. The roof looked like it was easily accessible, and Lee imagined some sandbags and a few machine gun nests up there could lay a pretty damn good field of fire on any attacking force.

Infected or otherwise.

Lee pointed up toward the big building. 'What do you guys use it for?'

'When we first got here, we all lived inside,' Bus explained.

'We very rarely left. The security of the fence was no big deal, because the building was our security. We welded the cargo-bay doors shut, which left only two sets of double doors to worry about – the ones you're looking at now and another set on the opposite side. We had everyone in there, but it was only about twenty people.'

They reached the double doors and Bus pushed them open. Lee noticed the smell first. It was the smell of the refugee camps outside Al-Waleed and the smell of a home-less shelter he'd once visited in D.C. It was sweating bodies and grimy clothes, exacerbated by the warm air. Lee could only imagine how much worse it smelled during the day.

After the double doors, a short hallway opened into the main portion of the building where Lee could see that the Ryder trucks had once been serviced. But instead of trucks and tools and lifts, Lee only saw another collection of shanties, these built less sturdily than the ones outside and more for the purpose of privacy. Lee thought there were about fifteen different dwellings crammed into the space, most of them with a lantern glowing inside. All the lamplight eking through wooden slats cast a kaleidoscope of light on the ceiling.

Bus guided the three of them to the right and they began to ascend a metal staircase. 'After the shit officially hit the fan and FEMA tucked its tail and ran, we started getting a steady trickle of survivors. We tried to take in only people who had something to contribute, but ...' Bus trailed off. 'It was tough. A lot of tough decisions had to be made.'

As they reached the top of the stairs, Lee spied a panel of glass to his right: a large window belonging to an office that overlooked the floor. In the dark window, Lee could see his reflection staring back at him and it almost stopped him in his tracks. He was thinner than he remembered; his neck and arms just bundles of taut cords with flesh stretched over them. His once-tidy crew cut was slightly overgrown and four days' worth of beard had grown in thick.

He was shocked to discover that the once gentle set of his face had turned into hard angles. His lips were pressed, the corners in a slight downturn, his jaw set as though preparing for a blow. The eyes that his last girlfriend, Deana, had always told him were kind now shone cold and savage. He forced his face to relax, and there he could see some semblance of the person he remembered. But it was only a grim parody. That person didn't exist anymore.

Lee realized Bus was still speaking and tore his attention away from the harsh visage in the window, refocusing on the conversation.

'I've always believed that we shouldn't turn anyone away – more manpower, you know? But a lot of people don't agree with me.' Bus opened the door to the small office overlooking the floor. Lee supposed it had once housed a foreman or supervisor. Inside, it was sparsely furnished with a few folding chairs, a large desk, and a big corkboard with a county map pinned to it. Bus stepped behind the desk but didn't sit. He continued speaking as he stood there, fishing through one of the desk drawers. 'Even being selective, we eventually got too crowded for everyone to fit in the building, so we allowed people to start making their camps outside. Seeing that it was safe, some of the people who were living in here decided to move out too. You think it looks cramped now, you should have seen it before.' Bus sighed. 'Pretty soon, we'll have too many for that, and then we'll have some real problem-solving to do.'

Bus finally found what he was looking for and pulled out

a bottle of whiskey. He smiled wanly at it and gestured his two companions toward the folding chairs. 'Have a seat, gentlemen.'

Harper and Lee both took a chair facing the desk.

Bus snagged the chair behind the desk and hauled it over to the front, so the three men were positioned in a small circle. He took his seat with a sigh, adjusting the straps of his holster. He leaned back and unscrewed the cap off the whiskey. 'Wish I could say it was good stuff, but it ain't.' He took a swig and offered the bottle to Harper, who accepted.

'So . . .' Lee tapped his fingers on his knee.

There was a long, awkward silence as Bus stared at Harper, who stared at the bottle in his hands. Harper seemed to take notice of the silence and looked up at Lee. 'Did we have a problem you were going to help us with?'

Bus leaned forward, elbows on his knees. 'Harper, we found a hole cut in the fence. Someone had put a CD player on the ground, playing an audiobook to attract infected. We think it was Milo.'

Harper deflated with a single long sigh. He leaned back and finally took a swig of the whiskey with a violent grimace on his face. Then he passed the bottle to Lee. 'Yeah . . . Milo.'

Lee smiled unsurely. 'What's the backstory on this guy?'

Harper looked to Bus and seemed to be waiting for him to take the reins.

'Uh-uh.' Bus folded his arms. 'You tell him. Milo's *your* brother.'